THE ARMARNAN KINGS BOOK 1:
Scarab – Akhenaten

By Max Overton

Writers Exchange E-Publishing
http://www.writers-exchange.com/

Scarab-Akhenaten Book 1 of the Amarnan Kings
Copyright 2009 Max Overton
Writers Exchange E-Publishing
PO Box 372
ATHERTON QLD 4883

Published by Writers Exchange E-Publishing
http://www.writers-exchange.com

ISBN   ebook: 978-1-921636-24-0
       Print: 978-1-921636-41-7

Cover Art: Julie Napier

Dedicated to the woman I love, Julie Napier, my wife, whose love of Ancient Egypt persuaded me to take a half-conceived story sitting around in the back of my mind and write it down.

Who's Who and What's What in Scarab

In any novel about ancient cultures and races, some of the hardest things to get used to are the names of people and places. Often these names are unfamiliar in spelling and pronunciation. It does not help that for reasons dealt with below, the spelling, and hence the pronunciation is sometimes arbitrary. To help readers keep track of the characters in this book I have included some notes on names in the ancient Kemetu language. I hope they will be useful.

In Ancient Egypt a person's name was much more than just an identifying label. A name meant something, it was descriptive, and a part of a person's being. For instance, Amenhotep means 'Amen is at peace', and Nefertiti means 'the beautiful one has come'. Knowledge of the true name of something gave one power over it, and in primitive societies a person's real name is not revealed to any save the chief or immediate family. A myth tells of the creator god Atum speaking the name of a thing and it would spring fully formed into existence. Another myth says the god Re had a secret name and went to extraordinary lengths to keep it secret.

The Egyptian language, like written Arabic and Hebrew, was without vowels. This produces some confusion when ancient Egyptian words are transliterated. The god of Waset in Egyptian reads *mn*, but in English this can be represented as Amen, Amon, Ammon or Amun. The form one chooses for proper names is largely arbitrary, but I have tried to keep to accepted forms where possible. King Akhenaten's birth name was Amenhotep, though this name can have various spellings depending on the author's choice. It is also sometimes seen as

Amenhotpe, Amenophis, Amunhotep and Amonhotep. I have used the first of these spellings (Amenhotep) in *Scarab*, and every name that includes that of the same god is spelled Amen-. The god himself I have chosen to call Amun, largely because the word Amen can have an alternate meaning in Western religious thought. The god of the sun's disk I have called Aten, though Aton is an alternative spelling. The City of Aten I have called Akhet-Aten (the Horizon of the Aten), rather than Akhetaten as it is normally written, to distinguish it easily for readers from the similar name of its king, Akhenaten.

The names of the kings themselves have been simplified. Egyptian pharaohs had five names, known as the Horus name, the Nebti name, the Golden Falcon name, the Prenomen and the Nomen. Only the nomen was given at birth, the other names being coronation names. The Horus name dates from pre-dynastic times and was given to a king upon his coronation. All kings had a Horus name, but by the eighteenth dynasty it was seldom used. The Nebti name dates from the time of the unification of Egypt and shows the special relationship the king had to the vulture-goddess Nekhbet of Upper Egypt and the cobra-goddess Wadjet of Lower Egypt. The Golden Falcon name conveys the idea of eternity, as gold neither rusts nor tarnishes, and dates from the Old Kingdom. It perhaps symbolizes the reconciliation of Horus and Seth, rather than the victory of Horus over Seth as the titles are usually non-aggressive in nature.

By the time of the eighteenth dynasty, the prenomen had become the most important coronation name, replacing the Horus name in many inscriptions. Since the eleventh dynasty, the prenomen has always contained the name of Ra or Re.

The nomen was the birth name, and this is the name by which the kings in this book are commonly known. The birth names most common in the eighteenth dynasty were Tuthmosis and Amenhotep. Successive kings with the same birth name did not use the method we use to distinguish between them – namely numbers (Amenhotep III and Amenhotep IV). In fact, the birth name ceased to be used once they became king and the coronation prenomen distinguished them. Amenhotep (III) became Nebmaetre, and Amenhotep (IV) became Waenre. In this book I have used prenomen and nomen, depending on the circumstance.

Another simplification has occurred with place names and titles. In the fourteenth century B.C., Egypt as a name for the country did not exist. The land around the Nile Valley and Delta was called Kemet or The Black Land by its inhabitants, and the desert Deshret or The Red Land. Much later, Greeks called it Aigyptos from which we get Egypt. Other common terms for the country were The Two Lands (Upper and Lower Egypt), and the Land of Nine Bows (the nine traditional enemies). I have opted for Kemet though I have used the other titles. Likewise Lower Egypt (to the north) was known as Ta Mehu, and Upper Egypt (to the south) was known as Ta Shemau.

Similarly, the king of Egypt or Kemet was later known as 'pharaoh', but this term derives from the phrase Per-Aa which originally meant the Great House or royal palace. Over the years the meaning changed to encompass the idea of the central government, and later the person of the king himself. The Greeks changed Per-Aa to Pharaoh. I have decided to remain with 'king' though I do use 'Per-Aa' from time to time, when referring to royalty larger than the person of the king.

During the eighteenth dynasty, the kings ruled from a city known variously as Apet, No-Amun or Waset in the Fourth province or sepat of Ta Shemau, which itself was also called Waset; or just 'nwt' which meant 'city'. This capital city the Greeks called Thebes. The worship of Amun was centered here and the city was sometimes referred to as the City of Amun. I have called this great city Waset.

The gods of Egypt are largely known to modern readers by their Greek names; for instance, Osiris, Thoth and Horus. I have decided to keep the names as they were originally known to the inhabitants of Egypt – Asar, Djehuti and Heru. The Greek names for unfamiliar gods can be found in the section *Gods of the Scarab books*, at the end.

Names and terms used in this and succeeding books will be unfamiliar to many readers. I have therefore included a section - *The Main Characters in Scarab-Akhenaten* – in which possible pronunciations and definitions can be found. This is to be found at the end of the book.

Prologue
Syria, 1959

Dr Dani Hanser stared out morosely at the sodden slopes steeply descending to the tiny rivulet, now in danger of becoming a full-fledged stream. Rain fell in misty swathes, obscuring the craggy rocks on the far side of the valley. She looked up from her position at the entrance of a large cave etched in sandstone cliffs, wiping the rain from her eyes and hair. Scowling, she turned back to her contemplation of the weather and the workers' campsite huddled at the base of the cliffs.

Soft footsteps in the dirt and gravel of the cave floor brought Dani out of her reverie. Turning, she caught sight of a lanky young man in tattered jeans and tee shirt picking his way through the rubble toward her, his face almost obscured by luxuriant growths of chestnut hair.

The man grinned, white teeth flashing in his full beard. "Not joining us, Dani? I thought you'd be eager to get what you can from our last day's dig." A cultured British accent belied his scruffy appearance.

Dani jerked her head toward the rain and the deserted-looking campsite. Despite her despondency, the man's youthful enthusiasm made her smile. "I'm just fed up, Marc, rainy day blues, I guess. And those lazy bastards down there."

Marc flicked his eyes toward the campsite and snorted. "What do you expect? The Syrian government is paying them whether they work or not. Besides, they don't have our lust for knowledge, the desire to wrest information from a few scattered bones and stone tools."

"That's just it, Marc. A few bones and tools is all we have to show for the last four months. I really thought we were going to find something important here. The signs are right; I know the Neanderthal migration route passed through this area. I thought this cave was a sure bet for our excavations." Dani kicked idly at the rubble on the cave floor, her head turning toward the muffled sounds of conversation from deeper inside the cave.

Marc shrugged. "Perhaps the cave wasn't so enticing thirty thousand years ago. Al says there are signs the walls were worked in relatively recent times."

Dani sighed and thrust her hands into the pockets of her parka. "I know. This whole cliff face has been quarried sporadically over the last four thousand years, yet there are Neanderthal remains here. We have evidence that it was used as a shelter."

"Just not the evidence the migration was coordinated rather than random." Marc smiled again and gestured toward the interior of the cave. "Never mind, Dani. This year may be a washout – literally, but there's always next season. Now come and join us, we have need of the guiding hand of our esteemed leader."

Dani grinned. "Will you be back next year, Marc? You'll have your doctorate by then. Maybe you'd rather be doing your own research rather than following a middle-aged frump into the Syrian Desert."

The young man turned his eyes up to the rock ceiling. "'Frump,' she says. And middle-aged yet." He looked back down at Dani and his face became serious. "Don't you know your loyal team would follow you anywhere, Dr Hanser?" He pursed his lips, considering. "Well, almost all. I can think of one exception."

6

Dani's grin slipped and she blushed slightly, covering it by turning away toward the cave. "Well, we'll see," she muttered.

Marc ambled along behind her. "Be careful by the wall over there. This rain brought down some earth and stone. I think water must be eating away at a fault in the rock." He reached out and gripped Dani's elbow when she slipped in the mud.

"I'm okay," Dani replied, stepping carefully along the muddy trail. She eyed the pile of rubble spreading out from a crevice in the cave wall. "I see what you mean. Well, it won't worry us this year, but we'll have ..." She broke off and peered into the gloom. "What's that?" She shook off Marc's hand and gingerly picked her way through the mud toward the rock wall. She picked something up and slogged back to the trail before examining her find.

"What is it? Another tool?"

Dani wiped the mud from the small rounded object in her hand and held it up to the light. "I don't believe it," she whispered. "What the hell is something like this doing here?"

"What?" Marc leaned over and took the object from Dani's hand. He turned it over and stared at the little carving wide-eyed. "It's gold," he breathed. "A bloody gold beetle."

"Not a beetle, Marc, a scarab, an Egyptian scarab." Dani shook her head and took the scarab back, peering at it in the dim light filtering back from the cave entrance. "It looks genuine enough. The workmanship is what I'd expect from, say, late Middle Kingdom or early New Kingdom, but ..." She turned the scarab over and picked at the mud caked between the moulded golden legs of the insect. "Holy mother!" she murmured.

7

"Egyptian, eh? Well, I suppose those gyppos got around. I seem to remember some of the pharaohs like Tuthmosis and Ramses got up this far."

"Not with something like this." Dani held up the scarab, displaying the underside. "See what's inscribed on it?"

Marc peered closely in the dim light. "A spiky ball?" he said doubtfully.

"The sun disc, the Aten," Dani replied, wonder in her voice. "This is the symbol of the Heretic King. The pharaohs after him tried to destroy all traces of him. What's his scarab doing in Syria?"

"Heretic king? Sounds interesting. Who was he?"

"Akhenaten, pharaoh of the eighteenth dynasty and possible father of Pharaoh Tutankhamen." Dani shook her head. "Scary times if you believed in the gods of Egypt. He tried to abolish all the old gods and set up a new religion worshiping the disk of the sun."

"Never heard of him." Marc grinned. "I've heard of old king Tut, though. Curse of the pharaohs and all that." He looked over his shoulder at the dark recesses of the cave. "What horror from beyond the grave will come to haunt us?" He broke into a peal of laughter and pointed a finger at Dani. "Beware, Dr Hanser, the mummy always comes for the pretty girl."

"Idiot!" Dani grinned despite herself. She gripped the scarab tightly in her right hand and pivoted slowly, searching the bare rock walls around her. "Get the others, Marc."

"Eh?" Marc sobered and he peered at Dani, his eyebrows coming together in perplexity. "What for? There's nothing here. We went over this section when we first arrived."

8

"Please, just get them." Dani waited until the squelching footsteps receded into the depths of the cave before relaxing her tense shoulders. She lowered her head and unclenched her hand, staring at the golden scarab. "It is true, then," she muttered. She paused, smiling self-consciously. "Nut, show me that which is hidden."

Several minutes passed in silence as Dani stared, eyes unfocused, at the rough stone walls of the wide cave. She blinked, and then shook her head when the sound of voices intruded on her. Turning, she watched her small group of graduate students negotiate the muddy track that led from deep in the cave system and the anthropological dig. Flashlights bobbed and danced, sending little disks of light skittering over the ground before fading into the gray light seeping from the cave entrance.

A small dark man with long, wavy, black hair sweeping down over his eyes led the group. He stared up at the tall woman standing by the rock wall, a sour expression distorting his features.

"Well, Dr Hanser?" he asked in a singsong voice redolent of Welsh valleys. "Why have you dragged us away from our valuable work? Is it just to look for golden treasure?"

"Damn it, Daffyd," muttered a male voice from the rear of the group of students. "Do you always have to be so objectionable?"

Daffyd turned, his jaw thrust out. "Objectionable is it, boyo? Just because I'm the only one who seems to take this dig seriously. Here we are at the arse-end of the season and everyone is losing interest. Well, I'm not and I resent being pulled away to search for Egyptian shit."

"Please, Daffyd," Dani said, "moderate your language. There are women present."

9

"Don't mind us," came a clear young voice. A tall blonde girl pushed to the front and stood, hands on hips in front of the tiny Welshman. A man's shirt and faded, ripped jeans covered in mud totally failed to conceal her feminine charms. She grinned, displaying a set of beautiful teeth behind her full lips. "We're used to Daffyd's coarser vocabulary. In fact," she fluttered long lashes, "it's quite a turn-on."

Daffyd flushed and stepped back. "You keep your foul insinuations to yourself," he muttered. "I'll not listen to them." He pushed away and stumbled a few paces back down the track toward the dig, before stopping and standing with hands in pockets, glowering at the group of young people.

Marc snorted. "Now, what's up, Dani? What do you want us to do?"

Dani held out her hand, displaying the golden scarab. "Look at this, all of you. It's Egyptian, end of the eighteenth dynasty or thereabouts and has no business being here."

The students gathered round, the light from the flashlights scintillating from the golden insect. The tall blonde poked a grimy finger at the artifact.

"It's beautiful," she said, stroking the scarab's etched wing covers. "But why shouldn't it be here? Egyptians got up this far into Syria. In fact," her brow furrowed, "didn't the battle of Kadesh take place near here?"

Dani nodded. "About twenty miles northwest of here. But that doesn't explain this." She flipped the scarab over, revealing the sun disk nestled between the carving's legs.

"A circle?" chipped in another girl. "What's exciting about that?" She straightened, pushing back lanky brown hair from her face. "I mean, the beetle is gorgeous but why is a circle so interesting?"

"Because, Doris, dear," said the blonde, "that is not just a circle. Look at the lines radiating from it. They end in little hands. This is an Aten."

"Very good, Angela." Dani grinned. She looked around the circle of faces. "Next question, guys – what is an Aten?" Marc opened his mouth to speak and Dani held up her hand. "Give the others a chance, Marc."

"A circle with hands," said a fresh-faced young man, grinning. He caught Dani's eye and blushed. "Sorry, Doc."

"Aside from Will's statement of the obvious," said Dani, "any other thoughts? Bob? Al?" Both men shook their heads. "All right, Angela. Tell us what an Aten is."

"The Aten is the disk of the sun and represents one of the gods of ancient Egypt," replied Angela promptly. "For a while, the Aten was the only god worshipped, then they overthrew his temples and went back to the old gods. I'm sorry, Dr Hanser. That's all I know."

"Not bad." Dani nodded approvingly. "Very little is known of the time or the events surrounding them. What makes this artifact so interesting ..." she held up the scarab, "is the placement of the symbol of the god Aten on the scarab. The scarab was the symbol of Khepri, an aspect of Re who was one of the most powerful gods in the Egyptian pantheon. Someone was making a statement here."

Daffyd, who had moved up to stand at the back of the group, listening intently, grunted his approval.

Al looked around the cave, scratching his unshaved face absently. "You think there might be other stuff here, Doc?"

11

"I know there is." Dani crossed the mudslide to the cave wall. She ran her hands over the fresh scars in the curved surface of the sandstone and over a vertical surface next to it. "The scarab fell from here. There is more."

Doris glanced at the others. "Er ... that's just a blank wall."

"That's right," agreed Marc. "Perhaps the scarab was just in the mud and we missed it when we searched this area."

"No." Dani shook her head, running her fingers over the smooth rock surface. "There is more here. I know it."

Angela frowned. "How, Dani?" she asked bluntly. "How do you know?"

Bob grunted and picked his way gingerly across the slippery mud to Dani's side. He held the flashlight close to the rock wall, throwing light sideways across the surface in a great yellow cone. Moving slowly he pushed past Dani, murmuring an apology, and illuminated the area on the vertical surface close to the recent rock fall.

"There, see it?" Bob pointed. "A tiny groove."

"Where?" Marc joined him, waving his flashlight around, peering at the rock.

"Not like that," Bob said patiently. "Hold it parallel to the rock face. See how the light throws irregularities into relief. See ... just there ... a thin straight shadow."

"Um, possibly." Marc looked round at Bob, one eyebrow raised.

"You're right," Angela agreed. She reached out and traced the shadow over the rock face from top to bottom. "What do you think, Dani?"

Dani nodded. "I think it's a doorway."

Al frowned. "Bit of a leap, doctor. I mean, extrapolating a straight line in a rock wall to a doorway ..." His voice trailed off.

Bob dropped to his knees, oblivious of the mud, and shone his flashlight directly upward, pushing his face awkwardly against the sandstone. He peered up for a few minutes, angling his head first one way then another. "A line, there." He pointed. "At right angles to the first one. I think you're right, Dani."

"Jesus H. Christ," breathed Al. "We got us a tomb, girls and boys."

"Now who's jumping to conclusions?" Dani asked, a smile on her face. "It's a doorway. Who knows where it leads?"

"So let's find out." Marc turned and started back toward the diggings. "I'll get a couple of pickaxes."

"Hey, hey," Al shouted. "We can't just go blasting into something like this. There are protocols to follow. Tell him, Dani."

Dani looked from one to the other, noting the eagerness on most faces as well as concern creeping across their features. "Al's right, guys. There are protocols to follow. We should report this to the authorities in Damascus."

Will snorted. "Once they hear of it, we'll be packed off home on the next plane. We found it. We should be the ones to excavate it."

"That's true, Dani," added Marc. "They'll hand it over to some government team and we'll be lucky if we ever hear what they find."

"Let's go for it, doc," Angela urged. She looked around at the others. "What do you say, guys? Bob? Doris? ... Dani?"

Dani grinned. "It's tempting." She held up a hand as Al opened his mouth. "I know, Al, we're not really qualified to open an Egyptian tomb but hey, we don't even know if it is one. All we've found are a couple of lines in a rock wall. It may be nothing."

"And we'd look awful fools if we reported a tomb and there was nothing there. Do you think they'd let us back next year?" Marc approached Al and punched him lightly on the shoulder. "What do you say? Can we at least see if there's anything there?"

Al scowled and rubbed his shoulder. "I guess, but I don't like it."

"Do you want to go back to the camp or the dig, Al?" Dani asked, her voice gentle. "If we get into trouble over this I'll tell them you protested my actions."

Al stared at Dani. "No way, doc. If you're determined to go ahead, I'm not going to miss a thing." He turned to Marc. "Go get the pickaxes, dear boy. We have work to do."

Dusk fell, the gray light draining away leaving deep pools of shadow. Bob and Will disappeared for a time before returning from the camp with kerosene lanterns that spluttered and hissed, spreading a golden hue over the sandstone walls. Shadows, demonic and distorted, leapt and plunged as Marc and Al swung their pickaxes. Angela and Doris raked back the chips of sandstone, clearing the debris piling up at the foot of the rock wall.

Dani sat on a boulder near the main path, her gaze fixed on the wall, her fingers stroking the golden scarab. Daffyd sat quietly beside Dani, a stubby self-rolled cigarette glowing in his shadowed face.

At last, Marc lowered his pick and stepped back, his flushed features glistening with sweat, his long hair and beard matted and dirty.

"It's a veneer," he said quietly. "A half an inch or so of plaster mixed with rock dust and sand hiding bricks."

Dani got up and dusted off her jeans before crossing slowly to the shattered wall. Her boots crunched in the fragments of plaster and stone littering the mud. She slipped the scarab into a pocket and ran her fingers over the rough serried brick.

"There are no seals," she whispered. "No cartouches, no symbols. Whatever this is, it's not a tomb."

"Damn," said Al. "I thought we were onto something."

"We are. Nobody goes to this length to hide something unless it's important."

"But if it's not a tomb, what could it be?" Angela asked. "And what about the scarab? Where does that fit in?"

"Only one way to find out," grunted Marc, hefting his pick again. "Stand back, guys. Time to make the bricks fly."

"Hang on, boyo," drawled Daffyd. "There's something you should do before you get all macho again."

Marc lowered the pick and swung round. "Yeah? And what might that be? I don't see you contributing much to this enterprise."

"That's because I believe in careful methodology rather than the cowboy antics I've seen so far." He got to his feet and flicked his cigarette stub into the shadows before turning to Dani. "Dr Hanser, at least take some photographs of the wall before you break it down."

"What for?" Al strode to the wall and flung out his hand, gesturing at the rough bricks. "They're only bricks, for God's sake, not some bloody artifact."

Daffyd smirked and pulled out his tin of tobacco and cigarette papers. "Dear, oh dear, Dr Hanser, some of

15

your students are showing a dismaying level of ignorance." He finished rolling his cigarette and stuck it between his lips. He slipped the tin of tobacco into his pocket, lit up and breathed a cloud of strongly-smelling smoke over his unwilling audience. "Let me enlighten you."

He strolled over to the wall, pushing past Marc and Al. "Doris, be a good girl and lift that lantern a bit higher." He crouched beside the wall and regarded Dani and the students crowding round. He smirked again. "Now, I'm an expert on the Paleolithic, not historical times, but even I can see that there are two types of bricks here." He stabbed a finger at the wall. "This is common mudbrick, sun dried, with an obvious straw inclusion. They've been making this type of brick in the Middle East for thousands of years. But this ..." Daffyd brushed some dust loose from the lower tiers of the wall. "This is worked stone. Brick-sized, much the same colour, but definitely worked stone. And a rather distinctive style, I might add."

"So what does that mean, Daffyd?" asked Angela.

"You want to tell them, Dr Hanser?"

Dani nodded slowly. "The dressed stone looks Egyptian. It is similar to the funerary blocks used throughout the Middle Kingdom and early part of the New Kingdom. Whoever started this did not finish it, though. The mud bricks were added later, by unskilled labourers."

"Or else we have a desecrated tomb, repaired by a later generation," added Daffyd. "Either way, we need to photograph this wall before we break through."

"We're still going to do that?" Doris queried. "I mean, if it really is a tomb, oughtn't we to ... er, tell somebody?"

16

Dani pursed her lips, her forehead furrowing. "I still favour going ahead, at least for now." She looked across at the tiny Welshman leaning nonchalantly against the brick wall. "You agree, Daffyd?"

"Oh, yes. Whatever we find, it should be interesting. Just take a few elementary precautions. Act like scientists for God's sake, not like a pack of children." He walked back to the path and sat down against a boulder. He stretched out his legs and put his hands behind his head.

"I'll get the camera," murmured Bob, hurrying off toward the cave entrance.

Used flash bulbs littered the ground before Dani expressed satisfaction. She called Marc and Al over to the wall and pointed out an area of crumbling mud brick at about waist height. "Keep the hole small, if you can, and if you break through into a cavity, stop at once."

Marc and Al went at it enthusiastically and after only a few strokes, stepped back. "Here's your cavity, Dani," Marc murmured.

A black hole yawned in the sandy coloured wall of brick, sucking in the yellow light of the lanterns. Dani moved closer and brushed the rubble away from the lip of the hole. A loose brick fell inside with a clatter that echoed and rang. She took the lantern from Doris and held it to the hole, peering past the light into the cavity.

"What can you see, doc?" Al asked.

Dani peered through the hole in silence for several minutes. "There's ... there's a chamber. I can't see the far walls, only the closest one, but there are pictures and ... and colours." She pulled back and stared wide-eyed at her students, her face pale. "We've got to get in there. Help me."

Marc stared back at Dani's shocked features for a few moments then shouldered past her and stuck his head

17

through the hole. A heartbeat later he ripped at the crumbling mud brick, pulling it loose in a billowing cascade of dust and dirt. Al joined him, then a moment later, Bob and Angela, jostling at the rapidly growing cavity.

A section of the brick fell away, into the room beyond the cave and a shaft from the kerosene lanterns, filtered through dust clouds, lit up the interior. A whitewashed wall, gleaming as if freshly painted, sent a coruscation of light back. Figures of animals and men danced on the wall as the dust billowed and settled.

Coughing and wiping the grit from their faces, the students stepped aside, letting their leader enter. Dani stepped cautiously across the threshold of dressed sandstone blocks and swept the beam of her flashlight over the walls and floors of the chamber. She let it rest for a moment on a jumble of wood and stone in a far corner before continuing her survey.

"Incredible," she breathed. "I've never seen anything like this."

The students crowded into the chamber, pushing and jostling, their bodies obscuring the lanterns, sending dark shadows leaping over the painted walls. They settled, staring about them, flashlights picking out the details.

"Look," cried Marc, pointing. "A hunting scene." A flight of ducks, wings spread, each feather painstakingly delineated, exploded from the surface of a lotus-covered lagoon. An archer, concealed among rushes and feathery papyrus, took aim. On the far side of the lagoon a skewered bird lay, its head raised in agony as another fell from the skies. The colours of the scene glowed and the shifting shadows lent movement to the hunt.

"My God," breathed Doris. "They look alive."

"And here," Angela said. "Is this the owner of the tomb?"

18

The others swung round to look at the opposite wall. A young woman, reddish hair cropped in a side lock, her large almond eyes blued and outlined in black, calmly regarded a large scarab beetle. The insect, rather than being a stylized representative of the sun god, was caught in the act of rolling a dung ball across the sand.

The students stared at the woman on the wall, taking in her fine features, her sheer garment and the studied poise of her carriage. Angela walked to the painting and reached up to it, touching the delicately hennaed feet. "She looks like you, Dr Hanser."

"Maybe a little," replied Dani. "My mother was Egyptian after all."

"No, really," said Marc. "I'd swear that was you."

"Whoever it is, we have a bit of a mystery here," Daffyd said softly. "The subject matter is typical New Kingdom Egyptian but the style is not. It is similar to Amarna-style art but with differences. Look how alive these paintings are. It's almost photographic the way the artist has captured movement."

Al spoke from near the entrance. His head bent close to the wall, his flashlight illuminated a small part of the surface. "The wall's covered in tiny hieroglyphics. Can anyone read them?"

Daffyd crossed over and scanned the surface. "Another mystery. These hieroglyphs are minute. Not at all like a normal inscription."

"Can you read them?"

Daffyd shrugged. "A little. These symbols in a cartouche ..." he pointed to a series of tiny marks surrounded by a lozenge-shaped line. "... represent royalty. If memory serves, this one says 'Ankh-e-sen-pa' something."

"Ankhesenpaaten," said Dani from across the chamber. "And the bit before it probably says 'King's daughter, of his body, his beloved.'"

"How the hell would you know that?" Al asked. "You couldn't possibly see it from over there. I'm standing right by it and I can hardly make out the squiggles."

"Because this is a tomb of someone connected with the worship of the Aten, and Ankhesenpaaten was a daughter of pharaoh Akhenaten." Dani pointed her flashlight at the ceiling of the chamber.

A great golden sun disk filled the ceiling vault, rays extending outward in all directions, becoming tiny hands holding the ankh, the symbol of life. One ray, longer than the rest, swept back into the shadows at the rear of the chamber. Dani's flashlight followed it across the roof and down the far wall to where it touched the head of a kneeling woman. Back turned to its live audience, the painted image regarded an array of beings facing it. Figures of men, of women, of beasts and strange combinations stood in a semicircle around the kneeling figure, their painted concentration focused on the young woman.

"The Great Ennead of Heliopolis," Dani said in a strangely flat voice. "The nine gods of ancient Egypt."

"I thought they had hundreds of gods?"

"They did, but the Nine embody all the others. Three was a sacred number to the Egyptians and three times three even more so." Dani walked closer to the rear wall and knelt down in the dust, her body hiding the painting of the kneeling woman. She raised her hands as if in supplication. "Atum-Re, creator god and sun god; Shu, god of air; Tefnut, goddess of water; Geb, lord of the earth; Nut, goddess of the heavens; Asar, lord of the dead; Seth, god of violence; Nebt-Het, mistress of the underworld and protector of the dead; Auset, queen, protector and sustainer ..." Dani's head slumped and she almost fell, leaning against the wall.

Marc and Angela leapt forward to support her, lifting her to her feet. "What the hell happened?" Marc asked. "Are you okay?"

"You seemed really weird there, Doc," Angela added.

Dani shook her head and disengaged herself from Marc and Angela. "I'm okay. Just a bit dizzy there for a moment. Now, what was I going to do? Ah, yes, have a look at this inscription." She pushed past the students to the wall where Al and Daffyd still stood. "Let's have a look, shall we?" Dani leaned close to the wall, flashlight in hand. She perused the hieroglyphs for several minutes, her lips moving as she muttered to herself.

"Yes, as I thought. This is a description of Ankhesenpaaten entering into the presence of her father at some ceremony or other ... doesn't seem to say which one ... maybe ..." She moved across the wall, her finger tracing the symbols. "... ah, the Great Heb-Sed festival. In the twelfth year of Akhenaten's reign."

Dani stepped back and scanned the wall, her flashlight beam lighting up the columns of tiny symbols covering the wall from ceiling to floor. She shook her head, her brow furrowed and eyes narrowed.

"This wasn't written by a scribe. The words are wrong; the tone is far too informal. It reads as though it's a letter to a friend. I've never seen an inscription like this."

"But you can read it?" Marc asked.

"What does it say?" Al gripped her arm.

"Tell us, Dr Hanser," pressed Daffyd quietly. "Start at the beginning and tell us what it's about." He guided Dani gently across the room to a clear space at the right-hand end of the wall. "The figures face to the right, so we read from the right."

Dani nodded and scanned the first column of symbols. She cleared her throat and traced the hieroglyphs with a finger.

"Know then that I, the last of the line of Amenhotep and mother of the Great House, the Lord of the Two Lands, he who is Seti son of Ramses; to him be Life, Prosperity, Health; do set down this account of my vengeance against the blasphemers and usurpers of the holy throne of Kemet. I, who was once counted as the least of the daughters of the king, have been blessed by the gods. Though I bear the name of the one god who was set above all others, yet have the true gods of my land used me to reassert their authority over all men. Know then that I am Beketaten, youngest daughter of King Nebmaetre Amenhotep, and of his Great Wife Tiye. I was born in a year of tragedy and hope ..."

Chapter One

I have sat on the throne of The Two Lands, *Ta Mehu* and *Ta Shemau*; *Kemet* and *Deshret*; known too as the Land of the Nine Bows and to people of the nations as the Nation; the sacred seat whence all power derives in that ancient land. It is the throne of the Great House *Per-Aa*, that name transferred to the king who is called Great One; God-on-Earth, beloved of Re, bringer of life and death, shepherd to the people.

They say that the experience changes a man forever. I would not know, for two reasons: First, I cannot remember a time before I sat on the throne, coming to it in the belly of my mother. And second, I am a woman.

I was born in the thirty-first year of the reign of Nebmaetre Amenhotep, Lord of the Two Lands. I am his youngest daughter, begotten on the body of his beloved wife and queen Tiye, yet he never knew me or received me into his holy presence. I was born six months after the gods struck my father down with an affliction that erased his memories and crippled his body. For eight years he remained thus until the gods called my father to take his place among them in the underworld.

The kings of Kemet are given five names. Secret names, familiar names, names by which they are known to those they rule and by which the nations of the world know them. My father Amenhotep was known by that name only to his family; it was a personal name, bestowed on him at birth by a proud father. In truth, he was the Living Heru, Strong Bull Appearing in Truth; establishing Laws and Pacifying; Golden Heru, Great of Valor, Smiting the Asiatics; King of Ta Shemau and Ta Mehu, Nebmaetre; Son of Re, Amenhotep, Ruler of the

23

city of Waset in the sepat of Waset, in our beloved Ta Shemau.

Women are only given one name, for though women are accorded equality within the Two Lands, unlike other nations, women themselves are regarded as ornaments. A woman may own property, divorce her husband, marry whom she chooses, and bring suit against a man in the law courts. A queen may hold great power within the land, may rule over a great household and, in the absence of the king, may even issue commands; yet she is regarded as a lesser being by her husband. How much less is a girl-child worth, one born without a father?

A royal boy, particularly an heir, is named by his father on the day of his birth, and on the next holy day receives a secret name known only to the gods and their high priest. Later, a king receives coronation names by which he is known to the nations. My father Amenhotep had the coronation name Nebmaetre, and my brother, also Amenhotep – at least as he was at the start – was known as Neferkheperure Waenre.

A girl also receives a name from her father, though this may be the only one she receives until she flowers into womanhood. Then, if she displays some great beauty, she may be called by a more descriptive name.

I, on the other hand, though a royal princess, had no father present on my birth date to give me a chosen name. No one gave me a name and, though my mother, Queen Tiye, told me later that my name was to have been Beketamen, the handmaiden of Amun, I was never called that. Later, when my brother became king, I received first a nickname, then a proper name at his hands. For a few years I was called simply No-Name. It was as well that I did not realize at the time in what peril I was, having no name. If I had died, my spirit would have ceased to exist, the gods would have turned from me. Later, though, I acquired other names – nicknames, names of endearment from family and lovers, names of awe from the common people, and names of hatred from my enemies.

Yes, I have enemies. One does not enter the royal house; become a member of the nobility, live intimately with kings and princes without making enemies. Just as my position is high within the Great House, so are my enemies among the highest and most powerful. I have fought against three kings, two of whom were members of my own family. They are dead now these many years and I have lived to see another family raised to the Great House, though few within it realize they are tied to my family by bonds of blood.

The Great House of Kemet is ancient. The scribes and priests maintain there has been a king in Kemet time out of mind, stretching thousands of years back to when Menes, the first God-on-earth unified and ruled this blessed land. That is not to say that my father was a direct earthly descendant of the first king. Many families have embraced the godhead, for the gods themselves desire strength on the throne of Kemet. Even the strongest and most virile young man will fade, passing by degrees into maturity and feeble old age. So it is with families too. A dynasty of kings will arise, full of power and strength, ruling Kemet with an iron hand for a time. Then as the generations pass, the strength leaves – dissipates – until the kings presiding over the decline of the family fade into obscurity and the gods raise a new family from the ashes of the old.

Our family has been a strong one, possibly one of the strongest. My great-grandfather Tuthmosis, the third of that name, was a great conqueror, making his name, and

Kemet's, feared amongst the nations. My father, too, has been a great king, though one devoted to building and beauty rather than to the destructions of war. Yet he was the last of the great kings of our family. For a time I believed my brother/nephew Smenkhkare would achieve fame but he had too many enemies.

Smenkhkare – ah, Smenkhkare – best of men. There was a man destined to become a great king but for the evil of his Tjaty. A son of my father's later years, Smenkhkare was not in the direct line of succession, yet he was raised to the throne by fate and the strong hand of his uncle. My father begat him on his daughter, my elder sister Sitamen, three years before my own birth. It may seem strange and unnatural to those of lesser nations that a man should have a child on his own daughter, yet in the Great House it is not uncommon.

Every king seeks an heir of his body, and more, as the future is known only to the gods. Yet too many sons and the peace of a household may be disturbed through unseemly rivalry. So, too, with daughters. It is unthinkable that a royal daughter of Kemet should be married off to some foreign prince, but if not a prince of the nations, who is she to marry? Many nobles of the Two Lands would be only too pleased to link their houses with the king's by marrying off a son to the king's daughter; but in that way, too, lies discord. Many an act of violence has been spawned by overweening ambition. Far better the king should marry his sister and his daughter and keep the strength of the Great House within the family. The gods themselves spend their seed only amongst sisters, mothers, daughters, being jealous of their power. Why should not the king, Lord of the Two Lands and God-on-Earth, do likewise?

My father Nebmaetre Amenhotep married a commoner, Tiye, daughter of the king's Master of Horse, Yuya, and by all accounts loved her deeply. He had other wives of course; no king would be respected unless he had a herd of wives to be serviced by the Great Bull of Heru; yet was my mother, Tiye, always his favourite. They had seven children together - two sons: Tuthmosis and Amenhotep, family names that reflect the strength and antiquity of our line; and five daughters: Sitamen, Iset, Henuttaneb, Nebetiah and me.

Tuthmosis was the eldest, crown prince and heir, beloved of my father. Strong of limb, bronzed and athletic, with a quick and sharp mind, he embodied all that was good and great in my family. People talked of him as a re-embodiment of his illustrious namesake great-grandfather and looked for mighty deeds when he ascended the throne. He became a priest of Ptah in the city of Ineb Hedj – first heir to the throne ever to be elevated to this position – but fell ill and died of the plague four years before my birth. His brother Amenhotep was raised up in his place. Being the only surviving son, my father raised him to the throne, making him a co-regent. However, as he had neither the inclination, nor the heart for kingship, the younger Amenhotep, now styled Neferkheperure Waenre, returned to Zarw where he ruled, with his advisors, over the Delta lands.

Amenhotep was everything Tuthmosis was not. A sickly child, he pursued activities more in keeping with a scribe's son rather than the son of a king. Poetry was his passion, never statecraft. He was raised in my mother's city of Zarw, far downriver from Waset, surrounded by our mother's kinsmen. Yuya, our grandfather was a foreigner, a learned man of the tribe of Khabiru from the

27

north. I believe it was from these people that my brother learned his strange ideas.

By puberty, it became apparent that the gods had not blessed Amenhotep with the strength that a king of the Land of the Nine Bows needs. He developed strangely, his swollen hips and thighs hinting at a female's sex rather than a male's. His head was oddly elongate and his face long. If he had not been the king's son, it was whispered that he might have been put away. However, he was an acknowledged son of the king's body and while hardly likely to succeed to the throne, he was cherished, though far from the king's side. It was whispered, too, that my brother Amenhotep was not the natural son of his father the king, but instead came from the loins of another man, a Khabiru, in the Zarw household of my mother. These whispers, however, were started by a man who had everything to gain from blackening the names of my family, and I put no credence in them.

My father, as I have already said, was not a great warrior. He successfully waged war against the Nubians but put more store on diplomacy. His constant negotiations led to many foreign marriages as he tied the kings of surrounding lands to Kemet's skirts. One such diplomatic wife, Ghilukhepa, daughter of Shuttarna, King of Mitanni, came to my father's bed in the tenth year of his reign. Yet even this sloe-eyed, raven-haired beauty could not distract my father long. He sired a child on her, then duty done, hastened back to my mother's side.

His eldest daughter Sitamen, my sister, married her father in his twenty-sixth regnal year, in a year of Jubilee. The jubilee was held early for a reason that is not remembered, perhaps just on the whim of the king. It would normally have been held in the king's thirtieth year. At the first great Heb-Sed festival of his reign,

28

where Nebmaetre Amenhotep went through a ritual re-enactment of his coronation, anointed with the white crown of the South and the red crown of the North, he proved his strength by running, in full regalia, around the great chariot stadium four times with the Apis bull beside him. Later, in the royal palace, he proved his continued virility by taking Sitamen as Great Royal Wife. He lay with her, even though by custom it was not required, and later that year rejoiced in the birth of his son Smenkhka-re.

He married his other daughter Iset four years later, after another Heb-Sed festival, making her, too, a Great Royal Wife. But he did not lay with Iset, as that very evening, while celebrating the marriage feast, my father was struck down by the god Set, ever the enemy of the Living Heru.

Heqareshu, overseer of the nurses, told me later that as Amenhotep stood in the great hall, his beautiful young bride on his arm, accepting the plaudits of the assembled nobility, he staggered and put a hand up to his head before collapsing. He remained asleep, unable to be aroused, for a night and a day, but when he at last awoke, it was as if the king had been replaced by a clay figure of a man. His muscles would not obey him; the left side of his face sagged and ran like a beeswax candle left out in the sun, and his voice, once so deep and powerful, was now slurred and unintelligible.

My mother, the queen, stepped in when it became apparent this malady would last, and for half a year managed the kingdom alone until their son Neferkheperure Waenre Amenhotep could be summoned from distant Zarw, anointed by the priests of Amun and crowned as full regent in Waset. This as close as I ever came to

the throne myself, being in the belly of my mother, except for – but I am getting ahead of myself...

Chapter Two

Waset, City of Amun, lay baking in the summer sun. Its mighty walls and towering temples and monuments, painted and ornamented, gleamed dully beneath the sheen of dust raised by the cheering crowds that lined the main thoroughfares of the city whenever one of the many processions of gods and priests passed by. For weeks, preparations for the coronation had occupied the thoughts and hands of every artisan, tradesman and peasant pressed into service by officials of the Great House. The former crown prince Tuthmosis, dead these past five years, had been much beloved by noble and commoner alike, but the past was past. The Gods had called him to the underworld and the Land of the Nine Bows moved on. At least there was another prince ready to step into his sandals and take his place on the throne of Kemet.

Neferkheperure Waenre Amenhotep was a virtual unknown, having spent most of his life in the Delta lands, close to his mother's kinfolk in Zarw. A younger son, disinclined to athletic pursuits and public life; nevertheless, he was son and namesake of his illustrious father Nebmaetre Amenhotep. Surely he was a worthy scion of the Great House. Rumor had it that his physique was not all that it should be, but what did that matter? Per-Aa, the Great House, king of the Two Lands was God-on-Earth and how the gods chose to portray themselves was their business. At least he would have his father beside him on the throne, though this was another source of disturbing rumor. Half a year had passed since the unknown malady had afflicted the king and though the priests offered daily prayers for his health, some whispered that he would never recover. None, from the highest noble to the low-

31

liest peasant, liked to dwell on the thought of Kemet without a strong hand on the reins.

Samu, street-sweeper of Waset, straightened his back with a groan and rested his worn reed-rush broom against a wall lining the Road of Amun, sometimes called the Avenue of Rams for the two large statues of the holy ram of Amun that stood on either side of the temple gates. The road led straight as an arrow from the North Gate to the huge temple of the god. Samu cast his gaze over the jostling crowds, already thinning as the heat of the day increased. Catching sight of a young servant girl of one of the minor noble houses, he stepped in front of her, blocking her way. He hawked and spat in the dust, disturbing the flies that swarmed about a piece of rubbish.

"A plague on these priests and their decorations. And for what, I ask you? So we might have the pleasure of having a stripling prince lord it over us." Samu picked up a painted scrap of papyrus by his feet and glanced up at the wall, trying to find where it might have fallen from. Failing, he shrugged and let it fall to the ground. "I swear I have swept this street since sun-up and it looks no cleaner now than when I started."

The maid opened her eyes wide in shock. "Guard your tongue, old man. If the priests hear your blasphemies against the Great House you will think your present job a pleasant one."

"You think I care?" Nevertheless, Samu glanced about him, his eyes open for the gleaming white linen worn by even the lowliest priests. Seeing only the begrimed and dusty clothing of the peasantry and city dwellers he grinned, displaying a mouthful of yellowed and broken teeth. "No one here cares. Truth be told, most would agree with me. Why do we need another

32

king? Is not the Queen managing well enough with her council? And the king, too, he will recover."

The young girl hesitated, wavering between stopping and talking with the gnarled old man and walking on. "You do not want the young prince to mount the throne?"

"As well as his beautiful wife?" Samu cackled. "Now there is a woman even I could find time for." He hitched at his stained kilt suggestively. "She is well named – Nefer the beautiful."

The girl's mouth curled down in distaste. "You do not think the young prince Amenhotep should be crowned?" she persisted.

"In time, yes. Though he is not the man his brother Tuthmosis was." Samu shrugged. "Well, no doubt the Queen's Council will not listen to me but they should. I am helping pay for all this."

"You?" The girl threw back her head and laughed; a high, clear song of mirth. "What would your share of the taxes be, old man? A copper shaving or two?"

"Maybe," Samu grumbled. "But when did the nobles ever care for we who enable them to live in comfort?" He eyed the young girl standing in front of him. "And where are you off to, pretty one? Come pass an hour with me and I'll buy you a pot of beer." He leered, his eyes dropping to her breasts, bared as was the fashion, her thin linen shift tucked under the bronzed swellings.

"Keep your evil thoughts to yourself, old man. I am about my mistress' business and have no time for such things." She sneered. "Even did I wish to, do you think I would choose a dried-up old stick of a man like you? I like my men young, firm of thigh and buttock and with a strong back."

"That rules you out then, Samu."

33

The old street sweeper started and looked round, relaxing as he caught sight of a younger man sauntering across the street toward him.

"Mahuhy," he acknowledged with a bob of his head.

Mahuhy swaggered up to the young girl with a broad smile. He loosened the kilt at his waist and flipped the end to one side, allowing her a brief glimpse of firm genitals. "If you are looking for a good time, pretty one, don't waste your time with old men."

The girl flushed then looked at the younger man with a considering eye. Tall, with dark features that hinted at Nubian ancestry, his black eyes sparkled above gleaming white teeth. "And who are you?" She waved a fly away with a slim brown hand.

"Mahuhy, a trader and businessman. And you?"

"Tio. Personal maid to my lady Sebtitis." She touched her upper lip with the tip of a tiny pink tongue. "In what do you trade, Mahuhy?"

Samu snorted. "Whatever you have stolen, he will find a buyer for. Or if you wish to sell yourself, he will be pleased to arrange it, for a price."

"Come now, Samu, old friend, you do me an injustice," Mahuhy said with a smile, one hand coming to rest on the old man's scrawny shoulder. "Have I not always let you in on my good fortune?" His grip tightened.

Samu grimaced with pain and grunted. "When it cost you nothing."

Tio glanced at the old street sweeper dismissively before focusing on Mahuhy. "I would not want to sell myself, but I am not averse to being entertained for an evening – if the young man interested me." She looked at him boldly.

"You know the tavern in the Street of Cloth? I am there most evenings around sunset. Ask for me. I am sure I can find you an ... interesting young man to amuse you." Mahuhy smiled knowingly, forcing another blush from the young girl. "On the other hand, if you need money, I can find buyers for almost anything. Trinkets, perhaps? There are fripperies that your lady would not miss?"

"Perhaps. I will think on it." Tio glanced down at Mahuhy's kilt and turned away with an exaggerated swing of her hips. "I will see you at the Street of Cloth one evening, Mahuhy. Then we shall see if you are enough of a man for me." Flashing him a quick smile, Tio walked away, her head high and body moving gracefully in her thin linen dress.

Mahuhy grinned and tugged at himself, adjusting the folds of his kilt. "She looks like she knows what she is about," he observed.

Samu grunted again and picked up his reed broom. "A whore who doesn't yet realize it."

"The best type. I shall enjoy introducing her to the pleasures of my establishment."

"Fleecing her of all she makes, too, no doubt."

"How else am I to afford my other business ventures? Anyway, enough of this, old man." Mahuhy glanced upward. "A little after noon, I think. What say you we find a shady tavern and rest our weary bones after an honest morning's work?"

***

The bed chamber of the noble lady Sebtitis was spacious and well-appointed. Facing the north, and shadowed by the Great Palace in Waset, it remained cool until well after noon, even in the height of summer. Polished granite floors held the cool of the previous night, stretching gray and pink and white in a wide expanse that reflected light and sound alike from the high, curtained windows looking out onto a walled courtyard. The lady's bed, made of carved ebony with ivory inlay, sat rumpled, decked with soft linen sheets, rugs and pillows at the far end of the room, beneath transparent gauze curtains that kept out the mosquitoes during the rains, and revealed enticing sights whenever Sebtitis felt in need of a lover. Chairs, tables and inlaid cedar chests lay scattered around the chamber, every available level surface cluttered with a profusion of tiny bottles, pots and unguent jars. A wicker cage stood in one corner, flashes of yellow flitting between the narrow cane bars as a small song-bird spoke tremulously of half-forgotten freedoms.

The lady Sebtitis herself sat, with her servants in attendance, on a wide cushioned stool near one of the windows, looking out on the courtyard. High brick walls surrounded a wide expanse of garden paved with flagstones, the edges softened by luxurious plantings of flowers and shrubs, an ornamental pool with lotus blossoms and a spreading acacia tree. An old man fished fallen blossoms from the pool with a piece of cloth attached to a long pole.

A sleek shadow slipped from behind the curtain and arching, rubbed against Sebtitis' bare leg. She looked down, a smile on her lips, her fingers trailing over soft fur. "Miw," she cried.

The cat crouched and leapt lightly onto the woman's lap, butting its head against her chin. Sebtitis laughed and scratched between the cat's ears, eliciting an eruption of purring. "I love you, too, Miw darling, but I must get ready and I cannot do it with you here." She picked up the spotted cat and handed it to a young, naked girl standing beside her. "Abar, take him down to the kitchens and feed him. Some fish, I think."

The girl hurried off with the unresisting cat, her bare feet slapping faintly against the floor. Sebtitis shrugged off her linen shift and sat naked on the stool. "You may start, Weret."

"Yes, my lady." Weret signaled and a young woman stepped forward with a small tray. Weret picked a small cloth from the tray and, dipping it into citrus-scented water, began gently to wipe her lady's face, clearing away any trace of sleep. Finishing, she dropped the cloth to the floor, where another naked girl quickly salvaged it. Weret dabbed the traces of moisture from Sebtitis' face and picked up the pot of powdered alabaster.

"A touch too much sun, my lady," murmured Weret. "However ..." she judiciously dabbed the powder onto her mistress' skin with a short stick crushed and splayed out at the tip like a brush. "... I think we can keep you fashionably pale."

"What would I do without you, Weret?"

Rouge came next, just a hint to raise the cheekbones, mixed with a touch of ochre. Weret examined her lady's face carefully, brushing away the excess. A girl stepped forward with the eye makeup, colouring creams for the eyelids with powdered lapis and malachite. Kohl followed, the black border accentuating the green and blue of the eyes, drawn out into an almond shape, with thick black tails extending toward the temples.

"With your permission, I will leave rouging the lips until just before you leave, my lady. You may require some refreshment and that would smear the colour."

Weret turned her attention to ears and throat, working with alabaster, ochre and rouge to create the impression of glowing health yet lightening the natural coppery tint of the skin. She rubbed a thumb over her mistress' breasts, from nipple to base of the throat, frowning

37

slightly at the faint loss of elasticity as the skin sprung back. She squatted and viewed the breasts from the side. "Aloe, my lady. I think we must use an astringent today."

The unguent pot was produced and the astringent applied. After a few minutes, Weret nodded and bent to the task of hiding all traces of the preparation. She finished by rouging the nipples. "There, my lady, your breasts will be the envy of the whole court, Queen Nefertiti included."

Sebtitis laughed; a clear tinkling cry of pleasure. "Surely not? I have heard her described as the most beautiful woman in the world."

Weret smiled. "Only one of the most beautiful, my lady. The men at court today will not be able to keep their eyes off you."

Sebtitis looked down, her fingers delicately tracing her flat belly and firm thighs. "I wish I could see myself properly, Weret. I can only see a glimmer in the bronze mirror."

"You will see your beauty reflected in men's eyes today, my lady." Weret beckoned to two young women standing by an open cedar chest. "Have you decided on your dress?"

"Show them to me again. I cannot make up my mind."

The women held up the two dresses to their naked bodies. Both garments were of the thinnest, finest linen, sheer and revealing, falling in clear cascades to the floor. Both were designed to be fastened beneath the breasts, lifting and firming. One had a thin strap that ran upward from the bodice, between the breasts and looped around the neck. Gossamer thin wings extended down over the shoulders, partially obscuring the breasts.

"I am not sure I like that one after all, Weret. If my breasts are so fine, I should not hide them."

"Indeed, my lady, yet sometimes a hint of pleasure is more exciting, more titillating than the plain view."

"Perhaps." Sebtitis delicately scratched her bald head with a long painted fingernail, her expression thoughtful. "If I was to wear it I should open the front. Pull the sides open a tiny bit, Weret, and I shall give them a glimpse of my belly."

"Inspired, lady." Weret signaled to the women and one dress went back into the chest while the other was rushed off to the seamstress. "And the wig, my lady? I would recommend the long black one. It will make you appear paler by contrast."

Sebtitis nodded. "Show me my jewels. Where is that lazy good-for-nothing? Hekenu, come here at once, you bad girl, or I shall have you beaten."

A scrawny young woman hurried in, a small chest clutched in her arms. "H... here, my lady," Hekenu stammered. "I was dusting the box, lady. Forgive me."

Sebtitis reached over and pinched the girl hard on her buttock, smiling as the girl yelped in pain. She took the box and opened it, pawing through the trinkets within. "Where is my lapis neckless, you wicked girl? Have you stolen it?"

"No ... no, my lady." Hekenu leaned over and pointed. "See, lady, and here it is. Let me put it on you ..." She lifted it from the box and deftly fastened it around her mistress' neck. "Beautiful."

"Beautiful," Weret echoed. "It matches your eyes perfectly." She hurried Hekenu away and picked out some other pieces of jewelry, laying them carefully on a low table. "Perfumes next, my lady?"

39

Sebtitis picked up a polished bronze mirror and held it up, turning this way and that, peering at the dull reflection. "Am I truly beautiful, Weret? As beautiful as the young queen?"

"Indeed you are, mistress. Why, the young king himself will not be able to take his eyes off you."

"Now that is an interesting thought. It would not be the first time a king has sought pleasure away from the arms of his queen. Perhaps I can entice the young king Amenhotep into having an affair."

***

Seti, judge and troop commander of the garrison town of Hut-waret in the eastern Delta of the Great River, sat back in his ornate, cushioned chair and regarded his only surviving son. The young man stood at attention, his bronzed, muscular body gleaming with a faint sheen of sweat, his linen kilt still crisp and clean despite the heat. Picking up a faience cup of watered wine, Seti sipped, his eyes all the while fixed on the young man's face.

"Your report, soldier."

The young man glanced quickly at an older man standing against a wall behind the judge, and then looked straight ahead again. "Sir. I proceeded as ordered to the Khabiru encampment outside of Zarw with a troop of my men. There we requested an interview with ..."

"Requested, soldier? The Khabiru are hired men, just one step up from slaves. You do not request, you command. You are an officer in the army of the world's greatest empire."

"Yes, sir. We interviewed Kishom, head of the council of Khabiru elders concerning the trouble in the city. He was, er ... persuaded to admit his men were at fault."

40

Seti leaned forward. "Persuaded? How?" He sat back again and waved his free hand dismissively. "Never mind. Carry on."

"One moment, commander, if I may?" The older man stared at the young officer. "What was the crime committed by these men?"

"They demanded higher wages of the king for their labours in building the king's city and demanded the right to take their wealth back to their own country."

The older man frowned. "And this is a crime?"

"No, sir, not of itself. When their demands were refused they became angry and rioting broke out. A child died."

"Ah. Go on with your report, soldier."

The young officer stared at the older man for a further moment before returning his gaze to his father. "Kishom identified the men responsible and we arrested them, six in all. We interrogated them on the spot and, after extracting confessions, removed them from the camp."

"You had no trouble taking the men?"

The young man allowed himself a small shrug. "Nothing we could not handle, sir."

The older man pushed away from the wall and stepped forward a pace. "Tell the judge the whole story, boy. There was a riot."

The soldier looked hard at the older man for a few seconds. "Yes, sir. There was a riot. A crowd disputed our right to take the men. I sent a platoon in with staffs to break a few heads. It did not last long. We removed the prisoners and brought them to Hut-waret. They are in the cells now."

"Your boy displayed a cool head, Seti, old friend. A lesser man might have panicked and shed unnecessary blood." The older man, his craggy face topped by a bald head grizzled with gray stubble, walked over and poured himself a wine from a side table.

Seti nodded, a faint smile creasing his lips. "So the six men have confessed and await trial?"

"Five, sir. One died during interrogation. Another ... well, he may not live to be executed."

"No matter. I will conduct the trial tomorrow. The executions will be carried out immediately after. I see no point in delay."

The older man sipped at his wine thoughtfully. "Wise," he agreed. "It is a custom for clemency to be shown on a coronation day. Our new king is part Khabiru himself and may well pardon the men if he gets to hear of their trial." He poured another goblet of wine and held it out toward the young soldier. "I think your son Paramessu has acquitted himself most creditably. Will you allow him to join us in a cup of wine?"

"Of course." Seti nodded. "At ease, my son."

Paramessu accepted the goblet and looked enquiringly at the older man. "Forgive me, sir, if I do not know your name. I was informed you would accompany my troop to the Khabiru encampment, but not who you were or why."

Seti rose and walked over to the older man. "This is my old friend Horemheb. We have been comrades for what, twenty years now? He has recently been promoted to General of the Eastern borders and is touring the garrison towns. I insisted he stay here a few days."

"And I am very glad I did. Tell me, Paramessu, do you concern yourself with the future of our To-mery, our beloved land?"

"Yes, general, sir. I am very proud to serve in the ever-victorious army."

Horemheb grunted. "The idealism and short-sightedness of youth," he muttered. "What do you see happening, now that the prince Amenhotep has been raised to full regent?"

Paramessu raised his eyebrows. "Happen, sir? Why should anything happen? Apart from the usual patrols," he added hastily.

"What do you know of the prince, boy?"

"Only that he is the noble son of an illustrious father. He was raised in Zarw with his mother the Queen, becoming co-regent shortly after his brother Tuthmosis – may his name live forever – was called to the gods."

"And of his policies?" Horemheb held up a hand. "Let him speak, Seti. I would have no secrets here. He is an intelligent young man."

"Those of his father, the great Nebmaetre Amenhotep, sir," Paramessu said slowly. "Though he has had no experience of war ... nor even hunting."

"His policies are those of peace," Horemheb stated flatly. "He takes no interest in the army and little in the affairs of the nations. All he concerns himself with is religion and beauty."

"You know the state of the garrison command here in Hut-waret, son," Seti added. "Most of the garrisons are as ill-equipped as we. Do you think a king who has no interest in the army will spend gold to strengthen it?"

"But that would be suicidal, father. Even now there is unrest on the borders. It would be foolish to weaken our armies further."

"That is why I have been appointed General of the Eastern borders," Horemheb explained. "I am to examine the state of our defences and make recommendations."

"So the king is prepared to act?"

43

"Not the king, Paramessu. The old king is still incapable of ruling us, and the Queen and prince Amenhotep are disinclined to soil their hands with such ugly things. No, it is the king's advisor, Ay, who has given me my appointment."

"The Queen's brother?" Seti frowned. "I thought such appointments could only come from the king or his Tjaty."

"The papyrus of appointment bears the seal of the Tjaty; however, our noble Tjaty Ptahmose is in his dotage. Ay increasingly holds the reins of power behind the throne. After all, he is brother to Queen Tiye and father of Nefertiti, the new queen."

"What manner of man is he? I saw him once, when he visited Zarw, but I was not introduced."

"A hard man and an ambitious one. Were he of noble birth he would go far."

"I would say that king's advisor was going far," Paramessu commented. "Especially as he is Khabiru."

Horemheb nodded. "Indeed, but were it not for the old king's infatuation with Ay's sister, and with their father the redoubtable Yuya, he would not have risen that far. As it is, Ay seeks to distance himself from his Khabiru origins. He lets it be known he is son of Hapu, a scribe."

"Yuya?" Paramessu looked at his father. "I do not know this name."

"He was a Khabiru prophet of their god El or Adon or something." Seti crossed to the table and poured himself some more wine. "He arrived in the Two Lands in the time of the old king's father Tuthmosis, and prophecied for him. Nebmaetre appointed him Tjaty, of all things, and there he remained until his retirement and death ten years ago, when Ptahmose took over the position."

Horemheb grunted in disgust. "And that is why we have so much trouble on our borders now. Not only do the Khabiru grow above their station, but the seeds of rebellion are sown in the allied nations to the north and east. However, I shall put a stop to that if the gods are willing."

"You shall have my help, Lord Horemheb," Seti declared. "Tell me how I may render assistance."

"Give me your son."

"My son? He is a capable soldier but young and foolish."

"Young maybe," Horemheb replied. "But not foolish. I saw him in a tight situation today, old friend. I can see his potential. I have a use for him."

***

Amenemhet, First Prophet of Amun-Re; Hem-netjer, High Priest; servant of the god in the centre of his worship in the great temple of Amun in Waset, rose naked from the waters of the sacred temple lake in the first light of dawn and stepped toward his servants. Totally devoid of body hair, even down to plucked eyebrows and eyelashes, his appearance was of an indolent over-fed courtier, his expression one of perpetual surprise. Yet outward appearance misled many, for Amenemhet was the most powerful man in the Land of the Nine Bows, more powerful even than King Nebmaetre Amenhotep, and he had long years of practice in wielding this power.

Stepping from the water, Amenemhet lifted his arms and allowed his body servants to wrap the clean, white, linen robes around him, adjust the leopard skin of authority around his shoulders, lifting his feet one by one for his new papyrus sandals. Somewhere behind the temple, the clothes he wore the previous day were already disappearing in flames and smoke. God's servant, like the god himself, wore new clothes every day.

The morning hymn rose sweet and beautiful to the heavens from the temple. Amenemhet nodded to the other prophets of Amun-Re, Aanen, Bakt and Haremakhet, before leading the way back into the temple. They walked through the dim echoing halls of the temple, through the throngs of priests and servants toward the innermost recesses, toward the home of the god. As ever, Amenemhet could feel the presence of the god, a prickling sensation as if the nonexistent hairs on the back of his neck strove to stand up. He glanced sidelong at the other prophets, noting similar awed expressions on the faces of Bakt and Haremakhet. Not on Aanen's though. *Why not?*

Dismissing it from his mind, Amenemhet strode into the inner room, the home of the great gilded-wood shrine to the god. Standing in front of the shrine were arrayed men and women, singers selected for their clear voices, arms upraised and mouths open – the last phrases of the Morning Hymn to Amun-Re dying away into the lofty recesses of the pillared hall.

The singers drew back, melting away on each side as the prophets walked up to the bolted and tied doors of the shrine. Haremakhet cleared his throat and, still facing the shrine, turned his head to address the room. One never turned one's back on the god.

"The Lord Amun-Re, most high, beneficent creator, has awoken. Let the doors be opened that we may greet him."

Aanen and Bakt moved forward, untying the fine flax cords that bound the golden bolts holding the doors of the shrine closed. They drew back the bolts softly and

46

swung the doors wide. A breathless sigh of awe swept into the shadows in the high-ceilinged room as the singers, watching from the entrance way, fell to their knees.

The supreme god of Waset, ram-headed, stared out of the great shrine, the light of the torches flickering and reflecting off his gilded features. Life-size for a man, though no doubt smaller than the actual god, this repository for the god's ka was surmounted by the solar disk, the double plumes and the royal uraeus.

Amenemhet stepped forward and after bowing deeply, stood tall and addressed the god with words of praise. "Amun-Re, Lord of the thrones of the Two Lands, Dweller in Waset, Great God who appears in the horizon, draw near to us and bless us with your holy presence." He stood as if listening for a few moments before saying. "Let the god be brought forth."

At once, Bakt and Haremakhet ran forward, slipping two stout wooden staves through openings in the plinth below the statue. With a muffled groan they took the weight and slowly inched out sideways as Amenemhet backed slowly away. Once clear of the doors of the shrine, they lowered the statue, withdrew the poles and replaced them in the shrine, closing the doors once more.

"Bring water, bring incense and fine linen," Aanen ordered.

Priests ran forward with golden bowls of fresh lake water, fine linen towels and crisp white linen skirts. Others held the incense bowls, lighting them with long tapers, the clouds of gray-white smoke wafting over the statue. The shadows cast by the flickering torches and incense made the gilded limbs of the statue appear to move. Fresh water bathed the god before he was dressed in new clothes, a deep collar necklace of enameled lapis and gold hung about him, a close-fitting tunic supported

47

by elaborately worked shoulder straps hid his naked form from the priests. Jeweled bracelets and armlets followed, and, last of all, a heavy gold ankh placed in his lowered right hand, and a golden scepter in his outstretched left hand.

Perfumes and cosmetics followed, until the room reeked of costly unguents. The priests bearing the cosmetic pallets withdrew and the lesser servants of the god bore in his morning feast. A pristine linen cloth covered the spotless stone floor and on this were laid smoking joints of meat, roast fowls, freshly-baked bread, bowls of fruit and vegetables, pitchers of wine and great bowls of beer. Amenemhet took a bowl of fresh lake water and dipped a feather in it, sprinkling the food with a libation, while Aanen lit the candle of feasting. The servants left and musicians trooped in, ranging themselves around the room, striking up a stirring melody to which naked dancing girls dipped and pirouetted for the enjoyment of the god. The prophets of Amun stood around to watch the god eat.

The candle burned lower and as the flame crept down to a pre-set level, Amenemhet clapped his hands. At once, the musicians and dancers left the room, backing out with heads held low. The servants entered once more, clearing away the untouched food and the linen floor-cloth.

The four prophets of Amun-Re bowed low and backed through the door to the inner sanctum, closing and sealing the door behind them.

Bakt grunted as they turned away, his stomach making a faint groaning sound. "I'm hungry. That roast duck smelled especially appetizing this morning."

"Just as well the god left you some then." Aanen smiled and led the way along passages toward the First Prophet's chambers.

The servants had left a good selection of the finest food from Amun-Re's meal on a table inside the chamber. Bakt descended on the meal and ripped off a leg from the roast duck, biting into the fragrant flesh. "I needed that," he mumbled through the food. He swallowed and took another bite, juices running down his chin. He wiped them away with the back of his hand and grinned.

Amenemhet closed the door carefully before pouring himself a cup of wine. He gestured toward the table. "Don't stand on ceremony." He waited until the others had helped themselves to food and drink. "We need to talk."

Aanen removed a sleeping cat from a chair and seated himself near the table, reaching out for a small bunch of grapes. "What about?"

"Neferkheperure Waenre Amenhotep."

"The regent?" Haremakhet frowned, chewing on a piece of bread. "What is the problem?"

Amenemhet sipped his wine and looked open-faced at Aanen. "Why don't you tell us, Second Prophet? What is it about the young prince that worries me?"

Aanen stared back. He spat grape pips into his hand and popped another one into his mouth before replying. "You refer to his parentage?"

"His parentage?" Haremakhet's eyes widened. "You are not saying he ... he is ... not ..."

"Of course not," cut in Amenemhet. "Use your mind. There is no doubt he is the natural son of Nebmaetre and ..."

"Queen Tiye," Aanen finished. "You are referring to her Khabiru roots." He looked hard at Amenemhet, attempting to stare him down. After a few moments he looked away. "And mine, First Prophet. She is my sister, as the king's advisor Ay is my brother."

"No one doubts your loyalty, Aanen, nor that of your brother and sister."

"What then?"

"Tell me of the gods of the Khabiru."

"God, First Prophet. They worship only one."

"Then tell me of him – or is it her? Do they worship a goddess?"

"You know they do not. Why do you ask me? We have talked of this before."

"Indulge me, Aanen. Also, I seek to instruct Bakt and Haremakhet."

Bakt looked up from the remains of the roast duck. "Do I need instruction, Amenemhet? About a heathen god of the nations?"

Aanen sighed. "Very well. Perhaps then you will tell us what this is all about." He paused and spat out another few grape seeds, one of which landed near the cat, waking it. "There is but one god now. No one knows if he has a name ..."

"What!" Haremakhet grinned. "Not even his priests?"

"No. He has never revealed a name but he is known as 'El' which just means god, and sometimes as 'Adon' which means lord. He is a god of the mountaintops and he used to be worshiped there."

"What is his form, his aspect?"

"He has none. The Khabiru have no statues of man or animal that they recognize as their god." Aanen shrugged. "He is a very nondescript god though some say

50

his face shines with a great radiance, too bright to look at."

"I thought you said he did not look like a man. How can he have a face then, shining or otherwise?"

"I do not know, Bakt. I only repeat what I have heard."

"So this shining god of the Khabiru is a sun god," Amenemhet said slowly. "He is known as Adon, which in Kemetu is pronounced Aten. The Khabiru worship the Aten."

"An interesting thought," Haremakhet said. "But how is it relevant? No doubt all the gods that other nations worship are really the true gods in another guise."

"What makes it relevant is that the old king Nebmaetre has brought the worship of the Aten out of obscurity, and, by a coincidence, his beloved Great Wife Tiye is Khabiru, a people who worship the Aten." Amenemhet drained his wine, crossed to the table, and refilled his cup. "That in itself would not matter. The Two Lands are replete with gods and who the king holds close to his heart is a matter between himself and heaven. No, what matters is his son, Waenre."

"How?" Bakt asked. He wiped his greasy fingers on a piece of bread and bit into it. "You just said it did not matter."

"Nebmaetre knows he holds the kingship with the blessing of Amun. All the kings of his line have accepted the throne from Amun and know that a balance must be kept; the Ma'at of the Two Lands must be maintained. But now for the first time we have a king who is a foreigner, a son of the Khabiru. Waenre is showing signs that his worship of the Aten is close to his heart."

"Again I ask; how is it relevant? As long as Amun is king of gods, what does it matter if the young king wor-

51

ships the Aten? The sun disk is just another aspect of Re after all."

"Haremakhet," Aanen chided. "Must you be sent back to school? It is not just a matter of worshipping one or another of our gods; it comes down to power and wealth. Put bluntly, the wealth that pours into our coffers."

"Succinctly put, Aanen," Amenemhet commented, "If somewhat cynical."

Aanen shrugged. "Kemet is stable under a strong line of kings because they have put Amun first." He reached down and scratched the cat behind one ear. It arched its back and purred.

Bakt finished his loaf of bread and reached for a bowl of figs. "And you think that will change under the young king Waenre?"

"It may," Amenemhet said quietly. "He is young, and idealistic, and close to his mother who openly worships the Aten. His father Nebmaetre will not recover his health."

"I think you make too much of it, First Prophet," Bakt mumbled around a mouthful of fig.

"Besides which," Haremakhet added. "There is not much you can do about it."

"Actually there is," Aanen said. "But I would not advise such a course."

Amenemhet put down the cup and stared at the Second Prophet. "Why not?"

"Eh?" Bakt's mouth opened and a half-chewed fig fell to the floor unnoticed by all except the cat who investigated the fruit, sniffing it delicately. "What do you mean, Aanen? What can be done?"

"The Hem-netjer of Amun is more powerful than the king." Aanen looked across the room at Amenemhet, his face impassive. "He can consecrate the king into Amun's peace, or refuse, which means Waenre cannot be king. Of course, that would throw the Two Lands into chaos as there is no other candidate."

"There are daughters," Amenemhet said. "One could be married off to a suitable noble."

"Sitamen is already married to her own father, as is Iset. Henuttaneb and Nebetiah are not yet old enough. That leaves Sitamen's young son Smenkhkare or Tiye's unborn offspring, should it be male. Both are too young. You cannot risk anarchy, First Prophet. You must consecrate Waenre this afternoon."

Amenemhet sighed. "Yes, I cannot risk our beloved land. Yet I fear for Kemet under this young king."

***

Neferkheperure Waenre Amenhotep, Lord of the Two Lands, god-on-earth, King of Upper and Lower Kemet, Son of Re who engenders Ma'at, Lord of Crowns, sat on a padded couch in his private rooms fondling his wife.

A tall man for his time, Waenre was shaved completely except for wispy eyebrows. His high domed skull protruded backward, balancing his long, slightly prognathous face with its long nose and chin, lips full and pouting, eyes heavy and hooded. He sat naked except for an almost transparent kilt knotted around his hips, his protruding stomach, pale and hairless, hanging over the fabric. Pendulous pectorals, hinting already at breasts though he was still a young man, spoke, together with his belly, of a rich diet and long days spent indoors in leisurely pursuits. His kilt did nothing to hide his growing tumescence as his long, thin fingers stroked the beautiful woman beside him on the couch.

The woman, too, was striking, though in quite a different way to the young king. Almost as tall as Waenre, she exuded health and youth and a vibrant energy. Head shaven like the king's, the dome of her skull was smooth and rounded, her face small with high cheekbones and delicate features. Her eyes, accentuated by the strong cosmetic enhancements of lapis, malachite and kohl, looked larger than life and more striking. Small rouged lips smiled enigmatically, her eyes glancing sideways at her husband. A long neck swept down to small firm breasts and a flat stomach, still taut despite the births of two daughters in the last three years.

Cousin to the king, the woman had been named simply Nefer – beauty – at birth by her proud father Ay, son of Yuya. On the occasion of her marriage as a nineteen-year-old to the newly-raised, co-regent Waenre Amenhotep, the old king Nebmaetre Amenhotep had exclaimed at her beauty during the ceremony, "A beautiful woman has come!" She had henceforth been known as Nefertiti, thought by many to be the most beautiful woman on earth.

Nefertiti lifted a hand from where they lay in her naked lap and slipped it under Waenre's kilt. "I will make you forget that awful lady Sebtitis. I thought she was going to disrobe in front of you tonight."

The king groaned softly, his lips parting as he thrust his fingers down between the queen's thighs, moving up toward her hairless cleft. "She is forgotten already," he gasped.

A discrete cough from the doorway distracted him and he turned to see his mother, Queen Tiye, standing just inside the room. He groaned again, this time with an edge of frustration in his voice.

"What do you want, mother? It is late and I really do not want to be disturbed."

"My apologies, son." Tiye swept into the room, as poised as any woman can be who is elderly and at full term. Wearing a deep blue robe of fine linen over a paler dress fastened below her pendulous breasts, she crossed to a low table underneath the large window looking out toward the river. Lights, soft and butter-yellow picked out the richer homes in the late evening, beneath a star-studded sky. Picking up an ornate faience goblet she poured herself a drink from a jug of cool clear water.

"Mother, I am king now, not just a co-regent, but full regent, acting not only on behalf of my sick father, but also on my own behalf. I want to be left alone with my wife." He withdrew his hand from between Nefertiti's thighs.

"Don't pout, Amenhotep," Tiye said mildly. "A king may have greater freedoms but he also has greater re-sponsibilities. Have the last four years as co-regent taught you nothing?"

With a murmur of endearment and after raising a slim finger to her husband's lips, Nefertiti arose from the couch and crossed to where Tiye stood by the window. She bent and kissed the old queen's swollen belly, then straightening, kissed her cheek before pouring herself a cup of watered wine. "You are well, beloved mother?"

"Yes, child. I have had children before; this one will arrive tonight or tomorrow. I can feel it."

"Then we must see you settled, mother. Let me call the midwives."

Queen Tiye shook her head, her crisply curled wig slipping slightly as she moved. "Time enough, daughter. I must speak with my son." She hesitated a moment, glancing at Waenre who sat glowering on the couch, then back at Nefertiti. "Both of you. This will concern you, too."

"This will not wait until tomorrow?" Waenre sighed and stood up, adjusting himself beneath his kilt. He crossed the room to a carved wooden box in the far corner. Positioning himself above the hole in the lid, he flipped back his kilt and directed a strong stream of urine into the pottery bowl within the box. Shaking the last drops off, he turned away as a young boy entered the room. The boy kept his eyes on the ground but lifted the lid of the box, removed the bowl, and replaced it with another one. He backed away carefully, taking care not to spill his burden.

"Well, mother? What is it you must say that will not wait?"

Tiye settled herself on the edge of the royal bed, locking her hands below her belly. For a woman who had ruled Kemet alongside her husband Nebmaetre for nearly thirty years and effectively by herself for the last six months, she looked ill at ease, uncomfortable. She fidgeted, avoiding her son's eyes.

"The ceremony of consecration went well this afternoon, I thought."

Waenre looked at his mother and said nothing. Nefertiti, her naked body gleaming copper-coloured in the soft lights of the room, crossed to her husband and put a slim arm around his waist.

"What is it you want to say, beloved mother, yet cannot?"

Tiye raised her head. "You really are a most beautiful woman, Nefertiti, my daughter. And wise beyond your years. I look to you to counsel my son."

"Counsel? Mother, I have any number of advisors and do not wish for more." Waenre's face took on a sullen expression. "I require my wife merely to be beautiful and to bear my children. I have two lovely daughters already but I need a son and heir to be king after me."

"Unless you are careful, Waenre Amenhotep, you will have no kingdom to leave to any future son and heir."

Waenre paled. "What do you mean, mother?"

"Why did you change the words of your coronation speech today?"

"He is king, honoured mother," Nefertiti interposed. "He may do as he wishes."

"That is what you are worried about? I added but a few words."

"Important words. What possessed you to add the Aten to your prayer to Amun?"

Waenre shrugged. "I like the Aten; he is a god of light, not like the other gods who live in dark temples served by their grasping priests. Why should I not pray to whom I like?"

"Who is the most powerful man in the Two Lands?"

Frowning, Waenre pursed his lips. "My father ... and I." He thought for a moment. "I am, now that my father is sick and cannot rule."

"No, my son, you are not. Amenemhet, Hem-netjer and First Prophet of Amun, is the most powerful man in the land. It is within his hand to grant the blessings of the god, and deny them. At the ceremony today, he consecrated you as king, but he could just as easily have refused. You would not now be king if he had done so."

"That is foolishness, mother. If he had refused, another man would now be First Prophet – your brother Aanen perhaps, and I would still be king."

"And how would you have removed him? You could only do so with the permission of the god Amun, as he is Hem-netjer. And who is the only person who can approach the god? Yes, Amenemhet." Tiye shook her head wearily. "You spend your days in idle pursuits, in search of beauty, but you pay no attention to the real world, to the men around you."

Waenre breathed out hard, his lips vibrating. "What of it? Amenemhet did consecrate me, so there is nothing he can do now."

"Not to you, but what of your future son and heir? What if he decides to terminate our dynasty and set another family in our place?"

"Never!" Nefertiti hissed.

"He would not do that ... he cannot. Our line is ancient and has the blessings of the gods. The people would rise up."

"Against the gods, my son? Amun is the king of gods here in Waset, and Amenemhet is his Hem-netjer." Tiye heaved herself up off the bed and waddled over to her son. She put her hands on his forearms and looked up into his sulky face. "My son, be discerning. Be mindful of the gods, Amun especially. Our family chose Amun as our god, above all others. Give him honour and riches, his First Prophet, too, and your reign will be long and glorious."

"I prefer the Aten. He is your god, too, mother. I learned of him as a child at your knee."

Tiye sighed, turned, and walked slowly back to the bed. "Yes. He is the god of the Khabiru, of my father Yuya, and I will always honour your father for allowing his worship to increase. However, do not let it go too far. Do not challenge the supremacy of Amun."

Waenre smiled, his full lips curving upward, though his eyes remained cold and bright. "And if the Aten is the only true god, what then? Have you ever seen a ram-headed god, mother? How about a green-faced god; or

58

one with a jackal's head, or a hawk's?" He shook his head. "Nor will you. They either do not exist or, if they do, are far from the land of men. Yet you can see the Aten, the solar disk, any day. Look up in the sky. He exists. Why should I not worship him?"

Tiye glanced at Nefertiti, standing with her arm around Waenre.

"He is my husband, beloved mother," Nefertiti said simply. "And king of the Two Lands. I will give him my love, my support and my belief. If he says I should worship the Aten, then that is what I will do."

Tiye sat in silence, head down. Into the silence came the drip of water, increasing. "My waters have broken," she murmured. "It is time."

Chapter Three

And so I was born. On the night of Neferkheperure Waenre Amenhotep's coronation, my mother Tiye ushered me into the world, the last but one child of Nebmaetre Amenhotep, now barely Lord of Two Rooms, let alone Two Lands.

I was brought before him, still slimed and blood-covered as was the custom, for my father to pronounce his blessing, to name his newest child. Of course, he could not speak but just lay on his bed staring, so Heqareshu, the overseer of nurses, said, and would not even look at me. So I was given no name and for the first three years of my life was addressed as "girl" or "you" or referred to just as "no-name".

I cannot tell you much of those early years for despite being precocious, as so many of our people are, I find that memory fades with the passing of the years – so many years now. I have lived to see another dynasty take its place on the throne of Kemet, our holy land made great again, and the death of every single person I knew as a child, save one. That one still lives, I think, though with a different name from the one forgotten by the world.

I have talked of my time as a royal princess in the Great Palace of Waset, and later of the Palace of the Aten in northern Akhet-Aten, yet few people can comprehend the realities. To live as a member of the royal family is to be separated from the common man, for even though we live, breathe and love surrounded by servants and courtiers, yet are they invisible, nothing but ghosts there to grant our every whim, no more noticeable than the furniture. To give an example: I have walked into a room and found my brother Waenre making love to his queen Nefertiti, while around them servants dusted, cleaned and talked. As far as they were concerned, they were alone in their bedchamber.

Having no name, and being beneath the notice of anyone important in my early years, I found myself in the company of the palace staff more than was strictly proper and I have always had this liking, almost a kinship with those of lesser station.

It may surprise you that my mother had little to do with me, as we Kemetu are known as a family oriented people. However, she devoted herself to her stricken husband and left me in the care of Heqareshu, the overseer of nurses, and the wet-nurses he provided for me. I was not neglected, just not loved – at least not for several years. I learned early to keep to myself. This, of course, made me quieter and more withdrawn. Any hope I might have had of obtaining a name by being noticed, receded.

As I have said before, my memories of the early years of Waenre Amenhotep's reign are patchy at best. There were many children in the palace, for although my father only sired seven children on my mother, he was, or had been, the Bull of Heru, with a herd of lesser wives. These offspring, too, were royal, though far removed from the line of succession. Their destiny lay within the boundless realms of court functionaries. They would become scribes and fan-bearers, stewards and masters of horse and household, being prohibited only from the succession. Only Smenkhkare was different. Five years older than me, he was the son of my father and his eldest daughter Sitamen.

I will mention here that my father had a sister called Sitamen, too. In the early days of his reign he had married his sister to enhance his title to the throne, but she died before bearing him any children. I have sometimes wondered whether he felt something for her, missed her perhaps, because he named his eldest daughter after her, later marrying her.

Her son Smenkhkare was a robust young boy with a wild sense of adventure. When I first left the baby-nursery and became a member of the palace children, he was their leader, though not the eldest. From the age of three to ten, the children were left to run free, though closely and unobtrusively watched at all times. Smenkhkare was a leader, often taking a select band of youngsters into parts of the palace out of bounds to children, or even outside the palace walls.

When he was caught, as he almost invariably was, not being able to keep quiet about his exploits, he was beaten. Even a prince, and son of the king, must learn discipline and his uncle Ay, the Queen's brother, had a heavy hand. After the first time, though, Smenkhkare bore his punishment stoically, refusing to shed tears or cry out until he was alone.

I was beneath his notice of course, being one of many young girls and him the leader of the older children. It was several years before he befriended me, but by then, circumstances had changed for both of us. He was being prepared as a possible successor to his brother Waenre and I for a fate of considerably less appeal.

We all ran naked, boys and girls alike, our heads shaved except for the side-lock of youth. Clothing is not necessary in our climate and, except for formal and ceremonial occasions, is often ignored, even by adults. This is not to say that Kemetu men and women lack modesty, but rather that we develop a carefree attitude to nudity and sex.

I was given my first name when I was four years old. I can be certain of my age as it was the year before the king Waenre, his beautiful queen Nefertiti and their three daughters, Meryetaten, Meketaten and Ankhesenpaaten moved to the new city of Akhet-Aten, dedicated to the new god of our house. The king started searching for a place that was special to his god as soon as he became regent. He started by dedicating a temple to the Aten near to Amun's grand temple. Then a report came from downriver of a place where the morning sun rose through a notch in the line of cliffs. It was a barren place, the nearest village being a place called Akhet-Re. He looked for himself and laid out the plans for a magnificent city on the crescent plain beneath the cliffs, dedicated to the sun disk.

I did not yet fully understand everything that was going on around me, of course, but I knew something terrible and disturbing was happening. People whispered and gossiped, falling silent whenever a member of our family appeared, even the children. I became uncomfortable in the presence of others at about this time and withdrew into my own company, shunning the other boys and girls, playing by myself in the palace gardens.

I should mention that the palace I called home was not the magnificent new one built by my father on the Western Bank, but rather the older one on the edge of the city of Waset that had been the abode of kings for centuries. When my father suffered his illness, my mother moved him back to the old palace to be nearer the centre of government. Naturally, the entire household moved with them, and so I knew little of the new palace until I was grown.

The old palace at Waset boasted a garden that was widely regarded as the most magnificent in the world. As well as stately trees and carefully tended beds of flowers and fishponds, was a menagerie filled with exotic animals from all parts of the kingdom and from foreign countries. Kings would send gifts to Nebmaetre, and for a while, to Waenre too; often including animals like a leopard on a leash and collar, a pair of hunting cheetahs, a rhinoceros or giraffe, or a baboon. These gifts, along with other animals captured by the king's hunters, ended up in cages in the palace gardens for nobles to gawk at and point.

I rarely visited the animals. Not because I did not like animals but rather because I could not bear to see them locked up. The ones that were not locked up, gazelles and baby animals, were popular with the other children and, being shy, I seldom put myself forward to pet them. I generally stayed at the other end of the garden. There was a fishpond there, set about with shrubbery and papyrus and shadowed by a magnificent tamarind tree. It dropped leaves into the pond, and pods. I would fish the pods out and break them open, sucking out the sweet-sour brown pulp.

There were animals there, too, though none that would interest a king or even the other children. Butterflies flitted above the flowerbeds, bees too, and a myriad of other insects. Lizards scuttled on the sandy paths, basking in the early morning and late afternoon sun, or seeking the shade in the heat of the day. Frogs lived in the ponds; and schools of little silver fish thrilled me with their precise movements as I lay on my belly in the dust, watching them. Kingfishers took their dues from the ponds and brightly coloured dragonflies hovered and darted, dipping down to the water surface or clinging like jewels to the tips of the reeds. A female cobra lived in the reeds and I sometimes glimpsed her black shiny eyes watching me, her tongue flickering like summer lightning. She never bothered me and I came to think of her as Wadjet, the cobra goddess. After all, the cobra is the symbol of royalty, the uraeus coiled about the brow of the king. I took her watchfulness as a sign that the gods still remembered me.

The air hung still in those days, heavy and scented with exotic perfumes from the flowers all about me. Left alone, I turned my mind to the tiny wonders that lay all about me. I have always been curious. When I started my schooling I would drive my teachers to distraction wanting to know about things for which there was no real answer. Why was the sky blue? Why were leaves green? Why did crickets sing but butterflies not? It was never enough for me to be told it was because the gods had made it that way. I looked at the frenetic ants, listened to the different songs of grasshoppers and cicadas, stared into the intricacies of a flower, smelled their varied perfumes, marveled at the shimmering colours in a tiny blue butterfly's wing, or watched, fascinated, as two lizards mated.

One day, on a day that I came to know as my first naming day, I played in the dust in the shade of my great tamarind tree, watching one of the great scarab beetles roll a ball of dung across the ground. It would back itself against the roughly-shaped ball, gripping it with its hind legs and pushing backward. Not seeing where it was going, it often ran into an obstacle, scrabbling futilely at the ground. Eventually it would let go of the ball and investigate the obstruction before taking hold again and trundling off in another direction. The beetle moved out of the shade and into the bright sun and I followed on my hands and knees, my attention riveted.

A shadow fell across me and I looked up to see the king Waenre Amenhotep and his wife Nefertiti standing over me. I sat back on my haunches and stared at them, not saying a word. The king smiled at me and, disengaging his arm from around his wife, squatted down beside me in the dust.

"What is your name, child?"

I shook my head, staring solemnly up at my elder brother.

"I think she is your youngest sister, beloved," Nefertiti said. "She does not have a name as she was never given one."

"And what are you doing, child? Out here, without even a nurse to look after you?"

I pointed at the beetle, now jammed up against a fallen seedpod. It heaved the ball of dung up, only to have it slip sideways and down again.

"He struggles so hard. I want to help him but I don't know how to," I whispered. "That is why I watch him, so I may learn."

Waenre laughed. "And what have you learned by watching him, little one?"

"He is beautiful. He looks just like a dull beetle but if you look close you can see lovely colours – green, blue, red."

"What else?"

"He works hard, never resting, pushing his ball of dung across the ground."

"And why does he do that?"

"My uncle Aanen says it is because he is the god Khepri and he pushes the ball of the sun across the sky each day." I was repeating what my uncle had said but I did not understand it.

"That is what the priests say." Waenre nodded. He put out a finger and removed the tamarind pod obstruction. The scarab resumed its journey. "It is hard to imagine this little beetle contains a god, though. What do you think?"

I said nothing, just screwed up my face in thought.

Waenre got to his feet and brushed the dust and twigs from his knees. "What about you, beautiful one?" he asked Nefertiti. "What do you think? Is this beetle a god?"

Nefertiti smiled, her eyes fixed on her husband's face, though one slim hand strayed to her left ear, lightly stroking the two fresh piercings in her lobe. "Perhaps a very small god."

Waenre laughed. "Yes, very small and without much power." He stared down at the insect by his feet for several moments. "I could stretch out my foot and crush him beneath my sandal. Would that mean I had killed a god?" He nudged the dung ball with his toe, sending the ball rolling and the scarab end over end as it frantically tried to recover its balance. "I wonder if other gods would be that easy to kill."

I put out a hand and touched Waenre's leg. "Please don't kill him."

He looked down at me, a bemused expression on his elongated face. "Why not, child? If he truly is a god, as the priests say, I could not kill him. In fact I would be struck down for my presumption."

"I love him," I said. "Please don't kill him."

Waenre nodded. "As you wish, though I have never heard of anyone loving a dung beetle. Perhaps you wish to be his wife?" He laughed loudly, joined a few seconds later by Nefertiti. "Let them be married, scarab and ... and no-name."

"Scarab and Scarab, beloved husband," murmured Nefertiti.

"Indeed, beautiful one, that shall be her name from this day. Scarab." Waenre grinned down at me. "How do you like your name, little one?"

I turned the name over in my mind. Although not a beautiful name like so many of the little girls I knew, it was at least mine. "Thank you," I whispered.

"Run along now, little Scarab. I wish to sit and talk to my wife in this beautiful shade."

I left them there, turning back as I entered the palace. They were still standing where I had left them, staring down at the ground. When I returned to my tree the next day I found the scattered wing cases and horny shell of a scarab in that spot, picked clean by the ants. I buried the husks of Khepri but thought no more of it at the time, certainly made no connection between the dead beetle and my brother.

It was only later that I wondered whether my brother had, on that hot day, in the dust beneath the tamarind tree, braved the gods of Kemet by killing a very small one beneath his sandal.

Chapter Four

Ahhotep, master craftsman of the glass-blowers guild, wiped the sweat from his face with one broad hand as he peered into the depths of the glowing kiln in the courtyard of his small shop. Waves of heat blasted out, rippling the air as if the desert sun had somehow been plucked from the sky and thrust into his ovens. He adjusted the position of the bronze cup that lay in the fiery bed of charcoal, wincing as the heat was transmitted through the wooden handles to his calloused palms. Naked except for a small leather apron, his bare arms, legs and torso were covered with a myriad of scars, mementoes of a lifetime spent in the proximity of hot glass.

A small naked boy, ribs showing through his cracked and blemished skin, sat to one side working a leather bellows with slow automatic movements, his eyes unfocused and staring. The blast of air from the nozzle pushed through a reed tube to a charred brick block set into the wall of the kiln. The air made the coals glow yellow-white in irregular pulses. Ahhotep pitched a small pebble at the boy, hitting him on the shoulder. The boy jumped; his pressure on the bellows faltering as he swung his head round.

"Pay attention, Djer. Keep a steady flow of air." Ahhotep watched as the boy redoubled his efforts, pumping a steady stream of air into the kiln. The coals became hotter.

Did I put enough alum in? He lifted his eyes to where his apprentice sat in the shade of the courtyard wall, idly tossing a pebble from hand to hand. "Nakht!" he called. "Get over here."

69

Nakht got up slowly and wandered across the court-yard, his bare feet scuffing up the dry, powdery sand. "Yes, Ahhotep?"

"The alum, Nakht. Fetch me the bag."

"Which one?"

"The one from the Dakhla Oasis, the pink alum."

Nakht turned away and disappeared into a lean-to wooden structure at the far end of the courtyard. He re-appeared a few minutes later dragging a sack behind him. Pulling it across to where Ahhotep sat, the youth dropped it. He stood back, dusting his hands. "That's the one, master. See, the merchant's mark." Nakht pointed at a series of faint symbols scorched into the sacking.

Ahhotep opened the sack and dug his hand into the contents, letting the fine pinkish grains sift through his fingers. He stared at the fine dusting of powder on his hand then abruptly reached a decision. "We add more," he muttered.

Lifting the bronze cup gently from its bed of coals, he set it carefully on a low shelf of charred and cracked bricks. He beckoned the apprentice closer. "See, Nakht. The glass is blue but it lacks that deep colour so loved by the nobles. We must add more alum."

Nakht screwed up his face, glancing from the sack of alum to the bronze cup shimmering on the bricks. "But the alum is pink, master."

"Just so, Nakht, just so. Yet by the intervention of the gods, pink turns to blue in the heat of the kiln." Ahhotep smiled and pointed at the molten blue glass still bubbling in the cup. "Ten parts of alum to a hundred of fine sand produced that. I think I must add more." He considered for a moment. "Twenty parts to start with." Taking up a wooden measure he dug it into the sack of alum, and then started sprinkling it onto the heated glass in the cup.

The dry alum crackled and spat as it hit the molten surface, sending Nakht leaping back to avoid the hot particles. Ahhotep stirred the mixture with a long bronze rod, carefully mixing in the powder, nodding with satisfaction. He withdrew the rod, bringing with it a glistening blue tear that cracked and popped in the relatively cool air of the courtyard. The blue tear fell into the dust near the small naked boy, who grabbed at it, yelping in pain as it seared his fingers.

"Patience, boy," Ahhotep growled. He pushed the bronze cup back into the coals and watched as Djer pumped a stream of air through the cracked leather bellows.

Nakht sat down cross-legged beside his master and peered into the depths of the kiln. "Why do you seek such a deep blue glass, master? Your paler colours sell well enough."

Ahhotep nodded. "True enough, but the demand is there. Mitanni traders bring in a deep blue glass from the north, but nobody knows how they make it. The Guild of Glass Makers seeks to imitate it. I have tried often enough, and I can make deep blue glass with the Dakhla alum but the glass is brittle. Something is missing, some ingredient known only to the Mitanni glass-makers. If I can find out what it is, I will make my fortune."

Nakht grinned. "I shall enjoy working for a rich man. There are always plenty of opportunities for advancement."

Ahhotep scowled and cuffed his apprentice, though softly enough not to cause any real pain. "You keep your light-fingered hands to yourself," he growled. "Did you think I was unaware of your petty thieving?"

71

Nakht's grin slipped for a moment and he eased himself out of range of his master's calloused hands. "No, master, but I have to eat, as does my family."

Ahhotep shrugged. "Just do not get greedy, Nakht. I have it in mind to adopt you. I have no son of my own and I want to leave my business in good hands when I cross the river and journey into the twilight."

"Not for many years yet, master." Nakht grinned again. "And when the time comes I shall make dutiful offerings at your tomb, as a good son should ... if I should happen to be a son."

Ahhotep smiled. "Then act like a good son and fetch me some water." He watched as Nakht crossed the courtyard and disappeared into the mud brick hovel that served as a home for himself, his wife Abana, the boy Djer, and an assortment of animals. Glancing toward the small naked boy working the bellows assiduously, he picked up the now cool droplet of blue glass from the dust. He spat on it and rubbed it on his apron before holding it up to the light. A pale, clear blue, it was flawed with darker blue inclusions of imperfectly melted alum particles. A crack ran across the bead, indicative of the brittle nature of the product. Ahhotep sighed and dropped the bead into the dust.

Nakht returned with a cup of tepid water which he offered to his master deferentially. Ahhotep drank deep, then noticing Djer looking at him, offered the last of the water to the boy.

"Why do you want to create this deep blue glass, master, if it is so hard to make? Surely it would be more productive to make what you know?"

"Times are changing, Nakht. The young prince from the north is an artist and loves beautiful things. Now that he is king there will be a big demand for beauty in his

72

court. If I can make the prized dark blue glass, I will become rich ... we will become rich."

Nakht laughed. "Then we must get to work, master. I would like to be rich."

***

The northern Anatolian summer was also hot and dry, though the parched countryside surrounding the Hittite capital of Hattusas still showed signs of the late spring rains. Crops ripened in the fields and the incessant rasp and whirr of insects filled the dusty air that hung over olive groves and yellowing fields of grain.

Within the city, in a squat stone palace that in Kemet would be considered an insult to the governor of one of the poorer sepati, the Hittite king Shubbiluliuma, held court. Despite the lack of furnishings and the bare stone walls, the king himself was dressed in fine wool and linen robes, threaded with gold; and bedecked with jewelry. Before him, on the cool dimly-illuminated flagstones of the great hall, a minor taxation official groveled, accused of embezzling a small sum from the taxes gathered in his region. Pale, and drenched with cold sweat, the official babbled out a long and involved story, pleading his innocence and begging for mercy. Around him stood courtiers and soldiers, their faces held in stiff neutrality as they waited for the king's decision. The king ignored the official, leaning slightly to one side on his carved wooden throne as he listened to the murmured comments of the young man standing beside him.

"I must have gold, Great King," the young man stated. "I have raised an army and wait only for your word to drive the Kemetu out of Syria."

Shubbiluliuma nodded. "Patience, Aziru, you shall have it, but my treasury is not limitless."

73

"It could be. Kemet is a land of gold just waiting for a strong man to take it."

"Kemet is an ally, Aziru. Amenhotep is a friend who has promised me much gold. Should I strike at the hand that offers me gold?"

"And where is this promised gold, Great King?" Aziru looked around the bare stone hall as if searching for overlooked riches. "It is many months since the king promised you gold, yet we have not seen it. Now there is news that the king has been struck down by his gods and his weakling son named as regent." The young man lowered his voice to a whisper. "Men are saying that Kemet will send you no more gifts of friendship, my lord, no more gold. Is this an act of friendship?"

Shubbiluliuma beckoned to a man in rich robes not many degrees less fine than those of the Great King himself. "Mutaril, you have heard the arguments of Prince Aziru the Amorite. What think you?"

Mutaril bowed low. "Prince Aziru speaks words of wisdom, Great King." He straightened and, turning toward the Amorite prince, bowed again, though limiting the honour given by inclining only his head. Aziru glared but said nothing.

"Yet he is a young man," Mutaril went on. "And young men, however wise, are not noted for their patience. Perhaps another letter to the old king, my lord? And one to the new regent also, reminding him that you keep the peace on the borders of Kemet, not the Kemetu army."

Shubbiluliuma inclined his head in agreement. "Have letters drawn up, Mutaril. Be friendly, but firm. Remind the old king that he promised me two statues of solid gold over a year ago." He turned and regarded the young prince thoughtfully. "Tell him also we have received

word that Aziru the son of Abdiashirta of Amori is raising an army. Tell him I will need gold if I am to remove
this threat to his realms."

Aziru stepped forward angrily. "Great King, I do this
on your command ..."

Shubbiluliuma raised a hand, stopping the prince in
his tracks. "Do not be a fool," he said coldly. "You may
be a warrior but you have a lot to learn about diplomacy
and the ways of kings. Amenhotep will pay, especially if
he thinks the threat is grave. When he pays, you will have
your gold and your army."

Shubbiluliuma waved Mutaril away and turned toward the still-babbling official on the flagstones of the
great hall. "Silence him."

A guard stepped forward and slammed the haft of his
spear into the prostrate man's side. The official cried out
in pain and half-curled his body, whimpering slightly.

"You are guilty of theft from your king," Shubbiluliuma said coldly. "Can you repay the money and mitigate
your sentence?"

The official forced himself to his knees and, gripping
his bruised ribs with one hand, stretched out the other
toward the throne. "Great King, I beg for mercy. Give
me time and I shall repay everything, and more."

"So I am to wait for my money? If I allowed this,
every official would do the same and my kingdom would
be bankrupted." He gestured toward a captain of the
guard. "Go to this man's house and confiscate his goods.
Take his wife and children and sell them into household
slavery. Then kill him."

The captain bowed, ignoring the howls of anguish
from the tax official. "It shall be done, my lord." He hesitated a moment. "My lord, his daughter Agippa is a
comely girl, some fourteen summers and ..."

75

"You wish her for yourself, captain?"

"No, my lord, but the army brothels would pay handsomely for her."

The king nodded dismissively. "Do so. And get that sniveling creature out of my sight." He watched impassively as the guards removed the former official, his mind already turned toward the on-going problems of Kemet, the kingdom of the Amorites and gold.

***

Pa-it raised his head in the pre-dawn darkness and stared toward the eastern horizon where Khepri, the Reborn Light already paled the stars above the cliffs on the far side of the river. He dropped his mattock onto the black earth between the rows of onions and lettuce, raising his arms in a silent prayer to the rising sun. To his left, closer to the river, he could hear the cockerels of his tiny village of Akhet-Re – the horizon of Re, welcoming the new day in their special way. Named for the notch in the eastern cliffs through which the sun emerged on its daily journey across the skies, the village had always felt a special kinship with the god. Farmers like Pa-it, who for generations had plowed and harvested Kemet, the rich black soil of the river valley, knew and revered the many gods of the Two Lands, but held three in special regard. Geb, as god of the earth, gave them all growing things; and Hapinou, spirit of the Great River, gave the water and the rich flood of annual silt on which all life depended; but above all there was the sun god in his several aspects; Khepri of the dawn light, Heru of the ascending light, Re of the hot sun of mid-day, and Atum of the unified light when the great boat of the sun sank below the western horizon. Complicating matters, the disk of the sun itself was the Aten, a minor aspect of the godhead,

76

but one which had assumed greater importance in the reign of Amenhotep.

Pa-it did not pretend to understand the subtle distinctions between the aspects of the sun – that was the job of the priests – but he had his favourite – Khepri, the Reborn Light, sun of the dawn, the gentle aspect of a fierce god. Breaking his silence, Pa-it raised his voice in a song of praise, welcoming the new day.

The disk of the sun rose above the eastern cliffs, the shadows racing toward the river, shortening even as Pa-it watched. Voices rose in the still morning air, happy voices on the road from the village. Pa-it picked up his mattock and walked down the rows of crops in his little field toward the small group on the road, his hand lifted in greeting.

Asenath, his wife, led the small group, carrying a basket of provisions for the noon meal. Behind her trouped their children, two daughters, Enehy and Imiu; and three small naked sons, Min, Khu and baby Pa-it. The elder Pa-it smiled fondly and embraced his wife, leading her over to the shade of a tamarind tree that bordered on their land. Although still cool, the air was heating rapidly and shade would be at a premium before much longer. Already other families were on the road, coming out to meet husbands and fathers in the fields.

Pa-it's wife took charge at once, leaving Imiu in charge of the baby under the tamarind tree, she directed Enehy to start watering the rows of cucumber vines. She picked up a heavy wooden bucket and walked off toward the irrigation canal. The two boys, Min and Khu were set to work pulling weeds and searching the plants for any chewing insects. These would be separated out carefully; any large grasshoppers placed in a wicker basket for later consumption, the softer and smaller caterpillars and bugs placed in a linen bag. At day's end, these would be released in the pastures near the river. Animals, insects included, could be killed for food or to protect one's family, but never wantonly. Life came from the gods; it was not for man to assume the rights of the gods.

Pa-it shouldered his bronze mattock, a prized possession, and marched out to the rows with Asenath. She carried an old wooden hoe, hardly more than a pointed stick with a crosspiece a hand's length from the tip to allow the weight of the wielder to pierce the black soil. They bent to their task, working slowly down adjacent rows, side by side, loosening the thick loam, allowing the plants to breathe and the water laboriously carried from the irrigation canal by Enehy, to reach the roots.

Heru the sun rose higher, the air starting to ripple as waves of heat beat off the ground. Sweat poured from Pa-it, running into his eyes, the salt stinging them. He stopped Enehy and drank from the bucket, beckoning Asenath over to share the tepid liquid.

"You have earned a rest, daughter. Go look after the baby and send Imiu to the canal for a while."

His daughter smiled and murmured her thanks, picking up the bucket and heading back to the tamarind tree. Pa-it watched her go, her hips swinging beneath the tiny linen kilt she wore. He frowned and turned to his wife. "You must talk to her, Asenath. Provocative behavior like that will not please the village elders."

Asenath smiled. "She is a woman, husband. What do you expect? We should be looking to find her a mate."

"But she is only twelve."

"As was I when I married." Asenath turned away, bending over her hoe once more.

Pa-it stood and stared at his wife, thinking back over the past thirteen years to his marriage, suddenly seeing

Asenath not as the firm-breasted girl he married but as the careworn, thin and shrunken woman she had become. His eyes moistened and he stepped over the row of cucumbers and put his arms around his wife, kissing her tenderly.

"What is that for?" Asenath queried. "Get away with you, husband. We have work to do."

Pa-it smiled and with a brush of his fingertips against her arm, returned to his mattock.

Re, the noon-day sun took up his aspect and blazed forth his radiance over the baking fields. Pa-it and his family retired to the shade of the tamarind tree for their midday meal of onions and flat baked cakes of unleavened bread. Min and Khu kindled a tiny fire and roasted a few large grasshoppers, their wings and legs curling and charring in the flames; their bodies crunchy with a soft centre tasting of herbs.

After the frugal meal they lay on the bare soil and dozed in the shade, waiting for the worst of the early afternoon heat to pass. Scattered over the patchwork of fields, other families could be seen taking advantage of other trees, tamarinds, palms and acacias. The buzz of cicadas soothed his tired family and they lay back, dozing in the hot, still air. Pa-it and Asenath talked awhile, of domestic affairs, of the business of the village, and the burden of taxes. He stroked her bare breasts comfortingly, neither of them aroused.

"It is always thus," Pa-it said. "Any special event that involves the nobles means extra taxes for us. The coronation of the prince just more so."

"I heard a rumor that the prince is not, well ... not handsome like his father."

"Oh? Who said this?"

"Herer."

Pa-it snorted. "How would she know?" He glanced over at his two young sons and smiled, gesturing toward them. Min and Khu had removed two large green caterpillars from the soft linen bag and were attempting to make them race along a branch.

Asenath sat up, a worried expression on her face. "Be careful, boys. Those things have a spine on their backs." She turned to Pa-it. "Will they sting?"

Min laughed and nudged his brother. "No, mama. Look." He prodded one caterpillar on its spine and it fell off the branch.

"They are harmless," Pa-it said reassuringly. "Or rather, they would only hurt our crops." He fell silent for a moment before turning back to the subject of Herer. "How could she know, wife? She has never set foot out of Akhet-Re."

"No, but her husband's cousin went upriver to Waset two months past and he says he saw the prince during the coronation procession. He said he was, well ... strange looking. Not like his father at all. Either he takes after his mother or ..."

Pa-it glanced around. "I would not voice those thoughts too much, wife. Such thoughts are dangerous."

"Yes, husband." Asenath sat quietly for a few minutes. "I would like to see for myself though."

Pa-it laughed loudly, waking the baby, who squalled until Imiu clutched him to her naked body and calmed him. "Very unlikely. We will never be in Waset, dear wife, and I cannot imagine prince Amenhotep coming anywhere near our little village of Akhet-Re. What possible interest could he have in this place?"

He settled back against the trunk of the tree and looked out across the fields and the river, toward the eastern cliffs and the notch called the Horizon-of-Re.

***

Nebhotep, physician, newly appointed to the court from the House of Life, prodded gingerly at the bloody mess in front of him. A Nubian slave had fallen headfirst from a tree in the palace grounds whence he was attempting to rescue a kitten belonging to the young daughter of a court official, and cracked his head open on a stone. The man was unconscious now, his skin a pallid grey beneath his glossy black skin, his skin cold and his breathing uneven.

"He will not live," said an older man, also in physician's robes. "It is a perfect opportunity to practice your skills. Open his head."

Nebhotep felt the bones of the skull grinding beneath his fingertip. He grimaced and mopped at the blood with an old already-sodden rag. "I do not like to play with a man's life, Shepseskare. If he is dying, then we should let him die in peace."

"Nonsense. Four out of five people whose heads are opened die of the experience within three days. The fifth may live a little longer. What have you got to lose by doing the operation?"

"If everyone dies, then would it not be better to do nothing?"

"Nebhotep, you are newly elevated to the illustrious ranks of court physician, largely, I am told, for your skill with the knife and your knowledge of herbs. Do not disappoint me or you will find yourself scraping out a living in some slum near the waterfront. Open his head."

The young physician picked up a sharp bronze knife and delicately shaved the slave's head, carefully guiding the blade around the swellings. When it was as clear of hair as he could make it he swabbed the surface with water and mopped up the oozing blood with a rag.

81

"Go ahead," Shepseskare said, pointing with his finger. "A cross-shaped incision here."

Nebhotep cut, a torrent of blood released by his knife, rapidly soaking the mattress. He pulled back the flaps of scalp, exposing the broken pieces of skull, the edges grinding together as he dabbed at the blood.

"Take the forceps and lift the pieces of bone out. That one first."

Nebhotep picked up the instrument, flicking a piece of dirt off with one finger, then gently inserting the tips and pulling a small section of bone free with a gentle sucking sound. A gush of dark blood erupted from the hole in the skull and the slave groaned. He removed another, then a third. The flow of blood lessened until the only blood issuing from the gaping wound was the fresh bright blood from the cut edges of the scalp.

"That is the brain," Shepseskare said, poking the bloody grey wrinkles with a finger. "Nobody knows what it does, but if you injure it, you die. Wash it out with water mixed with honey and garlic."

Nebhotep obeyed, moving deftly and carefully. The water washed flecks of congealed blood and tiny chips of bone from the surface of the brain. When it was clean, he gently dabbed the spongy surface. "We will need something to cover the brain. In place of the bone. Beaten silver would be best." As he dabbed, the blood trickling from the cut edges of the scalp lessened and stopped.

"Silver? On a slave? Even copper would be too expensive." Shepseskare lowered his ear to the slave's chest and listened. "Besides," he said matter-of-factly. "The man is dead."

Nebhotep stepped back from the body and placed his bloody knife and forceps back in his physician's linen roll. "Perhaps if we had got to him sooner?"

"As I said, he would still have died. Opening the skull is fatal but just occasionally it works." Shepseskare grinned and wiped his hands on the slave's kilt. "It is a really impressive operation too and as long as you recite lots of prayers to the gods, nobody will blame you for the inevitable death. It is in the hands of the gods, not yours. Were this anyone but a slave, we could command a fat fee. Still, it was worth it for the practice, Nebhotep. You did well." He hurried to the door, calling back over his shoulder. "Clean up and join me in the wine house. I will buy you a cup."

Nebhotep put away his instruments and washed the blood from his hands and arms. "There must be a way to do this so the patient lives," he muttered.

***

Khensthoth the scribe tugged at his clean white linen robe of office and pointed toward the marshes at the edge of the river fifty paces from where he stood. "Observe the ibis, sacred to the god Djehuti, patron deity of scribes. The god has chosen this place. We will sit here and be instructed by him."

Despite the presence of the sacred birds in the open spaces, Khensthoth led his small band of youths into the shade of a stand of palm trees a hundred paces further down the goat track. He sat on the closely cropped grass and gestured, waiting for the youths to seat themselves in a semi-circle around him.

"Take out your pallets and pens. We shall start with an exercise on the evils of strong drink." Khensthoth started talking; the syllables of the set composition flowing sonorously off his tongue. The scratching of reed pens on papyrus filled the air like a chorus of crickets. The only other sounds came from the wide river, where a fresh breeze from the south forced a barge traveling upriver to furl its sails and unship its oars. The grunts and curses of the rowers came muffled across the choppy waters.

Khensthoth came to the end of his recitation and waited until his pupils had waved their scraps of third-grade papyrus in the air, drying the ink. "Pepy, collect up the scripts, I shall mark them now." Opening the linen bag beside him he took out a sturdy copper cup and handed it to one of the youths.

"Menkure, you and Psamtek go down to the river and fetch me a drink of water. I thirst."

The youth bowed and accepted the cup. "Yes master." He turned and ran, the other boy at his heels.

"Mind it is from the river itself, Menkure," Khensthoth called after him. "I do not want stinking water from the marshes." He turned to the pile of papyrus and picked up the first one, running his eye over the symbols. Shaking his head, he scratched a comment in the margin before going on to the next.

While he worked, the other youths lounged in the shade and plucked grass stems, chewing them and talking quietly amongst themselves. It was a rare treat to be allowed out of the city and they made the most of it, enjoying the cool breezes and absence of prying officials. Khensthoth was an experienced and senior scribe attached to the court of Nebmaetre Amenhotep and they all realized the honour of being his pupils. Their fathers, court officials also, had called in favours giving their sons access to the learned man. Just as important, for the boys at least, was his fondness for the river banks and his interest in fresh air rather than the stuffy confines of the classroom. It sometimes led to outings such as this, and a relaxation of discipline for the day.

Khensthoth finished his marking just as Menkure and Psamtek arrived back from the river with a cup of cool, clear water. The scribe thanked them and drained the cup, smacking his lips with pleasure. He gathered the boys around him once more and went over the exercise with them, pointing out errors in their writing and sentence construction. At length, he motioned them to put their pallets and pens away.

"Let us think back to yesterday. Just before I was called away into the presence of the queen, we started to contemplate the hieroglyphs of protection. Who can tell me the names of these hieroglyphs? Pepy?"

"The Ankh, master. Also the Sa."

"Very good, Pepy. And the third? Re-wer?"

"Er, I'm sorry, master. I can only think of Sa and Ankh."

"Never mind." Khensthoth looked around his little group. "Menkure?"

"Shen, master."

"Very good. And can anyone tell me what these signs look like?"

Psamtek raised his hand. "The Ankh is like crossed staves with a loop at the top." He drew in the air with his finger. "It means life, master."

"Indeed it does, Psamtek, but more besides. Listen closely all of you. The Ankh represents the connection all life has to that which has gone before, the umbilicus. It is the sign of life infused into humans from the divine spark and thence from human to human. The Ankh refers to that which is protected, renewed and vitalized; it is the descent of the eternal principle, the Atum, into the physical plane."

85

"Master, you have told us before that every hieroglyph comes from a common object or animal. What does the Ankh come from?"

"Good, Pepy. The Ankh is a loop of rope bound to the horizontal bar of reality with the tail hanging down. It binds the spiritual to the earthly horizon." Khensthoth picked up a stick and sketched the symbol in a patch of bare earth, pointing out the parts of the hieroglyph. "Now, who can tell me about the Sa?"

Menkure raised his hand. "It is like the Ankh but without the crossbar, is it not, master?"

Khensthoth nodded. "It too derives from a loop, but this time of woven rushes." He looked around the group of youths. "Who has been on boats? PenMa'at? Your father is Controller of the King's Wharves; can you tell me of woven rushes?"

"Yes, master." PenMa'at frowned, thinking hard. "Fishermen use woven rushes to keep themselves afloat if they fall in the river."

"Just so. A woven loop of rushes, bound with a rope, protects fishermen from drowning. The Sa comes into being when the horizontal plane of reality is fastened by the cosmic cord, the divine principle, to form a protective coil. The universal force that binds all things together forms a centre, a mooring post, a place of stability binding heaven and earth."

"And the last symbol, master? The Shen?"

"The Shen is a circle, representing endless time, eternity, bound to a horizontal bar, the earthly plane once more. It protects life by isolating and enclosing it, defining that which it surrounds, defending it against hostile forces. Can anyone tell me where the Shen is most commonly seen?"

86

A slightly built youth with a cast in one eye shyly raised a hand. "I have seen it, master. My father has told me of it when he takes me to the king's tomb."

Khensthoth smiled. "Indeed, Raia. As son of the Controller of the King's Funeral Artists, I would expect you to know. Tell us all."

"It is the cartouche, master. The loop around the royal name."

"Indeed. The king, as god-on-earth, is eternal, and his name enclosed by the cartouche, by the Shen symbol, is defined and isolated from common men, protected against all disaster."

Menkure put up his hand, abruptly dropped it before raising it again tentatively. "But if the king is protected, master, how is it that he was struck down by the gods?"

"*Shh*. The gods had nothing to do with that. Amen-hotep is a god himself, would he strike himself down? No, it is the earthly principle that is the cause. All men die, even kings who are part-god and part-men. It is the earthly part that weakens their godhead and limits their span of years. Were it not for the protection offered by the Shen ..." Khensthoth's voice trailed off with a shudder. "That will be enough for today. Gather your palettes." He rose, brushing down his robes of office.

"Tomorrow, we have permission to sit in the law courts and observe scribes in action as the young king enacts justice. Chief Advisor Ay has been most gracious and I trust none of you will disgrace me in front of the king."

To a chorus of denials and protestations of trust, Khensthoth led his young charges along the goat track and up through the fields toward the towering walls of Waset.

Chapter Five

The young king Waenre and Nefertiti, their three young daughters accompanying them, strolled slowly through the gardens surrounding the two great temples of Amun. Behind them walked a nurse, holding their youngest child Ankhesenpaaten, and the king's advisor Ay. The royal family often went out together, particularly in the cool mornings or in the dusk, taking in the sights or just enjoying each other's company. The king's advisor and father of the queen, Ay, disapproved of this practice but wisely held his counsel close. This particular day, shortly after the rising of blessed Aten, the king had decided to visit the nearly-completed temple of his god.

Shortly after his coronation, Waenre diverted vast amounts of gold from the temples of Amun, over the protests of the priests and set about having the land cleared between the two principle temples of the god of Waset. The priests were outraged and stepped up their protests. The removal of their wealth was bad enough, but now this minor god Aten was to be flaunted within sight of the temple steps. Waenre listened politely to all the protests and complaints before saying quietly, "The god requires me to do this," and ending all discussion.

The sacred garden between the temples of Amun was leveled, the carefully tended shrubs and trees, the flowering plants and ponds were, without ceremony, uprooted or filled in, the site razed in preparation for the building. Vast quantities of stone poured in from the quarries – granite from Qerert and fine white limestone from Roan near Men Nefer – brought by barge before being dragged on rollers through the lands dedicated to the god Amun. Skilled stonemasons, artisans and architects saw to the construction and with the deep coffers of Amun at their disposal, the temple rose swiftly.

Waenre stopped in front of the building site and stared up at the magnificent stone temple rising from the scraped and bare earth of the former garden. Despite the imposing edifices of the existing temple complex, the one dedicated to the Aten stood out. Vast columns rose to an ornately carved rim bearing complex patterns of leaves, lotus blossoms and animals chiseled from the stone. Above the entrance, a huge disk extended rays downward, each ending in a stylized hand. Unlike the outsides of the other temples, the one to Aten blazed with bright colours – gold and red, green and blue. The radiance of the great gold sun disk above the doors caught the morning sun and reflected it into the courtyard, bathing the king in its brilliance.

Waenre raised his hands toward the disk, his eyes closed and long head thrown back. A long sigh escaped him. After several minutes, he lowered his hands and opening his eyes, turned to Nefertiti.

"The Aten is here, my beloved. He accepts his new home."

Nefertiti moved closer and put her arms around her husband, laying her head on his bare shoulder. "It is magnificent, husband. A truly worthy offering to our god." The two young princesses, Meryetaten and Meketaten ran over and hugged their parents' legs. Nefertiti lowered her arms to stroke her daughters' heads before lifting her head and turning toward the other onlookers. "Do you not agree, father?"

Ay turned from his contemplation of the temples of Amun and the gathering of white-robed priests watching them. "Indeed, majesties." He bowed stiffly. "It is an extraordinary building."

89

"Not just a building," said Waenre. "The abode of the Aten." He led the way up the broad steps and into the temple, passing between the giant pillars.

Ay looked up with some surprise. As a priest of Amun he was used to the cavernous gloom of the temples, the multitude of carved gods and paintings over every part of the walls flickering and moving in the torchlight. The interior of the temple of the Aten astounded him. Looking up, he saw the tops of the columns carved into stylized lotus blossoms etched against an azure sky. Sunlight, rich and golden-pure poured down, filling the vast interior with light and warmth.

"Where is the roof? And why are there so few pillars? The builders will not be able to lay stone across these gaps without it cracking."

Waenre smiled delightedly. "There will be no roof. I cannot worship my father without seeing him in the sky above me."

Ay grunted and turned on his heel, scanning the walls of the vast hall. Only a scattering of workmen remained, cleaning up scattered debris, sweeping the floors or painting the far wall. "Where are the artists, majesty? Where are all the religious paintings? I see only pictures of plants and animals. And the sanctuary where the god resides? I do not see it."

"No religious paintings, father," Nefertiti said. "Only the glories of the Aten's creation to lift up our hearts in a song of praise."

"There is no sanctuary either," Waenre added. "How can you think that the sun itself could live in a building when he is there before us in the sky?" He strode forward over the stone floor toward the great mural on the end wall.

Another great sun-disk blazed from the wall, near the top where the limestone facings cut a line across the blue of the heavens. Rays with hands extended down as with the one outside the temple, but these hands clutched the ankh, the protective sign of life, holding it poised about bas-relief carvings of human figures dressed in the robes and crowns of royalty.

Ay stared at the carved figures for several minutes before letting his eyes travel slowly around the vast chamber, seeing for the first time the statues set back into shallow niches. He glanced at the king then back at the statues, his mouth tightening as his forehead wrinkled in puzzlement. "The statues," he muttered to himself. "What have the sculptors done?"

Nefertiti crossed to her father and put her arm around the old man. "It is a new thing," she said smiling. "We portray life as it is."

"But this ... this is not seemly. No king of Kemet should be held up to ridicule. The sculptors must be punished." Ay put out a hand and ran it over the smooth stone face of the statue in front of him. The carving was of the king, without a doubt, but surely the king was not grotesque. Ay glanced at Waenre again, standing in the same pose as the statue, though a slight smile replaced the stern look of the stone. Looking away, he saw the statue for what it was. A long narrow face, angular nose and chin, with hooded eyes and pouting lips stared blindly back at Ay. He dropped his eyes to a narrow stone chest with more than a hint of breasts, a swollen belly and rounded hips above misshapen legs.

"Ma'at is truth," Waenre said softly. "Even art must follow the law of Ma'at. Without it there is only chaos."

"But what of respect, my lord, and honour? Why do we look up to the great statues of the kings that have gone before? It is because we can see their nobility and strength. I fear that ... that the people will hold you in less respect."

"They will come to see that truth is everything. In the clear light of the Aten, all things are made plain."

Ay bowed. "As my lord Waenre wishes."

"There is another thing I wish."

"Name it lord."

"The Aten showers his blessings down on all men but only those that worship him in beauty and truth will be rewarded by him in the afterlife. I would have you do that, Ay, brother to the queen my mother and father of the queen my wife."

Ay bowed again. "As my lord commands. What must I do?"

"Give up your priesthood of Amun and turn to your father the Aten."

Ay thought hard, his face impassive. Amun was king of the gods without a doubt but the king was god-on-earth. If he required him to follow the Aten then that was what he must do. There was no power without the king's favour.

Nefertiti clasped her father's arm. "Join us, father. My husband and I are the principal priests but we will need your firm hand on everyday matters."

"Become a high priest of Aten," Waenre cajoled.

Ay bowed his head. "What can I say? If my king desires it of me, I can do nothing else."

"Then the ceremony tomorrow will be complete. The three of us will officiate over the dedication rites."

"Tomorrow? So soon? Surely the temple is not yet finished?"

The next day, as the great disk of the sun rose in the eastern sky, the young King Amenhotep, dressed in the purest white linen robes, led a long line of priests into the temple. With Ay and Nefertiti to his left and right, he lifted up his hands and his voice in a great song of praise.

"I am your son, O great Aten. I satisfy you, I exalt your name above all the other gods of Kemet. Your strength and power are established in my heart. Hear O Aten, you are the living disk, the great one who lives from eternity to eternity."

As the king sang in the morning sunlight streaming into the new temple, Ay led a chorus of newly consecrated priests into a chanting praise song. The melody itself was recognizable to many as a song to Amun, though the words had been changed to reflect the worshippers' new allegiance.

"The Aten has brought forth his honoured son, Waenre, the Unique One of the Sun, in his own form. Let praises honour the Aten and his only son for the Son of Re supports his beauty."

A long line of young girls entered the temple, also dressed in white linen skirts, their bronzed breasts shining in the golden glow from the Aten disk above the altar. Nefertiti advanced to meet them, and then led them in a swaying dance through the temple precincts, weaving between the painted columns as clear young voices rose into the sky.

Waenre turned to the altar and scattered incense on the sacred fire, sending billows of sweet-scented smoke into the vast open-aired hall. Breathing deeply of the perfumed vapours, Waenre staggered and Ay reached out to steady his king.

"The Aten fills me with his glory," Waenre croaked. "My lungs are like the noonday sun and my eyes water as if I have been staring at the blessed god."

Ay pulled on his king's arm. "Come, my lord, come away into the clearer air."

Waenre shook his head, wheezing. "No. The god speaks to me." He breathed the smoke again, dissolving into a paroxysm of coughing. "O great Aten, I hear you!" He shook off Ay and lifted his arms high in the air, stretching out to the golden disk whose light seemed to pulse in the billowing smoke.

"O Aten, living Aten, the beginning of all life.
You appear most radiantly on the eastern horizon ...
the ... the horizon of heaven itself."

Waenre lurched and clutched at the altar, holding himself upright. He sucked in the heady vapors before calling out again, his voice strengthening with every phrase.

"When you arise, O living Aten, from the eastern horizon,
You fill the land with your radiance, your beauty.
O living Aten, you are great and glorious, gracious and glistening,
High over every land. Your healing rays reach to all lands,
All lands that you have made, for you are Re.
O living Aten, you have subdued all lands for your beloved son Waenre,
And though you are far away, your rays are here on earth ..."

Waenre stumbled again and almost fell and this time allowed Ay to lead him away from the altar into the fresher air of the main body of the temple.

"Did you hear me, Ay? Did you note my words? I could feel the power of the Aten singing within me. There is more, a lot more. I feel it bursting to get out of my heart. I must send for a scribe and write it down; it will be my hymn to the Aten."

"Later, my lord. Rest now." Ay hesitated, started to say something, thought about it for a moment before trying again. "It is the presence of the god, my lord. Any mere man would be rendered insensible by the Aten's glory. It is only because you are the son of the living Aten and a god yourself that you can survive this experience."

Waenre nodded. "It must be as you say, noble Ay." He frowned. "But then how is it that you survive?"

"Your holy presence sustains me, lord." He looked around, and spotting Nefertiti, beckoned her over. In answer to his daughter's enquiring expression, he leaned close to her and murmured, "Smoke." In a louder voice he said, "It is the ecstasy of the god. The living Aten has made himself known to his son."

"I must commemorate this blessing," Waenre cried. "Statues. I shall have statues made of myself, of my beautiful wife and of my glorious father. No, take statues that are already made, Ay. Have them suitably inscribed. Start with the one of my father outside the temple of Amun."

"It shall be as you say, my lord. What would you have me inscribe?"

Waenre thought. "The God Aten sheds his rays on King Nebmaetre Amenhotep." He nodded. "Yes, then similar inscriptions on my and Nefertiti's statues." He smiled and put an arm around his father-in-law. "You may put the same on one of your statues too."

"You honour me, my lord, but I do not have any statues of myself."

"Then we shall have to rectify that. Have the masons prepare your likeness and inscribe it."

Nefertiti embraced her husband before gesturing toward the priests and singers thronging the vast temple. "Husband, we must finish the dedication."

Waenre stared out at the throng, his eyes unfocused. "The temple is already dedicated. Aten has accepted my gift and spoken to me."

Ay squeezed his daughter's shoulder and stepped past her toward the priests. "I'll deal with this." He hurried forward his arms raised as the last of the singing died away. The dancers stopped and all eyes turned to the king's advisor.

"The Living God Aten has spoken," he declaimed, pitching his voice to carry to the far ends of the temple. "He declares himself well satisfied with this temple and blesses it and all herein with his beneficent rays."

A spontaneous cry of joy burst from the throats of the leading priests, taken up and expanded by the singers and dancers. Ay let the cheering and cries of praise die down before raising his arms again.

"The Living Aten, all praise be to him, wishes to converse with his son, our beloved Neferkheperure Waenre. The king bids you depart from his house of the Living God and partake of the feast that has been prepared in the palace. Rejoice, all of you, for the Aten embraces his son Waenre, and through him, bountiful blessings will flow to his people."

Laughing and chattering, the crowd of priests, worshippers, dancers and singers left the temple, passing out from under the perfumed rays of the sun of the interior to the brightness of the gardens. As the last of them left, Ay turned and walked back to his king and his daughter.

Nefertiti grinned. "Father, you surprised me. You handled that very well for a man who has been a High Priest of Aten for only a day."

Ay shrugged. "I have been a priest, and a high priest of Amun long enough to know how to handle people. I just had to change the names."

"Yes, names." Waenre looked at father and daughter thoughtfully. "I must think on names some more. My throne names mean "Beautiful are the manifestations of Re" and "The unique one of Re". These names are acceptable, as Re is an aspect of the Aten but the name that is on the lips of people is Amenhotep, or "Amun is at peace". This is not suitable for a son of the Sun."

"You would change the name your father Nebmaetre gave you? It is also the name under which you were consecrated as king." Ay frowned, and lowered his voice though they were alone in the temple. "My lord, think on this I beg you. Do not be precipitate in your actions. In the eyes of everyone in the Two Lands you were consecrated as king in the name of Amun. If you change your name, particularly to one without the god's name, some might question whether you still have the right to rule."

"Aten gives me the right to rule," Waenre said. "These are but the jealous mouthings of the priests of Amun. It is only right that as I owe my very life and being to the living Aten I should bear his name."

"Husband, if you take a praise name of our great Aten, then I shall too." Nefertiti smiled and placed her slim arm around the king's shoulders.

Waenre turned and kissed his wife, stroking her back. "Beloved," he said, between kisses. "We shall devise a name ... of beauty ... that will honour the Aten ... and sing your beauty to all."

"Come then, my husband." Nefertiti took Waenre by the hand and led him past Ay. "Come to the palace and let us show our love together. Then we can find names for ourselves that praise our god."

Ay watched the young king and queen leave the temple precinct, his face set in a worried frown. "I cannot stand by and do nothing if inaction brings disaster on Kemet," he muttered. "I must plead with Nebmaetre, if the gods grant him speech, or else his queen, my sister Tiye." He contemplated the empty temple for several minutes before a slow smile creased his face. "And yet, if he is set on this act, then a strong man, a determined man in the right place, could achieve much."

Chapter Six

Cicadas thrummed in the olive groves of Lebanon. The heat of the summer's day rippled the dusty air, creating mirages over the coastal plains. On the bare hillsides above the groves, where within living memory the great cedars had grown, goats grazed on the rank grass, tended by small boys. Dust, kicked up by the sharp hooves, tasted acrid and sour in the throat. The herd moved slowly, cropping the grass and weeds, prevented from straying too far by the vigilance of their herders. Always ready with a shout and a stone hurled unerringly from a leather sling, the boys herded their charges across the hillsides, seeking the shade of a stand of scrubby poplar trees in the shelter of one of the many stony-bedded streams dissecting the landscape.

As the day moved toward noon, the goats sought out the deepest shade and settled down, jaws moving incessantly and yellow eyes contemplating their domain. Three of the four young boys sat beneath a large boulder overlooking the herd while the fourth climbed atop the great rock, shading his eyes as he scanned the hillside. It was not unknown for leopards to come down from the mountains, even in the summertime.

The sun moved and the boy clambered down, one of the others taking his place. A thin wisp of smoke rose from beneath the boulder where the bloodied corpse of a rabbit lay across a bed of coals. The stink of burning hair was gradually replaced by the aroma of cooking meat. The boy atop the rock glanced down hungrily, his mouth salivating in anticipation. As he did so he missed the movement on the trail that led to the north.

He called down to his friends below, his cry of inquiry masking the rattle of a dislodged stone. Straightening, he turned for a last look round before descending for his meal. His eyes widened at the sight of a troop of Amorite soldiers running along the path toward him, the sun glinting off spearheads. With a yell of alarm, he jumped into the long grass, rolled and picked himself up, bolting for the meager cover of the streambed.

The other boys, startled by his wordless cry of alarm, issued from around the boulder, fitting stones into their slings. They ran right into the armed men and went down at once, their limbs pinioned and tied within seconds.

A burly man, dark complexioned and unshaven, pushed to the front and scanned the hillside, his eyes searching for movement, flicking as a goat shifted then away again. He grunted and pointed.

"There, by the tall rock, a few cubits downstream."

An archer raised his bow. "I see him, Jebu."

The boy ran, jinking and dodging through the long grass, hurdling the smaller rocks. The arrow took him high in the back, tumbling him over and into a small ravine. The archer trotted over to retrieve his arrow, emerging a few minutes later, wiping the bloodied arrowhead on his tunic.

Jebu ordered his men to rest. The small fire was enlarged and two goats were sacrificed to the men's hunger, the rest of the flock scattering. While the meat cooked, Jebu led his two junior officers up to the crest of the ridge. Crawling up to the rim, they peered over.

In the valley below, beside a small river, lay a fortified encampment. A low ditch and rough palisade of sharpened stakes surrounded a dozen ragged tents. A road ran through the encampment, while a flimsy-looking gate of brush and branches made pretence of blocking each entrance. Two men lounged by each entrance, leaning on their spears. Within the camp, men sat around attending to the day to day activities of soldiers, mainly eating, sleeping or indulging in games of dice.

"I count twenty, Jebu, including the four at the gates."

"There are twelve tents, Aram," Jebu growled. "Kemetu sleep four to a tent. Allow one for the commander, another for the priest and that still leaves twenty unaccounted for. I would like to know where they are."

"Asleep in their tents maybe? Or else on patrol."

Jebu hawked and spat down the slope. "Either way, we must winkle them out of there. Any ideas?"

"We could wait until dark and go straight in," Aram ventured. "Take them by surprise."

"You have a high opinion of our rabble. Unless they can see what they are doing they'll be killing each other. The Kemetu are more disciplined."

The other officer shook his head slightly, running the fingers of one hand through the stubble of hair on his head. He gestured toward the camp. "They don't look very disciplined to me, Jebu. See, there is an officer, yet they don't even stand when he addresses them."

Jebu squinted into the bright glare. He watched the officer, a glint of gold around his neck, haranguing his men, seemingly without much effect. "Very good, Simyras." He grinned, showing crooked and yellowed teeth.

"Perhaps a trap then?" Aram suggested. "If they are not disciplined, could we lure them out?"

"Perhaps. What would bring them out?"

"A fire," Simyras said. "The hills are dry enough."

"That would just alert them to our presence. Besides, why would they venture out if the hills burn? They are in the valley and safe enough."

101

"Send a few men down there. They run away when the Kemetu come out and lead them to the rest of us." Aram grinned. "I would enjoy that killing."

Jebu made a farting noise with his lips. "They would have to be idiots to fall for that trick."

"They might come out if they heard from someone else there were only a few of us." Simyras turned and looked at his leader. "One of the goat herders maybe?"

Jebu thought it over, then nodded. "It might work, provided we can trust the boy ourselves. What's to stop him telling them it's a trap?"

"I'm sure a little gentle persuasion will work." Simyras grinned and touched the dagger hilt in his belt.

Jebu led his two officers back down to the camp by the big boulder. The goats were now partly cooked and the men fell upon the meat, carving hunks off with their daggers. As they ate, Jebu questioned the boys and was delighted to find that two were brothers.

"I'm going to give you a chance to live, boy." Jebu addressed the older brother. "You will do exactly as I say or I will personally slit your brother's throat – and your friend's," he added.

The boy nodded, flicking a tear-stained glance at his weeping brother.

"All right, Aram, cut him loose." Jebu waited until the boy got shakily to his feet. "In the next valley is a Kemetu outpost. You have no love of Kemetu so you should not care what happens to them?" He looked enquiringly at the boy and, receiving no hint of disagreement, continued. "You'll run down there as if the gods of the underworld were after you and you'll tell them that bandits captured your brother and friend, killed another and are now busy eating the flock. You got that?"

The boy nodded.

"You were separated from your friends and we never saw you. There are six of us and we are eating but we have not even set a guard. Understand?"

"Yes."

"Good. You will lead them up here and will give them no warning."

"What if they don't want to come?"

"Then if you want your brother to live, you will persuade them."

Jebu watched as Aram led the boy up to the ridge crest and turned him loose. The boy disappeared over the rim at a run. He designated six men to sit around the fire and continue eating, and then carefully laid out the ambush, setting archers to cover the path leading down to the valley. "No-one must escape," he told them. He clambered up to the ridge where Aram kept an eye on the Kemetu outpost.

"Still only twenty men visible," muttered Aram. "The others must be out on patrol."

"Then pray to the gods they do not return too early." Jebu scanned the hillside and the valley. "Where is the boy?"

Aram pointed. "He went down along the streambed as if seeking cover. If the guards see him they will believe he is hiding from someone."

Jebu watched as the boy broke cover and headed out over the bare ground toward the encampment. The guards spotted him and rose to meet him, issuing a challenge. After a few minutes, one of the guards accompanied the boy into the camp. They disappeared into the commander's tent.

"How many do you think he'll send?" Aram asked.

Jebu shrugged. "Who knows? There are only supposed to be six of us so my guess is a dozen, no more.

103

He'll want to make sure of his capture but not empty his camp with the others away. That will give us odds of two to one."

They watched and waited. At length a man ran from the tent and out of the encampment, heading out along the road to the distant coast.

Jebu cursed, forcing a grin from Aram at his colourful language. "The son of a whore has sent for the patrol." He got to his feet, brushing off his tunic. "Nothing for us here then. Kill the boys and let's get out of here."

Aram waved his leader back down. "Something's happening. Look."

Jebu lowered himself again and stared down into the valley. A bustle of activity in the encampment caught their attention. The man with the glint of gold on his chest stood outside his tent with the boy as a squad of men with spears formed up in front of him. They set out at a trot, the commander and the boy in front, heading through the makeshift gate and toward the hills.

"I make it eleven, counting the commander," Aram murmured. "We can take them easily." They hurried back down to the streambed, where Jebu altered the positions of his men slightly. The men by the fire lay down in the shade of the boulder as if asleep while one sat up, leaning against the rock, acting the part of a somnolent guard.

Jebu lay in the long grass halfway up the slope, watching the point where the path crested the ridge through the stems. A slight breeze ruffled the vegetation, carrying the sour odour of wood ash to his nostrils, intermingled with the scents of roasted meat. Grasshoppers chirped and the cicadas buzzed from the stand of scrubby poplars.

A movement caught his eye. Jebu lifted his head slightly as a man, dressed in a plain brown military kilt appeared on the ridge, crouching down. He moved cautiously along the path, scanning the track ahead of him. The sight of the big boulder and the sleeping men froze him. He looked around cautiously, noting the apparently sleeping guard, before moving back to the ridge. A few moments later a file of soldiers moved cautiously over the top, walking swiftly down toward the boulder. The commander led his squad, the goat herder at his side.

The Kemetu soldiers quietly surrounded the rock, then, with spears at the ready, the commander called out. The guard raised his head and gave a cry of alarm, jumping to his feet. The 'sleeping' men awoke and stood, their swords still sheathed in their belts. They stared back at the soldiers, knuckling their eyes.

The commander called out again and his men advanced on their quarry. Jebu stood up and waved a hand. At once, his archers stood and loosed their arrows. The thud of the bronze-tipped missiles hitting flesh carried quite clearly to him, and Jebu jerked his sword from his belt and rushed down the slope, his men screaming beside him.

The Kemetu turned, even as three of their number fell in a tangle of limbs, raising spears to meet the threat. At once, the men behind them snatched up their swords and threw themselves on the soldiers. The ambush dissolved into a melee of struggling men. Kemetu spears proved no match for the close-quarter fighting of Jebu's men and shortly the soldiers lay dead at their feet.

Jebu wiped his bronze sword on the grass and sheathed it. "Anyone hurt?"

Aram indicated one of the men. "Sellu has a stab to his arm, otherwise nothing more than scratches."

"Right, strip them. Collect any jewelry they have, clothing and the spears. We are going to need everything."

Simyras frowned. "Why do we need their kilts? They're made of coarse linen. Nobody will buy that."

Jebu grinned. "Because you, my friend, are going to become a Kemetu."

Leaving a few of his men behind to remove the heads of the corpses, Jebu led the others along the trail toward the encampment. His plan, which he had considered brilliant when he first conceived it, had suffered in the execution. He had forgotten that Kemetu commonly shaved their heads and bodies. Consequently, the Kemetu soldiers that now trotted down the track seemed singularly hirsute to any but the most casual observer.

"We're never going to get away with this," Aram muttered. "Nobody is going to mistake them for Kemetu."

"Maybe not, but they won't be expecting anything. All their attention will be on our prisoners." Six men, lightly bound with nooses around their necks, stumbled along in front of the false soldiers. "I chose them because they are the hairiest."

"And if they are not fooled?" grumbled Aram.

"Then we cut and run. They have no archers and they're not going to come out after us. There are ten men left in camp and twenty of us."

Simyras, as one of the least hairy Amorites, wore the gold badge of rank around his neck, trotting at the head of his troop. Jebu, one of the hairier ones, brought up the rear. As they got closer to the fort they changed their angle of approach, herding the Amorite 'prisoners' ahead of them as a shield. Cries from the encampment told Jebu they had been seen and he risked a direct look at the fort.

The gate was wide open and at least half a dozen men crowded the entrance.

They drew closer and the welcoming cries suddenly ceased. One of the Kemetu soldiers at the gate yelled in alarm, grabbing for his spear. Jebu drew his sword and uttering a scream, ran past his men. With scarcely a pause, the others followed, the prisoners throwing off their ropes and snatching swords from their fellows. A disorganized rabble burst through the gates and started hacking at the soldiers. Jebu swung his sword and missed, tried again, hacking into the arm of a soldier. The man screamed and fell back, going down as another Amorite spitted him. He blocked a stab by a spear and closed with the man, grappling. Jebu kneed the man in the testicles, and then slashed down as he doubled over.

Two of Jebu's men went down and another three were injured but even the spirited defence by the soldiers was no match for the screaming Amorites. The Kemetu were outnumbered and the din of battle rapidly died away. Soon, the only sound was panting and muffled groans from the wounded. Somewhere, high above them in the heat-rippled air sounded the clear tones of a lark.

Jebu nodded and examined his wounded men. "All right. We have done what I set out to do. There is still a Kemetu patrol out there and I would guess, from the fact that a runner was sent after them, that they are not far away. Take the heads and we will leave." He watched as his men hacked at the necks of their fallen enemy with blunted blades. Others started to plunder the camp.

"What of our fallen, Jebu?" Aram asked.

"We leave them." He held up a hand as Aram opened his mouth. "We can do nothing else. Speak the words over them and sprinkle a handful of soil. Let the priests earn their keep when we return."

"And the heads? When have we mutilated the dead?"

"Special orders, Aram. All the way down from Prince Aziru. We are to annihilate any Kemetu forces we can and remove the heads. They are to be sent to governor Ribbadi of Byblos. 'Sowing the seeds of terror and dissension,' he says."

Jebu and his men gathered up the last of their booty and left the camp at a fast walk, a blood-stained linen bag containing the heads bouncing on the back of one of them. The Amorites disappeared into the hills and silence descended on the camp by the river.

The drone of flies grew in the summer heat, the hawks and kites circling for a while before stooping in a rapid descent. The returning Kemetu patrol arrived just before dusk, horror and unease appearing on their faces as they saw the carnage that awaited them.

Chapter Seven

The young king Neferkheperure Waenre Amenhotep stood in the bows of the great royal barge 'The Aten Gleams' with his wife Nefertiti as it sped downriver from Waset. For two days they had journeyed with wind and current to the north and now were nearing the point where the cliffs that ran close along the eastern bank of the river pulled back in a great half-moon plain, green with grass and dotted by clumps of palms and acacia. The cliffs themselves continued on straight and level except for one point where a dry stream valley cut through the sandstone. By chance, the sun rose through the notch in the cliff tops when viewed from the plain. The local farmers, living on the western bank in a small area of rich black earth trapped between stony rills when the river flooded, worshipped the sun as it rose through the notch, calling their village Akhet-Re or Horizon of Re. The young king, drawn by reports of the phenomenon, had visited the site the previous year. He ordered a city built on the broad crescent plain on the eastern bank, naming it Akhet-Aten or Horizon of the Aten.

"See beloved," Waenre murmured, his arms around his beautiful wife. "Already our city takes shape."

The wind, constant from the south for two days, veered and reflected back from the cliffs. The sails on the barge rippled and cracked before filling once more. Resuming its passage, 'The Aten Gleams' heeled over slightly and eased toward the eastern shore.

Nefertiti scanned the banks of the river as the barge pulled slowly into the makeshift docks at the northern end of the growing city. "It ... it does not look like much, my husband." Her voice faltered at the sight of the dust-

109

covered piles of mud bricks. Hordes of workmen clambered over the piles, adding more as lines of peasants staggered in from the workmen's village near the cliff face. Others carted bricks from the stockpiles to add to the rapidly rising walls of a maze of small buildings. The warm breeze carried with it the stench of open middens. "It is not how I imagined it."

Waenre smiled and kissed her cheek, his hand lightly brushing a naked breast. "A city is not built in a day. But it is important that something is built quickly. The workmen's quarters came first, then minor officials. Mud bricks will do for now. Stone buildings will come later. Already quarries are being worked to the south." He pointed toward the southern cliffs. "Somewhere over there is a good supply of sandstone. Worked granite is on its way. As soon as the outlines of the city are in place, the infrastructure, then we can start on the palaces."

"It just does not seem the glorious city of the Aten I dreamed about."

"It will be. I have a hundred architects working on plans and a thousand stone-masons and artists already at work. With the treasury of Amun behind it, the Living Aten will soon have a city worthy of his glorious name." He gestured toward the mud brick jumble. "Do not be put off by the brick. By the time I have finished I will have a city of stone that will make Waset look like a country village."

The barge drifted in close to the wooden wharf and naked sailors leapt ashore to tie the craft up, securing it firmly against the pull of the current. Waenre and Nefertiti strolled casually back to the awning shading the central part of the barge. There, in the shade of the linen awnings, their three young daughters sat with their nurses, playing with small carved animals and cloth dolls.

110

The eldest, Meryetaten, jumped up with a squeal of joy. "Daddy, Mamma, can we go ashore now? Anhai said we could." She waved in the general direction of her nurse as she spoke.

The nurse Anhai rose to her feet and bowed quickly, her eyes wide. "Oh, majesties, please. I did not mean to imply ... I mean, I only said we may be able to go ashore ..."

Nefertiti smiled. "I am sure you did not mean to presume. However, I think it would be better if you stayed on the barge. It is hot and dusty out there."

"Come, beloved," Waenre chided. "The girls have been two days on board. I am sure they are eager to see Akhet-Aten. It is their city as well."

"As you wish, husband." She nodded at the nurse. "You are charged with their safety, Anhai. Take some soldiers with you and make sure you have them back for their noon meal and nap."

Anhai bowed. "Yes, lady." She turned away, ushering the little princess back to the others. She called to the captain of the king's guard. "Hori, you heard the queen. You must give me men."

One of the other nurses, Tia, who looked after the princess Ankhesenpaaten, grinned and slipping a hand in front of her mouth, muttered to a third nurse, "Give me one man, at least, she means. And we all know which particular man she has in mind."

"Shh," said the third. "The princesses are listening."

Waenre watched as the nurses bustled around, making sure they had everything needed for the trip ashore. A squad of soldiers stood stoically by the side of the gangplank, waiting for the women and girls. One of them, a tall young Nubian, kept his eyes fixed on Anhai. Tia grabbed Ankhesenpaaten and hurried her over to the

111

far side of the barge, holding her over the side as a thin clear stream of urine arced into the water below. Lowering the baby girl to the deck again, she walked her slowly back to the others. Waenre took his wife by the arm and guided her away.

"The state chariot is waiting, beloved. I thought we could see the whole city together."

Waenre walked down the broad gangplank, arm in arm with Nefertiti. At the bottom, officials in clean linen pressed forward, the gold of their chains of office glinting in the harsh sunlight. The mayor of the fledgling city bowed low.

"Welcome, majesties. We are honoured by your presence." The mayor straightened, but kept his head low, rubbing his hands together as he spoke. "As soon as the royal barge was sighted, I ordered a feast to be prepared, great king. It is unworthy, I know, but we can offer cool refreshment ..."

"Thank you, Neferkhepruhersekheper," Waenre interrupted. "Maybe later. First, I wish to see the progress you have made with my city." He pushed past the officials to where his chariot stood, harnessed to a pair of finely caparisoned white horses. The king's charioteer, Besenmut, stood by the horses' heads, his firm hand restraining the spirited beasts.

"My lord." Besenmut inclined his head civilly, while flashing his monarch a quick smile. "The new horses, as I promised. You can see they are a fine pair, brothers. The one on the left is Raia, the other Reuser."

Waenre smiled and favoured his charioteer with a touch on the arm. "They are indeed beautiful, Besenmut. Are they swift?" He ran his hand over Raia's flank. The horse snorted, its sides shivering as it rolled its eye back to look at this strange new man.

"Like the north wind, Waenre. And as strong as the sun for which they are named." Besenmut held onto Ra-ia's bridle, stroking the beast, calming him.

"Excellent." Waenre turned to help Nefertiti up into the broad carriage of the ceremonial chariot. She stepped up gracefully and gripped the ornately moulded rail at the front. The king signaled to a fan-bearer and the man ran over, bowed, and clambered up behind the queen, bracing himself so he could keep the ostrich-feathered fan over her, shielding her from the worst of the sun's heat. Waenre got up too, and picked up the reins.

"My lord," Besenmut said, stepping away from the horses' heads and coming around the chariot. "It would be best if I drove."

Waenre stopped smiling. "You do not think I can handle them?"

Besenmut hesitated. "They are high-spirited, my lord."

Waenre said nothing, just picking up the reins. As the cords touched the horses' backs, they shied, dragging the chariot forward. Waenre pulled back hard and fought the horses to a standstill.

Nefertiti put out a hand to grasp her husband's arm and squeezed. "Are you all right, husband?" she murmured.

"Of course. I can handle them."

"Please, my lord, let me, I know them." Besenmut wore a frown now and flashed a quick glance at the watching officials. They avoided his eyes. Stepping forward, closer to the king, he put a hand on the chariot rail and looked up. "My lord Waenre. It was my understanding you wanted to see your beautiful new city. Would it not be easier if I was driving?"

Nefertiti stroked the king's arm, smiling up at him. "That is true, my love. I would like you to point out all the buildings to me."

Waenre scowled briefly, and then threw down the reins. "Perhaps you are right. Besenmut, you drive. I will stand with my wife."

The charioteer hid a smile by bowing. "Yes sir." He scrambled up into the chariot and picked up the reins. He wound them round his wrists and braced his feet in the leather loops riveted to the floor. "Ho, Raia, Reuser, on you brave ones." The chariot lurched as the horses leapt forward, before settling down into a steady pace. Besenmut guided the chariot through the swarms of workmen toward a building that was no more than foundations set amongst scarred vegetation. The workmen largely ignored the bouncing chariot though quickly got out of the way of the horses.

Waenre pointed at the foundations as they neared. "One of the palaces, beloved." He gestured off to the left, toward where the great cliffs veered to meet the river. "The city will continue to the north, as far as the cliffs. This will be the port area, where all the wealth of our great empire will arrive."

"It is very dry and barren now, husband," Nefertiti observed. "But I shall engage a thousand gardeners and turn this place into a paradise."

Waenre squeezed his wife and kissed her gently. He tapped Besenmut on the shoulder and pointed to the south. "Take us down the Royal Road."

Besenmut slowed the chariot and eased it into a turn, calling softly to his horses. He guided them through the piles of building materials and headed south toward the main activities.

"The city will extend all along here. This will be housing for all the artisans and ... and everyone that has business here." Waenre frowned. "It is a pity that this great city of Aten must have so many people but I suppose it cannot be helped."

Nefertiti smiled and slipped an arm around her husband's naked waist. "If we are to dedicate ourselves to beauty, there must be a lot of people to produce all the things we need. They will not intrude on us."

The chariot, churning up a great cloud of dust, arrived on the outskirts of the growing city. A wide street opened out in front of them, with buildings taking shape on all sides. A huge stone edifice with rough-hewn pillars loomed on the left, its walls unfinished and draped in scaffolding.

"The Great Temple of Aten," Waenre said. "Naturally it was the first thing to be built." Besenmut slowed the chariot and brought it to a halt outside the temple. "See how it is oriented to face east into the valley and the notch in the cliffs where the Aten rises each day. When it is finished it will be more magnificent even than the one in Waset."

"I am glad, husband. It is not proper that Aten's temple should be next to that of the false god Amun."

Besenmut caught his breath, not daring to even glance at his king and queen. He offered a silent prayer to Amun then stared straight ahead at the backs of his horses' heads. After a few moments, as the king gave no sign of wanting to alight, Besenmut shook the reins and turned the chariot once more down the Royal Road.

The road passed a number of small houses next to the great temple complex and a smaller stone building on the right. Next to it rose the foundations of another huge stone edifice. Though smaller than the Great Temple, it dwarfed all the other buildings.

"Another temple." Waenre nodded to his right. "And of course, the lesser priests need homes too. Then the royal palace."

The road narrowed abruptly as if a wall of mud bricks had been thrown across the open space. Besenmut slowed the chariot to a walk and steered for a gap in the wall.

"Is this right?" Nefertiti asked. "Does the road come to an end here?"

Waenre chuckled. "No beloved. On the right is the palace and on the left is the king's house. The two are joined by this great bridge so we will never have to go outside to get from one to the other."

"A bridge?"

"Yes, with a covered walkway on the top. In the middle there will be a room with windows facing out over the Royal Road in both directions. I call them the Windows of Appearance where we can show ourselves to the people."

Nefertiti clapped her hands with delight and hugged her husband again. In full sight of the people in the street she leaned close and kissed him, running her hands over his nearly naked body. He responded enthusiastically, leaving Besenmut to thread the chariot through the gaps in the bridge brickwork, his eyes fixed on the road ahead. The fan-bearer knew his job and kept the ostrich plumes firmly in place above the royal heads, his eyes carefully averted.

They emerged into the open road again and Besenmut picked up the pace, dust once more billowing in their wake as pedestrians scattered. Waenre gave Nefertiti a last lingering kiss, his hand still stroking her breast then pointed out the sights again.

"The river lies to the right here. I have planned a large garden for the common people. It is not enough that we enjoy the beauty of Aten, the common people also must see that all beautiful things come from the god." He turned to his driver. "Is that not so, Besenmut?"

Besenmut inclined his head. "Indeed, my lord king. The needs of the common people are quite simple. Food, and shelter, and the protection of ..." He faltered a moment before finishing. "... of the king."

Waenre frowned, catching the brief hesitation. "Poverty is always among us, Besenmut. Yet even the hungriest peasant can appreciate the beauty of the living Aten. I shall plant gardens filled with ponds and shade trees and flowering plants and incense bushes where even the lowliest person may contemplate beauty during his rest."

"What rest?" Besenmut muttered. "And I'm sure they would rather have public gardens planted with radishes and lettuce." Louder he merely said, "A most generous gesture, my lord. All of Akhet-Aten will praise your name."

"Turn left here, Besenmut. Head for the cliffs."

The chariot veered, threading through a warren of side streets filled with pedestrians. The buildings here were low and made of mud daubed over brick and wattle, many occupied and all seemingly advertising some form of trade. Nefertiti saw shops displaying cloth, jewelry and pottery before the chariot exited on the landward side of the city. The high cliffs reared up in front of them, the sun just short of noon not yet lighting the sheer rock face. Waenre pointed up at the creviced and shadowed wall of rock.

"My quarrymen tell me there are many good tomb-sites up there for the overseers and senior officials."

Nefertiti raised a hand to shade her eyes and scanned the cliff. "And royal tombs?"

Waenre shook his head. "There is a better place." He tapped Besenmut on the arm and gestured north.

As the chariot moved north once more, bouncing and clattering over the sand and loose rock at the foot of the cliffs, they passed a workmen's village ringed by a high brick wall. Beyond it, the cliffs receded to the north-east, dipping into a great dry valley that plunged back into the dry heart of the desert. Besenmut turned the chariot into the stream bed and guided the horses carefully and slowly to the east. The valley narrowed rapidly and before long, Besenmut stopped the chariot.

"I will have to stop here, my lord, else I will not be able to turn the horses."

"Very well." Waenre jumped down and helped Nefertiti to descend also. "Wait here. We will not be long."

"My lord, you should not go alone."

"Why not? What hand would be raised against me in all of Kemet? I am the son of Aten. He shines down upon me and protects me."

"At least take the fan-bearer, my lord," Besenmut pleaded. "Not ... not as protection but as an attendant upon the queen." He gestured and the fan-bearer jumped down, his fan held over the royal heads once more.

Waenre grunted and nodded, then, turning his back, strolled up the narrowing streambed, his hand in his wife's. The fan-bearer hurried after them, struggling to hold his fan aloft. Within fifty paces the way became rougher and they slowed, the king helping his wife over the boulders until they stood on a patch of sandy gravel looking up at a shadowed cliff in a small side stream.

118

Halfway up the steep stone side, darkness hinted at the presence of a cave.

"There is our future tomb, beloved. My masons tell me the cave itself only extends ten paces into the cliff but the rock is hard and sound. It can easily be extended into galleries and rooms. A few years and our eternal abode will be assured."

They turned and started back down the stream bed. Besenmut had turned the horses and was feeding them a handful of grain each from a small bag tied to the side of the chariot. He looked up as the king approached.

"All is well, my lord?"

"Of course. As I said it would be." Waenre helped Nefertiti up, then climbed into the chariot himself, waiting while the fan-bearer and Besenmut positioned themselves. "Back to the docks."

They rode in silence as they exited the notch of Aten and headed northwest across the plain toward the north suburbs of the city. As they neared the first mud brick houses, Waenre pointed off to the right, at the cliffs.

"There is another good site for tombs up there. As important as Akhet-Aten will become, we cannot have too many tomb sites for the court officials."

"And what of the common people?" Nefertiti asked.

Waenre shrugged. "They will do as they always do. The desert is vast and they will bury their dead in the sands."

The chariot bounced over deep ruts, almost unbalancing the king before turning north onto the Royal Road again. They sped past the North Palace and turned toward the docks and the royal barge.

***

Anhai, Tia and Kawit, the nurses of the three young princesses, walked down the gangplank with their charges

119

as the royal chariot disappeared in a cloud of dust toward the Royal Road. With them went a squad of soldiers under the command of Zemti, Leader of Five, the tall young Nubian. Tia and Kawit hurried ahead with their princesses, the soldiers dressed in their short red-dyed kilts trotting alongside them, spears in hand. Anhai dropped back with princess Meryetaten to talk to the handsome young Nubian Zemti.

"I see you, Anhai," Zemti said.

"And I you." Anhai grinned then leaned across and smacked the young man on his firmly-muscled buttock.

Zemti's eyes widened and he danced back a step before resuming his fast walk. He glanced at the interested face of princess Meryetaten. "Be cautious, Anhai. The young one ..."

"The young one knows when to keep quiet, don't you, my pet?" Anhai squeezed the princess' hand. "She loves me like a mother, particularly when I buy her sweetmeats." She winked at Meryetaten.

"Yes, Anhai." Meryetaten looked up at the young soldier trotting alongside them. "Are you and Anhai going to lie together?"

"Where did you hear such nonsense?" Anhai exclaimed. "That is not a proper subject for the ears of a young princess."

Meryetaten shrugged and smiled. "Tia and Kawit were talking this morning. They say Zemti has a very big thing. Do you, Zemti?" She peered at his brief kilt with interest.

Zemti rolled his eyes. He pointed to where his squad was pushing through a small crowd of people around one of the shops in the north suburb. "We must join them," he rumbled.

Anhai dragged her charge over to the other nurses and looked over their shoulders at the shop front. A man, his attire plainly indicating he was an artisan of some worth, was talking about his wares, laid out on trestle tables behind him.

"Gather round, good people." The man looked across at the squad of soldiers, recognizing the palace insignia bound around their left biceps. His eyes flickered across the three young women and the small girls. He smiled. "I can see we have someone from the palace here today. Give them room, good people."

The crowd muttered and grumbled but edged away, allowing Anhai and the others closer, the soldiers standing in a group around them.

"My name is Nesmut, good ladies," said the man. "I am an artisan and glass dealer, newly up from Waset where I have a thriving business. However, once I knew that the people up this way appreciated beautiful things, I knew I should bring my wares up here." He gestured at the trestle tables behind him.

"Observe, if you will, the cunning ways that I have combined gold, silver and copper threads with wonderful pieces of pure-coloured glass that are indistinguishable from gem stones. My partner in Waset, one Ahhotep the glassmaker, has recently perfected a technique of making the most beautiful deep blue glass." He picked up a necklace of woven copper threads set with beads of deep blue and green glass, holding it out to Tia. "Hold that against your skin, lovely lady ... ah, yes, see how the tone of your beautiful skin sets off the colours. It was made for you."

Tia tittered and preened, holding it against her throat and turning to the others. Anhai clenched her fists while voicing her admiration. She reached out and almost

121

snatched the necklace from the other nurse, holding it against her own throat.

"What do you think, Zemti?" she murmured. "Would you not want to see me in this? Perhaps only this?"

Zemti flared his nostrils and shifted his posture awkwardly. "How much?" he growled at the shop keeper.

Nesmut flicked his eyes from the soldier to the young woman, then to the young girls, considering. "Normally, a fine piece like this would fetch ten, maybe fifteen copper pieces." He lifted a hand as muffled groans of disappointment broke out from several women. "However, seeing as how the piece is destined for the palace, I will let it go for five. I make no profit on it at that price but ..." he shrugged.

"Two," said Zemti.

Nesmut laughed. "Come, soldier. You may be used to looting foreign lands but we are loyal subjects of the king. Four."

"Three," Zemti countered.

Nesmut thought hard. The copper thread and glass beads had cost him two copper pieces, and several hours work. "Agreed. However, you must tell everyone who admires it that it came from the shop of Nesmut the jeweler in North Suburb."

Zemti dug in a small pouch at his waist and passed over three copper pieces. Ignoring the look of hatred from Tia, Anhai fastened the necklace and twirled, grinning. The other women in the crowd jostled around the tables, admiring the other pieces. Nesmut immediately started bargaining, his attention diverted from the palace party.

Tia and Kawit turned away with a sniff of disdain, dragging their girls with them. The other soldiers, at a nod from Zemti, moved off after them.

"It is beautiful, Zemti. Thank you."

Zemti nodded again, his eyes fixed on the beautiful green and blue gems lying between Anhai's bronzed breasts. "You will see me tonight?"

"Of course, my strong one," Anhai purred. "When I have put the young princess to bed this evening. Where will I meet you?

"By the gangplank. We can walk along the riverbank."

Meryetaten tugged on Anhai's dress. "What about my sweetmeats?"

Anhai smiled down at the little princess, putting a hand on the girl's shaven head, stroking her side lock. "Come then, let us find you a treat."

Meryetaten walked beside her nurse and looked across at the tall young Nubian striding alongside. She stared wide-eyed at his kilt. "Zemti. You are getting bigger. Why is that?"

Chapter Eight

"I've seen you before, haven't I? You're No-name."

The little girl looked up from where she watched a cluster of ants dragging a dead grasshopper toward their nest. Still kneeling, she looked at the naked boy standing by the lotus pond. She regarded him with inquisitive but cautious eyes. After a moment, she nodded. "I have a name now. I'm called Scarab."

"Scarab? That's a strange name for a girl. Why are you called that?" He came closer and stood over the girl, looking down at the insects. He nudged the grasshopper with a toe, sending the ants into a frenzy of activity.

"Don't do that," snapped Scarab. "I'm watching them."

The boy grinned. "Is that why you are called Scarab? Because you watch beetles?"

"The king called me that. I think he wants me to marry the god."

"Which god?"

"Khepri of course, the scarab."

The boy nodded and squatted beside the little girl, watching as the ants resumed their task of dragging the grasshopper. He reached out a finger to disturb them, then hesitated and drew it back. "You probably will marry a god when you are older, Scarab, but not Khepri. It is more likely you will be God's Wife to the king."

Scarab made a face. "Ugh, he is an old man. Besides, he has a wife already."

"Nefertiti?" He shrugged. "The king is allowed many wives and it is common practice in our house for kings to marry their sisters. Maybe I'll marry you instead."

Scarab sat back on her heels and contemplated the small boy for a while. "Who are you? I've seen you, of course, but you don't usually play with the babies ..." She flushed and added "... younger children."

The boy grinned. "I'm your brother Smenkhkare. Well, half-brother anyway, though my grandmother is also your mother. I suppose you could say you are my aunt also."

Scarab nodded. "Yes, your mother Sitamen is my older sister."

Smenkhkare looked away, his eyes glistening. "Was your sister, little Scarab. She has been in the house of embalming for this past month." For a few moments, his shoulders shook with grief.

The girl looked down, her face twisted into a frown. She reached out and touched Smenkhkare's arm. "I'm sorry. At least she will be with the gods."

Smenkhkare wiped his eyes with the back of his hand, then pinching his nostrils with his fingers, blew hard and wiped his fingers on the ground. "Look," he said, pointing at the ants. "They are just like the men pulling blocks of stone to the temples." He laughed, his previous thoughts forgotten. "Except the ants are pulling in more than one direction."

"I've never seen men pulling stones. Where was this?"

"At the new temple of the Aten. You know the one?"

Scarab shook her head. "I've never been outside the palace and the gardens here."

Smenkhkare raised his eyebrows. "Really? I go all the time. More these last few weeks ..." His voice trailed off and he stared at the ground again. "My nurse and tutor are too busy to watch me. I like to go off by myself."

"Where to?"

"The city, the temples. I like talking to people and finding out what they do. I think a king should know about the common people."

Scarab gaped. "A king? But you are not a king."

"Of course not, silly girl. But I might be one day. My brother Amenhotep has only daughters. If he does not have a son, I may yet be king."

"That's not fair. Why can't a woman be king?"

"Because kings are men, silly. A woman can be a queen though. If I become king I shall marry you and make you my queen and we shall rule Kemet together."

Scarab laughed. "King Smenkhkare and Queen Scarab!"

"Well, we will have to find you another name by then. Perhaps you will grow into a beautiful woman and we can call you Neferkhepre – Beautiful Scarab."

"My mother says our father wanted to call me Beketamen, but couldn't 'cos he got sick. That's why I didn't have a name."

"That's a nice name. Maybe we can call you that when you get older?" Smenkhkare fell silent and for several minutes they watched the ants try to haul the dead grasshopper into the nest. When they started to dismember the grasshopper and take pieces in, he looked across at his little sister.

"Do you want to come into the city with me?"

Scarab's eyes grew round. "You want me to come?"

"If you want. I could show you the temple where I saw the stone blocks being dragged. It's not far. Come on." Smenkhkare leapt to his feet and started walking past the lotus pond, in the direction of the walled orchard.

Scarab raced after him. "Wait," she cried. "What if the nurses won't let me go?"

126

"Huh. Do you think we are going to ask them? I just go whenever I want. I know a way out of the garden."

Smenkhkare led the way into the carefully tended orchard. Several gardeners were weeding and hoeing the soil around fig and pomegranate trees. Others were pruning the vines tied to a trellis fence. The children avoided looking at any of the adults and walked quickly and purposefully toward the far end. "This way," Smenkhkare said. "We have to go round behind the house of Her-uben, the Head Gardener. He's all right once you ..."

"Boy!" A deep voice rang out from the doorway of the house by the orchard wall. An old man limped out, supporting himself on a staff. "Oh, it's you again. Off on another of your jaunts?"

"Yes, Her-uben. With your permission of course."

"With my permission? Don't be a fool, boy. If they find out I'm letting you wander in the city unsupervised, the chamberlain will have me whipped, despite my age. Not that I could stop you, young Smenkhkare. Just don't tell them I let you past if they catch you."

"I won't, sir."

Her-uben nodded, before fixing Scarab with a piercing look. "And who is this young girl? Anyone I should know about?"

"No sir. Her name is Scarab. She's a ... a friend of mine."

"Scarab, eh? Funny name for a girl." The head gardener shrugged and turned away to a bench by the wall. "Well, off you go then and be careful."

Smenkhkare grinned and took Scarab's hand, leading her at a run around the gardener's house and squeezing between the back wall of the house and the orchard wall. An old acacia tree had grown up right on the line of the wall, its roots splitting and tumbling the stone blocks, spilling them in a jumbled pile.

"You'll have to climb up these stones, then onto that branch there." Smenkhkare pointed and scrambled up ahead of his sister. "Watch out for scorpions though, they live under the rocks."

Scarab drew back, not wanting to touch a rock with a scorpion under it, but she saw an expression of scorn start to appear on her brother's face. Taking a deep breath, she started up the pile of rocks, then hauled herself onto the branch.

"Well done. You climb well for a girl. Now, follow me." Smenkhkare turned and lowered himself down the tree, from branch to branch. Scarab followed, more slowly as the branches were spaced almost at full stretch for her smaller body. After a few minutes they both stood on the grass underneath the tree, looking toward the imposing buildings of the temples of Amun.

"They're as big as the palace," Scarab said.

"Bigger. The palace only houses the king, though he is also god-on-earth. But Amun is the king of the gods; he needs a much larger home." Smenkhkare started walking toward the nearer temple. After a moment, Scarab joined him.

"We ... we're not going to see Amun, are we?" Scarab clutched at her brother's arm.

Smenkhkare laughed. "Not even his statue. We won't be allowed in that far. One of the young priests I know, Pa-Siamen, says they actually dress the statue every day and put food in front of it."

The two children crossed the large garden surrounding the temple and walked round toward the back of it. They passed several men in white linen robes that ignored them completely.

128

"See," Smenkhkare said. "Nobody minds us being here." He led his sister up to the small building at the back of the temple and rapped on a wooden door. A few moments later the door creaked open and a wrinkled face peered out, like the priests, completely hairless.

"What do you want, boy?" The words were indistinct, formed by toothless jaws and cracked lips.

"May I see Pa-Siamen, sir?"

The old man contemplated the boy, his tongue rummaging around in his toothless mouth. "Polite at least," he mumbled. "Wait here." He closed the door.

Several minutes passed. Scarab sat on the stone steps and watched a lizard on the wall as it sunned itself. Smenkhkare tapped his foot impatiently, then started pacing across the width of the small porch. Footsteps sounded indistinctly behind the door and they both turned.

A youth of perhaps fifteen floods opened the door and peered out. His hairless skull made him appear older but could not mask the bright twinkle in his eyes. "Smenkhkare. I thought it might be you." He looked past the boy at the naked young girl standing behind him. "And who is this?"

"Her name's Scarab. She's a friend of mine."

"From the palace?" Pa-Siamen frowned, staring at her face. "And with such an obviously false name. Nobody calls a little girl 'Scarab'. Well, never mind, have your secret games. You want to come in?"

The young priest led the way into the shaded hallways of the priest's residence, along echoing passages to a tiny room at the back. A small window space was almost blocked by a large bush planted outside, the daylight filtering through, green and cool. A handful of dried and yellowed leaves lay on the tiled floor.

129

Scarab looked around the tiny room with its sparse furniture. A narrow sleeping mat filled one corner and a stool by a small table sat underneath the window. An open chest completed the décor, a scribe's palette poking out of the top along with a linen robe.

Smenkhkare crossed confidently to the sleeping mat and sat down. "I wanted Scarab to meet you, Pa-Siamen. She doesn't get out much and needs to meet other people."

The youth smiled. "You are welcome in the god's house, little Scarab. Can I offer you some water?"

Scarab glanced around the room but could not see any source of water. "Yes please," she said doubtfully.

"I shall be but a few moments." Pa-Siamen left his room and disappeared down the corridor.

Smenkhkare patted the mat beside him. "Sit down. He is a good man, for a priest. He will tell you all you want to know."

Scarab sat but screwed up her face. "I don't know what I want to know," she wailed. "I thought we were just going on an adventure to see things, not talk to strange men."

Pa-Siamen padded back into the room, carrying a tray with three pottery mugs of water and a plate with a handful of ripe figs. He set it down on the floor next to the cot, helped himself to a mug and one of the figs, and then sat down on the stool. "Well. What would you like to talk about?"

Scarab said nothing, just hanging her head and biting into a plump fig. Smenkhkare grinned. "Whatever you like, Pa-Siamen. I brought Scarab with me because she hasn't seen anything outside the palace nor met anyone who didn't live there."

Pa-Siamen nodded. "It must be glorious to live in the palace, little Scarab, even as a servant or a child. To be in the presence of courtiers and officials, maybe to even see the king. Have you ever seen the king up close?"

"Yes," Scarab whispered.

"Wonderful. Your friend Smenkhkare has told me much about the palace, though no doubt because of whom he is, it is different from your experience."

"She's called Scarab because she likes beetles," Smenkhkare chuckled. "But I think she likes the god Khepri too. Tell us about the gods."

"Ah, one could talk all day about the gods. Scarab, you know you are in the house of Amun? He is the king of the gods and he has a special love for our beloved king Nebmaetre Amenhotep. I am indeed privileged to be a priest of Amun and one day I shall rise to become one of the god's prophets."

"Like my great-uncle Aanen," Smenkhkare said.

Pa-Siamen inclined his head with a smile. He bit into his fig and chewed.

"And what of the other gods?" Smenkhkare asked quietly. "What of the Aten? He has a big temple next to this one now."

The young priest scowled. "The Aten is a minor god, merely a sometime manifestation of Re-Herakhte, the physical disk of the sun. Why, before the time of Nebmaetre's father, he was nothing." Pa-Siamen shrugged. "However, it is the will of the king that the Aten be worshipped, so he must have his own house here in Amun's city."

"And between the temples of Amun, on Amun's own land, and funded by the wealth of Amun." Smenkhkare smiled, slipping his remark in like a dagger.

131

Pa-Siamen scowled again. "It is not just." He hesitated and glanced round at the open door behind him. "However, it is the king's will, so we obey, but ..." He shrugged and picked up the plate of figs, offering them to the children.

"Excuse me, sir," Scarab whispered. "How does a god who is nothing become a rich and powerful god?"

"Perhaps I overstated the case, little Scarab. I did not mean to say the Aten was nothing, just that he was a minor deity with few worshippers. We Kemetu have many gods that reflect every aspect of our lives and deaths, and the sun god is always important. The actual disk of the sun is a relatively minor aspect though, as Re's heat and light are what sustains us." Pa-Siamen settled back on his stool and took a long drink of water from his cup. "Nebmaetre's father had a foreign advisor, a man called Yuya ..."

"My great-grandfather," Smenkhkare said.

"Yes. He was a priest of the Khabiru, a tribe to the north and east of the empire. He prophesied for the king and the king made him his Tjaty. His daughter Tiye ..."

"My grandmother."

"... grew up in the palace and married Nebmaetre, our beloved elder king."

"And the Aten?" Smenkhkare asked.

Pa-Siamen laughed. "Patience, young lord, I am coming to that. The Khabiru worship the Aten. Yuya's god became an infatuation of the king and the worship of Aten increased. Nebmaetre, being married to a Khabiru himself, has pulled Aten from obscurity and set him among the major deities of Kemet." Pa-Siamen looked around again. "The younger king, Waenre, seeks to further raise the Aten's status, almost challenging Amun himself."

132

"But if Amun is king of the gods, how can he be challenged?"

"He cannot, in truth," Pa-Siamen said. "However, if Ma'at, the balance of our Two Lands, the natural order, is threatened, then we must face the wrath of the gods." The priest leaned closer to the children, putting his empty mug on the floor. "We are the god Amun's servants, doing his will. What do you think would happen if we neglected his worship? Failed to give him the proper respect, offer the proper sacrifices?"

Scarab shook her head, her eyes wide, too afraid to speak.

"He would withdraw his favour from the Two Lands and we would become just another nation, at the mercies of foreign kings and foreign gods. Can you imagine what life would be like?"

A gong sounded deep in the house, low and resonant. Pa-Siamen straightened. "It is the call to the midday ceremonies, children. I must go. Come, I will see you to the door. Quickly now."

Smenkhkare rose and bowed slightly toward the young priest. "Thank you, Pa-Siamen. We are indebted to you for your teaching."

The priest smiled. "A pleasure. Come again. I always enjoy our little talks." He put a hand on Scarab's head as she moved toward the door. "You too, little Scarab. If Smenkhkare brings you, you may come, but do not come alone."

The outer door closed behind the young priest and Smenkhkare turned to Scarab on the porch, blinking in the bright sunlight. "So what do you think? That was more interesting than anything you could do in the palace, wasn't it?"

"Um, I thought we were going to see men pulling great big stones, not talk to priests."

"Another time. We had better get back now before they miss us. The nurses will be looking for you."

Scarab stamped her foot. "I'm not a baby anymore."

"No? Well, we still need to get back." Smenkhkare set off across the gardens, walking fast. After a moment, Scarab followed, then as he outdistanced her, started to run.

"I'm sorry, Smenkhkare," Scarab panted. "Please, don't walk so fast." He slowed but said nothing. "Can I come out with you again? I won't complain. We can go anywhere you want."

"I'll think about it." They arrived at the foot of the acacia tree and Smenkhkare scrambled into the branches. He looked back at the little girl standing underneath with tears in her eyes. Grimacing, he moved back down and stretched out his hand, hauling her up onto the first branch. She rewarded him with a big grin.

On the other side of the wall they descended the stone blocks with care and ran back through the orchard to the ornamental garden and the large tamarind tree. Scarab turned to her brother with a searching expression.

"Thank you for taking me outside, Smenkhkare."

The boy stared at the little girl for a while before nodding. "All right, we'll try it again. Be here tomorrow at the same time." He turned and ran off through the garden toward the palace.

Scarab watched him go, a contented smile on her face.

Chapter Nine

My first meeting with my brother Smenkhkare changed my life, though at the time I could not see beyond the excitement of venturing outside the palace walls. Being a solitary and lonely child I lacked interactions with others of around my own age. I played with the other palace children sometimes but generally they avoided me, I think because I was a daughter of the king and above their station in life. Then Smenkhkare came along. Looking back, I wonder whether he wasn't also lonely. Although he was a boy and a natural leader, he seemed to have a hunger to teach and guide others. The other sons of court officials desired adventures, not learning and they gradually drifted away. My thirst for knowledge meshed with his desires and from that day in the garden, until Waenre's Heb-Sed festival, I saw my brother at least every few days.

In the weeks and months that followed, Smenkhkare took me to see many other people in the city. For a nine year old boy, he knew a lot of people. I think it was even then that he had an eye on becoming king one day and he realized a good king knows his people, noble and commoner alike. We visited many he knew and some that he did not. He was unfailingly polite and attentive and I think I must have been a real trial to him at times as my attention span was short and I was always looking for the next adventure.

Not all our outings were interesting however. We went back to Pa-Siamen again and met some of his fellow-priests of Amun. That was boring as I didn't understand half of what they talked about. The scribes too almost made me wish I hadn't come. One in particular,

Kensthoth by name, was a stuffy old man who delighted in tedious and esoteric details and the hidden meanings of words. He did say one interesting thing, though it was only interesting because it was to do with my name.

"Scarab, you say, little girl. Hmm ... ah, hmm. You know of the four elemental forces? Qebsenuf or Fire, Daumutef or Earth, Imset or Air, and Haapi or Water? Well, there is a fifth element called Khepri, the deity of unceasing renewal. Khepri is the sacred scarab, child, and it conveys the boundless emanations of Sa in the universe, the principal of divine protection." He fixed me with his glittering eyes and seemed to look beyond me. "Who gave you this name?"

"The king," I whispered.

"Indeed?" The old scribe raised an eyebrow. "Then the gods themselves have offered you their divine protection, young Scarab. The next time you come across the sacred scarab, listen to the music it makes with its wings. That unique humming is the universe talking to you."

I said I would and the conversation turned to other matters. He was a dry old man who tutored many of the older sons of court officials and I only saw him that once while I was a child. Our paths crossed again later, though many things had changed for me before they did.

Our other forays into Waset were more interesting. I got to see men hauling blocks of stone to one of the smaller temples of Aten, I watched as Ahhotep the glass maker fashioned delicate cups and jars of tinted glass and faience or made beautiful coloured beads in his special moulds. I sat for hours with Kenamun the toy maker as he fashioned simple children's toys and dolls from pieces of wood and cloth. He made me a small carved scarab out of some soft wood and I treasured it for a year before one of the other children snatched it and broke it. I wept for a day, then buried my little broken Khepri beside the old husk of the other one in the garden.

Not all our outings were adventures. Sometimes Smenkhkare would tell me at the outset that he wanted to spend time with a scribe, or a priest, or watch the soldiers training in their barracks. On those days, he would take me down to the markets and leave me in the charge of one or other of his friends, returning to pick me up as the shadows lengthened. I got to know the merchants quite well and they would give me small treats as I sat on a box, or bale, or just the dusty ground and watched them at their work.

Asheru sold fruit; figs, dates and pomegranates and sometimes grapes if one of the boats from down river made a swift trip. He was generous and would give me a handful of dried dates or figs to munch as he called out his wares, arguing and haggling with his customers. I learned there was no fixed price for his produce, each transaction being unique and depending on how much the customer was prepared to pay and what Asheru had paid for it from the farmers. The currency he received was fluid too. He might receive pieces of copper, or cloth, or a live pigeon. Once a servant from one of the minor noble houses bought a large basket of sweet figs and paid with a piece of silver, but more often it was payment in whatever the buyers had.

Meres, on the other hand, a grain merchant, was more miserly. Or it may just have been that he had little that was edible. He sat all day on a wooden stool under an awning, his belly hanging over his soiled kilt, making detailed notations on a large papyrus scroll. Some merchants employed scribes to keep their accounts, but Meres begrudged their earnings and had developed a system of his own. It had the advantage that nobody else could make sense of his scrawling and so dispute his calculations. The smaller farmers would bring grain to him in large rush baskets, tipping the golden stream of seeds into the open measuring jars and thence into the great storage bins.

These bins lay in a large building behind the small courtyard where Meres sat, high roofed, airy and filled with dust. I loved it, for the sunlight came through the cracks in the walls in solid bars of gold, a king's treasury all my own. Dust danced in the light and always there was the fluttering roar of birds' wings and the shrill cries of mice. I would lie naked in the dust, my chin resting on my hands and watch these tiny creatures scurrying about or sitting up, whiskers quivering, my own image reflected in their tiny black eyes.

There were cats too that roamed the grain warehouse. Lean and black as a starless night, or spotted like a leopard, or striped in shades of gray, their coats shone as they lay contented or hunted through the shadows, a thin shriek of agony telling of their success. They did not need to hunt to fill their bellies for cats are loved and revered in Waset, as they are throughout the Two Lands. People would leave offerings for these local representatives of the goddess Bastet, small portions of fish or a tiny amount of goat's milk in a pottery dish. They would bow and offer the food, muttering a prayer as they did so. It was understood that if a cat ate or drank the offering on the spot, the prayer would be answered. Most times the goddess looked favourably on the petitioner as they kept the piece of fish small, so the cats were always looking for their next meal.

Sometimes Smenkhkare would take me down to the docks where we would watch the boats unload. For a time I thought that only Kemetu vessels docked at Waset because all the boats were the familiar barges I had always seen on the river, with good Kemetu names like 'Heru Lives' or 'Eye of Re'. My father the king even had a barge of his own called 'Aten Gleams'. It did indeed gleam, being covered in thin, beaten gold and painted in bright colours. I traveled on it when I was older, but for now it was just another wonder to be viewed from afar.

There were foreigners in Waset, especially down near the docks. Huge muscled Nubians unloaded the barges from the south, while from the west came Libyans in robes, thin and hawk-faced; and from the north, bearded Syrians, robed Babylonians and strange looking dark-haired men from the Sea. Small and swarthy and as clean-shaven as any Kemetu, they wore brightly coloured kilts, gold around their arms and jewels in their wavy black hair. Strangest of all, they wore as much makeup as a woman, their eyes coloured in green and blue and lips rouged. When I first caught sight of one I thought it was a woman until it turned and I saw there were no breasts. Then the kilt parted and I knew without a doubt it was a man.

"Who are they?" I asked, pointing.

Smenkhkare snatched my finger down. "Cretans," he said. "People of the Sea. Don't point; they are very sensitive about their appearance."

The man had seen me point though and sauntered over, his mincing walk raising doubts in my mind again.

"Well, what have we here?" the man asked in a high, clear voice.

"I'm sorry if we caused offence, sir," Smenkhkare replied. "I am showing my sister around and she has never seen a Cretan ship before."

"Really? May I invite you aboard, young sir – for by your speech I can tell you are well educated. Your sister

139

too." He winked at my brother and laid a finger alongside his nose. "We can have some wine and dates and get to know each other."

Smenkhkare bowed. "Perhaps another time, sir. Regrettably I must get my sister back to her nurse."

I opened my mouth to protest as I was very interested in seeing the Cretan ship and the dates sounded appetizing but Smenkhkare dug me in the ribs and hurried me away. "What did you do that for? He was very nice."

"He thought I was your pimp."

I looked blank. "What's that?"

"Never mind. I'll tell you another time."

The docks were smelly, dirty places. Refuse lay everywhere and workers on the wharves, loading and unloading cargoes, stopped to urinate and defecate in the water, instead of finding a privy like normal people. Vermin abounded because of these habits with large sleek rats running along the decks or sitting on the bales in full sight of passers-by. Cats were here too, but not the contented cats of the grain warehouses. These were half-starved and mangy, not much bigger than the rats and tended to leave them alone. They hung about the fishing boats, darting in to steal a fish when a back was turned. Stray dogs hunted the streets in packs, getting bolder with each passing day until the people complained and the police would sweep through, killing as many as they could find and dumping the bodies on the city's refuse heap. Then the streets would be safe until they bred and built their numbers up again.

On one such trip to the city a strange thing happened – something new to us both. As we loitered by the side of the river, munching on a handful of figs given to us by a shopkeeper, a shadow fell over us. I looked up to see a bank of heavy cloud obscuring the sun. A few moments later I was astounded to feel small droplets of water strike my upturned face. A faint crackling sound washed toward me from the river as the smooth surface dimpled and jumped.

"What is it?" I asked. "What is happening?" I shrank back toward the shelter of a crumbling warehouse.

"Rain." Smenkhkare grinned, his face upturned like mine, his eyes wide. "I have heard water falls from the heavens though I have never seen it before today."

"What does it mean? Are the gods angry?"

"I don't know. I don't think so – look, it is stopping."

The fall of water eased and stopped, the cloud scudding eastward and breaking up, the sun shining out once more.

I shivered, despite the renewed heat of the day. "It – it feels unnatural."

Smenkhkare shook his head and bit into another fig. "It happens, though not often here in Kemet. Uncle Ay says the rain sometimes comes down so hard the tombs in the western valleys are flooded out. He says that in Nubia it rains so hard you cannot breathe."

I ventured a weak smile. "Now that I cannot believe, even having seen water falling from the sky." I took a fig from my brother's hand and sat down on the river's edge. Our talk turned to other matters.

Gradually, as the weeks and months unfolded into years, I came to know the common people of Waset almost as well as my brother – or so I thought. I certainly knew something of the wide range of trades and professions practiced in the city, but I still had a lot to learn about people themselves. That lesson would take longer, but I had a good teacher and I came to love my brother Smenkhkare. I have heard it said that the gods prepare us early for the part we play in their designs. I did not know

141

it then, but my schooling in Waset prepared me well for my later life.

Chapter Ten

Jebu the Amorite sat in the small rock shelter outside the Samarian village of Jerborah, nursing a clay pot between his knees. Around him, a dozen of his men sat with similar pots or with their swords drawn, sharpening them. He picked up a handful of dry twigs and, snapping them into little bits, fed them into the tiny, almost smokeless fire in the pot.

"Why do we wait?"

"Patience, Simyras. It is nearly dark."

"We did not wait for dark at the farm. Why do we have to wait now?"

Jebu put down his pot and leaned back against the wall of the stone shelter, idly scratching his groin. "God-cursed lice," he muttered. "They infest these sheep-shelters." He looked up at his subordinate. "The farm was a small one with only a few men. This village has maybe thirty men and they will have seen the smoke of the farm. They will be waiting for trouble but with luck will relax when it gets dark. Then we will strike with fire and sword."

Simyras grumbled inaudibly and sat down across from his leader. He pulled out his bronze sword and examined the edge, peering along it. "I will kill more men than you tonight, Jebu. I am feeling lucky."

Jebu laughed. "What will you wager? That silver brooch you took off that trader two days back?"

"Against your dagger."

"Done. But men only, Simyras. Women and children do not count."

143

"Boys if they hold a weapon is fair." Simyras turned to one of the other men to support him. "Isn't it, Joram? It was a boy nearly spitted you last month."

Joram leaned over and told Simyras in a harsh voice exactly what he should do with that sword of his. The men in earshot guffawed and tossed small pebbles at them both.

Jebu laughed loudly. "Boys it is then, Simyras, if they hold a weapon, but no women."

"I have other uses for women," Simyras leered.

Jebu nodded. "As you will, but make sure all the village men are dead before you start your pleasure. And be swift, I will not wait for you when we pull out."

"I will pull out when you do, Jebu," grinned Simyras. He made an obscene gesture and resumed his examination of his sword.

The sun set, dropping behind the hills toward the western sea, casting a dusky gloom over the land. Jebu and Simyras left the rock shelter and walked down the rutted uneven road to where it crested a low rise before sweeping down to the outskirts of Jerborah. Without a stockade or any defensive structures, the village lay exposed and vulnerable. A few men could be seen standing around where the road met the first buildings, looking toward the north where a dark smudge of smoke could still be seen against the darkening sky. The cries of livestock and children came faintly on the breeze.

"Not even an attempt at a wall. Twenty years of peace and they think the world is their friend," Jebu sneered. "Well, we shall disabuse them of that notion tonight. They will find that the Kemetu cannot protect them."

"What's the plan?"

"Come full dark, we attack from the north. Break the fire pots and set the thatch ablaze. When the men come out to deal with us, Aram and the others will hit them from the south. It will be a merry slaughter."

Simyras squinted into the gathering darkness. "Where is Aram anyway? Why isn't he here?"

"He is where I want him. He will attack when he sees the flames. Come." Jebu turned back toward the sheep shelter, scratching underneath his leather armor. He gathered his men together, and in the failing light, made an inspection of their weapons and the fire pots. At length he nodded, satisfied.

"Very well. Time to start. I have told you all before but I will say it once more so there are no mistakes. We approach the village along the road then spread out along the north side. Move quietly but steadily until you are in position, close by the outer walls of the houses." Jebu picked up one of the prepared torches, a crooked branch with the end tied with strips of cloth, soaked in pitch. "Look along the line for my signal. I will light my torch and hold it aloft. That is the signal for you to light yours. When all six are lit we throw them into the thatch. When the men come out, kill them."

He looked along the line of his men, all soldiers he had fought and bled beside this last year or more. He nodded, satisfied with what he saw. "Kill them all," he repeated softly. "We take no prisoners and we take no booty." Jebu grinned, his yellowing and crooked teeth showing in his luxuriant black beard. "Take your pleasure with the women if you must, but quickly. I mean to leave before moon rise." He doused the torch, kicking dirt over it to smother the flame and plunging the sheep byre into darkness.

A hundred paces short of the first house, Jebu halted and listened for any sign that the populace was on guard, ready for them. A myriad of sounds emanated from the village and the surrounding scrub – insect noises, dogs barking, children crying and a low indistinct murmur of voices, the screech of an owl as it made its kill – but nothing that even hinted of danger. He motioned with his arm and Simyras led his men quietly off the road and into the scrub, angling to the right, toward the houses in the village.

As the last man passed, Jebu followed, quickly taking up a position by a woven thatch wall. He could hear the movement of livestock behind the wall, muffled bleating and stamping of hooves. The night hung quiet and still around him, the darkness complete, lit only by the stars ablaze in the sky and a faint orange glow from the clay pot in the crook of his arm. The odour of pitch from his unlit torch mingled with the stale smell of sweat and the animals a few feet away. The man beside him shifted, his armor chinking softly as he moved. He looked along the side of the village but could see no-one, hear nothing.

Jebu thrust his torch into the fire pot, waiting until the pitch-soaked rags ignited before drawing it out. He raised it above his head, waved it. A few moments later a flicker of light glowed in the darkness behind the village, followed by another. Distinct across the intervening shadows came the sound of bronze swords whispering from their scabbards, the clink of metal on metal and a muffled curse as a fire pot fell and shattered on the rocky ground.

A dog yelped, then lifted its voice in alarm, followed by a chorus of others. A light flared in one of the huts and a man called out.

146

Without waiting for the last of the torches, Jebu swung his brand and tossed it in a high arc onto the top of the nearest thatched hut. The flames caught almost immediately, crackling and spitting as the dry material ignited. Along the northern rim of the village, Jebu saw other brands fire other roofs, heard cries of alarm from within the huts. He raised his sword and with a yell, ran between the burning huts toward the middle of the village.

Jebu dashed out into an open space beyond the first row of huts and collided with a man running in the opposite direction. The man fell with a cry of fear and Jebu staggered back, his blade swinging down. He felt a tremor run up his arm and he wrestled his sword free. The burning roof behind him fell in with a roar of flames, sending a pillar of sparks skyward to mingle with the stars. The screaming of trapped animals and the cries of the townsfolk almost drowned the yells of his men as they poured into the main street of the village to meet a resolute defence.

Unexpectedly, the peasants were better armed than the usual villagers. Several had spears and a few had old swords or knives, the rest pitchforks or staves. They rushed Jebu's men and forced them back by sheer weight of numbers. The Amorite soldiers fell back and consolidated in the lea of the burning huts, standing shoulder to shoulder as the village men faced them. Bursting flames lit the scene as if in full moonlight, though the leaping shadows and flicker of the flames fooled the senses, multiplying the foes facing them. Dark smoke billowed, enveloping soldier and villager alike, blinding the eyes and doubling them over in fits of coughing. Despite the discipline and superior weaponry of the Amorite soldiers,

147

three were already down and the ten remaining could not hold off more than thirty for long.

"Where's that bastard Aram?" screamed Simyras, fending off a pitchfork that came searching for his life. "Can't he see the fornicating flames?"

Jebu said nothing. He concentrated on two men with daggers in front of him, weaving his sword back and forth as they edged closer, looking for an opening. A gust blew spark-filled smoke over them and as one flinched; Jebu stabbed forward, feeling his blade rip into flesh. The man screamed and dropped his dagger, clutching at the sword in his gut with his hands. The unexpected action sent Jebu stumbling forward as he tried to keep his grip on the weapon, and the other man moved close and slashed. Jebu felt the knife rip through his shirt, turn on the leather and bronze studs of his armor, before scoring a stinging cut on his arm. He swore and let go of his sword, rounding on his assailant before he could recover from his stroke, hitting him on the side of the head.

The man staggered back and Jebu, blood streaming down his arm leapt forward, carrying the man to the ground. They rolled and punched on the ground, tangling in the feet of other fighting men. The man tried to stab Jebu and the soldier kept a hand, slippery with blood, on the man's wrist, striving to break his hold. A villager stabbed down awkwardly with a spear, missing them both, but as he did so, Simyras thrust his sword into the villager's throat. Jebu twisted and kneed the man hard in the groin, following it with a punch to the head that made the man drop the dagger, half-curling to protect himself. Jebu rolled and grabbed the fallen dagger, sweeping it up and into the man's chest. The man screamed weakly and belched gouts of blood over his chin before collapsing, his legs shuddering in the dust.

148

Scrambling to his feet, Jebu steadied himself against one of the as-yet unburned huts. He looked around at his men, hemmed in by a tide of villagers and cursed Aram out loud.

As if in answer to his curses, a great cry erupted from the far side of the street and a wave of bearded, armored men swept out of the darkness and fell upon the rear of the peasants. Some fell where they stood, others turned in an attempt to counter this new threat, others tried to run. Jebu rallied his men and attacked the remaining villagers, hacking them down. A few threw down their weapons and pled for mercy only to be slaughtered.

The fighting faltered and died, and Jebu took stock of the stinking dirty men in front of him. "Aram, where in Hades have you been. The fornicators nearly had us." He sniffed, his nose wrinkling in disgust. "You stink. Have you shat yourself?"

Aram cursed volubly. "The south side just happened to be where the middens are. The wind was behind us and by the time we nosed it, we were in it."

Jebu waved his sword at the burning village. "Finish this then and you can clean yourselves." Above the crackle and roar of the flames could be heard the wailing of women and children and the terrified screaming of the trapped and burning livestock. Black smoke rose in thick clouds, almost dimming the flames and the stink of charred flesh assaulted their nostrils.

Aram and Simyras led the attack on the remaining villagers. The Amorites went from hut to hut, systematically hunting down and killing the people. Old men and women died under the sword, children were gutted and left to die and young women wished for a death that only held back for the space of a brutal coupling.

A gibbous moon rose above the low hills before the village died. The soldiers dragged the bodies into the centre of the street and heaped them one upon the other where they lay soaked and streaked in black blood, eyes staring, naked bodies and limbs sprawled.

"Get a move on, curse you," Jebu yelled. "I wanted to be away from here before moon rise." He picked up a burning brand and pushed it into the thatch of an intact house. "Burn everything. Hurry."

"Five of ours dead, Jebu," Aram reported.

Jebu cursed. "Killed by fornicating peasants. Say the rites and scatter the earth, Aram. We leave them here."

Simyras sauntered up, the front of his tunic spattered darkly in the smoke-filled light. "Five, Jebu," he crowed. "Five and only one a boy. He had a knife too, so it counts."

Jebu snorted. "I claim five too, Simyras, but mine were all men. I win, I think."

Simyras scowled for a moment and then shrugged. He dug into the wallet at his belt and brought out the silver brooch, passing it to his commander. "No matter, I found a couple of nice bits of copper on the women."

Jebu nodded and turned away, exhorting his men to hurry. The last of the huts was set afire and any surviving animals turned loose. Before the moon rose its own breadth further, casting its silvery light onto the black smoke clouds hanging over the village, Jebu and his surviving Amorite soldiers were trotting eastward along the road, back into the hills.

At dawn a patrol of Kemetu soldiers arrived from the west, alerted by the plume of smoke smudging the dawn sky. They found the village of Jerborah in ruins, its people dead and livestock burned or scattered. They also found five dead Amorite soldiers neatly laid out on the

150

outskirts of the village, a coin in their mouths and dirt scattered on their bodies. The commander ordered the taking of the enemy heads, pocketing the death coins, then led his small squad back to the fort. As they ran, the commander started formulating the report he would submit to Ribaddi, the governor of Byblos.

Chapter Eleven

The time of the flood came and went. The gods smiled on the Two Lands once more, delivering a rich layer of alluvial mud to the farmlands near the river. Pa-it and other farmers of Akhet-Re, and villagers along the length of the river, spent the weeks of the flood mending equipment and sorting out, seed by seed, the viable ones from the insect-ravaged. Frogs bred in the flooded meadows, filling day and night with an incessant racket, making sleep all but impossible. Fish invaded the fields, swimming where the peasants had toiled only weeks before, feeding on rich algal blooms and aquatic insects, worms and detritus, fertilizing the ground in return.

Mosquitoes and biting flies flourished as the flood waters spread, particularly in the Delta region, but unless you had to work in the fields or in the great reed beds, they were not particularly bothersome. In the cities, the breezes from the deserts tended to discourage flying insects, though others crawled and crept into houses. The waters sent snakes and scorpions seeking higher, dryer ground and the months of Athyr and Khoyak saw many people bitten and stung. Those who could afford it treated their afflictions with a variety of physical remedies and prayer. Those who couldn't just prayed to the gods. Generally, people recovered unless the gods failed to listen to their prayers. The gods heard about as many prayers as they always did.

The waters receded as usual and Peret, the time of sowing, gripped Kemet. An early planting was essential for a good crop, allowing the plants time to grow before the heat and drought made life a struggle. The wheat fields burgeoned, promising a good harvest, as the year turned past the solstice and the festivities that welcomed the growth of the sun once more were especially fervent. Shemu, the time of harvest, arrived, and in the month of Payni, just after the equinox, further good news gladdened the hearts of all.

The old king Nebmaetre Amenhotep, all but dead these past five years, returned to life. Palace officials, those close to the royal chambers or who waited on the old king and his still active wife Tiye, had long been aware of the king's slow recovery. Struck down by an unknown malady that made his limbs weak, his speech slurred, and his mind wander, he lay on his great gilded bed, on sheets of the finest linen. Unable to rise, even to clean himself, the king suffered the indignity of being tended like a helpless baby, being washed and fed by trusted body servants. The queen too, danced attendance on her husband, caring for him and tending him with her own hands whenever she could take time from the government of Waset.

Officially never more than Queen, Tiye was in truth ruler of the Two Lands for the first six months of her husband's illness. The young prince Amenhotep, raised to the co-regency four years before his father's illness, and following the death of his elder brother, had ruled over Lower Kemet from Zarw with the help of a roomful of advisors. Truth be told, the young king and his beautiful young wife had little interest and less aptitude for rulership, being interested only in beauty and pleasure. When however, after half a year, Tiye could see that the great Nebmaetre was not going to recover soon, she took counsel with her brother Ay and the Tjaty Ptahmose. They decided that Kemet needed a king who could be seen to be king. There was no choice but to bring Waenre Amenhotep south to Waset and crown him full regent to act in his father's stead.

Then on that blessed day in the month of Payni, seven days after the equinox, Nebmaetre Amenhotep's eyes held intelligence once more. He turned his head to the servant gently cleansing his body with rose-scented water and spoke with slurred but intelligible words.

"'Ere iss my 'ife?"

Queen Tiye came at a run, forsaking her usual queenly demeanor, on hearing the news. She burst into the king's chamber, her brother Ay on her heels to find her husband, naked, sitting on the edge of his bed and staring round the room in bewilderment, a knot of servants kneeling around him.

"My husband," cried Tiye. "The gods be praised for your recovery."

Amenhotep stared at her, his brow knotted as he struggled to find words that meant something to him. "'Ere iss my 'ife? 'Ere iss Isset? I marry her, 'y iss sshe not 'ere?"

Tiye said nothing, turning to her brother with an enquiring expression.

Ay pondered a moment, then addressed the king.

"My lord, the Lady Iset is in the women's quarters as is proper. Do you wish her sent for?"

"Of coursse. It iss our ... 'edding night. Her place iss 'ith me."

"He thinks it is the day he married his daughter Iset," Ay murmured. "He has no memory of the last five years."

Tears brimmed in Tiye's eyes as she looked at her husband as he strove to rise. She glided forward and, putting a hand under the king's elbow, helped him to his feet, steadying him as he swayed.

154

"Fetch Iset," Tiye said to one of the servants. "Tell her what has transpired and escort her to the king's bed-chamber. Go. At once."

"What are you doing?" Ay asked.

"The king's wishes." Tiye led Amenhotep slowly across the room and sat him down in a carved chair, letting him slump against the backrest. She crossed to a table and poured a golden goblet full of water before bringing it back to her husband, helping him to drink. He sat, afterward, his mouth open and tongue lolling, a trickle of water escaping his mouth and dribbling over his hairless chest.

"I repeat, what are you doing?"

"Brother, the king has recovered from his malady." Tiye lowered her voice and approached Ay. "If he believes no time has passed, perhaps that is because where he was; no time has in fact passed. Who knows what happens with the gods."

"That is foolishness," Ay hissed. "The king has been ill, struck down by the gods. I have seen it in lesser men; it is a sickness, not a sign of the god's favour. Men seldom recover from this sickness and never for long." He jerked his head in the king's direction. "Look at him, sister. His body is wasted, and his mind is not there. The god is not present."

"Nevertheless," Tiye said, steel creeping into her voice. "He is my husband and the king. We will do as he wishes. If he says no time has passed, then none has."

"And what of the young king, Waenre, down in his new city of Akhet-Aten. Is he to be informed that the last five years did not take place? Will you remove the double crown of Kemet from his head?"

Tiye shook her head. "What is done cannot be undone. Nor would I wish it, Waenre is my son. However, Nebmaetre is also the king. We must obey him."

"And when he finds out that Kemet lies weakened under the rule of his son? Will he not seek to take the power into his own hands again?"

"Ah, I see your problem, brother. If my husband takes charge once more you lose what power you have over my son."

Ay looked away with a muttered curse. "I will not be thwarted in this, sister," he whispered. He gripped the queen's arm and pulled her round to face the old king as he sat drooling and humming in the gilded chair. "Look at him, Tiye. Even if he really has recovered, he is an old man. How long can he last? Waenre, with me as his support, is the future of Kemet."

Voices came from the hall outside the king's bed-chamber. The king's second daughter-wife Iset entered the room, her short-cut hair visible beneath her wig as she hurried in. She straightened her wig with one hand, tugging at her robes with the other, her expression panicked as her father called out, the word slurred and unintelligible. Catching sight of her mother she hurried over to her, her eyes wide.

"Mother. What has happened? Is that ... is that truly the king? What does he want?"

"Iset, my child. The king has awoken from his sickness and believes no time has passed. For him, it is your marriage day."

The young woman turned with an expression of horror. "What ... what does he want of me?"

"He wants to consummate his marriage," Ay growled. "You were chosen as God's Wife five years ago and you didn't seem to mind then. Why now?"

"I was young and ... and I obeyed like a good daughter. Now I ... Please, uncle, help me. He cannot ask this of me."

Tiye looked at her daughter carefully, noting the way her hands shielded her breasts. "You have fallen in love, daughter. Who is he?"

"Love," sneered Ay. "You are a royal princess; you do not 'love'. Besides which, niece, you are married, or had you forgotten?"

"It has been five years, mother," Iset wailed. "Father was never going to recover but I was just sitting around the women's quarters. What harm would it do if I looked for another?"

"Just looking? Or has it gone further? Who is it?" Tiye's voice hardened.

"There is nobody, mother, just a young noble I have spoken with. I will not speak his name. He is young and is of a good family. It is a good match. Please mother, intercede with the king, ask him to release ..."

Tiye's hand slapped Iset's face with a crack that rocked her head back. "Silence, girl. There is no good match for you. You are God's Wife, so spread your legs and do your duty. If the gods will it so, perhaps you will produce a son to be your father's pride in his old age."

Iset dissolved into sobs, her shoulders shaking. Tiye took her daughter and held her, patting her back and stroking her bare arms. "Hush child. Anyone would think you had been sold as a slave to a hard master. This is your father, Iset, and he loves you. Do not shame him." By degrees the crying lessened and Tiye led the woman over to the seated man.

Amenhotep looked up at the approaching women and smiled. "Tiye," he said. "And 'oo iss thiss?"

The queen smiled back. "My beloved husband, I greet you and thank the gods for your renewed health." She gripped her daughter's shoulders and pushed her forward. "This is your daughter-wife Iset, whom you called for."

Amenhotep nodded and struggled to his feet. "Isset, of course, my child. You are bew ... bew ... tiful." He looked around the bedchamber with a puzzled expression. "'Ey iss the bed not pre ... pre ... made with rose petalss and lotuss blossomss for my bride?"

Tiye hesitated. "It was on your orders, my lord. Do you not remember you changed your mind?"

Amenhotep shook his head. "I did? I do not 'member." He looked back at Iset, his eye traveling over her body. His member swelled slowly. "No matter. Come then 'ife. It is time."

Tiye pushed Iset forward and the young woman stumbled before catching herself. She quivered, and after a quick glance of entreaty at her mother, smiled tremulously at her tumescent father.

Ay clapped his hands and ushered the remaining servants from the room. "We will leave you then, my lord. May you have great happiness on your wedding day." He put out his hand to the queen. "Sister?"

Amenhotep turned from where he was running his hands over his new wife. He looked hard at Ay. "Thank you, er ... thank you."

Ay escorted his sister from the room and closed the double doors behind them. "You would have me be loyal to this man," he snarled as the doors shut with a hollow thud. "He did not even know who I was."

"No, brother. I would have you remember that he is the anointed king of the Two Lands, consecrated into

158

Amun. Your loyalty is between you and the gods – and the gods will judge you on it."

Ay fell silent. They walked slowly through the wide halls of the king's palace toward the queen's palace and the women's quarters. Servants bowed and backed away as they approached, fleeing as soon as they had passed. "There is another matter," he said at last. His sister looked questioningly at Ay, but did not speak.

"Our young king Amenhotep wants to change his name. To honour his new god, he says."

Tiye stopped and turned to look at her brother. "Does that matter?"

"Use your head, sister," Ay growled. "He was consecrated as king under the name Amenhotep, by the priests of Amun, under the protection of Amun. If he changes his name it could be argued that he is no longer king."

Tiye laughed until she caught Ay's expression and her laughter drained away. "Are you serious? How can anyone say my son Amenhotep, no matter what he calls himself, is not king? You were there, Ay. You saw the priests consecrate him, not the name. How can the name matter?"

"I could wish you had spent more time learning about the gods of Kemet rather than interesting your husband in this esoteric god of the Khabiru. It is his meddling that is the root of the problem." Ay guided his sister over to a divan on an open balcony overlooking the palace gardens. He dismissed the ever-present servants and looked round carefully to make sure no-one was in earshot.

"Your husband stirred things up by elevating the god Aten to a prominent position. As long as your El or Adon was only a god of a subject people – yes, yes, I know what I am – it was of no great concern. Even the previous king, Tuthmosis, who raised our father Yuya to Tjaty, only paid lip service to this god. It was Amenhotep who identified him as our Aten, and to please you, elevated him from a minor god to the place he now holds." Ay pushed his sister down on the divan and stood over her, legs astride and fists on hips.

"What were you thinking of?" he barked. "Aten is but an aspect of Re, one of the most powerful gods, but Amun is the god of Per-Aa, the Great House – your husband's family. His ancestors saw the necessity of wedding the two gods into Amun-Re so their house was seen to have the blessings of the whole pantheon, but you have upset that."

Tiye, drew back, startled by her brother's vehemence. "What are you talking about? How are things upset? Amun is still the god of Waset and my husband's family."

Ay turned and walked over to the balcony and stared down into the gardens. He watched idly as two small children, a boy and a younger girl, emerged from under a tamarind tree and ran off in the direction of the orchard. "As long as Nebmaetre was content to worship the Aten as just one of many gods, there was no problem. Other kings have been infatuated with one god or another but have never let it interfere with the balance, the Ma'at of Kemet. However, when your son Tuthmosis died and Waenre was made co-regent, you and your husband made a fatal error." Ay turned and rested against the stone balustrade, looking at his sister. "You sent Waenre to Zarw, where he was surrounded by our kinsfolk, all Khabiru, all worshipers of Adon. A father's infatuation became a son's mania."

Tiye frowned and shifted on the divan. She plucked at her robe, smoothing out the creases. "Mania? That is too strong. He is young and idealistic, I grant ..."

160

"What do you call it when he does away with the other gods and only worships the Aten?"

"What? He has not done that."

"The signs are there, sister. Already he has insulted Amun by robbing him of his wealth to pay for temples to Aten. Next he moves his capital from Waset, the city of Amun, to this Akhet-Aten, the city of Aten. Now he wants to change his name from Amenhotep to Akhenaten, 'He who is useful to the Aten'. Is this not mania?"

"It is worrying," Tiye said doubtfully. "But surely his advisors will guide him to appropriate action?"

"What advisors?" A note of bitterness crept into Ay's voice. "I am his principal advisor yet he hardly even listens to what I say, let alone act on it. He prays to Aten and follows the advice of his heart and his wife, my oh-so-obedient daughter Nefertiti."

"I still think you are making too much of this, brother. Waenre named his daughters for the Aten after all – Meryetaten, 'Beloved of Aten', Meketaten, 'Protected by Aten' and Ankhesenpaaten, 'Living through the Aten'. I did not hear you making any great objection to those names."

"They are only girls. What does it matter what girls are called?"

Tiye sniffed loudly. "It is still only a name. How does this ... this name Akhenaten change things?"

"I thirst," Ay muttered. He strode to the end of the balcony and bellowed down the hallway. "Wine. Bring wine." He listened for a moment to be sure someone was hurrying to obey him before turning back to Tiye.

"Your son was crowned king of the Two Lands as Neferkheperure Waenre Amenhotep, which as you know means 'Beautiful are the manifestations of Re, the Unique One of Re, Amun is at Peace'. A good and praiseworthy

161

name for a king, one that balances praise to Re and to Amun. A priest of Amun anointed him into Amun's peace and most importantly ..." Ay broke off as a servant ran onto the balcony carrying an ebony wood tray with two golden goblets and a pitcher of river-cooled wine. Ay noted the beads of condensation on the outside of the golden pitcher and licked his lips in anticipation.

The servant placed the tray on a low table, poured the wine and, with a bow, handed the goblets first to the queen, then to Ay. He backed away and stood quietly by the far wall, his attention pointedly fixed away from his masters.

"Get out," Ay said quietly. He waited until the servant left before sipping at the rich dark wine. "Most importantly," he went on as if there had been no interruption. "Do you remember the phrase the Hem-netjer of Amun used during the ceremony when the double crown was placed on your son's head?"

"There were a lot of phrases used, brother. You cannot expect me to remember all of them."

"No, I suppose not. The relevant phrase was 'the god Amun sets his servant Amenhotep over Upper and Lower Kemet."

Tiye sipped her wine and looked at her brother out of hooded eyes. "So?"

"The god Amun recognizes Amenhotep as king, not Akhenaten."

"Mere word play."

Ay shook his head. "You are mistaken, sister. When Akhenaten makes his name change official; in the eyes of Amun, in the eyes of the priests, in the eyes of everyone in Kemet; your son ceases to be king."

Tiye laughed. "I do not believe you. You are telling me the people will rise up and overthrow my son? That has never happened to any king, nor will it."

"No, not yet. Your husband was likewise crowned as Amenhotep and as long as an Amenhotep reigns over Kemet, we will have a measure of Amun's peace. But what happens when your husband dies? Will Amun protect your son then?"

Tiye shrugged. "Do not think to upset me by speaking of Nebmaetre's death. I know he must die soon. But I think you misjudge my son. He may turn from Amun but he has embraced the Aten and the Aten will protect him."

Ay snorted derisively. "The Aten can no more protect him than Amun or any other of the myriad gods of Kemet. The gods, if indeed they exist, play no part in the struggles of men here in Kemet or in the Nations."

"You ... you do not believe in the gods?" Tiye gaped at her brother. "Then what is all this you have been saying about Amun and Aten and coronation ceremonies? Was this all just empty words?"

"What I believe matters not a fig at a king's feast, sister. It is not I that will depose our beloved king Akhenaten. Nor will the gods." Ay crossed to the divan and sat next to Tiye. He leaned close. "When Nebmaetre Amenhotep goes to the next world, Kemet will be without a legitimate ruler in the eyes of the priests. That is not a situation that will bring peace and security to our country. The priests will look for another, one who will be a true servant of Amun."

"There is no-one else." Tiye paused, thinking. "There is only Smenkhkare and he is but a boy."

"Then the priests will look outside our family for a successor. Do you now appreciate how serious the situation is?"

"What can we do? Can we persuade my son to hold off on this decision?"

"I think it is too late, sister. I am told that he means to announce it in Akhet-Aten today. By now he is already Akhenaten."

"Then there is nothing we can do?" Tiye put down her wine goblet on the marble floor tiles, her hand shaking. "We must pray for Nebmaetre's health and long life."

"There is another way."

Tiye stared at her brother, her eyes searching his face. "What way?" she asked quietly.

"I am styled God's Father and a priest of Amun," Ay shrugged. "And of Aten," he added. "I think I could persuade Amenemhet, the Hem-netjer, and our brother Aanen to grant me power – unofficially of course – until such time as a permanent solution can be found."

"You want to be king?"

"Merely the power behind the throne until Kemet can be returned to the true worship of Amun."

"You are a hypocrite, brother. You admit you do not believe in the gods but would use them to attain power."

"I prefer the term 'realist'. Kemet will be thrown into confusion if Akhenaten is toppled. It is unprecedented that a ruling monarch is deposed, but a strong hand on the helm until a legitimate substitute can be found is of benefit to everyone."

"That legitimate substitute being you, I suppose."

"I have no interest in being king, but think on this, dear sister. What will happen to your only son if he is deposed? Do you think his successor will let him live? If I have the power though, I can ensure he lives on in

164

health." Ay clasped Tiye's hands and smiled encouragingly. "Akhenaten is not interested in governing. His only interests are in his god and beautiful things. Let him keep those, live out his life where he can do no further harm to Kemet, a king still, but a king only in name. I will bring the Two Lands back to the true worship of Amun."

Tiye withdrew her hands and folded them in her lap. "The army will oppose you. The generals swore allegiance to my husband and my son."

"They can be persuaded. Why already I have ..." Ay broke off. He got to his feet and walked over to the balustrade, leaning on it and looking down into the garden through the heat-rippled air. "Do not oppose me, sister. You have neither the power nor the experience."

"I sat on the throne of Kemet when my husband first fell ill."

"For six months. The country governed itself. Do not think you could manage a country in the throes of rebellion."

Tiye rose and crossed to where her brother stood looking out on the palace gardens. She put a hand on his arm and leaned her head against his bare shoulder. "Ay, brother, do not make me choose, I beg you."

"I am not offering a choice, sister. For as long as Nebmaetre lives, Kemet is safe, no matter what Akhenaten does. When he is gone, I will look after Kemet and I will make sure your son comes to no harm. You must trust me."

"I do trust you, brother."

"Then it is settled. Leave everything to me." Ay put his arm around his sister and held her close. He smiled, looking out over the palace grounds toward the city of Waset. His smile creased his face, but came nowhere near his eyes which coldly regarded the rooftops of the city, calculating the future.

Chapter Twelve

A dust cloud hung low over the well-used road that ran along the shores of the Great Sea, east and north out of Kemet. Through the cloud, stirred up by many feet, could be seen the sweat-streaked and dusty bodies of soldiers, grim-faced and determined, running despite the heat that blasted back at them from the road and surrounding rocky hills. Though still several thousands of paces from the recognized border posts, the region the men ran through was dry and desolate and regarded as part of the Nations, not the green and bountiful land that was Kemet.

A breeze sprang up, carrying with it a humid freshness from the sea, blowing the dust inland. The men turned heads to look at the sparkling expanse of water though they never missed a stride as they ran onward. The road dipped into a shallow gully where a trickle of fresh water oozed from the dry rocks, across the road and tumbled a pace or two into the lapping waves. The man running at the front of the column raised a hand and the men slowed to a walk, then stopped, remaining motionless on the road, awaiting orders.

The man wiped the sweat from his face and spat grit from his mouth. He raised his head and slowly surveyed the surrounding countryside, paying especial attention to the rock-strewn hillsides and the skyline. He nodded his gray-fuzzed head and turned to the young man beside him.

"We rest here, Paramessu. Have sentries posted on the ridgeline, and on the road, front and aft. You know the way I like it."

Paramessu saluted respectfully. "Yes, my lord general." He turned away, barking orders at the men. Pairs of men briefly dashed water in their faces and drank from the tiny stream before racing off to appointed guard positions.

The column of men disintegrated into groups of ten, each moving off together into whatever shade they could find, picking up twigs and dried dung to start a small fire, or reclining on the hard ground. In turns, the groups moved to the watercourse and washed the sweat and grime from their bodies, slaked thirsts and refilled hide water containers. Those lucky enough to find fuel, congregated around small cooking pots, making up gruel of pounded grains and a little dried meat. Other groups watched enviously, gnawing on hunks of bone-dry bread and meat.

Some men clambered down the rocks to the tiny beach and, stripping off kilts and headdress, waded out into the cool water. One or two men in each group remained on shore, guarding the clothing, kit bags and weapons of their fellows. At intervals, a man would emerge from the surf, scattering water joyfully, and relieve one of his fellows.

Paramessu strolled along the road, noting the disposition of each of the nine groups of men, and scanning the distance for the tenth group on guard duty. Satisfied, he turned back toward the stream and the presence of his general. As he approached he examined general Horemheb, sitting with his back to a tall rock and poring over a papyrus map. Although nearly twenty years his senior, Paramessu knew that the older man was still capable of running the rest of the day with the men in his Hundred, and fighting a pitched battle at the end of it if need be.

He smiled, respect tinged with affection for the gruff old gray head who had become his mentor.

Horemheb looked up as a rock clattered on the path. He saw the young officer, nodded and indicated a flat rock beside him before turning back to his examination of the map.

Paramessu sat down and stretched his muscular legs out in front of him, smoothing down his dusty Shendyt kilt. The grime of the road nearly obscured the stitched blue wool scarab design on the front flap of the brown linen kilt. He rubbed a thumb over it, flicking it to remove the dirt. An officer in the Blue Legion of the Re Division, Paramessu had applied for, and been granted, permission to adopt the blue scarab as an insignia of his Troop. All his men sported the design and having seen their new commander in battle, wore it with pride. Jumping two grades since his adoption onto Horemheb's staff, Paramessu now was Captain of a Troop, though only a hundred men were with him from the under strength Re Division. More importantly, in Paramessu's eyes, he was a confidant of the general.

"We are here." Horemheb tapped a gnarled finger on the map. "We have made better time than I thought." He sat back and watched as Paramessu knelt in the dirt and examined the map. "Can you read it?"

Paramessu nodded hesitantly. "Yes, sir."

"Don't lie, boy. Plead ignorance if you must, but never lie to me."

"No sir, I mean, I think I can read it but I don't know why you think we are here. This coast road all looks the same."

Horemheb smiled briefly. "Learn to look around you." He tapped the map again. "This morning, early, we saw this mountain off to our right. It now lies well be-

169

hind us, but this mountain here," he tapped another mark on the papyrus. "This one we have not yet seen. Look at the coast. The map indicates a large bay here. What can you see out there?"

Paramessu shaded his eyes from the glare off the water. "The coast curves, sir. It is the bay."

"I believe so. If it is, the fort that was attacked lies at the head of the bay; no more than an hour's run from here."

Paramessu leapt to his feet. "Then we must get ready, sir."

"Sit." Horemheb waited until his protégé sat down once more. "I want the men rested. It is not likely the raiders are still there, but I want the men ready for action anyway."

"They could be, sir. The runner found us last night; it was the night before that the Amorites attacked. That is less than two days. We have never been this close behind them."

"Yes, it was rather fortunate we were in the area. However, another hour will refresh the men. It does not pay to go into battle with a blunted blade."

"It will scarcely be a battle, sir. A gang of bandits will not trouble our men."

Horemheb bent down and picked up his hide water bottle, taking a drink of the tepid water. Unlike many of the new generals, Horemheb believed in sharing the hardships of his men, never asking them to do what he could not. Paramessu smiled to himself, knowing the old man could out-run and out-fight men half his age, and that on a handful of grain, a cup of stinking water and a few hours snatched sleep.

"They are not bandits, Paramessu. You will not have seen the reports from Waset and Hut-waret."

"No sir."

"They are Amorites under the control of Prince Aziru. There have been raids throughout our allied lands this past year or more, burning farms and crops, slaughtering people and livestock. Even our forts."

Paramessu frowned. "Why does the governor of these lands not control them? Surely it would be simpler for him to do so than to send for us?"

"He is helpless. Ribaddi of Byblos is the governor over Lebanon, down as far as Gezer, but he lacks troops and gold. He has petitioned our king but he does nothing, sends no-one. The old king Amenhotep would have sent troops or at the very least gold to pay for troops but our young king in Akhet-Aten ignores the peril."

"Is it bad, sir? The situation, I mean."

"Bad enough, and worsening. This last year Aziru has raided our lands unchecked. They strike where they will, killing and plundering. Now traders refuse to travel the roads, flocks are untended and farmers fear to sow or reap the harvest, sitting inside fortified villages waiting for their turn." Horemheb rose and moved behind a boulder, lifting his kilt to one side. He paused, waiting for a full stream before continuing.

"We cannot hope to stop it by ourselves, but a swift hard blow may at least make Aziru more cautious." He shook himself and readjusted his kilt, moving back around the boulder. "Get the men up, Paramessu. It is time to move on."

The soldiers formed up on the road again with very little fuss. Bathed, refreshed and with a little food in their stomachs, the men were ready for what the gods and their generals threw at them. Horemheb came down the columns lined up on the road, casting his eyes over the men and their equipment. With a nod, he set himself at

171

the front and Paramessu gave the order first to march, then to break into a steady run.

The road rounded a headland and plunged eastward around a deep but narrow bay. At the head of the bay another small stream debouched, a small fortified camp lying astraddle the road leading out of Kemet. Nothing stirred on the ground or in the sky above. Horemheb halted the columns three bowshots out from the fort and scanned the walls.

"The gates are open but there are no signs of life."

Paramessu pointed. "There, on the battlements, sir. Extreme left. Something moved."

Horemheb nodded. "I see it now."

The object moved again and opening its broad black wings, launched itself into the air. It flapped briefly above the fort before dropping out of view within its stone walls.

"A vulture," Horemheb said flatly. "Nothing lives within the fort else it would not join its fellows." He signaled to the men and led them forward at a trot.

As the soldiers approached the open gates, Paramessu turned and waved squads of ten men left and right to circle the fort. The main body he halted outside the gates and led another squad of ten inside to join the general.

Despite the intact walls, the inside of the fort was devastated. Timber housings around the walls remained only as blackened stumps poking up through mounds of sour-smelling gray ash. Scattered around the bare earth courtyard were a dozen or so bodies, lying naked for the most part though clothed in dried blood and their gaping wounds open to the scorching sun.

As Horemheb entered the fort a jostling, squalling mass of feathered bodies arose from the centre of the

172

courtyard, black vultures running and flapping in a pan-icked attempt to get aloft. Horemheb dismissed them from his mind. He had seen worse than this before on any battlefield and Nekhebet, the vulture, was a very nec-essary part of life and death. Not without reason was it held sacred, the bird of the sun, soaring so high that it disappeared into the sun's blinding light.

After a cursory examination of the closest bodies, Horemheb stood back and let the soldiers check the rest. A few moments later, Meny, Leader of Ten, came up to Paramessu and saluted.

"All dead, sir. Most have been fed upon too."

Paramessu dismissed Meny before walking over to where the general squatted beside the ashes of the living quarters. "The vultures have been feeding a while, sir. They are long gone."

Horemheb straightened and dusted the gray ash off his hands. "Not that long, Paramessu. Those vultures have not stripped the bodies which they could do in the day and a half since the attack, and that ash still has some warmth in it. I judge they left here half a day ago."

Paramessu grinned. "Then we can catch them."

"Oh, yes. We will catch them. Send out your scouts. Find which route they took."

A shout from the gateway made them swing round as a young man entered at a run, his sandals churning up the dry dust. He skidded to a halt in front of Paramessu and stammered out his report.

"Tracks, s ... sir. Leading northeast, away from the road and into the hills."

"Show me."

The young soldier led his commanders out of the gates and round the fort to where the shallow stream val-ley plunged back toward the hills. A path ran alongside the stream and at one place, where the path dipped down along the waterway, fresh prints of bare and sandaled feet, and horses' hooves, could be seen clearly in the soft mud.

"How many would you say, Paramessu?"

The young officer squatted and examined the path carefully, looking at the prints closely. "Thirty sir, maybe more. At least ten horses too. Cavalry?"

Horemheb nodded. "More like fifty and I think those are pack horses rather than cavalry. If they are only half a day ahead, we can catch them. Bring your men up, Paramessu."

Paramessu set up scouts in front of the main body of men as they trotted slowly up the path into the hills. The rough worn track soon left the boulder-strewn streambed and headed up toward the ridge of the hills. The scouts reached the crest and peered over cautiously before signaling for the others to follow. The general studied the terrain below them, his pointing finger tracing the winding path as it descended through a dry and stony hillside to the dusty plains below.

"There are one or two places that would allow an ambush."

Paramessu frowned. "Is that likely, sir? They have no way of knowing they are followed."

"Unless they had a lookout watching the fort." Horemheb smiled. "Very unlikely, I grant, but what would you do to circumvent the possibility?"

Paramessu stared down at the place where the path ran through a boulder field and another where low scrub pressed close around the track. "Scouts could cross upslope there sir, and there. If I sent a squad of archers, they would be in a position to threaten any ambush."

"Good. Do so."

174

They waited while the archers scrambled across the hillside to a position overlooking the two suspect areas. One of them waved back at the men on the hill crest. Paramessu nodded, sending his men down the track at a run.

They reached the plains without incident beyond a fall or two and a few bruises. The track turned north again, following the line of hills, the prints of feet and hooves plain in the dry soil. Horemheb and Paramessu led their soldiers at a brisk run along the path, traveling in single file except for a squad that spread out on the open ground to the east and a few that scrambled over the sloping skirts of the hills to the west.

The afternoon wore on and the burning sun dipped below the hills on their left, sending a great cooling shadow over their progress. Horemheb flashed a quick grin at his subordinate and picked up the pace, the dust kicked up by their heels settling in a low cloud behind them.

A cry came from one of the out-runners near the hills. Paramessu angled over to check, then halted the column of soldiers. Horemheb found him squatting by the body of a bearded man.

"An Amorite, sir. Dead of his wounds, by the look of it." He gestured at the bloodied rents in the man's clothing. He reached over and prized open the mouth, flicking a small coin out with one finger. "Here," he said, tossing it to the soldier who had found the body. "Your reward soldier." The man grinned and slipped the coin into his pouch.

Paramessu straightened and looked at his general. "The man was not left to die. He had the death offering."

"And the body has not yet fully stiffened. We are close behind them." Horemheb turned back to the path at a run.

175

Sunset found them at a point where the track, together with the sign of their quarry, angled away from the hills into the great open plains. Horemheb called a halt and the men collapsed where they stood, panting and groaning.

"We camp here. There is enough light for another hour's travel but I would rather we had the shelter of the hills tonight."

Paramessu nodded and set about organizing the bivouac. "No fires," he said. "We may be close enough to be seen." He sent a pair of soldiers up the hillside into the dusk. The moon had risen, a slender crescent, when one of the guards returned. He squatted beside his leader and put a hand on his sleeping form, shaking him awake.

"Sir. There are fires to the east."

Paramessu scrambled up the slope in the dark, slowly following the guard. Horemheb stayed on his heels, seemingly unconcerned by the steep climb.

"There sirs," the guard said, pointing. "And there."

A distant pin-prick of orange light hung in the night sky, low down on the horizon. To the right and slightly higher hung another, slightly larger and brighter.

"A star," Paramessu said with a tinge of disgust and disappointment. "A star or a wanderer ..." He broke off as he suddenly realized that what he had taken for a low bank of cloud was in fact a low line of hills. "You may be right."

Horemheb nodded, just visible against the lighter sky. "Campfires. The nearer one maybe two hours away, the farther ... maybe another hour."

"We could make the crossing and be on them at dawn, general."

"Assuming it is who we are after. However, I don't think there will be any others out here."

176

Paramessu took a bearing on the stars and led his men out in a double column at a slow trot. The ground was sandy and undulating, with patches of broken stony ground that slowed them to a walk. Two hours crept by, then a third as the stars slowly wheeled in the sky before a scout came running back with the news of a large body of men camped ahead. He halted the men and crept forward with Horemheb. The camp lay in the shallow depression of a meandering dry stream bed. A large fire now burned down to coals and glowing embers lay in the middle of a large encampment. Numbers of bodies lay curled up against the chill of the night, others sat, resting against boulders or stood on guard duty, dim against the first faint pre-dawn flush of the sky. Horses whickered off to the left.

"Are they those we seek?" Paramessu whispered.

"They have the look of Amorites," Horemheb answered. "Bearded. The armor they wear is what I would expect." The breeze shifted slightly, bringing the sour odour of wood ash and unwashed bodies to the watchers. "They smell like Amorites too," Horemheb growled.

"I count forty-three, sir. Maybe more if there are guards by the horses. How do you want to do this?"

"We outnumber them two to one. We surround them at a distance, put our archers in position on that rise there, and call on them to surrender when dawn breaks."

Paramessu looked round in surprise. "You will not attack them?"

"Fighting is over-rated, Paramessu. People tend to die, some of them your own men. I prefer to do things without fuss if possible."

A faint scrabbling noise came from behind them and they whirled, hands gripping dagger hilts. A scout eased out of the darkness and squatted beside them. "Sirs, another group of men, perhaps an hour away, also camped."

"Who are they? Could you identify them?"

"Yes, sir. Well, I think so, sir. Amorites like these here but the other ones are soldiers like. More discipline it seems."

"How many, soldier?"

"About a hundred. Leastwise I think there was. It were dark, sir."

"That alters the odds somewhat," Horemheb muttered. He dismissed the scout and returned to his contemplation of the camp site below him. "What would you do, son?"

Paramessu thought. "I don't see we can afford to take these men without fighting now, sir. And we cannot hope to guard them or take them prisoner with this large group of soldiers only an hour away. Two groups of Amorites must be more than coincidence; they are planning on meeting up. We must stop them."

"Very good. How?"

"This group below us are the ones that destroyed the fort. I say we surround and attack under cover of night. Surprise and numbers. With luck we can be away before dawn, without the soldiers even aware we were here."

"A night attack?"

"I know it is not usual sir, and if it were any but my own men, I'd hesitate. But they are well trained and disciplined. I'll take out the sentries then have the men rush in silently in three columns. We can kill most of them before they waken. With your permission, of course."

Horemheb nodded and Paramessu crawled back to give his orders. Before many minutes had passed he was back beside the general on the rise overlooking the camp, thirty men prone in the sand behind him. He listened,

178

counting off the minutes, then a hoopoe called off to his right, followed a few moments later by another on his left. He waited. At last the noise of horses stamping in the lines came to them and another hoopoe rent the pre-dawn air with its eerie cry.

"That's the other sentries taken out," Paramessu murmured. "Now there are just the two below us." He rose to his feet and unsheathed a long bronze dagger.

"You are doing this yourself?" Horemheb whispered.

Paramessu grinned, his teeth gleaming faintly in the darkness. "Did you not always tell me never to ask one of my men to do anything I would not do?"

Horemheb grunted. "You learn well, boy. Permit me to accompany you?"

"I would be honoured."

The two men crept down the slope, bent low and taking advantage of every shadow and hint of cover. They picked their feet up and slowly settled them before putting any weight on, creeping silently into position behind the dozing sentries. One of the sentries farted loudly, eliciting a laugh and a show of light-hearted disgust from the other. The flatulent man laughed and turned up slope, pulling at his leggings. He started to piss, his gaze following the stream to where it spattered on the sand in front of a man-sized figure. He stared at the darkness, his mouth opening in a cry of surprise, cut off abruptly as the shadow flowed forward and a sharp blade sought out his heart. He collapsed; the sound and movement bringing the other sentry's attention around. Horemheb brought him low with an arm around his throat and his own dagger in the kidneys.

Paramessu looked around in the darkness, listening. He lifted a hand and framed his mouth, imitating the hoopoe. He nodded as Horemheb tapped him on the

179

arm. "The fornicator pissed on me," he muttered. Lifting his hand once more, he gave the cry of the desert owl when it has made a kill. The night rustled around them as thirty men crested the rise and flowed down toward the camp like a silent black tide. Paramessu and Horemheb joined them, running ahead into the Amorite camp, stabbing and hacking at the sleeping men. Darkened forms flowed from the night on the other side of the camp too, joining the silent killing.

Paramessu's men were through the camp and turning back to sweep through again before the alarm was raised. A horrified scream, cut off as a sword slashed, sent other Amorites stumbling from their beds, hands scrabbling for weapons. The Kemetu tore into the camp from different points and the Amorites died. Within minutes of the desert owl's scream, the attack was over.

Horemheb ordered a sweep of the perimeter and a check on the horses before returning to Paramessu by the remains of the campfire.

"I'm impressed," Horemheb said. "That was efficiently done."

"And no injuries to the men sir, apart from a few cuts." Paramessu looked around the camp, the men and the sprawled bodies already clearer as the sky lightened. "It will be dawn soon. What do you want to do about the other group of Amorites?"

"We have reduced the odds," Horemheb grinned. "And we still have the element of surprise. I say we rid Kemet of a few more troublesome jackals."

"I was rather hoping you might say that, sir," Paramessu said. Then he frowned. "We will not have the cover of night and these others are disciplined soldiers. How will we surprise them?"

180

Horemheb considered a moment. "What is the worst thing you can do to a dead Amorite? Other than rob him of his death coin?"

Paramessu snorted. "Take his head, you mean? You think to anger the others?"

"Angry men do not think well. What would an Amorite do if he happened upon forty of his fellows, headless, and twenty Kemetu running away with the heads?"

"Pursue and attack at once, probably without stopping to think how twenty defeated forty."

"Exactly. Now if we can think of a way to lead them into a trap, we have them."

Paramessu set his men to the grisly task of taking heads, ordering that the bodies be laid out naked in rows. Then he sat down with Horemheb to plan the trap.

"There is a shallow gully about an hour's travel back the way we came," Horemheb said. He drew a rough plan in the sand with his finger. "I recall there were large rocks on one side ... here. If our men led them into the gully at this end, and through it, with the Amorites close behind, I think we could take them."

Paramessu nodded, studying the sand. "I'd like to get some others on this side too." He tapped the sand on the other side of the gully. "If we could conceal some archers here ..."

"That might depend on the nature of the cover. We won't know until we get there. There is another problem too. The horses. If we take them they might give our ambush away, but if we leave them, the Amorites may use them to pursue our men."

"I'd say leave them but hide their tackle. If we taunt them enough with the bodies they won't stop to saddle them, just pursue us."

"Let us hope so." Horemheb looked up at the graying sky. "Dawn soon. We'd better be heading off now if we are to set up the trap. Pick out twenty of your swiftest men, Paramessu and be sure to give them full instructions. They must know exactly what we expect of them."

"I intend to lead them myself sir. I can't think of anyone I'd rather have set the ambush than you, and I need to be with my men."

Horemheb smiled and clapped his officer on the shoulder with a great horny hand, before gathering the men about him, leading them off toward the west at a run. Paramessu had the heads gathered up into linen bags and distributed among the men in his squads. He detailed two to run to the east to give warning on the approach of the Amorites, taking the others up to the low ridge overlooking the camp and sitting them down.

"Get what rest you can. We'll be running for our lives soon."

The sun rose, leaping up from the horizon and casting colour back into the desert. Paramessu, like many other officers, was a lower-ranked priest in addition to his military duties, so he led his men of the Re regiment in the morning devotional to their titular deity. They settled back down again, seeking what comfort they could in the already hot morning, gnawing on hunks of dried bread and sipping from depleted flasks of water.

"Where are they?" growled one of the soldiers. "I don't mind fighting the hairy sons of bitches but I hate this sitting around."

A shout split the air and every head turned, searching to the east. The two scouts came racing back toward them, leaping and jumping over boulders, kicking up the acrid dust. "They're coming, sir," panted one of them as

182

he came to a halt in front of his officer. "All of them, but slowly."

"Did they see you?"

"Yes, sir. As you said to, we didn't hide. Made sure the bastards saw us, then ran." The scout hesitated then blurted out. "They got horses, sir. We saw eight."

Paramessu cursed long and fluently, drawing grins of appreciation from the men within earshot. He looked around him at the bare ground and lack of cover, the low ridge and the swell of the land to the east offering but scant protection. He called over his three archers and explained the situation to them.

"We have to kill their horses. If we try and outrun them, we'll just get cut down."

He positioned the three archers behind the ridge with the bulk of his men, then led six of them eastward at a trot. "This is going to be chancy," he explained. "We are going to run headlong into them, turn and run back over the ridge. I'm hoping the archers can take care of them."

They crested the low swell of land and came face to face with the vanguard of Amorites, clambering up the slope towards them. Paramessu spotted horses beyond, in the indistinct body of men threading their way between rocky hillocks. He dashed forward with a yell and slashed at the Amorite in the lead with his sword, wounding him and sending him staggering back. His men leapt forward, hacking and stabbing, scattering their foes. An outcry arose beyond them and Paramessu grabbed one of his men, preventing him from chasing the enemy.

"Run!" he yelled. "For your lives."

Paramessu bolted back over the swell, his men close behind him. He looked back as they ran and saw half a dozen horsemen in pursuit. Already they were urging their mounts up the slope toward them. The Kemetu

183

raced down the far slope, bypassing the bloodied camp with its rows of headless bodies and up the slope to the ridge and the waiting archers. The horsemen galloped over the rise then pulled to the left, away from the camp, seemingly intent on cutting off the fleeing men. Paramessu halted his men and cut back toward the camp, trying to draw the Amorites back. The horsemen changed direction again and urged their mounts along the line of the ridge, trying to herd the Kemetu back toward their main force.

The archers rose to their feet as the first of the horsemen passed them, less than ten paces away and slightly below. The first arrows plunged deep into the chests of the horses, sending them crashing to the ground, their riders flying. The horses behind reared and plunged, their riders struggling to avoid their fallen comrades, two more falling as arrows found their mark. The soldiers waiting with the archers screamed out and ran at the fallen Amorites, their lethal long-bladed axes tearing the life out of the fallen men.

The remaining three horsemen wrestled their mounts around and kicked them into motion, fleeing back the way they had come. A volley of arrows cut one down, the horse squealing in agony as the bronze barbs bit deep. One of the soldiers threw himself in front of the horses, slashing at the legs with his axe. The man, horse and rider went down in a welter of bloodied limbs. The horse was the only one to rise, hobbling on blood-soaked legs, head down and trembling. The remaining rider galloped out of sight, swaying in the saddle with an arrow in one shoulder.

The Kemetu soldiers made short work of the Amorites, putting the wounded horses out of their misery.

"Cut the tackle as well," Paramessu ordered. "Make sure it is useless."

The Kemetu soldier who had thrown himself in front of the horse was dead, his skull stove in by a flying hoof. The rider still lived, but not for long, and the horse was likewise dispatched and the bit and bridle destroyed.

The sound of drumming feet and the clattering of rocks disturbed them and Paramessu signaled the retreat, bringing up the rear as his men gathered up their weapons and the linen bags with the Amorite heads and fled toward the west. Paramessu paused on the ridgeline and looked back at the Amorites swarming over the hillock. Three horsemen were among them but they made no effort to get closer, contenting themselves with urging the men on foot to attack. Paramessu grinned and shook his arm at them, making a universally known gesture of contempt before trotting unhurriedly over the ridge.

Once out of sight he picked up the pace, angling toward his right to intercept his men. Catching up, he slowed the pace and corrected the direction of travel slightly. At the top of a slight rise he looked back to see the Amorite soldiers strung out in a ragged line about fifteen hundred paces back. He halted his men and allowed them to catch their breath then, leaving a few of the blood-spattered heads behind to enrage their pursuers, they jogged on.

Meny, Leader of Ten though now separated from his Ten, ran alongside Paramessu, their slowly shortening shadows preceding them as they angled slightly north of west, heading for the shallow gully and the rocks.

"They're not very good runners are they, sir," Meny grumbled. "If we went any slower we'd be walking."

Paramessu laughed. "That's because they are part-time soldiers, not professionals. They have not been

185

trained for it." He glanced over his shoulder toward the haze of dust that marked the Amorite passage. "Still, they are too far back. If they approach the gully slowly there is a chance they will see the trap. We must hurry them along somehow."

Meny shrugged. "Well, if you want to stop, I don't mind. I could do with a piss, sir." He looked across at his commander and after a few seconds of silence added, "Sir?"

Paramessu grinned. "You want to show us how fast you can run, Meny? You'll get your chance." He picked his speed up and overtook the rest of his men running in a tight bunch a few paces ahead. "See that rock up ahead? We are nearly at the trap. Stop there."

The men slowed and halted by a large boulder sitting in a puddle of sand. At once Meny and a couple of the others lifted their kilts but dropped them at a snapped order from their commander. "Wait. Now," Paramessu said with a grin. "I need the men with the fullest bladders." He selected five and bade them stand, fidgeting, to one side. "You others dump your Amorite heads here and run on through the gully, along its length. When you reach the end, form a defensive line. We will be with you shortly."

Paramessu nudged the blood-spattered heads into a loose pile, keeping an eye on the approaching enemy. "All right, grab a couple of heads each and wave them in the air. Make sure they can see what they are." He held two up by their bedraggled locks, judging the distance to the oncoming soldiers. "Drop them, men, lift your kilts and piss on them. Laugh. Show your contempt."

A roar of rage erupted from the Amorites and they surged forward, the horsemen who had been urging the foot soldiers on, swinging around the men and digging

186

their heels into their horses' sides, swords drawn and waving. Closer they came, the foot soldiers putting in a burst of speed, their bearded faces contorted with a killing hatred.

The streams of urine faltered and two of the men stepped back in alarm. "Shit!" one of them yelped.

"Not now," Meny growled. "You'll have to wait for that."

"Now!" screamed Paramessu as the first of the soldiers reached them. He parried the down-swinging sword and kicked the man in the gut, swinging round and stumbling into a run in the same motion. "Run! Run as you never have before." The men fled, only paces ahead of the enemy. Without looking back they leapt and vaulted over rocks, racing and slipping over loose stones, kicking up sand as they fought to stay ahead of eager death.

They descended into the dried streambed, the breath of the enemy hot on their necks. Paramessu caught a glimpse of the towering rocks on the south side and prayed to Re that Horemheb was in place. A man tripped and fell beside him, uttering a scream of terror. The others ran on but Paramessu whirled, nearly overbalancing, his sword arcing round to slice across the chest of the man behind him. The man fell back with a curse and Paramessu stepped forward just as the fallen soldier died, stabbed by three swords. He slashed at another man before turning tail again, a spear thrust scoring his hip and ripping his kilt from him. He ran on naked, down the shallow gully, the horde of Amorites on his heels.

The Amorite horsemen spurred their mounts along the northern lip of the gully, passing the fleeing man and urging the horses down into the streambed ahead of him. Paramessu looked up and saw his way blocked. He slowed without thinking and he half-heard the whistling

187

rush of air behind him of a descending blade. Throwing himself to one side, he rolled and lifted his sword in time to block the first blow, but saw others coming as the leading Amorite soldiers swarmed toward him, their eyes burning with rage.

"For Re and Kemet," Paramessu screamed, preparing to die.

A grimace flashed across the face of the first man as he slashed down at the fallen Kemetu. Then the man fell across Paramessu, two of his comrades' swords biting deep into his back. Paramessu fought the man aside, struggling to lift his own blade as another man fell, a look of surprise on his face, then another, a blue-quilled arrow deep in his throat.

Paramessu scrambled to his feet and grinned in relief as he saw a wave of Kemetu soldiers erupt from the rocky cover on the south side. Silently they rushed down the slope and bit deep into the loose Amorite rabble, their deadly long-handled axes wreaking bloody havoc. Paramessu joined in, striking at the backs of the enemy as they turned to face the new foe. A riderless horse trotted by, eyes rolling, and he knew the archers had once more proved their worth.

Already outnumbered, the far end of the Amorite column turned tail and ran, throwing their weapons aside for greater speed. Horemheb's men, fresh after their wait, rapidly overtook the fleeing Amorites and cut them down. A few threw themselves to their knees and begged for mercy, dying with arms outstretched. Within minutes, silence returned to the desert, broken only by the groans of the wounded.

Horemheb found Paramessu standing naked among the dead and dying save for his stained linen headdress, his bloodied sword in his hand.

188

"Never let me catch you doing that again, you young fool," Horemheb growled.

Paramessu's grin faded and he drew himself to attention. "Sir?"

"Risking your life for the sake of a few mangy Amorites. If I'd known you were going to do that, I'd have put Meny in charge. At least he knows enough to run when he's told to."

"I'm sorry, general," Paramessu said stiffly, staring straight ahead. "I did what I thought was right to lead the enemy into the ambush. If I have angered you, I ask your mercy."

Horemheb sighed and put a gnarled hand on the young man's shoulder. "I am not angry, Paramessu, just concerned. Kemet would lose a future general if you got yourself killed – and I would lose a respected colleague and a friend." He slipped his arm around him and started walking. "Come now, let us find your Shendyt kilt. A commander should preserve his dignity where possible."

Chapter Thirteen

"So where do you want to go if not to the priests?"

Scarab shrugged her thin shoulders and looked down, smoothing her clean new kilt. A necklace of lapis hung on her flat brown chest, a small blue scarab beetle with outspread wings and tiny eyes of red glass. "Somewhere interesting."

Smenkhkare regarded his young sister solemnly. The two years since meeting her had passed quickly, and his expeditions into the city, once a solitary pastime, had become a keenly anticipated adventure for the two of them. He enjoyed showing the little girl – *well, not so little now*, he thought – *now that she has her first kilt she looks almost grown-up, despite her side-lock.* "The priests *are* interesting," he said. "There are great things happening in Kemet and the priests know more about them than anyone."

Scarab shrugged again, drawing a line in the dust with one toe. They stood below the old acacia tree that had half-tumbled the ancient stone wall behind the head gardener's cottage. The temples and the priest's houses were barely a stone's throw away across a well-tended garden. The children were familiar visitors to the temples and could be assured of a welcome into shady vine-covered porches, a cool drink of water or milk, a handful of dates or figs, and conversation. But beyond, baking in the heat, lay the great city of Waset with its myriad delights.

"I don't know, maybe Ahhotep? I love his glass ornaments and beads. Or Kenamun, the toy maker?"

"We went there last week. Besides, you may still like to play with toys but I'm too old for that." Smenkhkare looked down his nose at his sister summoning up every ounce of dignity present in his eleven-year-old body. "We should go somewhere we can learn something."

"Pooh. I don't want lessons. I want to have fun, have an adventure."

"How about the House of the Dead?"

Scarab looked up and cocked her head on one side. "What's that?"

"Come on, you must have heard about that. It's also called the House of Embalming. It's where the bodies go while they are being prepared for burial."

"I've never seen a dead body."

"Well, here's your chance. There are always lots of bodies there, in all stages of preparation. I know one of the embalmers, Ipuwer. I'm sure he'll be happy to show you round."

"Do you know people everywhere, Smenkhkare?"

The boy grinned. "Not yet, but I'm working on it." He took his sister by the hand and started across the garden toward the temple gates that opened into the road leading into the city. They skirted around a small flock of ibis searching for food on the temple pastures, not because there was any need for caution, but in order not to disturb the sacred birds. "Seriously though, Scarab, when I'm king I want to be a good one. I think a king should know everything about his people if he wants to rule them well."

"Do you still think you'll be king one day?"

"Maybe." Smenkhkare shrugged. "King Akhenaten still does not have a son. I'm next in line if he doesn't."

"What about Iset's son, Tutankhaten? He's our brother and Heqareshu says ..."

"He's only a baby. A baby can't be king. Honestly, little sister, you must learn to tell real life from the stories of the nurses."

Smenkhkare led Scarab through the temple gates into the busy thoroughfare of the great Avenue of Rams running into the city, then onto one of the narrower streets running at right angles to it. They walked hand in hand, keeping close to the buildings on one side, out of the path of horsemen, chariots driven by nobles and the occasional ox-cart. A great crowd of men and women walked around them, chattering and talking, arguing and bartering with the shopkeepers on both sides of the road. Children ran and played too, but kept to themselves, wary of strangers. Dogs barked; oxen lowed as the whips cracked over their long-suffering hides and horses stamped and blew as they pulled the chariots through the throng. The hot sun beat down on them all, reflecting off the stone buildings and raising swarms of flies on the fresh dung and refuse in the roadway. The stink of the ordure mingled interestingly with those of cooking foods, fresh-baked bread, and the sweaty bodies of the workers.

Scarab sniffed the air, wrinkling her nose at the mixture of odours. "Why does the city stink so much?" she complained.

"Because there is so much going on." Smenkhkare pointed across the road. "You want something to eat?" Without waiting for a reply he led his sister across the road, darting between a wagon full of melons and a chariot carrying a haughty looking man. He stopped outside a baker's shop, smelling the delicious odours of freshly baked bread.

Leaning through the doorway he greeted the baker standing sweating by his open fires. "Ho, Teti. I see you." Smenkhkare sauntered into the shop, grinning at the wife of the baker who was serving a woman, and a teenage girl kneading dough on a great wooden slab. "This is my friend Scarab," he announced to the shop. "Scarab, this is

Teti and his wife Ruia. Also their daughter Nyla." He turned with a bow and a broader grin at the customer. "You, madam, I do not know." Scarab shuffled timidly into the shadows beside the doorway.

"Ee, a cheeky young scamp, isn't he?" the woman commented to Ruia. She turned, planting hands on her ample hips. "And who might you be, eh?"

Teti the baker coughed and came forward a few paces. "That be Lord Smenkhkare," he said. "He be a young lordling up at palace."

"Ee, a lordling no less. What are you doing down 'ere then? Come to see 'ow the poor people live?"

"Indeed I have, madam. I take an interest in the workers of Waset and wish to learn as much as I can about conditions and how men and women conduct themselves."

The woman shook her head and picked up a large conical loaf of bread from the counter, slipping it into a reed basket. "It seems to me, young lord whatever-your-name-is, it would be better if you learned a useful trade instead of gallivanting about sticking your nose into other people's affairs." She sniffed loudly and marched out of the shop.

Smenkhkare looked after her with his mouth open, then broke into a fit of giggles. "Perhaps I should learn a trade. What do you think I should be, Teti?"

Teti's face cracked into a wide grin. "I think you could be anythink you wanted to be, young Smenkhkare. Stay clear of baking though, young sir, it be powerful 'ot in 'ere." He lifted his apron and wiped the sweat from his face. "Nyla, love." He addressed his daughter with obvious affection in his voice. "You be getting back to your work." Nyla bobbed her head and resumed punching a great ball of floury dough.

193

"So who's your little friend?" Ruia asked. "Come over here dearie, and let's 'ave a look at you." She held out her hand, smiling, and Scarab felt encouraged, walking over to the counter.

"I'm Scarab," she whispered.

"She's my friend and well, actually, she's my sister too." Scarab turned and smiled at her brother, her eyes glistening with love.

"Well I never," Ruia exclaimed. "A lord and a lady in my shop." She leaned her head on one side and examined the children with a twinkle in her eye. "Would you be wanting something to eat?"

"Yes please, Ruia," Smenkhkare said. Scarab nodded.

"Well, then, come in the back and I'll see what I can find. Husband, mind the shop while I'm gone."

"What d'yer think I'm likely to do?" Teti muttered. "Burn the place down?"

"Mind the fires now, children, an' the baking pots; they're very 'ot." Ruia ushered them past the counter and into a one-room dirt-floored house at the back of the shop. Two beds, a large and a small one occupied opposite corners, large squares of material half-hiding them. A table sat in the middle of the room with trestle benches along each of its sides. Along one wall was another long table, laden with pots and pans. A rickety set of shelves occupied most of another wall. A hole in the brickwork functioned as a window and a chimney, letting the smoke that eddied from a large earthenware pot escape the room. "Sit yers down then."

Ruia rummaged in the cupboard for a couple of clay platters and set them on the table in front of the children before disappearing back into the shop. She returned almost immediately with a small conical loaf, golden-brown and smoking from the baking pots. She ripped it

194

in two and set the steaming halves on the platters. "Careful now, children. It be 'ot from the pots."

Smenkhkare thanked Ruia and bit into his half of the loaf, exclaiming and fanning his open mouth vigorously. "Hot!" he cried. "Very hot."

Scarab ate more slowly, breaking off a small piece of the dark brown grainy textured bread and popping it into her mouth. She chewed and swallowed. "It's very nice," she said politely. "Thank you." Taking another bite, she yelped as she bit into a bit of grit. She grimaced and removed the offending chip of stone. "It's got things in it."

"Not what yer used to, young lady?" Ruia asked. "Up in the palace the flour is properly ground in fine, smooth mills no doubt. 'Ere we 'ave to use what we can afford." She shrugged, then grinned broadly, exposing her chipped and broken teeth. "Bits of stone come off the grinding stones. I catches some of them but bits gets missed."

Scarab grimaced and picked up the loaf, turning it over. She examined it closely then dusted it down and prized a small piece of gravel from the crust, dropping it to the floor. Ruia raised her eyebrows but said nothing. Smenkhkare scowled.

"It's very sweet bread, Ruia," he said, distracting the woman from his sister's complaints. "Is this the bread you make beer from?"

"Why yes, it is, young lord. We crumbles it and soaks it in water with dates. When you is older you can try some."

"It's very nice, really." Scarab smiled uncertainly and took another bite, chewing gingerly. She found a few grains of sand which she spat out but no more pieces of stone, and finished up her half loaf quickly. "Thank you."

"Delicious," Smenkhkare exclaimed. "We thank you for your hospitality, Ruia." He slipped off the bench and dusted a few crumbs off his kilt. "We must be getting on though; I promised Scarab I'd show her the House of Embalming today ..." He glared at his sister for a moment. "... and I like to keep my word."

Ruia laughed. "You won't get nothing to eat there."

"Ah, but there are so many things to find out. Besides, I like meeting people and seeing what they do. It's boring up at the palace."

"Now I could live with that kind of boredom," Ruia said. "Well, you come again young lord. Bring your sister too if she can put up with me coarse bread."

"I'd like to," Scarab whispered. "I'm sorry if I offended you."

"No offence taken, little lady." Ruia stroked Scarab's side lock of hair tenderly. "You remind me a bit of me baby Abar. She would 'ave been about your age if she 'ad lived." She sighed deeply and looked away for a moment. "Well, off you go then."

Smenkhkare led the way out onto the hot and dusty street, turning left and walking westward toward the river. He looked straight ahead and ignored his sister. Scarab scampered after him, her face screwed up with worry.

"What's wrong?" she asked.

Smenkhkare stopped abruptly and turned to face his sister. "You don't have to be rude to them just because they are poor," he hissed. "These people are my friends and they welcome me into their houses and share because they are good people. I don't like it when others who have never done any work complain about how hard things are or about a few little bits of grit in their bread."

Scarab gaped. "But ... but you don't work either."

196

"No, but I shall. If the gods favour me I shall be king and I will work hard for my people. And even if I'm not, I will be a man, a ... a general or a scribe or a priest and work hard anyway. You are just a girl, a princess who will always sit around and have things done for her."

"I can't help being a girl," Scarab wailed. "And I don't want to sit around. I want to do things, see people like you." She grabbed hold of her brother's arm and gripped it tightly. "Please, Smenkhkare, don't be upset with me. I didn't know but I can learn; if you show me. Please."

Smenkhkare grunted and nodded, looking over the head of his sister at the passing crowds in the street. "All right then, but you must try and be conscious of who you are. Members of the Great House are privileged, but they also bear great responsibilities to look after the people."

"I will, I will." Scarab nodded vigorously and standing on tiptoe, kissed Smenkhkare on the cheek. "Thank you," she grinned.

"We'll forget what happened today then, but next time we come out you are going to pick a nice piece of jewelry from your box and give it to Ruia. Just to show you are sorry."

"Do I have to? I've only got this necklace, two others and a few bracelets and jewels."

"And how many do you think Ruia has? You saw that necklace of wooden beads she wore? That was probably all she had. They are very poor." Smenkhkare took Scarab by the shoulders and looked her in the eyes. "If you want to come out with me again you need to apologize to Ruia by giving her a present. I think your silver and onyx bracelet would do very nicely."

Scarab opened her mouth indignantly then subsided. "Yes, brother."

Smenkhkare smiled. "Good girl. Come on then, let's see if we can find the House of Embalming."

"What do you mean, find it? I thought you'd been there before."

"I have, little sister, but I've always gone straight there from the palace. Going to Teti's first has confused me a bit." He looked around then pointed down a side street. "Down here I think." Holding Scarab's hand, he set off down the street.

The shops in this part of the city were all concerned with producing the basic things of life. They passed another baker, a large brewery, and shops displaying linen cloth of a low grade, as well as ones selling furniture and wood carvings. Interspersed with the shops and tiny factories were dwellings, mud brick for the most part though a few of the evidently more affluent citizens had homes of stone with tiny courtyards. The crowd of people on the street thinned out and the two children in their spotless white linen kilts and jewelry stood out. A few heads turned to follow them as they passed.

"I'm not sure it is down here," Smenkhkare said. "This street does not look familiar."

Scarab skipped along happily beside her brother. "This is fun anyway. It doesn't matter if we don't find the Embalming House, we're having an adventure."

Smenkhkare tugged on her hand sharply. "Stop that, you are attracting attention." He bent down and whispered as she quieted. "It's not always safe on the streets, Scarab. You wouldn't want to be robbed ... or worse."

"What do you mean; worse?"

"We are going to have to ask somebody." Smenkhkare looked around, trying to decide who it was safe to approach. After a few moments he walked up to an old street sweeper sitting against the stone façade of an ale-house, nursing a pot of beer.

"Excuse me," Smenkhkare said. "Can you tell me the way to the East Gate House of the Embalmers?"

The old man peered up at them out of beer-fuddled eyes. A dribble of thick yellow pus streaked the outside corner of his right eye and he rubbed it away with the back of one hand. "You're a bit young to be getting em-balmed, aren't you?" he cackled.

"Yes, sir." Smenkhkare smiled weakly. "Do you know the way?"

The street sweeper looked the children over carefully, his gaze lingering on the girl's silver and lapis necklace and the boy's golden one. "What's in it for me, eh? Why should I bother to tell you unless I'm getting something for my trouble?"

"I'm sorry if we have troubled you then. We shall ask elsewhere." Smenkhkare turned away, steering Scarab away from the man.

"Hold on there," called the old man, scrambling to his feet. He spilt his pot of beer as he rose and he cursed fluently, staring down at the rapidly evaporating patch of liquid on the ground. "Who's going to pay for that then?"

"You spilt it," Smenkhkare said, backing away.

"Well, you made me." The old man smiled, his tooth-less gums spread wide though his eyes glittered with ava-rice. "You are two obviously rich children. I think you should pay me for my beer. One of those necklaces will do." He took a step toward them, his eyes wandering over Scarab again. "Or else perhaps the little girl would like to comfort me?" He made a sudden grab and clutched Scarab's arm. She screamed and tried to pull free.

Smenkhkare leapt forward and grappled with the old man, shoving him backward with an incoherent yell of rage. The man backhanded him, knocking him to the ground, and dragged the girl closer.

"What's going on here?" A deep voice interrupted the scuffle. Smenkhkare looked up from the ground at a tall young man standing behind the old street sweeper, his fists on his hips, legs spread.

"Samu, are you annoying these children?"

"They spilt my beer," Samu whined. "It's only fair they pay for it."

"We did not spill it," Smenkhkare yelled, scrambling to his feet. "He spilt it when he got up. We were only asking for directions and he wanted payment so we were leaving and ..."

"Enough. It doesn't matter who spilt it. Samu, have you forgotten who paid for that beer in the first place?" The young man's eyes glittered and his voice hardened. "Now let go of that young girl."

Samu grumbled but released Scarab, who retreated behind her brother, rubbing her arm. She watched warily as Smenkhkare confronted the young man and the old street sweeper.

"Thank you, sir," Smenkhkare said, bowing slightly, though his eyes never left the old man. "May I know your name?"

The young man smiled. "Quite the little lord, are you not? I am Mahuhy, a local businessman. And you? What is your name, young master? And that of your friend?"

"I am Smenkhkare, and this is my friend Scarab."

Mahuhy frowned. "Smenkhkare?" His eyes flicked over the fine white linen of their kilts and the jewelry. "There is a boy of that name up at the palace, a prince. Would your parents have named you after him?"

"No, Mahuhy, businessman of Waset. I was not named after anyone else. That is my name alone."

"Ah." Mahuhy smiled again, considering. "And the girl? A princess perhaps? Though she does not bear any princess' name I have heard of."

"A friend," Smenkhkare said firmly. "It would be wise to treat my friends well."

Mahuhy bowed mockingly, his smile never leaving his face. "Then how may I be of service, Prince Smenkhkare and Princess Scarab?"

"You may not. We were just leaving." Smenkhkare backed away, drawing his sister after him.

"They was wanting directions to the East Gate Embalming House," Samu muttered.

"Indeed?" Mahuhy said. "I can give you directions."

"No thank you. We shall ask elsewhere."

"Samu," Mahuhy said, without turning. "Go and get yourself another pot of beer." He dug into the pouch at his belt and flipped a small piece of copper at the old man, waiting until Samu had disappeared into the alehouse. "Come, Smenkhkare, my friend Samu has given offence. Let me make amends by directing you to your destination. I am heading in that direction myself, so it would be no trouble."

Smenkhkare considered, glancing about the street, seeing few other people. "Very well, but only by well-frequented streets. We will not go down any alleys or deserted streets with you."

"You think ill of me, young sir." Mahuhy's smile broadened into a grin. "Never mind. It shall be as you say, only crowded streets. This way then, if you please." He led the way down the Street of Cloth onto another narrower avenue also crowded with people.

A group of children ran by, naked as the day they were born, laughing and chattering. Scarab turned and watched them, thinking how nice it would be to be part of a group, off on a carefree adventure. Then she noticed that one of them limped badly and at least two others were covered in sores. Another had a swollen and inflamed arm, and all of them had weeping pus-filled eyes. "How can they be happy?" she whispered to herself. "How can they laugh?"

Smenkhkare relaxed slightly as they threaded their way through the crowds, following the tall Mahuhy. He still scanned the people they passed and Mahuhy, looking for any signs of recognition passing between them. Leaning closer to his sister, he whispered in her ear. "I don't trust him. If there is any trouble, I will delay him. You run, as fast as you can."

Scarab gripped his hand tighter. "Where would I run?" she quavered.

"Anywhere. Stop a woman and ask the way to the temple of Amun on the Avenue of Rams. You can get home from there."

"What about you? I don't want to leave you."

"I'll be all right. You can alert the temple guards if you like. They'll come and look for me." Smenkhkare shrugged philosophically. "Of course, when word of this gets out I'll be prevented from coming into the city again but it can't be helped."

The crowds thinned and Mahuhy turned onto a still narrower street that was peopled enough to allay their suspicions. The air grew thicker with the stink of rotting things and flies buzzed in black clouds above objects in the street that the children avoided looking at. Refuse of all sorts littered the street. The young man dropped back to walk beside the children.

202

"Are you really prince Smenkhkare?"

"Does it matter? Would you only be helping us if I was?"

Mahuhy laughed. "You expect me to help people just out of the goodness of my heart?"

"It is what the gods expect of us. When Inpu weighs your heart against the feather of truth, do you not want a good deed to lighten your heart?"

"That may work in the palace, boy, though I have heard many tales to the contrary. It certainly doesn't work that way in the city."

Smenkhkare guided Scarab around a pile of refuse on the street. Two pariah dogs, their flanks scarred by running sores, fought over scraps of rotting food. He screwed up his face in disgust.

"I have nothing to pay you with."

"No matter. When Prince Smenkhkare comes into his own, perhaps he will remember Mahuhy once helped him."

They walked on down the street and Mahuhy paused on the corner of the Street of Whores. "I have business down here," he remarked. "I shall not be long; I merely have a message to pass on."

Smenkhkare looked at the refuse-filled street they were on and the somewhat cleaner street facing them. "We shall accompany you."

"Are you sure, boy?" Mahuhy smirked. "You are a bit young to know about this. How old are you anyway, ten?"

"Eleven. And my education is broad. I know what passes between a man and a woman."

Mahuhy laughed out loud. "Come then." He led the way down the Street of Whores. It soon became apparent why the street was so-named. Although there were residences still, and shops, a number of the low mud brick buildings sported large open doorways thronged with heavily made-up women of all ages, sizes and skin tones, dressed only in diaphanous linen shifts and brightly coloured scarves. Men wandered the street, openly appraising the merits of this woman or that, laughing and pointing, uttering crude remarks. A number were foreigners and Smenkhkare recognized bearded Syrian traders, short-kilted Cretan sailors with hair in ringlets and muscular blue-black Nubian soldiers. The women in their turn called out to the men as they passed, offering their charms or just passing good-natured banter. Many of them seemed to know Mahuhy and called to him. Some of the remarks were addressed at Smenkhkare and Scarab though, and the children hurried along, pressing closer to their guide.

"Here we are," Mahuhy said, stopping outside a freshly white-washed building. "Wait here." He ducked inside the doorway and stood, still visible from the street in an open courtyard. He called out loudly. "Nefer, Inet, Tio – where are you?"

A woman's voice, low and languid, answered him from the shadows. "What do you want, Mahuhy? It is a hot day and I just want to sleep." The woman moved out into the sunshine, holding a hand up to shield her eyes from the glare. The heavy make-up and layers of clothing could not disguise the wrinkles and sags of a much-used body. Her name Nefer, 'beautiful', had not been accurate for many years.

"Come, Nefer," Mahuhy cajoled. "At least you get to lie down when you work. Where is Tio? I have a job for her."

Nefer jerked her head toward the shadows. "She is with a customer. Tio!" she yelled.

There was silence for a few moments before a muffled "What? I am busy." emanated from the shadowed building at the far end of the courtyard.

"Never mind, tell her when she finishes that Pamiu, overseer of the garbage collectors guild wants her." Mahuhy grinned. "The usual place. And tell her to be especially nice to him; he has paid me already."

"I'll tell her." Nefer looked out into the street. "Who are they? More youngsters you have persuaded to earn you money?"

"Never you mind," Mahuhy said curtly. He turned on his heel and walked back out into the street. He beckoned to the children and started sauntering back the way they had come. At the corner he turned into the Street of Potters. "Nearly there."

"Do they work for you?" Smenkhkare asked.

Mahuhy grinned. "Yes. You want one? It'll cost you though. I can get silver for my young ones."

"No thank you. I merely wish to know what manner of man I am talking to."

"Oh, very straight and moral aren't we? We all have to make a living, princeling, unless we are born in the palace. How I choose to make mine is no concern of yours."

"You have made your choice, Mahuhy. Have your women also chosen it or are they forced to it?"

Mahuhy shrugged. "They are free to leave as soon as they have worked off their debt to me." He pointed down the long street to where the massive walls of the city were pierced by a large gate. "There you go, princeling, you can't miss it. The city entrance to the East Gate House of Embalming is on the right, just by the gate. I will leave you here." He turned and walked a few steps before turning back. "Don't forget my name, young Smenkhkare; I will hold you to your debt."

Smenkhkare stared at the young man. "I will not forget," he replied softly. He turned away and, hand-in-hand, led Scarab down the street toward their destination.

The House of Embalming was a huge edifice of granite set into the outer walls of the city. As such, it had one small entrance that opened onto a city street and several that opened onto the plains outside where a broad, much-traveled road led to the funerary temples and the ferry of the dead that carried the mummified bodies across the river on their final journeys to the tombs on the Western bank. The newly dead were considered ceremonially unclean and any contact of the House of the Dead with the residential and business quarters of the city was looked on with disfavour. However, the realities of supply led to the House being as close to the city as possible without actually being in it. Consequently, the vast edifice devoted to the preparation of the dead was within the actual walls of the city.

The cedar wood door Smenkhkare walked up to was set into the polished granite facing, between two towering columns engraved with scenes from the Book of the Dead. He knocked softly, then after a few minutes, again, louder.

"They may be busy," Smenkhkare explained. "Ah, here comes someone."

The door opened with a creak and a flood of cool air laden with the rich heavy odours of spices, incense and resins flooded from the dim interior. A fat middle-aged man in a clean white kilt looked out at the street then down at the two children standing on the steps. The man smiled, recognizing the boy.

"Smenkhkare. What a surprise. What can I do for you?"

"Hello, Ipuwer." He pushed his sister forward. "This is my sister, Scarab. She has never seen a dead body and I thought maybe you could show us one."

"This is not a place of entertainment," Ipuwer said reprovingly. "In these halls, we prepare the dead for immortality."

"That is not what I meant, Ipuwer. She seeks to learn, as do I. If we are to prepare ourselves for eternity, surely we should know how we will face it?"

Ipuwer considered, one hand stroking his smooth chin. "There is merit in your argument, young sir." He opened the cedar door wider and beckoned them in. "Your sister, you say? I do not think I know of anyone by the name Scarab. Does she have another?"

Smenkhkare shook his head. "Nebmaetre and Tiye are her parents, though."

"Indeed?" The man looked at Scarab with interest for a few moments then shook himself. "Well, come in then. You wanted to see a dead body, young lady?"

"You have some?" Smenkhkare asked eagerly.

Ipuwer looked at the young boy until his enthusiasm waned before turning back to Scarab. "Now, young lady, you realize that the House of Death in the temple precincts of Amun is the parent body to all the other Houses? Their clients are the royal family and priests. This House is but one of many in the city, and we cater for more well-to-do customers. Well, the fees are high, but the quality of work that comes from this house is second to none." Ipuwer coughed and added, "Maybe second to the House of Death itself, but certainly of a very high standard." He started walking down a long hallway that ran parallel to the city wall. The narrow hall was dimly lit, with bronze lamps suspended by chains from the ceiling. Oil burned in the lamps, ill-kept wicks guttering to produce a sooty yellow flame. The smoke, together with the strong odour of burning incense, irritated Scarab's nose and she rubbed it with the back of one hand.

"Because we only cater to the nobility we never have many clients in our halls at one time." He pointed to large double doors on the left as he walked past them. "This is the Hall of Incision. We have nobody there at present, but last week Anahy, a local landholder, slipped in some cow-dung and hit his head. He died the next day and his son brought him to us, together with fifty deben of gold. We brought in the Cutter – you know about cutters?"

Scarab shook her head and sneezed. "Sorry. No sir, I don't."

"How about you, Smenkhkare?"

"He's the person that cuts open the body. Will we meet him?"

"No, you most certainly will not. The cutter is unclean and untouchable because he deals with the dead bodies before they have been ritually purified. He is brought in solely to make the abdominal incision in the flank, draw out the viscera and clean the brain from the skull cavity. He works under supervision of course. We have resident scribes for that."

"What do you do, sir?" Scarab asked in a tremulous whisper.

"I am an embalmer, young lady. A priest of the funerary temple, and I supervise the preparation of the body for eternity. I have had training in the House of Life as a physician and also in the House of Death." Ipuwer stopped outside another set of double doors.

"This is the first stage in the preparation. Do you want to see it?"

Scarab nodded timidly and Smenkhkare agreed with an eager grin.

Ipuwer threw open the doors and ushered the children inside, closing them again. "Welcome to the Place of Purification."

Scarab stared around in fascination and some trepidation, expecting to see bodies all over the place. Instead the large room was almost empty, dominated by a single granite slab raised to a man's waist height. A high, wide window on the north-facing wall let in a broad shaft of sunlight which lit the slab and the surrounding area, throwing the rest of the room into deep shadow by contrast. Her eyes slid away from the lit slab toward the shadows, expecting to see something terrible stalk out from them. As Scarab's eyes grew accustomed to the gloom however, she began to make out huge chests and coffers lining the walls, shelves groaning under a multitude of pots and bottles, urns and instruments.

A movement by the slab caught her eye and Scarab gave a start as she realized a small group of men were standing round the granite table, their attention riveted on the top. Ipuwer moved toward the central slab, silently beckoning the children to follow.

The men around the slab looked up as Ipuwer entered the shaft of sunlight, nodding in silent greeting before turning back to their tasks. Scarab looked at what they were doing but had trouble recognizing anything. It looked like a bundle of waxy yellow-white rags or parchment lay on the table, then as one of the men moved, his shadow slipped off the bundle and the sunlight lit up the unmistakable profile of a man. She gasped and drew back, clutching her brother's arm.

"Not what you expected, young lady?" Ipuwer moved closer and greeted the other men. "Rekhmire, fetch me two small stools." A young man immediately bowed and ran off into the gloom, returning a few minutes later with a pair of plain wooden stools. "Thank you, my son." Ipuwer placed them alongside the slab and motioned the children to climb up on them. "Leave us," he murmured, waiting until the preparers had left the room.

Scarab found herself looking down on the naked corpse of a small wizened man. The skin was a pasty yellow colour, darkening where the flesh pressed against the cold granite slab. The eyelids were shut over sunken eyes and the mouth hung open, the teeth white and even.

"You would not think; to look at him," Ipuwer said softly, "That this is PenMa'at, son of Pepienhebsed the Controller of the King's Wharves, a sixteen year old youth. He looks like an old man, does he not?" He leaned forward and touched the dead face, then the hands. "Look though at the teeth, still white and unbroken. He ate a rich man's diet with little grit in his bread. See too the hands, soft and uncallused. This boy was no common labourer. He lived in luxury and privilege but he died just the same. Of the running flux as it happens." Ipuwer looked across at the children, searching their faces, noting the eagerness in the boy's and the fear in the girl's.

"Death is not to be feared, young lady, nor are the dead. This which you see before you is merely the Khat, 'that which decays', the physical body that contained the Khaibit or shadow body which has now dissolved, and the Ka, or 'double'. When this man has been readied for his eternal life in the tomb, a funerary priest, the Hem Ka will consecrate a special statue of the deceased. This statue will house the Ka, but my job, and that of those under

210

me, is to prepare the physical body to house the Ba, the soul of PenMa'at."

"My teachers have told me of these things," Smenkhkare said. "But I do not think they explained it very well. It does not seem to be a pleasant prospect, locked in a tomb forever, living in a statue and an eviscerated body."

Ipuwer shook his head. "Your teachers should be punished if they cannot explain it better than that. It is a very complex subject as a person is made up of many bodies, many senses, each with its own guiding principle. The two principles you should focus on, children, are the Ka and the Ba. Leave the rest until you are older and wiser. When a man dies, his Ka travels to the underworld and is tested by the gods. If he has lived a righteous life, his heart will weigh less than the feather of truth and he will pass on to the Field of Reeds, where all good things await him. However, for him to enjoy food and drink and all the pleasures of this life, his spirit must have a connection with his body. The Ka statue enables the spirit to return to the tomb, where offerings of food and drink are left for him. There too there will be effigies of servants ready to carry out his wishes."

Smenkhkare frowned, struggling to comprehend the information. "And the Ba?"

"The Ba resides within the preserved body and enables the returned spirit to leave the tomb at night and go wherever it will, enjoying the good things of our Two Lands."

"What if ... what if the body is destroyed?"

"Then the Ba has nowhere to live and the Ka is prevented from enjoying all good things for eternity. The preservation of the body is essential, which is why my job is so important."

211

"What about poor people?" Smenkhkare asked. "I have seen the poor carrying the bodies of their loved ones out of the city to bury them in the desert."

Ipuwer nodded. "The poor can preserve the body after a fashion, by letting it dry in the desert sands. They have no priests to say the rituals, nor Ka statue; and the residence of the Ba is as wretched after death as it was before."

"That does not seem fair," Smenkhkare complained.

"Fair? What has fairness to do with it? From as soon as we comprehend the fact that we must die, every person in Kemet is striving to make his eternal home the best he can. We live for what, fifty or sixty years if the gods favour us? We are dead for eternity. Surely we should make every effort to make our eternal years pleasurable? What is a lifetime of work if we can live in luxury after death? So a peasant, a poor man, refuses to better himself, to put aside a little for the funerary priest to make the offerings for him. Should we pity him? It is his responsibility."

Scarab put up her hand hesitantly. "Excuse me," she whispered.

Ipuwer smiled. "What is it, young lady?"

"W... why would anyone want to live in a body like this?" she asked in a small voice. "I think it would be dreadful to look like this forever."

Ipuwer chuckled. "Ah, little lady, there you have it. Who indeed would want to live in that?" He pointed at the corpse of PenMa'at. "But that is not what will go into the tomb. Look here." Ipuwer drew his finger down the body's left flank, tracing a long double line that, on closer examination, resolved itself into a neatly incised opening into the abdominal cavity.

"When the body first came to us, it was cleaned thoroughly and the cutter made an incision here. He removed the internal organs and the important ones were placed in the organ jars after drying in natron. You know about the organ jars?"

Smenkhkare nodded. "They are jars that are under the protection of four demigods, the Sons of Heru."

"Very good. The four sons of Heru look after specific organs and make promises to the dead person. Imset cares for the liver and promises to make the person's house flourish, Haapi looks after the lungs and protects the head and members of the body, Daumutef is in charge of the stomach and promises to raise you onto your feet, and Qebsenuf is in charge of the intestines, promising to set the heart in its proper place within the body."

"Is the heart not put in a jar then?" Scarab asked, remembering her nurse saying that organ was the seat of emotions and intellect.

"The heart is left in the body cavity. Now, where were we ..." Ipuwer tapped his chin with a forefinger for a few moments. "Ah, yes. The organs are removed through the incision in the flank, and another one here, in the chest. The cavities are washed out thoroughly and packed with dry natron and resins. The brain is removed through the nose, or sometimes we cut the back of the skull open to extract it, though increasingly embalmers are leaving the brain in the skull."

"What do you do with it?" Smenkhkare asked. "Does it go in another jar?"

"Whatever for?" Ipuwer smiled. "The brain performs no discernible function except perhaps to produce mucus, and the Ka will not need it. It is thrown away, together with anything else that is taken out of the body.

213

So, everything is removed, the body is washed with palm wine and spices and packed with natron before being sent to the House of Waiting where it spends the next forty days in a great tub of dry natron. This removes all the water and fat from the body, leaving it pure and dry as you see it now."

"It is not unclean anymore?"

"No, young lady, else I would not be touching it now. It was removed from the natron and washed to remove all traces of the salts and any debris that might have been missed during the evisceration." Ipuwer picked up one of the body's arms and flexed it. "Note how supple the body is now, despite being dehydrated. We can straighten out the limbs ready for burial."

Scarab watched as the embalmer demonstrated the flexibility of the body. Despite her initial nervousness that bordered on a fear of the dead, those ideas were rapidly disappearing in the face of Ipuwer's calm explanations. She leaned closer and touched the body with a fingertip, marveling at the cool solidity of the flesh. She pressed a finger into her own warm side for comparison, then back to the body once more, rubbing her finger slowly over the cool dry skin.

"What happens next?" she asked.

"We make the body as lifelike as we can. We have teams of specialists that pack linen soaked in resins beneath the skin to plump the tissues up again. Others apply makeup to restore the tones of life to the complexion. The body and the brain cavity are packed with spices and resins to fill and preserve. Finally resin-soaked cloths will be wrapped tightly about the limbs with special prayers written on scraps of papyrus and amulets. Then the family will collect young PenMa'at, who will now be for-

ever young in the halls of eternity, and take him for burial."

Scarab smiled and clapped her hands softly. "That is
a beautiful thought, Ipuwer. Thank you for showing me.
When it comes time for me to die, I want you to embalm
me."

Ipuwer stifled a smile. "You will far outlive me,
young princess. Besides, the royal embalmers would have
something to say if I stole one of their clients."

"I will let it be known that I desire to be purified in
this House of Purification. My brother will do the same,
won't you Smenkhkare?"

"Perhaps, little sister." Smenkhkare gazed sadly at
Scarab. "Only the gods know the future, and you should
not be concerned yet with death. You and I have scarcely
begun to live." He grinned. "I will be a great king first
and you will be my queen and we shall build a magnificent tomb that rivals that of the great Khufu."

"Indeed you will, young master," Ipuwer said. "And
you too, young lady. But for now I must ask you to excuse me. My servants and fellow embalmers must prepare the body of PenMa'at. I will have my son Rekhmire
escort you back to the palace. The hour grows late." He
peered up into the high vaulted ceiling to where the daylight streaming through the wide windows was dimming,
the shadows in the corners of the great room creeping
forward.

"May we come again?" Scarab piped up as they left
the room, the young Rekhmire holding the door for
them.

"Yes, young princess." Ipuwer bowed and extended
his hands parallel to the floor at knee level. "I would be
honoured. But come with your brother, never alone."

215

As Rekhmire closed the door, Scarab caught a glimpse of Ipuwer and the other embalmers advancing from the shadows toward the pale body of PenMa'at as he lay on the cold granite slab, awaiting the touch of eternity.

Chapter Fourteen

Death is not a thing to be feared, at least not for a Kemetu, and still less for a member of one of the great families. We Kemetu have always loved festivals and religious feasts and see no reason why death should interrupt our enjoyment. We have many gods, several hundred in fact if you separate out all the aspects and incarnations. The sun god Re, for instance, was one of the major gods until Amun rose to prominence. He then assimilated other gods and took on the aspect of the creator god Atum, becoming Atum-Re. Later on he merged with Amun to become Amun-Re. Khepri, the sacred scarab beetle is another subtle manifestation of the sun god, as is Harakhte, and Heru. Then of course there is the sun disk itself, the Aten.

Don't ask a Kemetu to tell you about the gods. He will just shrug and point you toward a priest, and the priest will talk your ears off without making you any wiser. All most of us know is that the gods exist and we need to worship them. Every day has a god sacred to it, sometimes more than one, and each god must have his own celebrations. Of course, this is not to say that every day is spent in festival, for if this were so, everything would stop, no crop would be farmed, nothing would be made or business conducted. Most gods have settled for minor festivities limited to a few people, or to a particular town that boasts a temple to the deity. On the other hand, there is one festival of Amun that lasts for eleven days, during which the city of Waset shuts down and everybody eats, drinks, and spends the days and nights in frivolous entertainment.

At a time of festival, particularly of one of the major gods, pilgrims will flock in from all over the country, sometimes traveling for weeks to get there. The king, or the priests if the god is a rich one, will provide food and drink during the festival days, usually just bread and beer, but sometimes more. Many of the rites take place within the temples and are known only to the initiates and the priests, though the king, as a higher priest even over the god-chosen Hem-netjer of the deity, must also attend and often participate in the rites. The processions are the public aspect of the festival days. The god emerges from his temple, carried by strong young priests and is borne through the streets. Crowds run before the statue, shouting praises, uttering prayers and petitioning the god incessantly. The king often accompanies the god, riding high on a throne made heavy with gold and precious stones.

The king, as the incarnation of Heru and the son of Re, is god-on-earth, the divine heir, and in the eyes of the people the only intermediary between the gods and mankind. Many people consider the rituals to be effective only when performed by the king. In reality he cannot be everywhere at once and delegates most of the rituals to priests, senior officials and other functionaries. He still performs the rites for the major festivals though, and attends the consecration ceremonies of every temple.

Kemetu believe that the living, the dead, and the gods – the three parts of creation – all share the same basic needs for shelter, food, drink, rest and recreation. The living are found in houses, the dead in tombs and the gods in temples. Divine rituals performed by the living supply the needs of the gods, and the funerary cults, also performed by the living, provides for the needs of the dead. On festival nights, long torchlight processions wind through the streets of Waset from the great temples of Amun as scores of priests, masked and robed, bathed in the sacred waters of the temple lake, visit the dead. Barges carry them over to the West Bank, the realm of necropolis and tomb, desert and jackal, to bring necessary food and drink to the dead.

The great Amun festival takes place around the new moon in the second month of summer, Khentkhety. This is an especially joyous occasion when the city blazes with light all night long. Oil-burning lamps are lit and fastened outside each door to guide the spirits of the dead home to visit their living relatives. Flowers are gathered in profusion from the surrounding countryside and adorn homes and tombs alike. The rich take gifts of food and drink to be offered, meat and bread and beer set out on mats in front of the false doors of the tombs. The less affluent take what they can afford, often doing without, so that their dead relatives might feast on this one day of the year. The poor take nothing at all, having neither gifts nor tombs to visit. Instead, they offer up scraps of papyrus with messages on, or scrawl pictures of food and drink, taking them to the temples for the priests to offer on their behalf.

I did not understand this custom the first time I saw it but Smenkhkare explained the reasoning to me.

"The poor cannot afford a tomb or preparation of the body such as Ipuwer showed us. The dead body is taken out to the desert and left in a shallow sand grave with whatever meager possessions they can afford. The shifting sands hide the body or jackals dig them up. Either way, the relatives have nowhere to take their offerings so they offer them at the temple so the priests can make sure it gets to them."

"But it's only words or a picture. The dead can't eat that."

"Remember the dead do not eat actual solid food, any more than the gods do. They eat the spirit of the food. The priests say a picture of food, or words describing food are as tasty and pleasing as the real thing, to a dead person."

We Kemetu focus on the dead, often spending our lives preparing for our deaths. It is not so strange when one remembers that one lives for maybe fifty or sixty years if you survive childhood, but one is dead for eternity. As soon as we can, we start preparing our tombs. The rich organize rock tombs cut into the solid cliffs near the Western necropolis, bring in teams of masons to carve out rooms, painters and scribes to portray scenes from this life and the next, inscriptions to petition the gods and praise the owner of the tomb. As a princess, that would have been my fate, had my life turned out as I thought it would. When I was a young girl I thought that I would marry my brother Smenkhkare, become queen when he became king, live a long and satisfying life raising my children and ruling Kemet and at last be prepared by skilled embalmers like Ipuwer to spend my death being praised and having my children's children bring offerings to my grave. A full and satisfying life leading to a full and satisfying death. It is very important that one dies and is buried close to relatives, for unless one is properly embalmed, the spirit cannot return to the body, and unless the offerings are made, one cannot enjoy death.

Until I saw the body of the youth PenMa'at, son of Pepienhebsed, Controller of the King's Wharves, lying pale, shrunken and eviscerated on the cold granite slab in the House of Purification, I had never seen a dead body. It made it doubly strange for me in that I had seen

220

PenMa'at once before, though I doubt he saw me. No-body pays attention to a little girl. He was one of the pupils of the scribe Kensthoth and though I only spoke to the scribe once in my early life, I would sometimes see him from a distance with his pupils.

PenMa'at was my first dead body, but I have seen many more since. I have walked through plains strewn with the dead; bodies piled and cast about like a wheat field after a summer storm. I have sent my share and more to their own personal eternity, and I have spoken with the dead. Yes, I know: it is easy to speak to the dead, harder to get them to answer. Yet I have done this. He could tell me nothing of what lay beyond, but to be fair he had not long been dead, having still the wounds of his passing fresh upon his body. So I no longer fear death, having seen it in its myriad forms and knowing that every one of us must embrace it.

Lest you think that we Kemetu think only of death, let me hasten to add that while we live we strive to enjoy life to the fullest. It would be true to say that the average person does not think of death often. Perhaps it is because he cannot afford to prepare for eternity but while he has his health he eats, drinks, works, and raises a family that he might have sons about him in his old age, daughters to care for him. We love our families and re-joice in having children around our feet, infants dandled in our laps, toothless grandparents sitting gossiping in the sun by the front door, aunts and uncles visiting with their own families, sharing the goodness of life. I have seen families, rich and poor alike, in the many parks of the city, sitting on the grass or strolling among the flowering shrubs and exotic trees, their children screaming and laughing around them. Feast days and festivals bring out the joy that lies in all hearts. Kemetu love animals too. It is a rare home that does not boast at least one cat, for cats must be our favourite animal. Sacred to the goddess Bastet, these little animals are prized for their vermin-catching abilities and for their calming presence. Dogs are common too, though these tend to wander the streets in packs and sometimes become a public nuisance. The rich have more exotic pets. Some of the nobles display wild cats in cages, monkeys, gorgeously coloured parrots. In the palace grounds we enjoyed a menagerie that included leopards, ostriches, baboons, gazelles of various types and a wild striped horse from the southern lands. I doubt there is a single house in Kemet that does not have some sort of pet. I have seen beggar children nursing a twig on which swayed an insect that looked remarkably like the twig to which it clung. Others treasured a tortoise, a mouse or even a fly.

Of course, it is not always like that. Some families live more in a state of armed truce, much as the nations do. My own family was like this. Smenkhkare and I loved each other, as did my father Nebmaetre and mother Tiye, and there is no doubt that my brother Waenre Akhenaten loved his wife and family, at least at the beginning. But other members of my family displayed a darker side. Husband fought wife, brother fought and killed brother, daughters ousted mothers and uncles betrayed all. Perhaps it is the effect of great power and wealth. Having it, one desires more. There is not much love left over for pets in houses like mine. Akhenaten's children enjoyed baby gazelles, leopard cubs until their claws grew, or a lamb – and of course there were the ubiquitous cats, but though they played with these animals I never saw much love displayed toward them.

I was never given a pet, so I found my own. I adopted a scarab beetle, grasshoppers and butterflies, crickets and ants, but never caged them, preferring to watch them as they lived their lives unrestrained. In return, they taught me the lessons of creation, how to work unceasingly and how to lift up one's voice in song, to have a reverence for all life.

The gods give us life for a short time but leave it to us to decide how we live it. One day they will demand of us an accounting when our hearts are weighed against the feather of truth in the Halls of the Dead.

Chapter Fifteen

Ay, God's Father, brother and father to two queens, hurried along the long colonnade that led over the bridge spanning the Royal Road in Akhet-Aten. Arriving in the new capital city only a few short hours before, the news had come to his ears circumspectly, filtered through several layers of slaves and servants, finally whispered by a junior priest in the small Mansion of the Aten, next door to the King's Residence. Ay did not give much credence to the rumor – *how could he* – but even the thought of it brought a return of the heart flutterings that plagued him off and on. It brought, in turn, lightheadedness and a feeling of tiredness.

As soon as his duties as priest of Aten permitted, he hurried out the back of the temple to the small House of Life by the Records Office and consulted a physician. Unfortunately, his own consultant, Intef, was out on a call so he suffered the ministrations of another charlatan who plied him with a foul-tasting concoction and offered up a prayer by way of treatment. Ay cursed and left the House of Life, the flutterings having eased of their own accord as they so often did. Ay considered the rumor again, consciously fighting down the feeling of panic in his breast. He must see the king; he would know the truth of it.

The King's servants in the Residence were their usual unhelpful selves. Akhenaten reigned with a light hand and the palace servants knew exactly how far they could carry their disdain and contempt even for the highest in the land. He had seen behavior that under the old king would have brought an instant flogging for the first offence and death for the second. Yet Akhenaten merely smiled and ignored the veiled insults. Nor would he listen to complaints from the visiting lords and high officials. Only once had Ay seen justice meted out for such flagrant disrespect.

Ay smiled despite his worry, remembering the visit the previous month from Horemheb, General of the Eastern Borders. A servant had kept him waiting for no reason other than to demonstrate the power he held over all visitors to the King's Residence. Horemheb had said nothing, merely noting the man's name. After his audience, Horemheb had the man abducted by his own soldiers, flogged senseless and left on the palace doorstep with a papyrus note attached to his loincloth which read 'Learn Manners'. Naturally the man had complained to the king, but as with other complaints the king had done nothing. Unfortunately, manners had not been learned, though Ay suspected Horemheb would not be kept waiting next time.

Perhaps I should emulate the worthy General, Ay thought. He sighed, shaking his head. *Who would I get to do it? I have no soldiers at my command.*

And so he hurried over the bridge, past the Window of Appearance where the servants were cleaning and bringing in chairs and tables laden with food and drink. Through the Window itself, Ay could see crowds starting to throng the thoroughfare, gathering beneath the arches of the bridge.

In the West palace, he found an old scribe whom he recognized sitting on a stone bench in the gardens. "Nedes," he cried, thinking how men are sometimes given names that eventually mock them. This old graybeard could no longer be called 'young' but must forever be called that. "Have you seen the king? I must speak with him."

"I think he is in the Women's quarters, friend Ay," Nedes mumbled. "If you ask in the palace I am sure they will tell you."

"The servants tell me nothing these days. If ever there is a crisis, it will be over before the king hears of it." Ay turned to leave. "Do you know where in the Women's quarters?"

"He visits his daughters, I believe, so the North Harem."

Ay muttered his thanks and ran back into the palace, turning left along the long pillared portico that ran the length of the palace. He passed the South Harem, the normal abode of the queen, his daughter, when she was not with the king, nodding a greeting to the unsmiling Nubian guards. He reflected on the customs of other lands as he looked at the tough, virile guards. Some kings would have eunuchs guarding the women, but not in Kemet. Here, all women are regarded as untouchable unless they give their assent. And who, of the king's wives would dare give assent to anyone but the king?

He found the king with his daughters in the gardens of the North Harem, together with Queen Neferneferuaten Nefertiti and the nurses of the younger girls. The guards recognized him and let him into the sweet-scented gardens. The princesses, Meryetaten, Meketaten, Ankhesenpaaten, and the youngest, Neferneferouatentasherit were playing a game, running along the paths between the flowering shrubs and around the ornamental fish pond, under the watchful eyes of the nurses.

Ay greeted Akhenaten, bowing low with his hands held out in ritual supplication, then after a moment, performed a similar obeisance toward his own daughter.

"Rise, father," Akhenaten said with a fond smile. "The father of my beloved does not have to bow to me.

226

Come, sit beside us and drink, you are indeed welcome here."

Nefertiti came across, dressed in a diaphanous gown and drew her father upright. "Greetings, father, and welcome back to the city of Aten. I hope your journey was a pleasant one?" She examined his taut face with its wrinkled brow. "What concerns you, father?"

Akhenaten laughed and approaching his wife, put his arm around her, hugging her closely. He too was dressed in a filmy gown that looked more like a woman's dress than raiment more suited to a king. The thin fabric hid nothing and despite having seen it before, Ay found himself wondering at what trick of the gods had given the king such a body. Thin-chested and broad-hipped, his swollen thighs made the king waddle like a duck as he walked. It was hard to look at the man and see a god, the anointed ruler of the Two Lands.

Ay hid his thoughts and smiled disarmingly. "Why, daughter, nothing concerns me now that I am in the exalted presence of my beloved king."

"Then come and sit beside us, father, and enjoy the beauties of the Aten's creation." Nefertiti took her father's arm and drew him over to the fishpond, where they all sat on the raised stone lip of the pond and watched the antics of the children. "Something is troubling you, father. Tell us."

Ay shrugged, wondering how to broach the subject of the rumor. Instead, he prevaricated, talking of something else he had noticed on his journey down the river from Waset. "There has been an increase in crime, my lord. When we put in for the evening, we were set upon by brigands who quite openly rob and kill."

"You were unharmed, though, father?" Nefertiti looked concerned.

227

"The soldiers saw them off, killing several." Ay noticed the king's look of distaste, and hurried on. "Beloved king, I fear these are criminals who were released under your mercy."

In the months following his accession to the full throne of Kemet, Akhenaten had celebrated the love and beauty of his god by emptying the jails and the quarries of criminals and slaves. His view was that under the gentle influence of the Aten, all men would learn to live in peace and harmony. Predictably, the crime rate soared and there were areas of Kemet where one did not travel without an armed escort. The Medjay police did what they could but as penalties had been reduced at the same time, there was little incentive for hardened criminals to work for their bread and beer.

"There have always been those who do what is wrong, father. But as they learn to live in truth, so they will not want to live by hurting others." Akhenaten turned to his wife and took her hands in his. "Beloved, I think the people need to see more of us. Let us make a procession throughout the Two Lands so everyone can see how the Aten has blessed us. When they see our blessings they will embrace the Aten's truth more closely. Why, within a few months we may be able to disband the Medjay."

Nefertiti smiled and gazed admiringly at her husband. "Indeed, husband. We can take the girls too so that they may see this Kemet of ours."

"Then that is settled. Ay, you will make the arrangements. We will leave ... when is your moon blood, dearest?"

"In ten days time, beloved," Nefertiti said without embarrassment.

"Then we will leave in sixteen days, Ay."

228

Ay bowed his head. "It shall be as you wish, my lord."

A deep rumble issued from the king's copious belly and a twinge of pain crossed his countenance. He broke wind, and sniffed openly at the noxious odour. "I must empty my bowels," Akhenaten said. He stood and indicated the Harem. "Will you accompany me?"

Ay raised an eyebrow but said nothing as the three of them crossed the close-cropped lawn to the balconied colonnade of the Women's quarters. They entered through the wide columns and turned aside to the Chamber of the Bath.

"I have had this wonderful new device installed throughout the palace. I have two of them, the queen has one and this one was put in for my daughters three days ago." Akhenaten laughed. "Tell me, father," He waved his arms around the cool tiled floors and walls of the Bath Chamber with its sunken tubs and fountains. "We are in the room where the bowels are voided, but can you detect either the odour of the body's decay or the strong disguising scent of perfume?"

"Er, no, my lord." Ay looked around, not quite sure where the conversation was leading.

Akhenaten broke wind again, the sound reverberating in the large tiled room. A stench of excrement wafted over them. The king walked over to a raised ebony and ivory chair, inlaid with the figures of golden animals, in one corner. A raised channel lay on one side of the chair and a lowered one on the other. Akhenaten pointed at the seat. "See father, it is like any other Seat of Relief, save for this one thing, a small pool of water in the bottom."

Ay peered into the bowl and nodded. "I see it, my lord, but I do not comprehend its purpose."

229

Nefertiti laughed and clapped her hands with delight. "Show him, husband. I cannot wait to see his face."

Akhenaten swept his gown up and aside and sat down, positioning his buttocks over the hole in the chair. He concentrated and frowned, several small splashes following. He got up and peered into the bowl. "There, father. What do you see?"

Ignoring the smell, for in truth he had smelled worse, Ay peered in at the royal turds. He nodded wisely. "Good, my lord, firm but moist. As the physicians would say – 'Of superb consistency'. This indicates your bowels are healthy."

"Ah, but now comes the new thing." Akhenaten crossed to the wall and pulled on a flax cord. A small sluice gate rose where the higher channel met the tiled wall and a tiny flood of water gushed down the chute, swirled through the bowl and carried the excrement away down the lower channel where it disappeared into another opening in the wall. The king released the cord and the gate closed, shutting off the water.

"Remarkable." Ay examined the bowl, finding only a small pool of fresh water. "Where does the channel lead?"

"To a large pot in the next room," Nefertiti said. "Disebek the builder tells us he can run the channel completely out of the palace eventually, but it will mean digging up a lot of the flooring. He is going to get it done when we are next away."

"And the water source has to be filled by slaves," Akhenaten added, slapping the tiled wall with one hand. "No longer do we have to put up with the smell of defecation even for an instant. This is but one of the innovations Disebek and his assistants have come up with. Think of it, father Ay, for centuries our Kemet has done things simply because that was the way they were always done. Now, under the impetus and fire of the Aten, new things can be seen in the Two Kingdoms." Akhenaten started to pace about the room, throwing his arms about, his voice echoing off the walls of the Bath Chamber.

"Take art for instance. You have seen the new drawings and paintings that the court artists are creating? New colours, new styles, new ways of representing the world – all in truth, the truth that is Aten. The statues that they make of me, accurate and truthful, down to the last detail. I will not be represented as some stiff, lifeless king identical to every other, the body held just so, this leg forward, this arm raised. My artists have been instructed to show me as I am." Akhenaten stopped and waved his hands down his body from his head to his thighs. "My beautiful wife too, and my daughters. They are the most beautiful things in all of Aten's creation and I want the world to see her beauty and envy me. I have commissioned a huge pair of statues of the two of us, naked, that all may appreciate every beautiful part of her."

"Alas," Nefertiti said softly. "I am no longer the beauty I was as a young woman. Already my body fades."

"In truth, my wife, in Aten's truth, your breasts sag and your belly protrudes more than it once did. Wrinkles line your face in the mornings before your ladies have attended to you and your delightful bottom and thighs are also creased. The statue will show these things, but also in truth, I love you as much as I ever did."

Nefertiti frowned. "Truth may be carried too far," she muttered.

"Still, enough of this, let us go back out into the garden – unless you would like to use the device, father?"

"Er, no thank you, my lord." Ay joined the king and queen as they walked slowly back to the garden. They

231

stopped in one of the balconies and watched the young princesses at play. "My lord ..." He hesitated, and then tried again. "My lord. If Aten is truth, then how ..."

"If?" Akhenaten interrupted, all the good humor leaving his face.

"My apologies, son of Aten." Ay bowed, extending his hands in silent supplication once more. "I am overcome by the amazing sight I have just seen and I spoke without thinking. Forgive me."

Akhenaten waved a hand nonchalantly. "You are forgiven. What was it you meant to say?"

"Only that with Aten being the truth; how are we to interpret the release of criminals and the army cutbacks?"

The king frowned. "Explain yourself, Ay."

"Criminals do not live by the truth, my lord, yet they were convicted by the truth of witnesses and law. Yet they, who do not live by truth, are now released by truth." Ay essayed a smile. "In truth, my lord, I am confused."

Akhenaten frowned again. "I am the son of Aten, the son of truth. Do you think I have done wrong?"

"Of course not, great king, only ... perhaps there should be some division made between those capable of knowing the truth and desiring to follow it; and those who know the truth yet disregard it. There are a number of murderers out there that prey on your innocent subjects, my lord."

Akhenaten rounded on his wife. "And you, beloved. Tell me, have I done wrong by releasing these poor ones of the prisons?"

Nefertiti stroked her husband's arm gently and spoke softly. "You are king, my husband, ruler of the Two Lands, Lord of the Nine Bows, you can do no wrong. Your word is law; your word is the perceived truth. Our father in the heavens inspired you to an act of great mercy. Our father on earth is mistaken."

Akhenaten nodded. "You are wise, my beautiful wife, yet I do not want to leave my subjects groaning in the grasp of murderers and thieves."

"Then have your police round up and imprison any who have abused your leniency and the Aten's great mercy. Thus mercy will have been shown, yet justice will also be served."

The king pursed his lips. "I shall think on it. Your words are sensible yet subtle." He looked back at Ay. "You said something about the army? Do you accuse them of being murderers too?"

"On the contrary, my lord. Just the opposite. Kemet is and always has been beset by enemies, the Nine Enemies, other nations envious of the riches the gods ..." – Akhenaten's eyes narrowed – "... have bestowed on us. The kingdoms of Syria, Lebanon, Byblos, Gezer and Sidon have been a buffer, a shield against the depredations of the wild men, the Hittites, Amorites and Hyksos. Yet to defend these lands, our army needs men and gold. At the very least, faithful men like Ribaddi of Byblos need gold that they might defend themselves, and us, against the enemy."

"The Aten is a god of peace. By spreading the words of peace through the nations around us we shall achieve brotherhood and unity without the need for war and bloodshed. Nor will we need to find much gold for the armies and our allies."

Ay frowned. "My lord has seen the reports that come in almost daily from the frontiers?"

Akhenaten yawned. "These things bore me. There is always some general or governor of some little town prattling on about the troubles he has. And always want-

233

ing gold, ever more gold." He turned away and watched his daughters at play. A movement in the shrubbery caught his eye and the king extended a finger, laughing with delight as a bright green mantis, about the length of two finger joints ran up onto it and stood there swaying gently from side to side. Akhenaten lifted the insect aloft, positioning it in the bright sunshine as he examined it. "Look how it folds its arms to its body as it faces the sun, beloved wife. It too worships the Aten."

Nefertiti put her hand on her husband's wrist and pulled it down so she could see. "It is looking at me," she cried in delight.

"And no wonder, beloved wife, for it too appreciates your beauty." The king turned and called to his children. "Daughters, quickly, come and see this delight. An insect worships the Aten as we do."

Ay coughed gently. "My lord, it is imperative we discuss the army."

"Later, Ay. It will keep. See, daughters, how this insect has come to me to dance and pray to Aten."

The girls clustered round, wide-eyed, exclaiming at the wonder. "I have seen one of those before, father," Meketaten said. "They eat other insects. I saw one eating a grasshopper it caught." She poked a finger at it and the mantis unfurled delicate green and pink wings and took flight, whirring into the garden. With a scream, Neferneferouaten-tasherit raced after it, the other girls laughing and calling as they followed.

"My lord, I received a report from Horemheb, your general of the Eastern Borders, that incursions by Amorite raiders are assuming epidemic proportions. He says he must have more men and ... and more gold if he is to resist them." Ay saw growing anger in the king's face and gritted his teeth.

"There is no need to discuss this further. The reports are blown out of all proportion. I have other reports, from the high priest of Aten at Zarw for instance, that says soldiers are sitting around idly, drinking and causing mischief. I have decided to disband these units."

"My lord, I beg you to reconsider ..."

"Enough, Ay. You try my patience with your prattling. The generals and governors are exaggerating the problems to get more gold but I have better uses for it. Now, the matter is closed."

Faced with the king's anger, Ay could do little else but bow, hands extended once more, and keep silent.

Akhenaten and Nefertiti stood together, arms around each other, looking out on the tranquil garden and domestic bliss. The girls were, under the watchful eyes of the nurses, playing by the fish pond. Ankhesenpaaten stood knee-deep among the water lilies, bending and trying to catch the little silver fish that darted amongst the weed. The others danced around the edges, yelling encouragement and advice. Neferneferouaten-tasherit slipped and fell headlong into the pool, to emerge spluttering. A moment of stunned silence followed as the little girl tried to comprehend what had happened, before she erupted into howls of rage and embarrassment. The older girls laughed loudly and the nurses hurried over and gathered the little one into their bounteous arms, soothing her tears and drying her with their linen dresses.

A gong sounded softly behind Ay, from the cool depths of the Women's quarters. He turned and saw a slave slipping quietly back into the shadows, a bronze plate in one hand and a cloth-tipped stick in the other. A courtier stood in the doorway, his white linen robe immaculate, eyes painted and the hair on his head slick and reeking of unguents. He bowed low, his voice honeyed.

"O Great King, son of the Living Aten, the Window of Appearance is readied and awaits your royal pleasure."

Akhenaten turned with a look of anticipation. "Excellent. Go and prepare the way. I and my family will be there in a short while." He dismissed the courtier with a wave of his hand and called to his daughters to ready themselves.

The nurses gathered their charges and ran off into the Women's quarters, urging the princesses onward with a mixture of empty threats and small promises. The king and queen walked through into the empty halls of the palace harem, Ay bowing again as they passed.

Akhenaten stopped and regarded Ay's bent head. "It pains me to quarrel with you, father. Will you keep silent and follow me? Great things are about to happen in this Kemet and I would have you with me."

"I will, my lord," Ay murmured, falling in behind his daughter and son-in-law. The three of them slowly walked through the palace corridors and rooms, any whom they met bowing low and pressing themselves against the walls if they could not otherwise remove themselves from the royal presence. It was as if the myriad inhabitants of the palace were all elsewhere, leaving the king and queen to walk in solitary splendor. They turned left onto the long ramp leading onto the bridge and the Window of Appearance and it was here that the princesses joined them. The girls were no longer naked as they had been at play, but were robed in thin fine linen like that of their parents that concealed nothing. Meryetaten and Meketaten, as the eldest, wore richly braided wigs with gold intertwined. The younger girls still wore the side lock of hair on an otherwise shaven head, signifying their youth.

Together, and in silence, the royal family walked up the ramp into the broad chamber that lay behind the two Windows of Appearance that faced North and South over the Royal Road.

From the broad street below came a muted roar as if from a great wind storm, the street being crowded with people, peasants and shopkeepers, soldiers and slaves, tradesmen and nobles jostling together, staring up at the vacant Windows in vociferous anticipation.

A large table was set up in the middle of the wide room, out of sight of anyone standing in the street below. It was laden with fruits, roast meats, goose, fish and steaming breads. Jugs of river-cooled wines, beer, mead and water, together with beautifully inlaid faience cups waited to assuage the thirst. The young princesses uttered cries of delight and descended on the food and drink, grabbing figs and dates and rich honeyed loaves. Nefertiti moved to control their appetites while Akhenaten looked on affectionately.

"Ay, join us."

"Thank you, my lord." Ay took a ripe fig and bit into it, relishing the sweet and gritty texture.

"Come children," Akhenaten said. "It is time for the Appearance. Put down the food and let us show ourselves to the people. Afterward we can feast on the bounty provided by Aten." He moved with Nefertiti to the north window.

A roar went up from the crowd, laughing and cheering, the soldiers stamping their feet and clattering spears on shields.

The king waved and smiled, talking quietly so none but those close to him could hear. "You see, Ay? My people love me. Is this the reaction of people who be-

237

lieve I am too lenient or do not have the interests of our Kemet at heart?"

"No, my lord," Ay said. *But it is the reaction of those who have been paid to be here*, he thought. This was one of the rumors he had heard within minutes of arriving in Akhet-Aten this morning – that the king would announce something momentous from the Window of Appearance at noon and that all that came to listen would receive a deben of silver.

Akhenaten made quieting motions with his hands, waiting through the long minutes as the babble and roar of the crowd diminished by degrees until it finally fell away into a hush. High above, lost in the glare of the noonday sun, a solitary falcon cried out, and its piercing whistle sent a murmur of superstitious awe through the populace.

"People of Akhet-Aten," Akhenaten cried out into the silence, priests repeating his words below him on the lower tier of the bridge, and others in the street itself. "Let us give praise to the Living Aten from whom all good things flow." He paused for a moment, gathering himself, then launched into the Great Song of Praise to the Aten.

"O most wondrous and majestic god,
You appear most beautifully on the horizon of heaven,
O Living Aten, the originator and beginning of life!
When you rise on the eastern horizon,
You fill every land under the heavens with your beauty.
You are gracious, great, glistening, and high over every land;

Your rays encompass the lands to the
limit of all that you have made:
As you are Re-Harakhte manifest,
you reach to the end of every land;
You subdue them for your beloved
son..."

Ay groaned inwardly as the sonorous chanting went
on and on. *He is going to sing the whole thing.* He stepped
back and edged sideways behind the king and queen toward the table, filching another fig. Only
Ankhesenpaaten saw him, one slim finger up her nostril
as she looked around, bored already.

"The Two Lands rejoice in you every
day, O Living Aten,
Awake and standing upon their feet,
the people rejoice,
For You have raised them up.
They wash their bodies, they take up
their clothing,
They raise their arms in praise at your
appearance every morning ..."

Having sung the hymn many times himself in the
morning devotions, Ay knew he was in for a long wait –
and this before the king got onto whatever was the point
of his message. He bit into the fig and wondered what it
was that the king wanted to announce. *Surely it couldn't be
... no, not even this fanatic king would be that foolish.*

"O sole god, only god, before you
there is no other!

Behold, there is one god, the Aten,
and one son, his servant Akhenaten.
You created the world according to
your desire,
While you were alone: All men, cattle,
and wild beasts ..."

Ay snapped out of his reverie, his head swiveling to the king standing in the window, his wife and daughters next to him. The bright sunlight pouring through the broad window rendered the fine linen of their robes completely transparent.

Did he just say...? He knew the words of the Hymn varied, depending on the occasion and who sang it. In fact, it made his life a lot easier. The songs of praise to the other gods had to be sung perfectly. A line, a phrase, even a word wrong and the whole thing had to be sung again. He remembered a time when, as a young man, he listened to a priest sing the same praise song to Amun over twenty times before he got it right. The old king, Nebmaetre Amenhotep, had been furious at being made to stand for hours in the hot sun, banishing the priest to one of the border outposts. How much easier were the rites to the Aten. A word wrong, even whole sentences, and nobody minded, least of all the sun god. He still rose every day, whether or not the priests got his rituals right.

The hymn of praise wound down to its conclusion, praising the king and queen as the only direct beneficiaries of the Aten's love.

"... Since you created the earth and all
that is in it
And exalted them for your only son,
Who came forth from your body:

240

the King of Upper and Lower Kemet,
Neferneferure Waenre Akhenaten,
And the Chief Wife of the King,
Neferneferuaten Nefertiti,
living and youthful forever and ever."

The king's voice died away, followed a few moments later by the more distant voices of the priests. Akhenaten lowered his arms and cheering broke out from the crowd once again. He let the tumult continue; obviously basking in the love and praise of his subjects, then raised his arms once more, waiting for the noise to die away before speaking again.

"People of Akhet-Aten, City of the Living Aten, it has long been a sorrow to me that the other gods of this Kemet are remembered and praised in people's names. I have sought to change this where I could, altering my own name from Amenhotep which exalted the false god Amun ..."

False god? Ay's eyes widened. *Lesser god I can understand, but false god?*

"... To my new name of Akhenaten, the servant of Aten. I was sorrowful that this obvious step was unappreciated and that no-one else sought to change their names to exalt the only true god, whether as his sublime manifestation as the Aten, or his lesser ones as Re-Harakte. However, the Aten has illuminated the minds of my subjects and I can now introduce to you ..."

The king turned and gestured, beckoning forward two men who stood in the shadows, behind the press of servants and courtiers. The Grand Tjaty Ptahmose and General Horemheb stepped forward and joined their king in the Window of Appearance.

241

Horemheb glanced at Ay as he passed; his eyes hooded and unreadable while Ptahmose tottered on old legs, a bemused expression on his face.

"... The man who has been my faithful servant, and the servant of my illustrious father on earth, my Tjaty Ptahmose – who will henceforth be known as Ramose." Akhenaten embraced the old man and, after a brief hesitation, kissed him on his spittle-flecked lips. A servant stepped forward with a copper-bound box and the king lifted a heavy gold chain from it, fastening it about the neck of Ramose.

"Behold. I reward my faithful servant Ramose with a golden chain of praise, a weight of one hundred deben of gold."

The old man bowed then tottered backward out of sight of the crowd. General Horemheb stepped forward, tall and powerful, his great bronzed chest gleaming against the white of his formal kilt. Gold armbands and an enameled pectoral caught the sunlight, and Ay could hear murmurs of appreciation drifting up from women in the street below.

"I present also my General of the Eastern Borders, known to you as Horemheb. He is promoted to General of All the Armies of Kemet and will henceforth be known as Paatenemheb." Akhenaten took another great chain of gold from the box and reaching up, hung it about the general's neck. "I award him too, a golden chain of praise, one hundred deben of gold."

Paatenemheb bowed low, the gold chain swinging, and stepped back from the window. He glanced at Ay again, a tiny smile of amusement twitching at his full lips. The king called to Ay, beckoning to him.

"I heap praise upon Ay, son of Yuya, father to my beloved wife Nefertiti and in truth, God's Father. I award

242

him the position of Court Chamberlain and Fan-bearer on the King's right hand. Furthermore, he is named Deputy Tjaty and Overseer of the King's Horses." Akhenaten pulled out another gold chain and hung it about his father-in-law's neck. "Fifty deben of gold." He leaned forward and kissed Ay full on the lips, whispering, "Will you not change your name too, father?"

"I ... I must give it some thought, my lord. I would wish for the perfect name to reflect my faith."

Akhenaten smiled and turned back to the open window. "Then go and think on it. You are dismissed." He raised his arms again and waited for the hush. "Others among the court and nobility of Akhet-Aten have changed their names to honour their living god. To each of these I award ten deben of finest gold." He started to recite a long list of names.

Ay caught Horemheb's eye – *Paatenemheb*, he amended. "You knew about this?"

The general drew Ay to one side, out of earshot of the servants and courtiers. "Of course. Didn't you?" He looked quizzically at Ay. "No, I see you did not."

"Changing your name? I would not have thought you would stoop to deny Heru like that. And for the man who refuses to strengthen the armies."

Paatenemheb shrugged. "I have been made General of All Armies and," he flipped his massive chain of praise. "I have some gold at least. Plus I have the king's favour and the king's ear. I think I will achieve more now than as a mere general of the East. As for the name, well, I can live as well under this name as any other and Heru is an understanding god."

"And have you heard the rumors?"

"What rumors? Rumors abound like mice after the harvest."

Ay hesitated and glanced about the broad room before edging closer to the general. "Rumors of an announcement," he murmured. "Rumors concerning the gods."

"Only that Kemet now lives under the supreme god Aten and other gods are in a lower position."

"Only lower? Not ... not forbidden?"

Paatenemheb stared at Ay. "Are you mad?" he whispered. "Gods are gods. One may worship whom one wills but one does not deny their existence."

"Then I pray it is just rumor."

A burst of applause and cheering interrupted them. Akhenaten and Nefertiti stood in the balcony of the Window of Appearance, their daughters beside them, waving to the crowd once more. "See beloved," the king exclaimed. "Truly my people love me."

"How could they not, husband?" Nefertiti smiled up at her love. "Extend your bounty, gracious king, as we talked about earlier."

Akhenaten nodded and spread his arms again for silence. When the roar fell to an acceptable level he spoke again. "Good people, the Living Aten shines down upon all men and women, showering blessings and life. To give honour to my father in the heavens, I will give a deben of gold to any man, saving of course slaves, who will change his name to honour the Aten." Cheering erupted again from the street below, with much stamping of feet and clattering of spears on shields.

"One thing more, good people of Akhet-Aten. It has long been in my mind that the priests of every god live well in their temples and their houses, feasting upon every good thing offered up in honour of the gods, sucking the poor and the needy of the very sustenance that the Aten provides. Well, no more."

Akhenaten's words sank like a smooth stone into a still pond, the ripples of interest in his words dying away before even the priests of Aten had repeated his words. A sea of faces looked up at their god-king standing above them.

"The Living Aten provides every good thing that men need and enjoy. He gives us the sunshine, the days, our beautiful river and black soil, the food we eat and the very breath within our lungs comes from our heavenly father. What need have we of other gods when we have Aten? From this instant, the old gods which you worshiped before the truth of Aten was revealed stand exposed as worthless. The public worship of any god other than the Living Aten is forbidden, though I will still allow their names to be known in inscriptions."

The silence from the street below was almost tangible. Even the stridulation of insects in the gardens of the city faltered as if aghast at this pronouncement. Paatenemheb caught Ay's eye. He mouthed 'You knew?' Ay shook his head vigorously, his face pale.

"Only the false god Amun do I except from this edict," went on Akhenaten. "Too long have the priests of Amun gathered power and wealth in their god's name. Too long has Kemet suffered under the tyranny of this false god. The public worship of all gods except Aten ceases this day, and the wealth of the temples becomes that of the Aten. Public inscriptions of the old gods will remain as their lack of power will highlight the beauty that is Aten. Only Amun do I except from this. The wealth of the temples of this false god is forfeit utterly. The temples will be cast down, the images of the god broken up and his name is to be removed from every temple, building, tomb and monument throughout the land. Amun is no more."

The silence grew. Akhenaten turned to Nefertiti with a puzzled frown. "Why are they silent?"

Nefertiti looked down into the street. "I do not know, husband. Perhaps they are amazed at your wonderful vision of the future. Maybe ..."

A groan started somewhere in the crowd where the peasants stood in grimy loincloths, their weather-beaten faces pale and vacant-looking. The sound of lamentation swelled and a voice called out, cutting through the grief.

"Give us back our gods."

At once the cry was taken up, the crowd chanting the words in unison, clapping and shouting, an edge of panic and horror creeping into their voices.

"Give us back our gods."

The minor nobles out there in the crowd, their slaves around them holding parasols and fans above them, started pushing back, moving away from the source of the disturbance. The motion increased as the common people jostled the nobles, upsetting a litter. An attendant slave pushed a free man and was beaten to the ground. Other slaves were set upon and the crowd roared its rage and anguish. A woman fell to her knees, struck from behind and her screams fueled the frenzy.

"We want our gods."

Akhenaten stared at the scene below him, panic and anger wrestling for control of his face. He turned to Paatenemheb. "General, control this crowd. Send in your soldiers."

Paatenemheb strode to the Window and took in the riot below him. He nodded and whirled, running toward the ramp into the King's residence. A few minutes later he emerged onto the street in command of two Tens of his soldiers. He shouted a command and the men formed up in ranks, shields high and spears leveled. The crowd drew back, the chanting faltering as they stared at the armed men.

"Disperse," Paatenemheb bellowed, the gold of his chain of praise bouncing and gleaming on his brown chest. "On the King's orders, disperse now."

The crowd, outnumbering the soldiers a hundred to one, swayed and drew back. Around the edges, men and women eased away from their fellows before scurrying for the safety of the side streets and the public gardens. The off-duty soldiers in the crowd formed up into rough ranks but milled about uncertainly, wondering whether to join the general's men or just to slip off before anyone in authority recognized them.

"Disperse," Paatenemheb said again. "Men, forward one pace."

The threat of the sharp spears sent the front lines of the crowd reeling back and the mass of people shivered as if breaking up. Then a stone hurtled out of the back and thumped against the shield of one of the soldiers.

"Give us back our gods." More stones appeared, showering the soldiers. One fell with blood streaming from his head. Paatenemheb dragged him back and took his spear, taking his place in the line.

"Steady," he growled. Another shower of stones clattered on shields and the crowd surged forward. "Ten paces," Paatenemheb shouted. "Charge."

The soldiers gave a blood-curdling yell and leapt forward. The eighth pace carried them into the front ranks of the crowd, the shields slamming into bodies and heads, the spears slashing forward, stabbing deep and pulling free in a welter of blood. On the tenth pace the soldiers stopped dead, the crowd reeling back in a panic, leaving their dead and dying in the dusty street.

"Disperse."

This time the crowd obeyed, pulling back, then as the space between the motionless soldiers and the people increased, turning tail and running. Within minutes, the street was deserted except for the bodies of the dead and wounded.

Paatenemheb led his soldiers off the street and back into the King's residence at a trot, leaving the physicians to save those they could.

Akhenaten stared down at the empty street with tears in his eyes. Beside him, the younger girls clung to their mother, sobbing. The older girls, Meryetaten and Meketaten looked down at the casualties with great interest. The king sighed and put his arms out to gather his family to himself. He turned them away from the Window of Appearance and led them back toward the Harem and the Queen's residence.

A few minutes later, Paatenemheb walked into the broad room, rubbing blood stains off his hands with a clean napkin. He threw it at the feet of a servant and strode over to the table, ripping himself off a handful of roast goose.

"You are hurt?" Ay asked.

Paatenemheb shook his head, chewing his food noisily. "Not mine. Those are good soldiers," he added. "Disciplined. They should be rewarded."

Ay nodded. "I will see to it." He motioned the servants away and moved over to the table, pouring a cup of beer. "Has the king taken leave of his senses?"

"It would appear he has, but the king is still the king."

"He cannot destroy Amun, he is a god."

"If he is a god then he cannot be destroyed. If he is only something the priests have dreamed up to gain power, then ..." Paatenemheb shrugged. "I am just a soldier; I obey the orders of my king."

248

"You do not believe in the gods?"

"I don't know. I have never seen one." He ate the last bit of goose and poured himself a cup of beer, swallowing it in three gulps. "Ay, you should be careful what you say. These are delicate times and strong opinions either way could land you in trouble."

"And what of the old king, Nebmaetre Amenhotep? This action of his son has just robbed him of his name and his power."

"I don't think that will be a problem much longer."

Ay raised his eyebrows. "Why not?"

Paatenemheb smiled. "You have just come up from Waset. You tell me."

"The old king is dying? He was well when I left."

"A messenger arrived last night. Overland by horse. No doubt he overtook you on the river. Amenhotep has been struck by the gods again. He is lying senseless in his bed and the physicians have been summoned to open his head. It is not expected he will survive long." The general shrugged. "He may already be dead."

Chapter Sixteen

Waset lay silent and subdued in the heat, like a wounded lion panting under the African sun. The city itself showed signs of neglect – no pennants flew from the palace, no smoke from the sacred fires spiraled heavenward with offerings of incense for the gods, and the streets lay littered and unkempt, the docks crowded with goods from all parts of the crumbling empire. The people carried on their normal lives as best they could, if only because few could afford not to, but there was little enthusiasm shown. Only the elderly could remember the last time a king had crossed the river and none could even imagine a time when the gods had been rendered so powerless.

King Nebmaetre Amenhotep lay in the House of Death. For forty days he had lain in the natron, giving back the water of his body to the land, relinquishing the yellow fat built up over a lifetime of good living. Now he was back in the temple of his namesake god, titular god of his House, his organs dried and placed in costly alabaster jars, his body cavities packed full of rich and expensive spices, his eyeballs shrunken and sunken behind brittle eyelids, turned back in his head as if in contemplation of the resins and incense that filled his cranium. His limbs were swaddled in fine linen, wrapped and bound with interspersed printed prayers and invocations to the gods, amulets and fine jewels, gold leaf, beaten silver and copper, each layer fixed in place with resins and naphtha.

The Uadjat amulet was placed above the right eye, the Ursh, or 'amulet of the pillow' placed under the neck, the Usekh collar fixed in place and the Ab, made of hard green schist placed over the heart, ensuring that this vital organ would remain with the soul in the inner life. The Djed pillar, made of finest carnelian and gilded, was dipped in the juice of ankhamu or rose flowers and placed above the stomach, in line with the vertebral column. The priests of the House of Death continued the wrapping, chanting the prayers and blessing the amulets as each protective emblem was placed in its designated position. The four sons of Heru, then the Thet, Uadj, Shuti, Shen and Sa followed, each piece carved of durable mineral or fashioned from glowing gold. Finally the Ahat, a round gold disc, was placed beneath the head. It was inscribed with the four sacred names that preserve the body's heat and its power would cause flames to burst forth from the king's head in the shadow world, granting him entry to any portal.

The body rested now, arms crossed over his chest, bandaged hands clutching the crook and flail, symbols of royalty. A golden mask, sculptured and painted, in formal Nemes headdress, the two guardians of the royal crown prominent, covered the smoothed and rounded featureless face of the body. Nekhebet, the vulture, shaded the royal head with outstretched wings, and Wadjet, the cobra reared as if to strike any that would disturb the king's rest.

Amenhotep lay in the House of Death, adjunct of the temple of Amun, despite the edict issued by his son Akhenaten two days after the old king's death. Although the young king had ordered the temples closed and the name of Amun to be removed from the sight of men, no-one had yet dared to enforce his command. Akhenaten stayed in his city of Akhet-Aten, and the priests of Amun refused to give way to a man who they openly called heretical and cursed by the gods.

Between the two opposing forces that threatened to rip Kemet asunder, the old king lay awaiting his burial, perhaps dreaming of happier times. No-one doubted his Ka had already passed through the trials and tribulations of the underworld and was at one with the gods. His heart had been weighed against the feather of truth and found to be lighter, for Amenhotep had been a good king, an upright and honest man, a god in whom even the lowliest peasant could trust. If he could be faulted for any one thing, it was for leaving his beloved Kemet in the grip of his only son.

Seventy days Amenhotep lay dreaming in the House of Death and now it was time for his burial. His body, wrapped and preserved for eternity, encased in golden coffins in the likeness of the king, was transported across the river to the West bank where it lay for a day in the grand funerary temple. The rock tomb lay waiting in the dry Valley across the river where all the kings of the Two Lands spent eternity. Since the king died, the tomb, on which work had started nearly forty years before when Amenhotep succeeded his father Tuthmosis, had been the site of intense activity. It was cleaned thoroughly, every trace of rock dust and rubble removed, the paintings touched up so every colour gleamed as if new, the soot on the ceilings from years of smoking torches scrubbed off, the tomb furnishings sorted and dusted, arranged for occupancy. Hundreds of Ushabtiu dolls, models of every servant the king could possibly need in the afterlife, were blessed and imbued with life by the priests and placed where the king could call on them when Ka and Ba were reunited. Tables were laid out for the funerary food and drink that the relatives would consume, though the food and drink itself: rich wines, roast meats, baked breads, freshly fermented barley beer and delicious fruits, still lay in the palace kitchens, waiting to be transported across the river in the royal barge, together with the foods that would accompany the dead king in his voyage through eternity. All was in readiness. Only the king was missing, the new king, the successor, the 'one-who-opens-the-mouth'.

On the seventieth day, king Akhenaten and his queen Nefertiti arrived on the royal barge from Akhet-Aten. Despite being the dead king's only living son, saving the young princes Smenkhkare and Tutankhaten, Akhenaten had stayed away from Waset during the period of Preparation, leaving all the details to the care of his mother Tiye and uncle Ay. Now he arrived in the somber city in the late afternoon, the cliffs of the Western desolation already casting long shadows across the river.

On the royal wharf, a delegation of white-garbed priests met the royal party, representatives of all the gods, the priests of Amun prominent among them, their wealth and position openly flaunted. Akhenaten's eyes opened wide at the sight, then his fists clenched on the railing of the barge and his eyes glittered in rage. He strode down the gangplank onto the wharf and confronted Ay.

"What are they doing here?" he growled. "I gave orders that the worship of all gods was to cease and their priests disbanded. The false god Amun was to be destroyed and his wealth confiscated. I pronounced this two months ago. Why are the priests here now, mocking me?"

"They do not mock you, golden one," Ay replied, bowing low. "It is just that your illustrious father Amenhotep must be buried with all the rites attendant on his position as God-on-earth, and who else can perform these rites except the priests? In your absence, your holy mother and I took it upon ourselves to rule on this."

253

Akhenaten ground his teeth and glared at the company of priests. Amenemhet, the First Prophet of Amun caught his eye and bowed with a small smile on his face. The king turned away and strode across to the waiting litters with Nefertiti and climbed inside, drawing the curtains. Slaves rushed them up to the palace.

The king and queen emerged just after sunset and walked down to the wharf, attended by Ay and Tiye, together with all the immediate members of the royal family. Smenkhkare, his side-lock of youth newly shaved off, walked in quiet dignity behind the adults, Scarab followed, together with Iset, daughter and wife of the late king, and a nurse carrying the toddler Tutankhaten. Notable by their absence were the daughters of Akhenaten and Nefertiti. On being asked, Nefertiti had explained.

"They are too young and I do not wish them to be tainted by the presence of the old, false gods."

The royal party boarded the barge and they cast off, teams of slaves rowing them swiftly across the river in the gathering darkness to where a blaze of red-gold torches burned in the City of the Dead. The body of the dead king was brought out from the funerary temple built by and dedicated to Nebmaetre, a team of slaves manhandling the heavy gilded sarcophagus onto the funerary sledge. Oxen pulled it away over the sands and loose rubble into the Valley of Kings, the mourners following behind. Jackals shattered the silence as they entered the valley, their eerie cries calling to Inpu, the jackal-headed god of death. They passed the entrance to the main valley where so many kings of the Two Lands lay dreaming in death and made for the lonelier Western Valley where the old king had his tomb waiting.

Priests of Amun, wearing the ceremonial white robes and specially prepared papyrus sandals, leopard-skin capes draped over their shoulders, carried pottery lamps, twisted flax fibers dipped in a reservoir of fine oil casting a reddish flickering light over the procession. Akhenaten followed, his features cast in mixed expressions of sorrow and anger, Nefertiti on his arm and the grieving widow Tiye by his side. Ay came next, walking alongside and supporting the ancient Tjaty Ramose, then Smenkhkare, and lastly the lesser women of the family, Iset, Scarab and the nurse Abar, with Tutankhaten in her arms. Behind them, not part of the procession but present to perform necessary manual tasks, walked dozens of strong slaves. A military escort surrounded them, Paatenemheb leading, though he commanded out of respect for Amenhotep rather than necessity. Paramessu accompanied him, watching the royal family in fascination. The two officers had brought down an honour guard from the Northern Legions, trusting their own men above the doubtful abilities of the local Amun Legion.

Far above them, on the crumbling cliffs surrounding the burial grounds, other eyes watched the funeral procession. Several groups of shadowy figures watched with great interest the proceedings unfurling below, their hearts beating fast at the thought of all the gold and jewels that lay buried in the open tomb. For now, they would watch and wait, but in the nights that lay ahead, when the first fervor of the guards wore off, they too would pay a visit to the sealed tomb of king Amenhotep, breaking down the doors so they could stare at the sarcophagus, wonder at the treasures buried with him and plunder his belongings as a fee for their trouble.

The procession arrived at the tomb. Amidst the wasteland of rock and rubble, stone steps descended into the valley floor. From the chambers beneath, a rich golden light flooded out, bathing the surrounding landscape and casting deep shadows. Paatenemheb's soldiers spread out to guard the king's resting place while the slaves hauled the ponderous gold sarcophagus off the sledge and down the wide stone steps into the First Corridor. The priests of Amun followed, Amenemhet, Aanen and Bakt, then Akhenaten and Nefertiti and the rest of the royal family. The nurse Abar handed the young prince Tutankhaten to Iset and waited outside. Scarab, before descending into the tomb, looked up at the night sky and saw from the stars that the steps led due east toward the rising sun. The stairs led into a corridor that sloped steeply downward and Scarab held her brother's hand tightly as she shuffled down the incline. More steps followed then another sloping corridor and more steps into the well chamber. Small and square, the chamber floor receded into black depths. Sturdy wooden beams bridged the gap between the entrance corridor and the next chamber. Scarab crossed the beams quickly, though the wood was obviously strong enough to bear the ponderous weight of the gold sarcophagus that preceded them. The funeral party entered a broad, brightly-lit chamber, the roof of which was supported by two broad rock pillars.

The body of Amenhotep was removed from the golden sarcophagus and propped up at the far end of the room. The lifeless gold mask of the king stared out at the splendors of his last palace. Queen Tiye, wife of the dead king, knelt before the standing mummy and offered up the ritual lamentations, taking cold gray wood ash from a small jar and strewing them liberally over her hair and face, whitening her brown arms. Her keen of grief was the only sound in the tomb.

Akhenaten stared at the wall paintings, grief and anger battling for possession of his features. "This will be the last burial involving the old gods," he stated flatly, to no-one in particular. "In deference to my father, I allow this to happen, but from here onward only the Aten will be pictured on tomb walls."

The now empty sarcophagus and the attendant priests made the slow journey deeper into the tomb. Scarab released Smenkhkare's hand and looked around the room, avoiding looking at the dead king and his grieving queen. She was fascinated by the glorious paintings on the walls and ceilings. An image of Amenhotep, leading ranks of priests, led the prayers to the sun, Re-Herakte and Aten, as images of the sun god in his golden boat sailed above them. Stars and images of lesser gods crowded the walls and ceiling. Along one side was a trestle table covered with fine linen and bearing dishes laden with the funerary feast. Pictures of everyday life formed a backdrop to the feast: bread-making, brewing of beer, the feeding and slaughtering of animals and hunting scenes where wild fowl, desert gazelles and lions fell beneath the bow in the king's hand. Toward the back of the room, near the doorway to the next room, stood the great Ka statue, a full-sized likeness of Nebmaetre Amenhotep, stern-faced and regal, the double crowns of Kemet, Deshret the Red and Hedjet the White on its head. In its outstretched hands the Ka statue held the symbols of kingship, Heka the Crook and Nekheka the Flail. Scarab jumped when she first saw the staring eyes of the Ka statue and, wide-eyed, crept closer to her brother Smenkhkare again and slipped a hand into his.

At the end of the chamber, niches were oriented crossways, being the 'Sanctuaries in which the Neteru of the East and West repose'. They held figures representing the inner life spirits and the walls were covered in texts from the Book of the Dead, serving to guide the deceased through the intricacies of the afterlife. It was also the point through which the Ka would come back to the tomb to eat and drink, and to return to the spirit world afterward.

Smenkhkare motioned to Scarab to stay where she was and approached Akhenaten. He whispered to the king, receiving a nod of agreement. Returning to his sister's side he said "Come," and led her past the niches into the third descending corridor. "Akhenaten said I could take you through to see the rest of the tomb."

Scarab glanced back over her shoulder at the gathering in the first chamber. "They won't leave us here, will they?"

"Don't be silly. Now, pay attention." He pointed at two life-size statues standing on either side of the room. "Those are the 'Two Doorkeepers'. They symbolize the soul's entry to divine life and its return to earth. See the walls?" Smenkhkare pointed out the lavish paintings of every sort of manufacturing process: metal working, bead making, carpentry, weaving, and glass blowing. He tapped the painting of the glass blower. "Who does that remind you of?"

"Ahhotep," Scarab cried.

"*Shh*! Loud voices disturb the harmony of the spirits. In these deep niches here are funerary goods, everything the king could possibly need. A portion of his treasury lies in the room off the first chamber, as much gold as he will need in eternity. More lies in the treasury rooms next to the burial chamber, his House of Gold. We can't see in there as the doors will already be bricked up and sealed. Costly woods, ivory, jewels, silver and bronze, even an iron dagger worth more than gold is in there – Ay told me. In another one there are urns filled with salted meats, jars of wine and beer, baskets of fine bread, fruit and vegetables. The king must have everything in abundance."

Scarab looked dubious. "A room full of food is a lot, I suppose, but it still wouldn't last long. I mean, if it is to feed the king for eternity ..."

Smenkhkare chuckled. "The spirits do not eat solid food. Remember how the young priest Pa-Siamen told us about the feeding of the god Amun each day? A feast is set out for him to eat, but after he has had his fill, the food appears untouched. It is because the god feeds on the spirit of the food, not its body. In the same way our father Amenhotep will feast on the spirit of this food for eternity. That is why they have made sure there is everything he liked here. All those sweet things he liked, but no toothache to deny him pleasure." They reached the end of the descending corridor and walked down several steps into another smaller chamber.

"Since we left the first chamber, we've been going north," Smenkhkare commented.

"Why? I thought tombs were supposed to be straight."

"Normally, yes, but the builders hit shattered rock so they bent the tomb to follow the fine-grained limestone."

Smenkhkare pointed at the opposite sides of the chamber. "Look at the walls Scarab, and learn. Everything in our beloved Kemet is paired, especially in this chamber of the Two Doorkeepers. Kemet is made up of Two Lands, Ta Mehu and Ta Shemau, better known as Kemet, the Black Land and Deshret, the Red Land – Delta and Valley, Papyrus and Lotus, Bee and Sedge plant, Cobra and Vulture, Gold and Silver, Sun and Moon – the list is endless. Remember this, little sister. Our lives are in two parts."

259

The young prince led his sister through into the next chamber, the burial chamber. A broad room needing the support of six stone pillars, its long axis was oriented to the east again. Lamps containing the purest, nearly smokeless oil, burned throughout the chamber, lighting for the last time the wonderful paintings adorning the walls. A star-studded sky covered the chamber, with the goddess Nut – the Neter of cosmic birth – overhead, her arms and feet touching the floor at opposite ends. Scenes on the walls showed the dead king overcoming all carnal aspects of life in his quest of the spiritual realm. Around the walls, Amenhotep pursued lions from his royal chariot, harpooned hippopotamus from a boat, dealt the deathblow to ranks of stylized enemies kneeling before him.

Smenkhkare leaned against a wall just inside the entrance. Motioning his sister to join him, they watched the bustle of activity in the chamber of the 'House of Gold'. The room was crowded, with slaves wrestling the nested golden coffins into a beautifully polished rose quartz sarcophagus. The sarcophagus itself lay in a trench carved into the floor of the chamber, and at its foot lay another excavation in which the priests of Amun carefully positioned the carved alabaster jars containing the dead king's dried organs. The lid of the great box hung suspended on ropes above it, the timbers of the scaffolding groaning under the great weight. The priests of Amun moved slowly around the chamber as the labours of the slaves permitted, making sure that every inscription on the walls, every carving in the lustrous gold of the shrine walls was exactly right. Amenemhet, as First Prophet, chanted prayers of protection over the great golden caskets in their pink stone sarcophagus. Aanen and Bakt uttered the responses, scattering pure water and powdered incense at intervals.

Smenkhkare pointed toward several small doorways that led off the burial chamber. "The treasure storehouses," he whispered. "He's even got his favourite chariot in one of them, and furniture in another." Squeezing Scarab's hand he jerked his head back toward the entrance. "Come on. It must be nearly time for the funeral feast." They moved back toward the entrance chamber with Amenemhet and Aanen accompanying them. Bakt stayed to oversee the slaves as they finished up preparations in the House of Gold.

Akhenaten glared at the priests of Amun as they reentered the First Chamber but remained silent, allowing them to continue the rites unhindered. The other members of the funeral party stayed quiet too, watching and waiting, though Iset was occupied keeping the young Tutankhaten quiet. Amenemhet started the ceremony of 'Opening the Mouth'. The High Priest stood in front of the Ka statue, ignoring the mummified body of the king, and washed the statue with purified water. Lustrations of oil followed, while Aanen chanted the sacred phrases in a low voice. The ceremony dragged on and the watchers, despite the importance of the ritual, felt their senses reel in the incense-laden air.

Amenemhet stood aside and handed a forked instrument of rose quartz to Akhenaten. He took the instrument, the Pesheskef, and held it to the lips of the Ka statue, uttering the ancient prayers in a low voice, then handed it to Aanen. The Hem-Netjer then handed the king an adze made of sky iron – 'that which falls from heaven', the Seb Ur scepter, which was tapped against the lips of the statue, again with the utterance of complex phrases. Lastly the Ur Hekau scepter was passed and held to the statue's cold lips, Akhenaten leaning close and whispering the prayers before the ceremony was complete. The watchers relaxed and the tension eased.

Scarab tugged on her brother's arm. "Why are the statue's lips opened and not the king's," she asked, looking at the mummy propped in the opposite wall.

"Because the Ka will return from the underworld and inhabit the Ka statue," Smenkhkare whispered. "Only the Ba lives in the body itself, but the Ka must be able to eat and drink. The Opening of the Mouth enables it to do so."

The funeral feast started. Now that the dead king's mouth had been opened, he could join his family in the last meal they would enjoy together. For several minutes the sounds of eating and drinking dominated the room, though conversation was kept to a minimum. At a signal from Ay, the remains of the meal were gathered into flax baskets and stacked against the wall. The linen tablecloth was folded and the table taken apart and leaned against the wall.

Bakt came through with the slaves and supervised them as they lifted the mummy and carefully carried it through the descending corridor to the House of Gold. The family followed, spreading out into the burial chamber. The priests of Amun advanced toward the great rose quartz sarcophagus in its carved pit in the floor, with Akhenaten, Ay and Tiye following close behind. At a nod from her brother, Scarab and Smenkhkare eased around the other family members and watched the proceedings from behind one of the pillars.

Laying the mummy in the chamber in front of the sarcophagus, the slaves drew back to allow Queen Tiye a last farewell of her husband of nearly forty years. She knelt by the perfumed and spiced mummy and murmured fond endearments, remembering some of their happy times together. Lifting the golden face plate with a little difficulty as the resins clung to it; she gently kissed the bandages above the dead lips of her husband. She replaced the golden mask and rocked back on her heels, holding out her arms in supplication. Her voice shook and tears streamed down her ash-covered face.

"Wait for me, beloved Amenhotep, in Sekhet Hetepet, the Field of Peace; and Sekhet Iaru, the Field of Reeds; the land where all good things are enjoyed by those the gods love, for all eternity."

The slaves lowered the mummy into the nested gold coffins, replacing and securing each lid in turn. Grasping the ropes firmly, they slowly lowered the great rose quartz lid onto the sarcophagus. It chunked into place and with a chorus of grunts and groans, the ropes were eased out and the lid ground into position. The ropes were coiled and stacked to one side and the slaves slowly started disassembling the wooden framework of the scaffolding, stacking the timber neatly to one side. A golden shrine which had lain against one wall was erected around the sarcophagus. One by one the doors of the shrines were lifted into place, the bronze pins were hammered into position and the full glory of the carvings on the surface of the gold doors became apparent. Great winged goddesses knelt at the corners, holding hands, their wings outspread and covering the king's body. Scenes from his life lay between the outstretched wings, of Tiye kneeling at Amenhotep's feet, of his sons and daughters, of his hunting and fowling exploits. Inscriptions and prayers covered the rest, imploring the gods to receive king Amenhotep into the afterlife.

The priests of Amun tied the doors closed with the sacred linen cords, washed them with holy water and fastened them with the sacred knots. The slaves filed out past the royal watchers and disappeared toward the entrance, accompanied by the Third Prophet Bakt. Amenemhet and Aanen tidied the crowded chamber, placing other sacred objects around the gilded tomb of their king, items he would need symbolically for his journeys in the afterlife, or ones that held special meaning for him.

Here were placed small cedar wood chests, bound with gold and copper, inlaid with lapis and malachite, containing the mummified bodies of two dogs and a cat, favourite pets of the late king. Bouquets of flowers lay on the floor, love offerings from a widowed queen, an old favourite pair of sandals, a fly whisk trimmed with ostrich feathers, the handle of ivory bound with gold wire, and a ceremonial bow and arrows. Magic bricks were placed at the four corners, each specially fashioned with inscriptions designed to guide the king's soul and afford it protection.

Bakt returned with masons, each of the slaves carrying a wicker basket heaped with bricks. Ay, Tiye and Akhenaten left the tomb as the masons set about bricking up the doorway to the burial chamber. Smenkhkare pulled Scarab to one side and held a finger to his lips. The children watched in silence as the masons worked, mixing the mortar, fitting the bricks in place as the wall slowly rose. Just before the last few blocks were set in place, Scarab could see the top of the golden shrine gleaming in the light of the torches left burning in the House of Gold. The light flickered and died as the last brick scraped into place. A layer of mortar was spread over the wall and the seals of Amun and the mortuary temples were carefully set in place, officially sealing the tomb.

Everyone moved back to the next chamber and the process started again, the slaves moving back and forth, fetching more bricks and mortar. One by one the rooms were sealed off, the official imprints bearing testimony that all was carried out in accordance with tradition and decency. The beams across the well were removed and dropped into the pit, the well now becoming a dangerous obstacle for anyone daring to desecrate the tomb. Finally the last wall was finished, the last seal set in place and the priests ascended the stone steps to the cool desert air. Scarab looked up at the star-studded heavens in some surprise. Already the first faint glow of dawn stained the sky over the rocky wall of the Western Valley and Akhenaten and Nefertiti stood facing the place where their god Aten would rise, arms uplifted in greeting. The priests spared them a quick, contemptuous glance and directed the filling in of the stepped entranceway with rubble.

As soon as the entrance to the tomb had been filled and the traces of the night's activities swept away, the priests and masons departed with the slaves and the soldiers formed up around the royal party, preparing to escort them back to the barge and the palace. A small detachment of soldiers moved off into the cover of a timber shelter where they would guard the tomb. Akhenaten murmured something to Nefertiti, then called Paatenemheb and Ay over to him.

"Send the others back to the barge, Paatenemheb. You and I need to have a talk."

Paramessu gave the orders and the troop of soldiers marched away in the first rays of the new day, matching their speed to the slow pace of the old Queen. Akhenaten watched them go then turned angrily on Ay.

265

"I gave orders that all priests of all gods were banned, especially those of the false god Amun, over two months ago. Why was I disobeyed?"

Ay bowed low, extending his arms at knee level in submission. "My lord Akhenaten, the orders were given, but in light of your commands after ... after the bloodshed at Akhet-Aten, I did not dare enforce it."

"I am not pleased, Ay. You are my Deputy Tjaty and a high priest of Aten. Can you not see that this situation is displeasing to me?"

"Yes, my lord. But what would you have me do? I tell the priests their temples are closed but I have not the means to carry your edict out. I tell the people the old gods are finished and that the Aten now rules over all." Ay shrugged. "They listen politely then go back to the temples which are still open."

"Give me free rein and I will enforce your edict, my king," Paatenemheb growled. "A few broken heads will convince them."

"I will not have the blood of my people spilled. You were overly zealous in Akhet-Aten. I will not have that happen here in Waset."

"Then with respect, my lord, how do you expect me to enforce your commands? If I cannot use force, the priests will just ignore me and the populace will hold me and my soldiers in contempt."

"It is true, my lord," Ay added. "People respect strength."

Akhenaten turned away, facing the east and the rising sun. "You will close the temples, Paatenemheb. You will restrain the priests, arresting them if necessary, and you will issue my edicts to the people on every street corner. My priests of Aten will explain to the people why I do this. There will be no blood shed in the streets of Waset."

"And if there is? I can command my soldiers and they will obey, but what if they are attacked? Will you allow them to defend themselves?"

"I repeat; no blood is to be shed. The Aten is a god of harmony and peace. Now go and do as your king commands."

"At least let me wait until tonight, my lord. Under cover of darkness ..."

"No. The Aten is a god of the day. All things I do in the Aten's name will be done in the light of day and in the sight of men. Carry out my orders, General. Cleanse Waset of the false god Amun."

Paatenemheb bowed and strode off at a military pace, Akhenaten and Ay following more slowly. Ahead of them, across the wide expanse of the Great River, lay ancient Waset, City of Amun, a black and brooding silhouette against the brilliant light of the rising Aten.

Chapter Seventeen

Paatenemheb arrived back in the city while it was still early morning. He found Paramessu waiting for him on the royal wharf when the barge docked. Akhenaten also disembarked and gathered his family about him, hurrying up to the palace without a backward glance at his general or his father-in-law. Paramessu looked at Paatenemheb's stony expression with a certain amount of curiosity.

"What happened? What did he want to see you about?"

"He wants me to cleanse the city of false worship. We are to remove the priests, close the temples and prohibit the worship of any gods but the Aten – and all without violence."

"By Set's hairy balls!"

"I do hope you are not referring to our king," Ay put in mildly.

"We need a plan of action and we need it fast, Paramessu. We don't have our own legions so we are taking over the city troops. You are promoted to command of the Blue company of the Amun legion – their General Psenamy won't have the stomach for this. Djedhor and Khui will take over the command of the Red and Black companies too; we are going to need a lot of strength for this, and I want officers I can trust in charge. Meet me at the barracks in an hour."

"What do you want me to do?" Ay asked.

Paatenemheb scratched his armpit and stared at the old man. "You want to be part of this? Why?"

Ay shrugged. "Akhenaten is our anointed king for all his fanatical stupidity. If I can help avert civil war, I will consider my duty done."

Paatenemheb nodded. "Very well. Find the priests Amenemhet and Aanen. Bring them to the barracks if you have to bind them and drag them behind a chariot. One hour." He strode off leaving Paramessu and Ay to do his bidding.

It took longer than an hour to find and persuade the priests of Amun to accompany him to the central barracks. Ay and the priests walked in through the main gate to a desultory challenge from the guard on duty. He passed them in with a nod of his head and a wave in the general direction of the large stone building of the officer's quarters. They crossed the courtyard, viewing the activities of the soldiers with interest. The open area was huge, and acted as a parade ground and exercise and training yard as well. Pairs of soldiers fought with wooden swords or spears under the close supervision of an officer; archers filled straw effigies with arrows and other soldiers wrestled in the dust. Paramessu was waiting at the main portico of the officer's area and conducted them up the broad steps to an upper room. Guards at the doorway saluted Paramessu and opened the cedar doors, letting them into the cool room beyond.

Paatenemheb stood at a broad table covered with rolled sheets of papyrus. He and two other gray-headed men were bent over a large detailed map of Waset and the surrounding countryside, pointing and murmuring. He looked up as the doors opened and rolled the map up quickly, coming around the table toward the priests.

"My lords First and Second Prophets," he said smoothly. "I am honoured that you could attend upon me. Lord Ay has told you the reason?"

Amenemhet shook his head, glancing at the other military commanders quickly before focusing on Paaten-

269

emheb. "Only that it was a matter of quieting unrest in the city."

"Good. I would like to explain this myself. You will take wine? Or beer perhaps?"

Amenemhet considered. "You understand that drinking with you does not imply acquiescence to your schemes?"

Paatenemheb smiled and inclined his head.

"Then I will take wine." The high priest crossed to a group of cushioned divans by the window overlooking the training courtyard and sat down, arranging his robes. Aanen and Ay followed, the former sitting alongside his fellow priest, Ay sitting to one side. He chewed on a finger nail and kept glancing around the room.

Paramessu served wine to the priests and Ay and a big pot of beer to his general. He and the other two commanders remained standing by the table as Paatenemheb sat down opposite the priests.

Amenemhet lifted his goblet of wine. "May the blessings of Amun be upon you," he said softly, watching the old general's eyes.

Paatenemheb stared at the priest for a long time then grudgingly nodded and drank. "Why are the temples still open? King Akhenaten gave the orders that they be closed two months ago."

"That is what this is about?" Amenemhet sipped his wine. "I serve the god, not your king in this."

"He is your king too. Have you forgotten you crowned and consecrated him yourself – and swore a holy oath of loyalty?"

"My predecessor anointed a king called Amenhotep and later, when I succeeded him in the service of the god, I swore my oath to him. We buried him last night."

Paatenemheb held his face impassive, staring at the high priest. "And of his son, Akhenaten?"

"He has turned from the gods of his fathers. Why should the gods honour him?" Amenemhet drained his wine and put down his goblet, standing up. "And why should I? The temples will not close, general, not on the orders of a heretical king."

"Sit down!" The general glared up at the priest before continuing in a gentler voice. "Please, Amenemhet, sit down. We have much to talk about and, I assure you, you will benefit from our discussions."

Amenemhet remained standing, Aanen too as he had risen to his feet a moment later. After a minute they sat down again. "Very well. Say what it is you want."

Paatenemheb smiled and signaled to Paramessu to re-fill the goblets. He drank from his beer pot again and smacked his lips with enjoyment. "I prefer beer to wine, it is much more refreshing." He pointed across at the men standing by the table. "May I introduce to you, in order of seniority, Djedhor, commander of the Red company, Khui, commander of the Black company and Paramessu, commander of the Blue company, all temporarily within the Amun Legion of Waset. This is Amenemhet, First Prophet and Hem-Netjer of Amun, and Aanen, Second Prophet of Amun. Ay you know already."

The commanders bowed and received polite nods of acknowledgement from the priests. Paatenemheb got up and walked over to the window where he stared down at the soldiers exercising. "This morning, Akhenaten gave me orders to enforce his edicts. I intend to carry those orders out. At noon, the Black company will move through Waset and close down the principal temples, barring and sealing the doors. The Red company will maintain order in the streets and I, with the Blue company will take possession of the temples of Amun. The doors will close and will not re-open."

Aanen leapt to his feet in consternation. "You cannot carry out this sacrilege, general."

Amenemhet sat quietly, putting out a hand to restrain his fellow priest. "The people will resist you, general, as will the priests and the gods themselves. The streets of Waset will flow red before the temples close, no matter what the Heretic King demands."

"It will happen," Ay said softly. "Make no mistake, Amenemhet, the king is adamant and will not be swayed. He insists the Aten will be the only god in Kemet."

"You were once a priest of Amun yourself," Amenemhet sneered. "How quickly you turn on your god. And you, Horemheb – for I would not honour you by your changed name. Have you renounced Heru your god for this lesser manifestation of Re?"

"Enough," Paatenemheb growled. "I am telling you what will happen because I believe you want peace as much as I do. You will tell the priests at the temple not to resist my soldiers and you will quiet the people if they start to cause trouble."

"And if I do not?"

"Then it will be on your head."

Amenemhet got to his feet, Aanen joining him a moment later. "So the heretic desires a blood sacrifice to his god, does he? Well, if he so wishes, he shall have it." The priests strode to the door and walked out.

Paramessu turned to his general in the silence that followed the departure of the priests. "What are your orders, sir?"

"Djedhor, Khui, you have your orders already. You know what to do. But staves only, gentlemen, no weapons. I would not object to a few cracked heads but my orders are no killing. Paramessu, the same goes for the Blue company. You will come with me to the main temple complex." He turned to Ay where he sat worriedly playing with the hem of his robe. "Go to Akhenaten. Tell him his orders are being carried out at noon and plead with him not to tie my hands in this. Tell him there will be bloody violence unless he gives me leave to act with force. Tell him I have but three companies, under strength, of a single legion. Bring me word of his answer."

By the time Paatenemheb and Paramessu met up with Djedhor in the courtyard below, the troops of the Red and Blue companies were forming up on opposite sides of the training ground. Most were armed with solid wooden staves or cudgels, though the rest were knocking the bronze points off spears under the supervision of the junior officers. The general positioned himself in the middle of the open area between the legions and addressed the troops.

"Listen up you dogs of Set. We are here to do a job, an unpleasant job, but one given us by the king himself. I expect every man to do his duty without question and without hesitation. The Black company has the duty of closing the temples of all gods throughout the city and by now they will have started. You men of the Red will move through the city in groups of ten under your Leaders and maintain the peace. That is your sole duty. If citizens start to gather, you will disperse them. If they fight you, you have my permission to crack a few heads, but there is to be no killing. Understand that, you mangy dogs. If any man kills a citizen I will have him flogged senseless." Paatenemheb moved closer to Paramessu and the Blue company and lowered his voice. "You men will be tackling the hardest task. We move on the temples of

Amun to close and bar their doors. This is where I expect the most opposition and it is precisely for this reason I need the most disciplined troops. Don't betray my faith in you."

The general stepped back and waved his arms. "Red and Blue companies – move out. Commanders, you have your orders, obey them." He raced to the front of the Blue company and, with Paramessu, led them out the gate into the broad military road, southward toward the Amun temples. The Red company, under Djedhor and his officers, exited also, splitting up into smaller groups, dispersing through the city. The curious crowds lining the streets near the barracks ran for cover, cowed by the massed might of the legion.

The running troops of the Blue company attracted notice as they pounded into the Avenue of Rams, heading toward the massive temple gates. People started pouring from the side streets, running alongside and behind the troops, staring at them in silence as they ran. More moved north from beyond the temple precincts, forming up in a wide semicircle around the gates. As they drew close to the crowd, many armed with spears, knives, cudgels and farm implements, Paatenemheb barked an order and the front ranks of the legion lowered their staves into a solid wall and drove into and through the encircling crowd.

The silence of the citizens shattered into screams and cries of rage, the people falling back. A barrage of stones and bits of wood rained down on the soldiers but they continued through and into the temple precinct. Paramessu at once had a hundred men turn and face outward, blocking the temple gates, while the others, in groups of a hundred or more, fanned out to invade the temples and the maze of other buildings.

"Stop!" Amenemhet appeared on the steps of the main temple, in full ceremonial regalia, the other Prophets of Amun with him. Lesser priests in their white robes flooded out from the temple, covering the wide columned verandahs and broad steps. "Men of Kemet," he cried. "Would you fight against the gods?"

A groan of superstitious awe went up from the soldiers, several of them falling to their knees as the god himself, life-sized and adorned in fine clean linen, clutching the emblems of power, ram-headed and wearing the sun disk and double-plumed headdress, swayed out of the gloom of the temple. Several priests, clutching the poles of the great ceremonial boat, staggered under the weight of the god but still brought him down the wide steps and onto the paved courtyard. There they set him down in full view of the milling Blue company and the steadily growing crowd massing out on the Avenue of the Rams.

"Children of Waset," Amenemhet called out, his voice carrying easily to the front ranks of the crowd. "Children of the City of Amun, will you allow your god to be taken from you by the supporters of the Heretic King? Come to the defence of your god. Rise up and protect his person that his blessings may continue to flow." The priest strode forward toward the gates, raising his arms high.

"Silence him," Paatenemheb growled. "Quickly."

Paramessu grabbed a Leader of Ten standing nearby and pointed at the High Priest. "Take him, Wadj, bring him to me."

The man started forward with a yell, screaming for his men to follow him. They pushed through to Amenemhet and struck at him with their staves, knocking him to the ground.

275

"Not that way," Paramessu yelled. He cursed and raced forward, shouldering soldiers and priests aside, knocking Wadj and one of his men down. Another stood over the fallen priest his staff raised. Paramessu grabbed the wood, preventing the blow from falling.

He dropped to his knees and cradled the priest's head, pressing a cloth to the man's bleeding scalp. Amenemhet stared up unfocused at Paramessu.

"You ... you will not take him," he said, slurring his words.

Paramessu dragged the priest back and put him in the care of one of the army doctors, then ran back to Paatenemheb's side.

"That was a fornicating mess," the general growled. "If you can't control your men better than that ..."

A roar erupted from the Avenue of Rams and the crowd surged forward. Staves rose and fell and screams of pain joined the chorus of anger. The line of soldiers buckled and broke, falling back in disarray as the mob streamed into the temple courtyard, pouring round on both sides of the square ceremonial lake.

"Fall back," Paramessu bellowed. "Form defensive ranks."

The soldiers rushed to form up around their commanders, the mob hard on their heels. They formed a ragged line, staves at the ready as the angry citizens seethed and shouted a few paces from the line. A man rushed out of the crowd, a cudgel held high in one fist, an incoherent cry on his lips. He was met with a spear butt to his midriff and a staff cracked down on his skull, splitting his scalp and laying him full stretch on the ground.

"Easy," Paramessu called. "Defence only. We are not here to hurt anyone."

Paatenemheb made two soldiers kneel on all fours and he clambered onto their backs straddle-legged, holding onto Paramessu's shoulder for support. He looked out over the heads of his soldiers and scanned the temple precincts. Another group of soldiers was surrounded near the temple steps and, shading his eyes against the noon-day glare, he could make out Meny, newly promoted 'Greatest of Fifty', talking to members of the mob around them. Closer at hand, the priests were arrayed around the great statue of Amun, chanting and praying. Many of the crowd of citizens also knelt in prayer, though others milled around shouting, working themselves up into a frenzy.

"Citizens of Waset, hear me," Paatenemheb called. "Disperse. Go home. You have no business here."

A chorus of replies erupted from the crowd.

"Yes, we have."

"Go home yourself." Laughter followed.

"You shall not take our god." Someone shouted out the god's name and it was repeated, over and over, the volume swelling as the mob used the name to work up their courage.

"People, think, I beg you," called Paatenemheb. "I am ordered by King Akhenaten himself to do this. Do not oppose the king or it will not go well with you."

The roar of Amun's name increased, drowning out the general's voice. The crowd was growing by the minute, pouring in from the city as the news spread. Already the soldiers were outnumbered and the odds were growing.

Paatenemheb clambered down and pulled Paramessu to one side, whispering in his ear. "This is not good. We cannot enforce the king's orders unless we get back to

277

the barracks and arm ourselves. Prepare the men; we are going to have to break out."

"That could be suicide, sir. The crowd won't let us go – and they are better armed than us."

"So what do you suggest?" Paatenemheb snarled. "Wait here to be butchered?" As if to punctuate his question, a stone sailed into the packed square of soldiers, striking one on the arm.

Paramessu's eyes fell on the High Priest, still under the care of the army doctor. "I have an idea, sir." He ran across to Amenemhet and gripped his robe, hauling him unceremoniously to his feet.

"Amenemhet, you have been found guilty by a military court of fomenting riot and rebellion against your king. You are hereby sentenced to death by strangulation. Do you have anything to say before sentence is carried out?"

The High Priest paled and stepped back, flapping his hands ineffectually at the soldier's grasp. "You cannot," he gasped. "I ... I am Hem-Netjer of Amun, I am above military law."

"Under normal circumstances I would agree, but you have stirred up riot against your king's direct orders. For that, you die."

"The Heretic is a man of peace. He would not condemn me."

Paramessu smiled grimly. "Probably not, but you'll be dead by the time he finds out."

Amenemhet licked his lips, his eyes darting from Paramessu to the soldiers around him. "The crowd will kill you if you touch me."

"Very likely, but they will probably kill us anyway. It would give me personal satisfaction to kill you first."

Paramessu shifted his grip to the priest's neck and squeezed.

Amenemhet uttered a strangled shriek and fell to his knees, dragging Paramessu down with him. "Please, Paramessu, be merciful," he gasped out. "Take me to the king, let him judge me. I will do whatever you ask."

Paramessu maintained his pressure, watching the priest's face slowly darken, the man's hands scrabbling at his own, then abruptly let go. Amenemhet fell to the ground, whooping for air, but Paramessu hauled him to his feet again. "Talk to the crowd, priest of Amun. Convince them to let us through or you will still die."

"Why should I? You will kill me anyway."

"No. You have my word on it. You will accompany us to the barracks but then you will be free to go."

Amenemhet stared at the commander's face then glanced at the impassive hooded eyes of Paatenemheb. Abruptly he nodded. "I will do what I can."

"Do more," Paramessu said grimly. He pushed the priest through to the front rank of the soldiers, maintaining an iron grip on the man's shoulder.

Amenemhet raised his arms and gradually the mob fell silent, the men in the front ranks quieting the ones behind. "Citizens of Waset, faithful followers of the great god Amun ..." Paramessu squeezed his shoulder hard, making the priest wince. "This is not fitting behavior for the temple precincts."

"They want to take our gods from us," a man called out angrily.

"But they have not, and cannot. I ask you not to let blood be spilled in the temple. Let the soldiers depart in peace."

"Blood has already been spilled," yelled another man. "I saw a man cut down in front of me and many more are injured."

"Then let the king mete out justice, for I know that he gave specific orders that none were to be hurt. Do not compound this folly, good citizens. You have shown the king by your actions that your faith in the gods is strong. Surely he will now relent and allow his people freedom of worship?"

The front ranks of the crowd grumbled, wavering in their resolve. Then a man called from the back somewhere. "We cannot trust the king and his Aten."

"Tell them the king will keep his word if he swears on his god. The king will be made to listen." Paramessu shook the High Priest. "Tell them."

"The commander ..."

"Not me, you fool. It comes from you."

Amenemhet swallowed and cleared his throat, starting again. "I will make sure the king hears of your concerns. He will listen to me and rescind this senseless order. If he swears by his Aten, he will keep his word." He raised his voice and called out above the muttering crowd. "Aanen. Can you hear me? Priests of Amun. Answer me."

"I hear you, First Prophet." Aanen's voice, clear and resonant, carried over the hubbub. "What would you have us do? Clear away these sacrilegious soldiers?"

"No, Aanen. You will clear a path through this rab ... through these good people. The soldiers are to go free." Silence. "Aanen, do you hear me?"

"I hear you, First Prophet. It shall be done as you request."

A disturbance started at the back of the mass of people, white-robed priests pushing through and linking

280

arms to form a corridor through the sullen-faced people. Aanen came striding down the empty space to confront his High Priest and the soldiers. His eyes flicked over the rumpled, dust-smeared robes, the bloody-bandages and the bruises forming on Amenemhet's neck. His eyes narrowed in anger.

"Who has dared to do this to you, Hem-Netjer? He will feel the wrath of Amun."

"Peace, brother," Amenemhet muttered. He glanced over his shoulder at Paramessu. "Are you ready to leave?"

Paramessu nodded. "Blue company, form up in five ranks, smartly now. Follow me." He pushed Amenemhet forward and stepped out into the open, General Paaten-emheb one step behind. Aanen reluctantly stepped aside and the column of soldiers moved through the crowd, a thin film of priests guiding them, leading them, flanking them, and linking arms behind the last of them. Other groups of soldiers joined them as they moved steadily toward the temple gates.

Aanen stopped at the entrance to the Avenue of Rams. "My priests do not go beyond this point. Release Amenemhet."

Paramessu looked around at his column, the lightly armed soldiers crowding close, eyeing the mob warily. There were hundreds more people out in the streets and more gathering. "Amenemhet comes with us until we reach the barracks."

"No." Aanen waved the priests back and they melted into the crowd, which pressed closer, a muted rumble issuing from thousands of throats. "You want bloodshed, soldier? You shall have it."

Paramessu slipped a dagger from his belt and pressed the point up under the High Priest's chin, the sharp point pricking the soft skin. "Then your First Prophet will be the first to die."

"Do nothing precipitate, Aanen," Amenemhet grated, wincing as the movement of speaking sent the knife deeper into his neck. "I will accompany them to the barracks. See that we are not followed."

Aanen scowled but obeyed, stepping aside and allowing the soldiers past. Paramessu, Paatenemheb and Amenemhet led the way at a trot, the soldiers crowding behind, their staves at the ready. Despite the priest's instructions, the crowd ran alongside, keeping pace as they passed down the Avenue of Rams, back into the depths of the city.

"I will remember your deeds this day, Paramessu," Amenemhet panted as he wiped the blood from his throat.

Paramessu smiled grimly, his hand firmly on the priest's arm, hurrying him along. "Then remember too that I refrained from killing you. I hate neither you Amenemhet, nor your god. I am a soldier; I am sworn to obey my king."

The column moved deeper into the city where the signs of violence became more common. They saw the first dead soldiers, their heads beaten in, some by their own bloody staves which lay beside them. The red stripe on their brown military kilt revealed their company colours and Paatenemheb shook his head angrily.

"Someone will pay for this."

Amenemhet laughed. "The Heretic? He is to blame."

Paramessu turned his head as they ran, sizing up the mood of the accompanying crowd. "Do we stop for the bodies, sir? It might be possible."

"Leave them. Our first duty is to preserve the legion and report to the king. We will retrieve them later."

They turned into Military Road, within sight of the barracks, small groups of soldiers with red stripes on their kilts running in ones and two ahead of them. A mob burst out of one of the side streets just behind a group of five soldiers, rapidly running them down and clubbing them to the ground. The crowd caught sight of the hundreds of soldiers bearing down on them, flanked by another mob and, after a moment's hesitation, gripped their weapons and hurled themselves forward, screaming with rage.

Paramessu yelled to his troops to form a defensive square. He pushed the priest behind him and caught a glancing blow on his shoulder from a piece of wood. He stumbled and almost fell as an evil-smelling fellow sprawled on top of him. Struggling to his knees he plunged his dagger into the man and heaved the shuddering body to one side, grabbing the man's staff as he lurched to his feet. The mob pressed the soldiers but their training was taking effect. They fell back into rough lines, their staves swinging and probing, forcing the howling citizens back. Already the ground was littered with bodies, most trying to drag themselves clear of the melee but others lying ominously still.

"Move toward the barracks."

Slowly, the body of soldiers, some four hundred strong, heaved and shuffled toward the barrack gates. Staves slashed and stabbed and ordinary citizens, trying to avoid the hard wood, or desperately parrying the strokes with whatever came to hand – furniture, pieces of wood, the occasional spear – nevertheless fell howling to the dusty ground or staggered back holding wounds. Soldiers fell too, increasingly, and their comrades hauled them inside the disintegrating square.

Paramessu saw the press of the crowd was getting the better of his poorly armed men. He leant his staff in the crook of his arm and cupped his hands. "Spear formation, Blues. On me, form." For a few moments nothing happened as the incredulous men tried to grasp what their commander wanted.

Paatenemheb put a hand on his arm. "What in Set's arsehole are you doing? This isn't a chariot regiment."

"And they're not professional troops out there. They just outnumber us." Paramessu shook off the general's arm as the square fell apart, the men closest to him trying to get into a semblance of a spearhead, never having performed the maneuver, only having seen it from a distance. He pointed his staff at the most belligerent part of the crowd. "Charge!" he yelled. "Come on you dogs!" Leaping forward with a bellow of rage and desperation, Paramessu launched himself at the mob. A breath later, four hundred men followed, smashing into the crowd, hacking and slashing with spear handles and staves, trampling men and women under foot.

Fifty, sixty, seventy paces, blood spattered Paramessu as he swung his staff, then suddenly the pressure eased and the people were running, streaming away from Military Road and the City barracks, away from these madmen with the killing rage in their eyes. Ten paces more and a space opened up in front of him. Paramessu halted, breathing in great whooping gusts. "Halt," he cried. "Halt you motherless sons of donkeys."

The onrushing tide of screaming soldiers faltered and drifted, clutching bruised and bleeding bodies but with triumphant grins starting to form. Cries of victory rose into the air.

"Back," Paramessu commanded. "Back to the barracks, men."

284

The soldiers streamed back inside the compound without further incident. About a hundred of the Red company had already returned and more were coming in by dribs and drabs, running the gauntlet of the streets, but so far, none of the Black company. Paatenemheb set a troop to man the gates and keep a look out for returning soldiers before ordering the rest to the army physicians and to prepare food. He told Paramessu to bring the High Priest then marched ahead into the upper room.

The general poured himself a pot of warm beer from the jug on the table and drained it, spilling rivulets down his broad chest. He belched and turned, regarding the two men standing in front of him.

"Unorthodox, Paramessu, but it worked." He dismissed the matter with a wave of his hand and addressed the priest.

"Amenemhet, I am going to talk to Akhenaten and I assure you he will give me permission to arm my soldiers. When we return to the temple we will close it and destroy the god – if we find him." He stared at the priest impassively. "I have no wish to commit sacrilege, and of course I cannot do so if I cannot find him. I would imagine I'll be leading my troops back to look for him in about three hours. Do you understand?"

The High Priest nodded slowly. "This heresy will pass and Amun will remember those who helped him." He glared at Paramessu. "And those who fought against him."

"Don't be a fool, Amenemhet. This man saved your life today." Paatenemheb shrugged. "He was a bit direct and zealous but I encourage my officers to think for themselves. Now, I should by rights hold you here until you can answer charges of inciting riot and blasphemy against the Aten and his son, but with one thing and another, you seem to have slipped off in the confusion." He turned away and poured himself another beer, waiting until the priest had gone before turning back.

"Sir, was that wise? He could be dangerous."

"Extremely dangerous, Paramessu, but this Atenism will not last forever. Sooner or later the old order will return and it pays to have friends on both sides of the fence. Now, what are we going to do?"

"What can we do? We need the king's permission to arm our men before we can try again."

"Of course, and I shall see to that myself. I think I can slip into the palace unseen. What will you do to prepare?"

Paramessu thought. "Medical first – get the injuries seen to – then food. After that, open the armory and get everybody fitted out for hunting lion."

Paatenemheb nodded. "If the streets quiet down, you might see if you can find any more of the Red and Black companies. We are going to need them."

The general left through a small door at the back of the barracks building commonly used by slaves when they emptied the latrines. The passageway and alley stank from spilled effluent but the same stink discouraged onlookers. He disappeared in the direction of the docks.

Paramessu opened up the store rooms and got the army physicians tending the wounded. Only a handful had sustained serious injury but many held soothing compresses to bruised and split skin before the supplies of ointments and herbs ran out. The kitchen staff organized huge pots of barley gruel and beer and soon lines of men formed up in front of them before moving off into whatever shade they could find to consume their meal.

Men from the Red and Black companies straggled in as the afternoon wore on. Djedhor arrived early on, with a hundred men and an hour later Khui turned up with nearly two hundred soldiers in kilts with black stripes. Paramessu ordered the men fed and tended, then took the commanders upstairs to talk.

"That was a fornicating pig's meal," Khui spat. "We closed down half a dozen smaller temples, Ptah, Sekmet, Tefnut and such, put the seals on the doors, and then the crowds started turning up. It was all we could do to extricate ourselves without too much bloodshed."

"Where are the rest of your men?" Paramessu asked.

"The gods only know," Khui sighed. "And yes, I say gods because this Aten of the king is certainly not going to help us. I thought there might be trouble so I sent them off in groups under my Greatest of Fifties. I hope they had the sense not to push the issue when the mobs turned up."

"And you Djedhor?"

Djedhor drank deep from his flask of wine before answering. "My orders were to send men out in tens to every street corner, so my men were spread out too thinly to be effective when the trouble started. I tell you, I won't be making that mistake again, orders or no. I lost men out there today, good men, some of them."

"What happened?"

"Pig-shit! You know what happened. We got jumped on and beaten by fornicating peasants and shopkeepers. Luckily I saw what was happening and started rounding up my men, running through the streets ahead of the mob collecting stray soldiers. With luck there will be others in soon, those that haven't run off." Djedhor poured another flask of strong wine and gulped it. "I'll flog those fornicators for desertion."

287

"Paatenemheb is up at the palace getting permission to arm ourselves and do this properly."

"Not before time," Khui said, looking out of the window. "Look there in the city." The other commanders joined him and saw the spiraling columns of black smoke starting up above the roof tops.

"Why is it every time there is trouble, these stupid fornicators set fire to their own city?" Djedhor raged. "Well, I'll be sorting out a few arsonists before the day is out. Hang 'em all from the walls, I say."

Paatenemheb returned an hour later, by the same route he had left by. His first action on arriving back was to wash thoroughly and change his kilt. He refused to speak until he broke his fast, helping himself to a large bowl of barley gruel from the kitchens and a huge pot of sour beer. Having eaten, he took the beer up with him to the upper room where he faced his eager commanders.

"Well?" Djedhor inquired. "Do we have permission to smash these bastards into the dust?"

Paatenemheb grimaced. "Not really. Akhenaten bleated on about how his god is a god of peace and one that hates violence and even disagreement. I pointed out that the Aten may hate these things but the supporters of Amun don't. He saw my point, albeit reluctantly."

"So we can use force to close the temples?" Paramessu asked.

"Yes and no. We can arm our men and we can display our might to intimidate the opposition, but we are not to hurt them."

"Set's breath! What's the point of that?" Djedhor slammed a fist onto the table, overturning a wine cup. Dark red wine spilled out like blood.

"Well, I did wring one concession from him. If we see any arsonists or looters, we can take any steps necessary to apprehend or stop them." Paatenemheb grinned. "What would you wager that any group that opposes us is really looting the city?"

Khui barked out a hoarse laugh. "That will do. Let's get started then."

Paatenemheb nodded, looking out at the sun and the length of the shadows. "Soon. I want to get the city tied down by nightfall if possible. How many men do we have?"

"I have four hundred Blues," Paramessu said. "Khui has about three hundred and Djedhor four hundred and fifty. Three badly under-strength companies with many still missing."

"It will have to do. Make sure every man is well-armed. Spears and swords, bows for any trained as archers. Basically the same instructions as before but this time we stay in large groups and hit hard and fast. Khui, take the temples in the eastern quarter first, then the north. Djedhor, you take the west part of the city then swing south to back me up. The Blues will take the temples of Amun again. Any opposition at all, from anyone, you treat them as looters. Drive them off if you can, kill if you have to. I want the streets clear of citizens by nightfall." Paatenemheb looked at his commanders and nodded grimly. "You have your orders, get to it."

The barrack gates swung open and hundreds of armed soldiers trotted out into the street, turning in both directions. A small crowd of onlookers gaped at the sight then melted away, disappearing down back alleys. The companies of Khui and Djedhor vanished toward east and west respectively, and Paramessu's Blues started back down the Avenue of Rams toward the Amun temple complex. The avenue was deserted and silent but for the heavy tramp of four hundred men.

289

As the temple gates hove into view, people started appearing from side streets, pushing forward in front of the gates and blocking the way. Several white-robed priests appeared and moved through the crowd, haranguing the people. Paramessu stopped his force fifty paces short of the crowd and stepped out in front.

"Men of Waset," he cried. "By order of King Akhenaten, this temple of Amun is to be closed. Disperse and go to your homes."

A jeering laugh rose from the mob. "Go home yourselves," somebody yelled. "Or you'll get worse than you got last time."

"Do not be mistaken," Paramessu called back. "If you do not lay down your weapons and disperse, you will be judged rebels and looters and dealt with accordingly."

"Go fornicate with that god of yours!" A brick smashed into the dirt beside him, followed by a barrage of missiles. One struck Paramessu on the arm and another narrowly missed his head.

"Blue Company! Archers – a single volley left and right." Bows twanged in unison, arrows plummeting into the crowd. "Blue Company, spears down, forward one hundred paces, count off." With a yell, the men of the Blues leveled their spears and leapt forward, counting off the paces as they ran.

The crowd, already thrown into chaos by the arrows snuffing the life from so many, wilted, falling back so it was seventy paces before the first spears bit deep. Screams and shouts rent the air as men fell beneath the onslaught, trampled under foot as the count continued. One hundred paces and the soldiers stopped as one, their spears still leveled and ready. People streamed back toward the temple gates, clutching wounds but leaving the dead and bleeding behind them.

Paramessu stepped over the corpses with a grim expression. "Archers. Take aim centre."

The mob howled and ran, some into the temple precinct, others down the Avenue then vanishing into the side streets.

Paramessu looked around at the street, now deserted except for some twenty dead and maybe three times that wounded. "Close ranks," he ordered. "Move into the temple. Meny, take your Fifty and secure the gates."

Paramessu led the bulk of his men at a trot up to the main temple steps, sending another hundred over to the smaller Amun temple. "Search it," he said. "Find the statue of the god." Soldiers disappeared inside and after a while reappeared.

"Can't find it, sir. The shrine be there but no god in it."

"We dids find a priest though," said another soldier. He dragged a white-robed man forward. "You wants me to kill him, sir?"

Paramessu frowned. "What is your name, priest? Where is the statue of Amun?"

The priest drew himself up, shaking off the hand of the soldier. "I am Haremakhet, Fourth Prophet of Amun. You would be wise to pay the proper respect for my position."

"Your god is overthrown, priest, so you have no position. I repeat, where is Amun?"

Haremakhet smiled. "Gone. When word came of the approach of men of violence, the god Amun walked out of the temple and disappeared. You will not find him."

The soldiers within earshot cringed, their mouths open in amazement. They made protective signs against strong magic and edged away from the priest.

"Stand fast, you fools," Paramessu snapped. "All that happened is that the priests moved the statue." He looked back at Haremakhet. "So Amenemhet took advantage of the delay, did he? But why are you here, instead of with your god?"

"I am here to warn you, Paramessu, son of Seti." Haremakhet moved closer, lowering his voice. "You would do well to remember Amun. The days of the Heretic are numbered and Amun has a long memory."

"I am loyal to my king. I took an oath to obey him and as long as he is king, I will do so."

"Your loyalty is commendable, Paramessu. Just be careful you do not follow Waenre Akhenaten into oblivion." He stepped back with a smile. "May I go now?"

Paramessu nodded and watched as the priest sauntered off toward the gate. He saw Paatenemheb hurrying toward him.

"You have the temples secure? Did you find the statue of Amun?"

"Yes, and no. Fourth Prophet Haremakhet was here. He says the god left."

"I saw the priest. Well, nothing to be done about it then. Chain the temple doors, then withdraw and seal the gates. I've just come from Djedhor in the western city. There's trouble starting. I'll need you as backup."

Paramessu saw to the chaining and sealing of the temples without further incident before leading his troops away down the Avenue of Rams, then westward toward the docks. He found Djedhor and the Reds fighting their way slowly along the river, from street to street and house to house. The hovels in this, the poorer quarter of the city, gave scant protection to their owners as the howling troops ran from home to home, harassing the citizens. Many lay dead and dying on the streets or in

292

doorways of their homes as the trained soldiers beat down the opposition. Every now and then a fresh wave of people would erupt from a street, brandishing whatever weapons they could find. The fighting would intensify, then the mob would break up and run, leaving more dead and wounded behind. Fires broke out as cooking fires were scattered, or as arsonists took advantage of the disorder to sow a little extra mayhem.

The arrival of Paramessu's men tipped the balance and the soldiers of the Amun Division swept through the western city, carrying all opposition away. As the fighting eased, Paatenemheb led his troops on a sweep north and east to link up with Khui's Black Company, closing and sealing off the temples as they found them.

As the troops passed, men came to their senses and the city watchmen started organizing brigades of men and women with jars and pails, fetching river water to put out the growing flames. Small groups of Amun supporters still harassed the fire-fighters, chanting and throwing stones, but troops of soldiers easily dispersed them.

All through the night the troops fought to clear the streets and close the temples and behind them the charred and smouldering remnants of the city slowly came under the control of the authorities. Aten rose golden over the three hills east of the city, casting his light over a shaken city. By mid-morning, Akhenaten and his god controlled Waset.

Chapter Eighteen

With this one step, Akhenaten doomed his religious revolution.

We Kemetu love having gods and over the years have collected vast numbers of them until there are more gods than there are days of the year in which to celebrate them. Now the king was asking, or rather ordering the people to give up all their gods in favour of just one, the Aten.

As long as the king's Aten was just one of many gods, no-one was concerned. There is complete freedom of worship in Kemet – even foreigners are at liberty to worship their own deities provided the rites do not involve anything that might disturb the peace. Some years ago, I think it was in the time of my grandfather Thutmose, a group of Ammonite settlers in the river Delta area brought in the worship of one of their tribal gods – Molek. The rites of this bloodthirsty god involve feeding human infants to the fires in the statue's belly. This was frowned on by the authorities but not banned as it was the settlers' own infants who fed the god. However, the settlers were few in number and eventually they turned to offering up stray infants from the surrounding communities. The authorities acted swiftly, stamping out the practice and sending the priests of Molek to meet the gods of the underworld and explain matters to them in person.

My father Nebmaetre brought the worship of the Aten to the fore, doing it for the love of his queen, Tiye. His youngest son Amenhotep was raised among his mother's people, the Khabiru, and had his mind warped by their strange religious beliefs. Amazing as it may seem, this tribe worships a single invisible god who lives on mountain tops and creates the thunder. What is more their god has no name and apparently never has had one. They refer to him as 'El' which just translates as 'god' and 'Adon' which translates as 'lord'. And here lies the coincidence that almost brought Kemet to her knees. The 'd' sound in the Khabiru tongue is very like the 't' sound in ours and to young Amenhotep's ears, Adon became Aten, a minor aspect of Re, who is a major deity. Being raised among the Khabiru, he adopted their worship and when he came to power, he pushed his god with gathering strength to the front ranks of our pantheon.

He picked the wrong city to introduce the worship of Aten. Waset has long been dedicated to Amun, the most powerful god among our many, particularly when worshiped as the composite god Amun-Re. Every house of kings, every family line adopts a god as their royal patron and state god, and Amun was the god of our family. As long as my father just worshiped Aten as one god among many and held due reverence for Amun; Ma'at, the divine balance, was maintained. The Aten's role as creator of mankind, animals and plants and, as the sun, shining down on foreigners as well as Kemetu, was nothing especially new as these ideas had been incorporated in Amun-Re's worship. What was new was Akhenaten's insistence that the Aten was the only god, that all others were false. This brought the priests of those gods, and especially the extremely powerful priests of Amun, into active opposition.

Akhenaten instituted religious intolerance for the first time in our long history. Withdrawing to his city of Akhet-Aten, the king set up his cult of Aten, under which he was the son of the sun and the sole beneficiary of the blessings that poured down from the god. Akhenaten believed it offered something for the common people

295

but in fact it did not. It did not offer any sort of moral philosophy or laws, nor did it offer a comforting afterlife. The citizens of Aten's city at least had the semblance of a religious life with the king active in his self-centered worship, but the rest of the country did not even have that.

The priests of Amun were extremely rich and influential before Akhenaten's edict and, faced with the confiscation and redistribution of their wealth, started to foment dissatisfaction and incite riot among the populace. Coupled with the weakening of the army, Kemet tottered on the brink of anarchy.

I was present in Waset during the riots. Returning from the burial rites that saw our father interred in his tomb in the Valley of Kings, Akhenaten summoned his General of Armies, Paatenemheb, and instructed him to enforce the edict of obliteration without delay. He then proceeded to hamper his general by denying him the force he needed to carry out these orders.

We waited in the great palace in Waset, the whole royal family with the exception of Akhenaten's daughters who had stayed in Akhet-Aten. We heard the quiet become a mutter and the mutter grow by stages to a roar. Many years later I was by the Great Sea when the gods sent a wave, a great towering one that rushed in with a roar that loosened the bowels and froze us in our tracks. The wave of outraged humanity in Waset that day brought fear to our hearts like the wave of water would years later to mine. It was the cry of a people cut adrift from the stable land of their familiar gods. Akhenaten heard the people of Kemet that day. I know he did, for young as I was, I saw indecision in his eyes, and fear.

If Paatenemheb had arrived to talk to the king then, instead of an hour later, the course of our lives and Kemet's fate may have been very different. He did not though, and Ay talked instead, bolstering his courage and strengthening his resolve to put down the rebellious priests of Amun. Without our uncle's advice, Akhenaten may have given in to his fear and allowed the old gods to remain, rescinding his edict. Then Akhenaten would have retired to his new capital city to follow his own personal god and the rest of Kemet would have gone their own way. Perhaps this step away from extremism and intolerance would even have led to a change in foreign policy.

Ay advised the king to stand firm, to force the priests to stand down, by the use of force if necessary. He portrayed the uprising as a rebellion against the Aten rather than for the gods; and hardened the king's heart. I did not understand then why my uncle Ay did this, for he most certainly was not a dedicated Aten supporter. He had been a priest of Amun while it brought him power and influence. Now he was a priest of Aten for similar reasons. In retrospect, I believe Ay stood to gain by weakening Kemet and even then saw clearly his own role in the future.

Ay spoke calmly but forcefully and when Paatenemheb came to plead for arms for his troops, Akhenaten agreed almost immediately. He would have preferred a quiet demolition of the old order, with the people rejoicing over the triumph of Aten, but if forced to it, he would show strength. The statues of the gods were to be destroyed, the priests disbanded and exiled and if anybody got in the way of the king's troops, they too would feel his righteous fury.

For the first time I saw Ay as a power behind the throne, twisting words to alter ideas, modifying actions to achieve the results he wanted. I know Smenkhkare saw it too for he muttered angry words to me later.

"Who is king in Kemet, sister? Our brother Akhenaten was anointed yet it is Ay who makes the decisions."

"He is the king's advisor," I replied, quite reasonably I thought.

"Advisor, yes. But he put words in the king's mouth. When Akhenaten gave his orders to Paatenemheb, it was Ay's words that he heard, not the king's."

"Does it really matter? The riots will be quelled."

"Of course it matters," Smenkhkare snapped. I took a step backward, my mouth quivering at his tone. He did not see my reaction, being too busy pacing, thinking his own thoughts. "When I am king, he will not rule me. If he thinks he can rule Kemet through me, he must think again."

He looked up then and saw I was about to cry. At once he changed from fierce prince to kind-hearted brother. Putting his arm about me, he explained.

"A king is anointed by the priests to act as a bridge between the gods and men. He represents both sides of the bargain. In times long gone in Kemet, and still in some of the more backward countries, the king will offer himself up as a sacrifice in times of pestilence or drought. The voluntary spilling of his sacred blood pleased the gods and they would relent, sparing the people. The king was a herd-master, tending his herd. Now, imagine if the real power rested not with the anointed king but with someone who had not entered into this agreement with the gods? Who then stands for the people? I tell you, little sister, when I am king I will stand for my people, my Kemet, against any who seek power for their own ends. That includes uncle Ay."

From where we stood in an upper room in the palace, we could see part of the temple complex. Presently the roaring of the crowds grew loud again, the screams beginning as the soldiers poured in, their thick wooden batons rising and falling in unison, spears thrusting and swords slashing. They secured the temples and moved on, out of our sight, but we could hear their progress through the city. By late afternoon thick columns of smoke arose as buildings were torched by rampaging mobs that had lost sight of their aims and had descended into mayhem and violence. We heard the deep-noted bells of the city watchmen as they turned out in force to fight the fires.

Dusk fell and it was almost like the festival of the dead, for it seemed as if lanterns burned throughout the city. The glow of fires paled the stars and the smoke, white against the night sky, obscured them. We stayed by the window all night, sitting hand in hand on a couch carved in the form of Taweret, the hippopotamus goddess of childbirth. I did not recognize the irony until much later, but one of the old gods was presiding over the birth of a new age in Kemetu history, one in which she, along with all the other gods, would play no part.

The sun came up over the three hills to the east of Waset, but as it rose through the smoke, the light dimmed so we could look at the perfect unblemished disk as it seemed to swim through the air. Re hid his heat and light but Aten looked down at the horrors being committed in his name and by mid-morning, as the fires and smoke died down, the army finally gained control over Waset.

Akhenaten did not stay in the city that had defied him. He boarded the royal barge at noon, descending below decks before the sailors even cast off. He never saw the destruction wrought in his name for he never returned to Waset as king, content to live out his reign in

299

his god's city, ignoring anything that might disturb his illusions. Ay ruled in all but name.

Chapter Nineteen

Unseasonal rains in the hills and mountains to the east and north swelled the streams to bursting point, flooding the plains to the north of Gezer in a sheet of muddy brown water. The floods receded quickly, soaked up by a parched and sandy soil but the plant life of the region, geared to the vicissitudes of an arid climate, burst forth in the water's wake, creating another flood that covered the plains in green. The herds followed and increased: sheep, goats and cattle, the nomads of the dry regions spreading out to follow the gift of the gods. Others trailed the herds – predators – animal and human alike.

Jebu the Amorite had prospered over the years. A successful captain in King Aziru's informal army, his ruthless attacks on Kemetu troops, his persistent depredations of defenceless farmers, and his atrocities against villagers in the north of Syria brought him to the notice of the king himself. Gifts and honours followed, and increased power. Once the leader of a handful of cutthroats and bandits, he now controlled half a thousand men who were slowly being shaped into a disciplined fighting force.

Aziru's patronage had brought Jebu power and wealth – his armbands were now gold rather than copper and he drank wine as often as beer – but at heart he was still a bandit chief. He much preferred to leave the organization of his small army in the hands of his officers, Aram, Simyras and Jezral, and head off into the hills with a small band of men for a bit of relaxing rape and slaughter.

On one such trip, Jebu found himself overlooking the coast road a day's hard horse-ride north of the Kemetu garrison city of Gezer. Normally, the traffic on the road, despite being the only true route north out of Kemet, was light. Caravans passed north and south, the rich ones guarded well by mercenaries, the poorer ones almost unguarded but scarcely worth the trouble of taking. Spices, faience, trinkets and carved wood may bring a decent profit if you were a trader, but what was an honest bandit to do with a camel load of such things? Once the traders had been killed and their women enjoyed then killed, the only gains were the meager handfuls of copper and occasionally silver they carried. Spices were tipped out onto the dusty ground to mingle with the blood, pottery smashed and everything else burned. Sometimes a trinket or knife with a fancy hilt caught the eye, but generally there was little to show for one's efforts. Still, it was better than drilling the men or organizing food and equipment for Aziru's fledgling army.

A rasping cough broke through Jebu's concentration and he turned from his contemplation of the deserted coast road to look at his friend and lieutenant, Aram. His forehead furrowed in concern at the sight of the man doubled over and retching. One or two of the men supported the Amorite officer and offered a flask of water.

Aram waved the water away and straightened, panting. "I'm alright, you motherless turds. I just feel a bit sick, that's all."

"Something you ate?" Jebu asked. "Or have you been drinking again?"

One of the men standing nearby guffawed. "That'll be the day. Aram can drink unwatered wine and match cup for cup most men who are just drinking beer."

Laughter erupted with several other men making similar observations of Aram's prowess.

"Maybe you were poxed by that woman four days ago," another man observed. "If there's one thing Aram likes more than wine it's a bit of pink, even if she's half dead."

Jebu frowned again, thinking back four days.

His small troop had jogged out of the hills into a small Khabiru village expecting to find provisions and a bit of rest before the next stage of their journey. Khabiru favoured the Amorites over their putative overlords, the Kemetu and could usually be persuaded to part with food and drink – and the occasional young girl – for a few copper pieces. However, this village was different. The stench of death met them a hundred paces out and the silence was broken only by the muted roar of flies. Jebu's first thought had been of another raiding party. Aziru's soldiers seldom knew what other parts of his sprawling army was doing.

They entered the Khabiru village, cloths held over their noses to find the population, maybe thirty men, women and children lying dead in their huts, bloated and fly-blown, their stink enveloping them in a noxious cloud. One or two bodies were relatively fresh but even these showed swellings in the groin, neck and armpits. An Amorite soldier muttered "Plague," having seen it in Byblos once, he said. They avoided the bodies after that, plundering a few scraps of metal and a bag or two of grain from what had apparently been the headman's hut.

On the way out of the village, a noise from one of the outlying huts sent Aram in, sword drawn, to investigate. A few moments later he had hauled out a middle-aged woman by her hair and thrown her to the ground with a shout of pleasure. Ripping her dress he threw him-

303

self on top of the weakly-struggling woman and raped her. Finishing, he drew his dagger and penetrated her once more, this time in the chest, before rising to his feet and adjusting his clothing.

"Are you mad?" Jebu had asked. "These people died of the plague."

"Not this one," Aram grinned in reply. "She died of Aram." He tore off the woman's clothing and pointed. "See, there is no plague in her." A moment later he slapped at his leg and swore. "Fleas. That's all I caught from her."

Three days later Aram complained of the heat, though in truth the sun was no hotter than it should be at that time of year. He griped of an ache in his groin too, though he ruled out the pox as his water passed without pain. Chills followed, and a headache that had him seeking surcease in wine the previous night, to no avail. Now he coughed and retched as muscle cramps racked his body.

"It is plague," Jebu said flatly.

The soldiers around Aram stepped away hastily, their eyes widening in fear.

"Nonsense," Aram grunted. "You were all in the village breathing that foul air but nobody else is sick. I just have a fever. Maybe I drank some bad water." He hawked and spat, one of the men jumping back quickly to avoid the phlegm. Clutching his head, Aram groaned.

"It was the woman," Jebu insisted. "She had the plague and you were the only one who used her. She gave it to you."

"She wasn't plagued. You saw her – she had no swellings." Aram doubled over again, panting. He sank to his knees and wrapped his arms about his body as a wave of uncontrollable shivering swept over him. "Oh, gods, I feel awful ... but it is not plague," he added, a note of desperation in his voice.

Jebu stared at his lieutenant, knowing he was already dead. Nobody survived the plague. It was in the hands of the gods as to who caught it, though coming into contact with a victim seemed to increase the chance. It was almost as if the dead person wanted company and somehow made others around him sicken and die. Nothing would cure plague but fire would destroy it, and distance would safeguard them – if they were not already dead men. He drew his sword silently, moving round behind Aram, his men scattering as they divined his purpose.

Aram retched and spat, blood-flecked sputum streaking his lips. "Jebu," he whispered. "Help me, old friend."

"Go to the gods," Jebu answered gently. His hand blurred and his curved sword bit deep into the back of Aram's neck, severing the bone and opening the windpipe. An explosion of bloody froth erupted, spraying Jebu before he could step back. Aram buckled and fell forward, his head flopping forward on tendons and muscles suddenly limp. His feet kicked out in spasm, sending dust and gravel flying. He rolled on his side, his blood-soaked beard matted and sodden. The eyes flicked open and widened as if in surprise then slowly shut as the body shivered and stilled.

Jebu's men stared at their leader askance. One pointed at Aram's blood which speckled Jebu's face and clothing. "Plague," he croaked. "You'll get it next."

Jebu wiped his face with one hand, smearing the flecks. "Nonsense. Aram was my friend. He has no reason to require my death. I did him a service." He looked around at his troop. "Which of you would not have a friend do this for him if he could?" he challenged.

Squatting, Jebu wiped his blade clean on a clump of grass and sheathed his sword. He rolled Aram's body onto its back and sprinkled a handful of earth over the bloody face, slipping a small coin into the bloodied mouth. Getting to his feet he clapped his hands sharply.

"Get ready. We move south immediately."

Jebu whirled and crossed to where his spear and bedroll lay, picking them up and settling the first comfortably in his left hand, the other across his back. He walked south along the ridge before dropping down onto a goat track that led toward the coast road, breaking into a trot as his men joined him.

Behind, on the high bare ground of the ridge, the first flies appeared, drawn out of nothingness by the merest hint of cooling flesh. Above, the vault of pristine blue sky became marred by tiny black specks as one after another, vultures and kites gathered and descended.

Jebu halted at sunset, leading his men into a tiny derelict way station, erstwhile manned by Kemetu troops in the days of empire now long gone under the Heretic King of Akhet-Aten. One wall remained standing and sufficient rubble remained to form a shelter against the cool breeze that blew after the sun dropped below the horizon. Jebu allowed his men a small fire deep within the shelter, but also insisted on a watch being kept on the road. It was unlikely anybody would be moving in the night, at least before moon rise, but he did not intend to be taken by surprise.

The evening passed without incident and as the moon rose silver and horned above the eastern hills, Jebu ordered the fire put out. As their eyes became accustomed to the darkness, the road stood out pale and straight in a darker landscape of burgeoning new grass and shrubs. Nothing moved on the ribbon of packed earth and nothing could be heard except the soft sigh of the wind and the call of a solitary cricket among the rubble. Jebu watched and waited, straining his eyes to catch any movement, his ears to detect anything out of the ordinary. A sharp piercing scream came distantly on the breeze, making one of the younger men start and finger his spear nervously.

"An owl," Jebu murmured. "He eats well tonight."

"What are we waiting for, Jebu?"

"A spy. Now keep quiet and watch, Ephras. The rest of you get some sleep."

Neither sight nor sound alerted Jebu as the moon rose to its zenith, the eastern sky paling with the approach of dawn. Despite the unwashed presence of a dozen men and his friend's blood on hands and clothes, Jebu detected a faint odour of animal dung. He sniffed the wind, moving his head this way and that in the chill air, before tapping Ephras lightly on the arm. As the man turned his head, Jebu signaled for silence and pointed into the darkness to the north.

"He comes," Jebu hissed. He cupped his hands and uttered the plaintive call of a plover, paused, and repeated the cry. A screech of an owl answered him, followed by a soft clattering of stones as the figure of a man separated from the darkness.

"What kept you?" Jebu asked sourly. "We've been here all night."

The man shrugged and yawned, revealing blackened, decaying teeth. "There are a lot of soldiers in Gezer. I had some problems getting away unseen."

Jebu nodded. "Come and eat. I have meat and wine."

The man followed him into the shelter of the tumbled down way station and squatted against one wall while Jebu rummaged in a pack for a hunk of dried meat

307

and a flask of sour wine. Accepting the food and drink, the spy took a long pull of the wine before worrying off a chunk of the meat. He looked around at the other men in the shelter, raising an eyebrow quizzically.

"You can talk in front of them, Ashraz," Jebu said. "What did you find in Gezer?"

Ashraz swallowed and took another long drink before answering. "A lot of soldiers. They've come up in response to Aziru's attacks. As you already know, the king of Kemet is not interested and is disbanding the army, but the general – Paatenemheb I think his name is – is doing his best with what he has. The legions are under strength but well trained."

"How many men?"

"In Gezer? About five hundred soldiers. A lot of traders too, and of course the envoys."

"What envoys?"

"You haven't heard? No, I forget, Jebu. You've been too busy pillaging to listen to what is happening around you." Ashraz gnawed off another piece of dried goat meat and chewed noisily. "The King is holding a Heb-Sed festival in his new capital city even though he hasn't reigned thirty years. It seems he is celebrating the overthrow of the gods of Kemet."

"How do you overthrow a god?" Ephras interrupted.

Ashraz looked at the soldier but did not reply.

Jebu nodded. "I'd like to know that too," he said softly.

"He has closed down all the temples of all the gods, confiscated all their riches and is spending everything on that new god of his, Aten." Ashraz laughed. "May all our enemies have such gods. He is a god of beauty and love and hates violence. That fool king has even emptied the

308

prisons of murderers and thieves who now roam the countryside doing what they will."

"Getting back to the envoys?"

"Envoys from all the vassal cities and states appear before the king at a Heb festival and reaffirm their allegiance. That is what we are seeing now – envoys and ambassadors from every land that is still technically Kemetu or pretends friendship. The Hittites are there too, believe it or not."

"They do not profess to love Kemet."

"No," Ashraz agreed. "However, a few presents and some meaningless words and this King Akhenaten will go on doing nothing while his empire crumbles around him. Even Aziru has his representatives going to the festival."

"But King Aziru has a price on his life. The governors of Byblos, Sidon and Smyrna have all accused him of capital crimes. What purpose can possibly be served by sending envoys?"

"Am I one of the king's councilors that I should know his mind?" Ashraz shrugged and bit into the meat again. "Perhaps he just plays for time with a king that believes the best of everyone."

"So most of these armed caravans are ambassadors moving south?"

Ashraz nodded, chewing on the last of the meat. "Some traders too, but yes." He looked up at Jebu. "It would not be wise to attack the ambassadors."

"I have no intention of that. My sole concern is a little plunder from undefended parties. Anything else I should know about?"

"There is talk of plague. There have been no deaths in Gezer yet but word has come in of plague in the towns to the north."

309

Jebu grimaced. "We have seen it too. My lieutenant Aram died yesterday."

"Of plague?" Ashraz asked sharply.

"He would have, but I spared him the trouble."

"Good of you," Ashraz grunted. The spy got to his feet and brushed the dust off his clothing. "I must go before it gets full day. I have many miles to go before I can make my report."

Jebu stood too and gripped Ashraz's arm briefly. "I appreciate you taking the time to find me and tell me the news."

"I pay my debts." Ashraz hesitated. "Would you seek to be in my debt, Jebu?"

"How?"

"I have news of a rich but small caravan leaving Gezer for the north."

Jebu grinned and his men stirred with excitement. "Go on."

"A Syrian trader with seven camels and a dozen men leaves Gezer at dawn. He carries spices and copper."

"Not much use to us, Ashraz. Copper is useful but heavy and I don't want to get burdened down with it."

"There is of course, the gold."

"What gold?"

"Under the copper. In the panniers beneath a false bottom. My informants tell me there is over five hundred deben in gold links."

One of the men whistled appreciatively. "Five hundred deben divided among twelve is ... is ..." The man shook his head in wonder. "We could get a lot of beer and women with that."

"We owe you, Ashraz," Jebu murmured. "I will not forget."

The spy nodded and left the shelter, walking into the early morning shadows. He turned north and set off along a goat track, jogging. Within minutes he was out of sight. Jebu ordered his men to break camp and led them down toward the deserted coast road to wait for the caravan.

The caravan came just after noon, the camels plodding in single file along the dusty road, heads down as if dispirited by the heat and the monotony, several paces between them. The accompanying men, fifteen in all, robed after the manner of the desert folk, walked beside the beasts in two or threes, some talking quietly but none on watch. A few carried spears but that appeared to be the limit of their weaponry.

Jebu scanned the road in both directions carefully before stepping out from the cover of a large boulder into the road in front of the lead camel. He wore his sword in his belt, pushed ostentatiously to the front, and planted himself spread-legged in the middle of the road, his fisted hands on his waist.

"Good day to you," he called. "May I enquire as to your business?"

The man leading the front camel started, pulling back on the rope with a jerk. The beast responded with a mournful bellow before standing and regarding the man in front of him with a supercilious expression. The man shouted back down the caravan then strode forward to confront the Amorite on the road.

"My business is my own. What reason do you have to accost me?"

"Come friend," Jebu said pleasantly. "I merely offer greetings to a fellow traveler."

The man looked around him nervously, scanning the boulders and ravines alongside the road. Several men ran

311

up behind him, some with spears and the man visibly gained courage. "Why should you name me friend? I do not know you. What is your business? Banditry? Do not think you can rob us."

Jebu sighed. "Ah, bandits. There is so much evil in the world isn't there? I suppose it is only natural to think the worst of those we meet. I am no bandit, friend. I merely wish to trade with you."

"Trade? What do you mean?" Two of the caravan men stepped out with leveled spears and advanced on Jebu. The leader of the group gained courage and walked closer, raising his voice. "Come, answer me. What do you mean by trade? What do you have that I would want?"

"It all depends on what you consider precious. Some desire gems, others gold or ivory." Jebu shrugged. "For myself, I find the breath in my lungs the most desirable thing."

"You talk in riddles. Answer me quickly or we shall kill you and be on our way." The spearmen raised their weapons.

"Very well." Jebu bowed slightly. "I offer a trade of your lives for your gold. I mean to take one of them."

The man laughed; a harsh braying sound that shook his body though it did not lighten the glint in his eyes. "Gold? We have no gold." The other men added their mirth.

"What of the gold that lies beneath the copper in your panniers?"

The laughter cut off abruptly. "Where did you hear that?" The man shook his head. "No matter. You will not live to talk about it to others. Spread your arms out wide, if you please. Keep them far from your sword."

Jebu smiled. "As you wish." He raised his hands, spreading them wide. The air rippled, a high whiffling

312

sound sped past him and the two spearmen dropped in their tracks, transfixed by arrows. The other men leapt back in alarm, hands darting to daggers beneath their robes. Three more fell before the rest backed themselves into a rough circle on the road, spears and knives pointed outward, nervously wavering.

The Amorite troop swaggered out onto the road, swords drawn and arrows fixed on the caravan men. Jebu walked up to the circle, staying just out of reach of a spear thrust.

"I offer you a trade. Your lives for your gold." When they hesitated, he added, "Or we could just take it. I am an honest man though, I would prefer to trade." He flashed a disarming smile.

"How do we know you will honour your word?" the leader said gruffly.

"You don't. But you must learn to trust your fellow man. Come, put down your weapons."

After a long hesitation the leader rapped out a command and threw his dagger to the ground. The other men followed suit, scowling blackly. Ephras hurried them to the side of the road and sat them on the ground, their hands on their heads, leaving four men to guard them. Jebu meanwhile, organized the unloading of the camels. The gold was where Ashraz had said, stored in small spaces at the bottom of the copper containing panniers.

Jebu counted out the gold links, hefting a few to judge the weight. He frowned as he counted out the last of the links. "There is only about three hundred deben here. Where is the rest?"

"That is all there is," declared the caravan leader sullenly. "Take it and go."

"I was informed there was over five hundred deben."

"Then you were misinformed."

313

Jebu tossed the gold links to the ground and got up, walking over to the prisoners. "There are ten of you but only three-fifths of the gold we agreed to trade for. That means only six of you can live." He looked over the prisoners and pointed. "Ephras, bring those four out here."

With a struggle, Ephras and the other Amorites pulled the four men out of the group and forced them to their knees in the dusty road. Jebu walked slowly in front of them, looking calmly into their terrified eyes.

"I repeat; the gold you have given me only buys the lives of your six friends. Where can I find the gold that buys your lives?" He walked behind them, tapping the blade of his dagger on his palm. He leaned over and stroked the head of one of the man, making soothing noises as the man jerked at his touch. He moved to the next one. "It really is very simple. Tell me where the rest of the gold is and you live. If not ..."

Jebu stepped quickly up behind one of the kneeling figures and gripped the man's hair, jerking his head back. With a smooth motion he drew the blade of his knife across his throat, slicing through blood vessels, windpipe and tendons.

The man thrust forward in agony and terror, his hands scrabbling at his open throat, a bubbling scream choking on the gushing blood. He collapsed to the ground in a welter of blood, his eyes starting from his head as he faded into death.

"So unnecessary," Jebu murmured. "Who will be next, I wonder? All you have to do is tell me where the rest of the gold is and you all live." He moved behind the next man in line who was shifting, moving his knees to keep away from the growing puddle of blood beside him. His hand stroked the head of the flinching man.

"It is on the last camel," screamed the man, a hot flood of urine staining his robes. "Beneath the clothing. In the name of Ishtar and Bensu, have mercy, I beg you."

Jebu patted the man gently, his knife to one side where the man stared at it as he would a venomous reptile. "Check the camel," he called.

One of the soldiers cut the saddle girth sending the load crashing to the ground. He pulled the bundles apart, scattering clothing and rolls of fine linen. He held up a sack that clinked metallically. "It is here."

"Bring it here." Jebu signaled to Ephras to return the men to the other group of prisoners, then busied himself counting out the gold links in the sack. He looked up smiling. "All here. Five hundred deben of fine gold. You have bought your lives."

A whistle came from the north. Jebu looked up to see one of his men running back down the road, waving his hands frantically. "A caravan," he gasped out as he got within earshot. "A large one with soldiers."

"How far?"

"Two thousand paces maybe."

The caravan men tensed, one or two of them half rising. They all put their hands down and they started muttering to one another. Jebu strode over and kicked one of them. "Silence," he roared. In a quieter tone he continued, having caught their attention. "We will be leaving you now. Do not think to stir from this spot until we are out of sight. If you feel tempted, remember I have archers and you have seen their skill." He pointed toward the dead men on the road.

Turning to his men, he snapped out orders, sending his men trotting to the south, and then angling across the plains toward the low hills. As they left the road, Ephras

315

looked back and saw the caravaners running north as fast as they could go.

"Jebu, they are up. Shall I order the archers to shoot?"

Jebu grinned. "Leave them. They can do us no harm."

"What of the soldiers? They could pursue us if they are told which direction we took."

"And leave their own caravan unprotected? I think not. They will suspect we are but part of a larger body." He clapped the soldier on the shoulder. "Relax, Ephras. Think about how you are going to spend your share of the gold."

Chapter Twenty

Within ten years the royal city of Akhet-Aten rose from the dust to its present glory as one of the newest and cleanest cities in all of Kemet. Not yet complete, the building program set in place by its young king occupied the outer reaches of the city where building supplies; mortar, timber and brick almost leapt from stockpile to finished building within days. The city proper, mud brick and quarried stone, especially the great Avenue of the Aten with its magnificent temples and open breeze-cooled palaces, glowed in the bright morning light. Fresh new paint covered plaster walls, and wonderful bright murals blazed from every surface, proclaiming the brilliant new portrayals of man and beast. Gaily-coloured linen banners festooned the palace facades and everywhere the glint of gold shone from gilded images of the god – the blazing, many-rayed arms of the sun disk.

In the twelfth year of the reign of Neferneferure Waenre Akhenaten, Lord of the Two Lands; the king felt quite overcome by the feeling of power that was engendered by the death of his father Amenhotep and the abounding wonders of his intimate relationship with the Aten. He decided to celebrate Kemet's birth into a glorious new future by holding a Heb-Sed festival in Akhet-Aten.

Akhenaten's announcement caught everyone by surprise. Although there was nothing to forbid an early celebration of Heb-Sed, this festival usually marked the thirtieth anniversary of a king's accession to the throne. It was a celebration of the king's health and strength and by extension, of the Two Lands. It served as a reassurance of the continuing fitness of the king to rule over the nation. The recently deceased king Amenhotep had celebrated Heb-Sed three times, in the twenty-sixth, thirtieth, and thirty-fourth years, though the last festival was in name only as Amenhotep was unable to rise from his bed to attend it. It was unusual therefore, if not unheard of, for a king to hold a Heb-Sed as early as his twelfth year, particularly as all twelve years had been spent as co-ruler rather than sole king. However, Akhenaten was undoubtedly king, and if he chose to celebrate his reign early, it was his prerogative.

More uncertain was the form the celebrations would take. Traditionally, the gods Ptah, Min and Wepwawet were honoured, and in past festivals Amun of Waset figured prominently. However, under the new regime, the overthrown and toppled gods could scarcely be asked to bless Akhenaten and the land of Kemet. The king made it quite plain that it did not matter; the Aten was the only god that would feature in this Heb-Sed festival.

The people of Akhet-Aten did not especially care either way. For them, a festival was a time of full bellies, of entertainment and a little licensed debauchery. The capital city was well supplied with bread, vegetables and beer and if there was only one god in his many temples instead of several gods, well – that was the king's decision.

The people of the rest of the Two Lands were less sure. For them, the overthrow of the gods had produced nothing but trouble. As well as being unsettled in their minds and unsure of what would happen to them after death if the gods were not there to protect them; the fall of Amun had released vast tracts of land from the control of the priests and delivered it into the ownership of thousands of people who had no knowledge of how to farm or herd cattle. Crops rotted in the fields because city-dwellers were ignorant of their culture and failed to

318

harvest them; herds strayed, sickened and died for lack of care, and the grain already harvested succumbed to mould and mice in the temple granaries now uncared for. As a result, only months after the great change, starvation loomed on the horizon for a large part of the city population.

The economy of the land changed. Artisans of every sort derived much of their livelihood by creating beautiful objects for the temples or the tombs – from figurines, pots, jewelry and furniture, to statues, tomb reliefs and paintings – all tied to a worship of many gods. The market for these things collapsed and apprentices were laid off. The rich still had silver and gold but the middle classes, the shopkeepers and artisans lacked the means to earn a living. The poor fared worst of all. As businesses struggled, as trade decreased and increasing numbers of soldiers found themselves out of a job, the poor drifted more into crime. Mobs rioted, thieves operated in broad daylight without fear of retribution, prostitution increased and grave robbing became blatant. Without gods to hold people accountable, everyone did as they pleased, without thought for the rights of others.

The wealth ceased to flow and prices rose. Discontent grew and the police forces of the city, as the army was steadily weakened, found its resources strained as it tried to keep the peace and uphold law and order. Ma'at, the holy balance of Kemet, crumbled. The priests did not help. Out of work and unsupported by the confiscated wealth of their temples, they roamed city and country whispering, complaining, and stirring discontent. They found willing listeners as more and more people talked openly about the Heretic King.

In Akhet-Aten though, King Akhenaten remained blissfully unconcerned with Kemet's problems. He was not ignorant of them. Scarcely a day went by without Ay or one of his court officials coming to him with some pressing problem or other, but the king just smiled and changed the subject, asking the official what they thought of the new hymn he had composed in praise of Aten, or showing them some new painting or sculpture one of the court artists had just produced.

It was different when the subject turned from governing his lands to the organization of Heb-Sed. Here Akhenaten showed great interest, though his ideas appalled the more conservative elements at court, of which there still were a few.

"No, I have told you before; I will not go beyond the boundaries of Akhet-Aten. This is the city of the Aten and every good thing is found here. I have no need to leave it, for anything."

"It is customary," Ay murmured. "The initial rituals ..."

"Will take place here, in the Great Temple," Akhenaten interrupted forcefully.

The mayor of Akhet-Aten, Neferkhepruhersekheper, wrung his hands anxiously. "Your majesty will still inspect the building works? And the herds? These things are always part of the festival."

"The buildings, certainly. I am most anxious that the Aten's glorious city should be finished as soon as possible. As for the herds, talk sense, will you. I told you I will not leave Akhet-Aten and I am not having a herd of smelly cattle pollute my lovely clean city."

"But your majesty, a census of the cattle and an inspection is essential. Cattle are represented by the Apis bull which your majesty will run with later in the ceremony and ..."

"Have the herds counted and bring a selection of the best animals to the city. I will inspect them here – but I will not be running with any bull, Apis or not."

Maya, chancellor and fan-bearer on the king's right hand, stirred in his chair. "My lord Akhenaten, it is not enough to examine a selection of beasts. Cattle are sacred to Ptah, himself represented by the Apis bull."

The king stared at his chancellor for several long moments. "Who?" he asked coldly. "I do not recognize this Ptah."

Maya gulped and glanced across at the mayor's impassive face. "I ... I just meant to say that ... that cattle are ... I mean ..."

The overseer of the Treasury, Sutau, cleared his throat softly. "I fear chancellor Maya has not expressed himself well, your majesty. I think what he was trying to say was that many people in Kemet still hold to mistaken and out-dated beliefs in false gods and will look askance at this festival unless the truth of the Aten's changes are made plain. That is what you were trying to say, wasn't it Maya?"

Maya flushed. "Er, yes, that was the gist of it."

Akhenaten inclined his head. "Then we shall have to make sure the people understand why I ... why the Living Aten changes the festival. See to it Maya. I charge you with this matter."

"There will be no problem adjusting the ceremonies to cater for the Aten's truth," Ay added. "We shall find the purest and cleanest cattle to present to our king as a symbol of the purity of our worship." Ay met Akhenaten's smile with one of his own. He bowed low before continuing. "Next is the procession where the king appears before the people in the Sed cloak." He held up a hand as the king opened his mouth to speak. "I have re-

321

searched the origins of the cloak, my lord, and I find that there is no connection with any false god. Royal scribe Apy will bear witness to this fact."

An old man in a creased white kilt looked up from his contemplation of a large tabby cat curled up by the window. He nodded slowly. "That is so, your majesty, though it is perhaps ..."

"Thank you, Apy," Ay interrupted. "The appearance in the Sed cloak is the perfect time to introduce the royal family, my lord. What an example of family bliss to see the king with his devoted wife Nefertiti and his six loving daughters."

"Yes." Akhenaten nodded enthusiastically. "They have had new robes made especially for the occasion. They are of the finest, whitest, sheerest linen imaginable. Every eye will be upon them."

Mahu, the chief of police, grunted. "I would not let my wife and daughter wear robes like that," he muttered, careful not to be overheard.

"Then comes the procession. I have worked out a route, my lord." Ay held out a papyrus sketch map of Akhet-Aten for the king to see. "As you can see it covers most of the important parts of the city. You and your family will be transported in great high thrones lifted high so every eye may see your glory."

Akhenaten peered closely at the papyrus. "What is this?" He pointed.

Ay came around and looked over the king's shoulder at the map. "That is the Great Temple, my lord. It is where you start and end the procession."

The king nodded dubiously, turning the map this way and that. "Then what?"

"When you return from the procession of honour through the city where the people will praise you and sing hymns, a light meal will be served and afterward the ceremony of rebirth and regeneration will take place in the Great Hall. I have here," Ay held up a scroll. "... The form of the ceremony. I have adapted it so it involves only that which is sacred to the Aten."

"You are a good and faithful servant, God's Father," Akhenaten enthused. He stood up and embraced his father-in-law, kissing him on the lips. "Such loyalty must be rewarded. Sutau, you will go to the treasury and find a chain of honour of one hundred deben of gold. Bring it here that I might put it about my faithful servant's neck."

Sutau bowed. "At once, my lord." He hurried out.

"You do me much honour." Ay bowed low, then, as the king resumed his seat, consulted his notes. "The governors of every sepat in the Two Lands will gather to pay homage, my lord, renewing their vows of obedience. So too, will representatives of every artisan guild and workers group assemble to honour you."

"That is good, father Ay. Please continue."

"Another procession takes place then. Your family will wait behind while you and the sepat governors parade down the Avenue of the Aten to the Great Temple where you will lead them in worship, singing such hymns as you deem appropriate."

"I shall give the matter some thought. Go on."

"You return to the palace where you join your family at the Window of Appearance where the common people present themselves to you for your blessing."

"The blessing of Aten."

"Of course, my lord. Delivered through his only son." Ay stopped and swallowed. He indicated a side table with water and wine jars and fine faience cups. "If you will permit me, my lord, I will clear my throat." Receiving the king's permission, Ay crossed the room and poured himself a cup of rich dark Syrian wine. He drank deeply then, putting the cup down, crossed back to stand in front of Akhenaten.

"Following the presentation of the people comes the swearing of allegiance by the governors of all the vassal cities and kingdoms throughout the empire. At this time too, the envoys and ambassadors of foreign lands present themselves and offer gifts of friendship."

Akhenaten nodded amiably. "That sounds acceptable. I will be able to show them the glories of Kemet through the truth of Aten."

"The foreign dignitaries will then accompany you during the rest of the festival."

"Acceptable."

Mahu, the chief of police, got to his feet and bowed. "Rest assured, my lord, my men will be on hand to afford you protection, willingly offering up their lives for your comfort and peace of mind."

The king frowned. "The Aten will protect me. I do not want to display any distrust of my friends from other nations."

Mahu fluttered his hands in agitation. "My lord, not every man is a friend ... or trustworthy."

Akhenaten nodded slowly. "Not every man knows the truth of the Aten. Very well, Mahu, you may have six men near me but they are not to be armed. They can only carry staves."

Mahu bowed low, his hands outstretched at knee level in acquiescence, though his tufted white eyebrows came together in a look of concern. "As you command, my lord."

Akhenaten turned his attention back to his Tjaty. "What comes next, Ay?"

"Here arises a difficulty my lord, which I hope you in your wisdom, can help me with." Akhenaten inclined his head and waved Ay on.

Neferkheprubersekheper leaned closer to Maya, keeping his expression carefully neutral. "Amazing, is it not," he whispered. "He plays the king like a fine instrument."

Ay flicked his eyes at the mayor before continuing. "In previous er ... pagan festivals, the celebrations of Min take place now. This raises a difficulty, my lord, as while there is no need to follow the old false ceremonies of praise; the people have come to expect the rituals that follow."

Akhenaten looked puzzled. "What are these rituals, Ay? I don't really remember."

"That would be because the rituals are more suited to those of, well shall we say, coarser sensibilities. As you know, Min is the ... was the false god of fertility and sexuality. Part of the ritual involves the pairing off of men and women to er, copulate in honour of the god."

"I seem to remember a certain Tjaty enthusiastically taking part last time," Maya murmured. "But then he no doubt has coarser sensibilities."

Ay shot the chancellor a vicious look, then turned back to the frowning king. "If you decide to keep this aspect of the festival to appease the common people, you can be assured it would not be unseemly. The copulations always take place within the confines of the temple of Min."

"We do not have a temple of Min. Even before my edict I saw no reason to have one built." Akhenaten thought for a few minutes while Ay waited patiently. "I really cannot see anything wrong with husbands and wives expressing their love together during the festival.

We just need to find a better place for these conjugal activities."

"The copulations are not between married people, my lord." Ay looked away, seeking a way to express himself that would not upset the king. "Most men are faithful ..." He ignored a snort of derision from the mayor. "... and most women too. The Min rituals are traditionally a time when men and women can, without censure, seek to quench their lusts outside of marriage. That is why it is so popular."

"I cannot understand that. Since we were children, the queen and I have sworn to be faithful to each other, excluding all others. As Lord of the Two Lands I have many wives, yet I make love only with my queen, my beloved Nefertiti."

"You are indeed blessed, my lord. I do not doubt that it is your special relationship with the Aten that lifts your abilities and desires far above us poor mortals."

"Yes, I am sure that is the reason," Akhenaten leaned back on his gilded throne and made a steeple of the long fingers of his hands. His hooded eyes took on a dreamy unfocused look. "However, being at one with my father, the Aten, I can be benevolent toward my subjects. I will allow these rituals to take place until such time as the people come to see fidelity in marriage as a perpetual blessing."

Ay bowed, a look of surprise on his face. "And the place, my lord? In the absence of a temple of Min?"

"Let them offer up their lust to the true god of fertility, the Living Aten. Have mats set out in the Great Temple after the governors and I have paid homage to our god. They shall offer themselves in the sight of Aten, under the heavens rather than hidden shamefully away in the recesses of a dark temple."

Ay gaped, his mind racing at the thought of the spectacle this would provide for the many foreign visitors at the Heb-Sed festival. Behind him he could hear a rising swell of concern from the other councilors. "The king has spoken," he intoned formally. "As the king commands, so shall it be." The mutterings died away behind him.

Akhenaten inclined his head politely. "What is next, Ay? My bladder vexes me and I am tired."

"Traditionally, the visit to the chapel of Wepwawet where you anoint the standard."

"We Kemetu had so many gods it is a relief to only have one now," Akhenaten sighed. "Which one is Wepwawet? I do not remember him."

"The 'Opener of Ways', my lord. Jackal-headed and the god of war and funerals. A deity not much worshiped by the people."

"Then he will not be missed. The Aten is not a god of war but of love and peace. We will miss this part out. Next?"

"The running with the Apis bull."

"Remove that too. I have already said I am not going to run anywhere."

"My lord," Apy the scribe interposed. "A run, whether with or without the Apis bull is essential. It is a sign to all that the king is fit and healthy, and capable of rulership."

"I am fit and healthy. Everyone will be able to see this at the Viewings from the Window of Appearance. As for being capable of rulership, the Aten gives me that right as the sole channel between his beneficence and this beautiful land of ours. I repeat; there will be no running."

Ay bowed again. "The king's word is law." He straightened and consulted his notes. "All that remains is the offering of cattle to the ... Aten, and the final procession through the city."

"Aten does not require blood sacrifices, so we will do away with that also. The procession can remain. It will cheer the people up to see their king so often on this happy day. Now, if there is nothing else, you may go."

The councilors stood and remained with heads bowed respectfully as Akhenaten left the council room. The king paused in the doorway and looked back. "Sutau has not returned with your gold chain of honour, Ay. When he does so, have him bring it to me and accompany him yourself. I will be with my wife in her palace rooms."

Chapter Twenty-One

The day of Heb-Sed arrived. The city groaned with the numbers of people that packed into it, people journeying from all parts of the kingdoms to take advantage of the king's largesse, or just to see the fabled magnificence of Akhet-Aten for themselves. Bread and beer were given freely to all comers at dawn each day for a week prior to the festival, thousands thronging the forecourt of the Great Temple to the Aten to eat and drink and listen to the strange high-pitched quaverings of the king as he greeted his heavenly father at sunrise. Although any priest of the Aten could greet the sun disk, Akhenaten alone sang the great Hymn to the Aten, which he had composed. People came from all parts of the kingdoms, from all trades and walks of life save one – no priests graced the proceedings with their presence. The old gods of Kemet withheld their blessings from the Heretic King and his upstart god.

On the actual day of Heb-Sed, the king led the hymn of praise in the Great Temple at dawn, as usual. The congregation of common people, clutching their loaves of still-warm bread and jugs of beer, fidgeted, waiting for the services to finish so they could enjoy the day's festivities. The hymn wound down to its drawn out conclusion as Akhenaten spontaneously added a few more verses. He then proceeded to intone a complex litany of prayers written by acting-Tjaty Ay, adapted from the old foundation rituals that praised the false gods. The old Tjaty Ramose was in bed, the court physicians attending to him, though it was not expected he would survive the day.

The ritual of foundation closed and Akhenaten walked through the throngs of cheering citizens to the great columned portico of the temple. A huge gilded throne stood twice the height of a man, its base pierced with wooden poles. Eighteen stalwart Nubian soldiers stood by the poles, their faces impassive and their oiled muscles glinting in the morning sun as they flexed their arms before lifting. The king stepped onto the base and mounted the steps to the throne, seating himself.

Maya, the royal chancellor, followed his king up the steps to the throne and placed the double crown of Kemet upon Akhenaten's head. Ay came next after Maya descended and placed the crook and the flail of royal authority in the king's hands. Descending once more, Ay called out to the soldiers.

"Take your places...ready...lift." With a fluid motion, the throne swayed up and onto the soldiers' broad shoulders. "Advance."

Ay led the way into the broad Avenue of the Aten and turned north, walking slowly as the eighteen-man team of soldiers lurched and stumbled under the weight of the throne before settling into a steady slow march along the thronged street. Men and women shouted and cheered, many of them holding up their free pots of beer in a salute. Children ran and ducked between the legs of the adults, packs of pariah dogs yapping and snarling as they got caught up in the excitement. A company of court musicians walked behind the swaying throne, striving to make their music heard above the roar of the populace.

The procession reached the North Palace and turned away from the river toward the new housing and the streets that ran parallel with the main thoroughfares. The gaudy banners and fresh new gaily-coloured paintwork of the Avenue of the Aten was left behind and they entered an area of fresh new white-washed mud brick houses.

Akhenaten looked at the new houses with interest, nodding his satisfaction with the way his beautiful new city was taking shape. Fewer people lined the streets here but the noise was no less as hundreds followed the procession, pushing and shoving to be close to their strange young king.

As they left the area of new housing, Akhenaten sat back in his gilded throne and stared straight ahead, his back stiff and head held high, maintaining a very proper regal dignity. Above him the morning sun blazed, growing in intensity by the minute, drying every hint of the morning dew from the foliage in the parks and in pots outside the wealthier buildings. Dust, churned up by the milling feet of the following crowd, drifted in an acrid cloud over the procession, sticking to the oiled bodies of the Nubian soldiers and turning them pale, almost paler than the bronzed men and women lining the route.

The procession entered the business district to the southeast of the palace and temple complex that was the heart of Akhet-Aten, moving past shops and storefronts, where trestle tables laden with examples of the manufactured products of the city's trade lay exposed for the king to see. Akhenaten looked straight ahead, seeing neither the prepared display, nor the minor riot that started as some of the poor peasants from the countryside started to loot the stalls. Mahu led his policemen into the throng, their wooden clubs rising and falling. Within minutes the disturbance was quelled with only a few broken heads and limbs as a result. The king did not see the blood spilled behind him either.

The cattle yards lay to the south of the city, tucked into the entrance of the broad valley that pierced the surrounding desert cliffs. Beyond, the track led to the quarries that supplied the building stone for Akhet-Aten, but today the focus of attention was the broad expanse of beaten earth surrounded by a painted barricade. Around this expanse, several hundred cattle milled and lowed in small enclosures, churning up another great cloud of dust. The stink of dung hung heavy in the air, the valley walls deflecting the pleasant breezes that blew through the city. Above the bellowing of the cattle and the happy chatter of the crowds, a muted thunder gathered in the valley, generated by a myriad of flies drawn to the rich fare of cattle dung.

Ay signaled the lowering of the dais and the throne swayed downward. Akhenaten dismounted, maintaining his dignity with a little difficulty as he came down the steep steps. He walked over to the raised platform erected in front of the cattle yards and seated himself on the broad divan. Behind him, fan-bearers held aloft broad ostrich feather parasols to protect him from the growing heat of the day. A minor official sat just behind the king with a fly whisk made from the tail of a giraffe, waving it to keep the flies off his monarch. A table set with delicacies and drinks stood to one side and servants hurried to supply the king with anything he should need. Setting aside his crook and flail of office, Akhenaten accepted a cooling cup of citron mixed with wine and regarded the spectacle in front of him with a small moue of distaste.

The crowds that had followed from the city spread out on both sides of the viewing platform, chattering and pointing at the herds of cattle in the small pens around the central expanse. The dust hung low over the whole area, mingling with the rank smell of sweat and dung. The Nubian soldiers formed a line behind the platform, waiting stolidly until their services were required again. Servants brought them refreshing draughts of water, some of which was used to wash the dust from their limbs. They murmured to one another in the tongues of their homeland, the sight of the cattle bringing back memories of an earlier life.

Mahu and his police force spread out in a ring, pushing and shoving the crowd back, allowing the king an unobstructed view of the proceedings. The first pen was opened and twenty fine black bulls trotted out into the open, several naked herdsmen with whips maintaining the cohesiveness of the herd. The bellowing from the other pens reached a crescendo as the excitement of the herders transferred itself to their beasts.

The Overseer of the King's Herds, Wakare, consulted a papyrus scroll and leaned over to whisper in Ay's ear. Ay nodded and cleared his throat.

"Neferneferure Waenre Akhenaten, Lord of the Two Lands, King of the Land of the Nine Bows, Ruler of the Land of Sin, Syria, Kanaan, Lebanon and Asia; we present to you the wealth of Kemet, the noble and countless herds that are your property, that you might acknowledge that your humble servants are performing their duties." He bowed low to the king before resuming his recitation of the facts being whispered to him by Wakare.

"From the sepat of Men Nefer in Ta Mehu, the kingdom of Lower Kemet, come twenty fine black bulls representing the royal herds of two thousand, one hundred and eleven beasts."

The herdsmen urged the bulls close to the barriers where they stamped and bellowed belligerently, threatening the herders with their wickedly sharp horns. One raised its tail and splattered the barrier with its dung. The king clapped a perfumed cloth to his nose and waved at the flurry of flies that rose from the ground in a black cloud. Ay signaled them away and the herders ushered the bulls back to their pen with some difficulty. They were replaced by another small herd of cattle, this time red-brown beasts with large pendulous dewlaps and up-turned horns.

"From the sepat of Khensu in Ta Mehu come twelve milk cows from the royal herds of the pastures of Ausim. They represent seven hundred fine beasts belonging to the king."

The cows were herded closer, the beasts ambling amiably forward, their dewlaps swinging. They lowed loudly at the king and at Ay's nod, were herded back to their enclosure. The process went on, new animals being herded forward to be presented to the king, followed by a recitation of the sepati or governing districts and the numbers of beasts they represented.

The morning wore on, Akhenaten becoming increasingly uncomfortable with the stink and the flies. By the time the presentations were halfway through the sepati of Upper Kemet, he was no longer paying attention but lolled on the cushioned divan, his eyes closed and the perfumed cloth held firmly over his nostrils. The double crown of Kemet lay on its side by the divan, stimulating several of the court officials to make the now outlawed gestures to the old gods to avert the evil omen.

The crowd was becoming restless too, standing out in the hot sun, so Ay hurried the proceedings along, bringing some of the smaller herds out together, not worrying if the beasts mingled or were herded back into the wrong pens. The sepati of Atef-Pehu and Maten brought forth their cattle for presentation and accounting. Ay sent them quickly back and announced the grand total of all the king's herds. Akhenaten opened his eyes and stood, picking up his crown, crook and flail before walking with un-seemly haste back to his carrying throne. The Nubians hoisted him once more on their shoulders and the procession started back toward the city.

When the procession cleared the confines of the lower valley, the heat, dust and stink of the cattle yards blew away on the sweet moist breeze that came from the river. The mood of the crowd lightened once more at the prospect of the midday meal and refreshment out of the glare of the hot sun.

The king's throne arrived outside the king's palace next to the Lesser Temple of Aten and Akhenaten dismounted. Waving to the remnants of the fast-disappearing crowd, he entered the cool, shady colonnades of the palace, together with his entourage of court officials.

Ay trotted up beside his fast-walking king. "My lord Akhenaten. The census of the royal herds took rather longer than anticipated. We should move immediately to the Great Temple for the donning of the Sed cloak and the royal procession."

"I am hot and I stink of cattle. I am going nowhere until I have had a bath and a cold compress put on my head." He turned into the royal apartments. "Where is the queen? Send for her at once. And the maidservants. I will bathe immediately."

Ay withdrew, noting the edge of petulance in his ruler's voice. He drew Maya and Sutau aside. "Change of plan. We are already running behind schedule and everything must be complete by sundown. Bring the Sed cloak to the palace and shorten the route of the Sed procession. From the temple north then back again on the main Avenue. End it at the Great Hall. The procession will start and end there instead of at the Temple."

The chancellor and treasurer hurried away to give the required orders. Ay grabbed a servant and sent him scur-

335

rying to find food and drink, walking through into the Great Hall of the palace while he waited. The servant returned with the food and Ay went carefully over the decorations and seating arrangements, a pot of beer in one hand and a roast goose leg in the other. He nodded in satisfaction, handing the empty pot to the servant and wiping his greasy hand on the man's kilt. "Find the chancellor and bring him to me, then find out if the king has bathed," he ordered.

Maya entered a few minutes later, the Sed cloak over his arm. "The priests are upset at the change in plans," he observed.

"They'll live with it," Ay grunted. "You have the cloak?"

Maya held it up. It was of fine white linen, stiffened with papyrus fibers around the neck to make it project above the shoulders, fastening in front with an ivory clasp. Against the chancellor, the cloak extended nearly to the marbled floor but Ay knew that on the king it would not even reach to his knees.

"Good. Fold it over the back of the throne." He looked round as the servant re-entered the Hall. "Has the king bathed?"

"Yes, my lord Tjaty," the servant said, bowing low. "He is presently with the queen, dressing."

"Very good. Bring me word when he is dressed."

"Yes, my lord Tjaty. Er ... there is another matter." Ay raised an enquiring eyebrow and the servant hurried on. "The envoys and ambassadors, Tjaty Ay. They were shown into the Chamber of Foreigners as arranged, and supplied with meat and drink but they grow impatient. The ... the Hittite ambassador is threatening to leave Akhet-Aten unless he is paid the honour due to him."

336

Ay cursed under his breath. "I will see him. Maya, you will accompany me?" Without waiting for the chancellor's reply he left the Great Hall in the king's palace and hurried toward the ambassadors' quarters. The rooms set aside for foreign dignitaries lay at the end of a long corridor within the king's palace. Despite Akhenaten's trust of everybody, especially of foreigners accused by his own governors of fomenting rebellion, the rooms were well guarded.

Paatenemheb, on his previous visit to Akhet-Aten a few weeks before had lost his temper when he saw the security arrangements of the palace. A lesser general might have suffered for his outburst, or a stronger king have imposed a penalty against the rudeness of a subject; but Akhenaten had merely smiled and nodded, asking Paatenemheb what he thought of a new mural in the Audience Chamber. The general controlled himself with difficulty, dismissed the king-appointed incompetent officer in charge of security and imposed his own system, manned by picked soldiers from his finest legion.

The ambassadors' quarters were effectively isolated from the rest of the palace. Fully armed men unobtrusively guarded every doorway and ground level window, ostensibly to prevent citizens importuning the important visitors, but in reality to prevent any foreigner from coming near the king unattended.

Ay and Maya passed the unofficial checkpoints in the corridor with a nod of recognition from the officer on duty and hurried into the large Chamber of Foreigners. The room measured nearly a hundred paces in length, a forest of sculpted pillars supporting a high ceiling. Despite the time of day and the presence of large open terraced windows on this upper floor, the room was dim and flickering torches cast moving shadows within the columned interior. As the doors opened, several robed men turned toward the sound, their faces set in expressions of anger and determination.

Mutaril, first minister of King Shubbiluliuma, the Hittite, scowled at Ay as he entered; his eyes dark and glittering in his beard-covered face. Long woolen robes hung about him despite the heat of the day and his forehead glistened with sweat.

"Why am I kept waiting, Tjaty Ay? Does your king seek to insult me?"

Ay bowed; a pleasant smile on his lined face. "Rest assured, minister, king Akhenaten has nothing but high regard for you and your king."

"Then why am I ... and these other high-ranking ambassadors," he waved an arm negligently toward the other dozen or so men in the room. "Why are we kept waiting? I was informed that your king would listen to king Shubbiluliuma's words this morning."

"Regrettably, minister, the Heb-Sed festival follows a strict schedule and the events of the morning took somewhat longer than anticipated. The king is bathing and will shortly don the Sed cloak and show himself to the people. Following this ..."

Mutaril's complexion darkened. "I am kept waiting while the common peasants command his attention?" He balled his fists and took a step forward.

Maya interposed himself smoothly, stepping between the two men. "My lord minister, in Kemet, particularly at the Sed festival, the king attends to matters in order of increasing importance. This morning he inspected his cattle. Next he shows himself to the common people, followed by the governors of the forty-two sepati, then last of all to your Excellencies. No insult is intended, rather it is a compliment."

"Then your customs are backward, as are your people."

"Come, minister," Ay encouraged. "I hope that you will change your view of us before the day is out." He walked past Mutaril to face the other robed men in the room. Very few actual governors of the Kemetu cities were present, Ay noted, but most, even those of the blockaded ones had managed to smuggle a representative out and send him with pleas for help to the king's Heb-Sed festivities. Mingled with these were envoys from hostile states – Mitanni, Babylon, the Amorites and the Hittites.

"Gentlemen, I beg you to be patient," Ay said, smiling reassuringly. "King Akhenaten will shortly be showing himself to the people of the city, followed by the presentation of the sepat governors. In no more than two hours, you will be invited to the throne room where you may greet the king and offer up such gifts as you have brought, and receive the king's bounty in return. Naturally, the occasion is more of a ceremonial nature than a working one, but you may rest assured that all your petitions, your letters and concerns will be dealt with in the days ahead. In the meantime, I urge you to refresh yourselves and prepare for your audience with the king."

The envoys and governors nodded and murmured to one another, starting to move off into small groups as servants hurried in to offer wine in fine goblets and trays of appetizing foods. One of the governors' representatives, Iduma of Hazor, coughed loudly, his hand up over his mouth.

"Can you send one of the court physicians, Tjaty," Iduma asked, his breath wheezing as he spoke. "I really am feeling rather unwell."

339

"I will see to it at once, Excellency." Ay cleared his throat to regain the attention of everyone. "King Akhenaten invites you to follow his procession to the Great Temple after the audience that you might see for yourselves the glories of his god Aten, and the love that his people have for his son."

Ay bowed low again to the assembled dignitaries and once again to Mutaril before leaving the chamber with chancellor Maya.

"What is the king thinking?" Ay muttered. "Those men are not friends of Kemet. They are wolves waiting to rend the carcass of our beloved land."

"Why can he not see that?" Maya asked. "Strength is needed against Shubbiluliuma and his allies, not appeasement. Did you see the envoy from Aziru? Standing in the back watching everything with that supercilious smile of his?"

"I saw him," Ay agreed grimly. "And for now we can do nothing except obey our king. One day though ..." he added beneath his breath. He beckoned to a servant and bid him find one of the physicians and send him to see Iduma of Hazor.

The two men walked quickly back down the corridor toward the king's quarters, hoping Akhenaten was ready for the rest of the day's activities.

He was. The king and queen stood outside their suite, five of their six daughters around them, giggling and playing. All wore the most transparent gowns imaginable, revealing every curve of their young bodies. Meryetaten looked every bit a woman, wearing an adult wig, her side lock of youth having been shorn the year before, but the other girls still looked like children. To one side stood the other members of the royal family among them Queen Tiye, looking her age at long last. A vital, vibrant woman

340

devoted to her husband Amenhotep, she had lost her zest for life following his death. She too was coughing and her wan appearance sent a twinge of concern through her brother Ay. With Tiye were the royal children from Waset, the princes Smenkhkare and Tutankhaten, and princess Scarab.

What a ridiculous name for a royal princess, Ay thought. He looked closer and saw that the girl had grown up in the last few months. Twelve years old now, her body showed the onset of adulthood. Her hips curved appealingly and tiny breasts with rouged nipples showed through the diaphanous linen robe she wore. Other people had evidently noticed the change too. Ay saw that her side lock of youth had been shorn and the young woman wore an elegantly made up wig. *Yes, she is turning into a beautiful woman, it is time she had a proper name. I will speak to the king.*

Akhenaten turned from his earnest conversation with Nefertiti as Ay approached. "Where have you been, father? I thought there was some urgency in commencing the rituals."

Ay bowed. "Indeed, your majesty." He told a servant to run and fetch the Sed cloak from the throne and asked Maya to fetch the regalia before looking around the royal party again. "The princess Meketaten? Where is she?"

"She is not feeling well, father," Nefertiti said. "She has a headache and a fever. I have told her to rest in the hopes that she will recover to enjoy the rest of the festivities later today."

"I p'omised I would tell her about it," piped up a small voice behind the queen's robes. "I said I would stay with her but she ... she 'sisted I go."

"That was very thoughtful, Neferneferouatentasherit," her mother said, hiding a smile. "Now run

341

along and get your sisters together. It is time for the viewing." The little girl scampered off to her sisters, pulling and pushing them along the corridor to the Window of Appearance.

The Sed cloak arrived and Ay put it around his king's shoulders, fixing the ivory clasp securely. Maya arrived back with the crook, flail and double crown, handing them to the king who then led the way up the sloping ramp to the bridge over the Avenue of the Aten. Trumpets sounded as they entered the central room and from the window came a great roar of anticipation and approval. Akhenaten stepped up to the window and raised his hands, letting the cheering wash over him. The queen and their daughters joined him to increased cheering, which only died away slightly as the old queen and the royals from Waset joined the party in the broad Window of Appearance.

Nefertiti gleamed and shone like the sun herself in her dazzling white robes that hinted at her still-firm body. She laughed and shook her head, the glossy black wig flying out, the sun glinting off the many golden pitcher-shaped *Nefer* beads sewn into the fabric of the headdress.

Ay stood back and watched the royal family, marveling that his oldest daughter was queen and mother to such beautiful princesses. *All girls*, he thought, a shadow passing over his heart. *No sons of my own and now no direct grandsons either. Smenkhkare will inherit, or Tutankhaten.*

Akhenaten turned from the window, his arm around his wife. "Come, my dear, girls, it is time for the procession. Our chairs await us below." With squeals of excitement, the youngest four girls rushed for the ramp leading down into the king's palace.

"Such a pity Meketaten could not be here. She would enjoy the spectacle." Nefertiti stroked her husband's arm

342

as they walked together with Meryetaten after the young girls.

"Yes," agreed Akhenaten. "There will be a chair vacant." He thought for a moment and turned to the other members of the family. "You can join us," he said, pointing at Scarab. "You are of an age with Meketaten and a beautiful young woman." His eyes roamed appraisingly. Then he frowned. "What is your name, girl? It seems to me you had some outlandish name."

Scarab bowed elegantly. "You gave me my name, your majesty. When I was a little child you named me Scarab."

"Did I indeed? Well, you cannot be called that any longer, you are a woman, not a child." He turned to Tiye. "Mother, why does this lovely woman not have a proper name?"

Queen Tiye coughed raspingly before replying. "She was born after your father's affliction. He did not give her the name we had chosen, so she could not be named formally."

"What name had you chosen?"

"Beketamen, Handmaiden of Amun."

"That is not a suitable name. Let her be called Beketaten, Handmaiden of the Aten."

Chapter Twenty-Two

And so I became known as Beketaten. Some even said later I was a daughter of Akhenaten, having been named by him, a custom normally carried out by the father. As I was undoubtedly the daughter of Queen Tiye, the calumny was magnified by the assertion that he begot me on his own mother. While father-daughter and mother-son marriage did occur in my family it was always for dynastic reasons. Akhenaten would have gained nothing by marrying his mother. He was already royal; she was not, being the daughter of Yuya, a commoner. Besides, he promised himself exclusively to his childhood sweetheart Nefertiti and at the time of the Heb-Sed festival he still remembered his vows. For all his faults and short-sightedness, his fanaticism and blindness, Akhenaten was my brother, closer by blood than even my beloved Smenkhkare.

In my twelfth year I was no longer the carefree child tagging along behind my adored older brother, investigating the mysteries and complexities of Waset. Four months earlier my breasts began to swell and I woke terrified one morning to find my bed spotted with blood. The nurses compounded my terror by filling my head full of fearful and unlikely images of my future, for despite the openness of sexual relations among Kemetu, I was still largely ignorant of what passed between a man and a woman. I knew that what lay between the legs of a woman was of great interest to men but I imagined no man would want a woman who bled from that place. My mother belatedly remembered her duty and took me aside, drying my tears and explaining matters to me. She initiated me into the day-to-day mysteries of woman-

344

hood, the daily rites of bathing, makeup, dressing and perfuming, shaving the armpits and pudenda, new ways to walk and comport myself, and how to talk to men.

My side lock of youth was shorn and taken away and my mother had two wigs made for me, one of long straight black hair for everyday wear, the other more fashionably of a series of tightly pressed black ringlets descending in vertical rows. Both had gold and silver wire woven through the locks and looked very fetching I am told. I might mention here that my natural hair colour is brown with strong reddish tints, a colour that is uncommon in Kemet but was perhaps passed down to me through my mother's family. Many of the Khabiru have reddish hair. I later grew my hair out and I found as I got older that it became a deeper, richer red-gold.

So I found myself in my brother's city of Akhet-Aten, my new name sounding strange to my ears and the unexpected adulation of the crowds filling me with excitement as the panoplied thrones were borne aloft on the shoulders of strong young soldiers. The king and queen led the way, looking severe and regal. Meryetaten followed as the eldest daughter and to my embarrassment I found myself carried along just behind her. I told myself it was only because I was taking Meketaten's place in the procession, not because of any special honour being given to me. The young princesses followed behind, screaming with excitement, waving and yelling at the crowds.

All my life I have been nobody, a person without a name before being named for an insect. Only my brother Smenkhkare believed in me enough to open my eyes to Kemet and my place in it. Now, in the space of an hour, I had become a royal princess with a glorious future opening up for me in my brother Akhenaten's court. Is it any wonder that first procession sped by me almost unseen in the turmoil of my thoughts? I could not say where we went, nor if we saw anything special. All I know is that I found myself at last in the throne room, standing with my nieces, the princesses of Akhet-Aten, watching as the still considerable wealth and power of Kemet prostrated itself at the feet of the king.

One by one the governors of the sepati of Kemet came forward, a scribe announcing their name, the sepat they governed and the nominal wealth of their province. They prostrated themselves on the hard marble floor in front of the throne, swearing their loyalty to Akhenaten and the throne of Kemet in a loud voice before retiring to the back of the room.

The governors of the vassal cities followed, Simyra, Tunip, Biruta, Kadesh, Tyre, Akko, Megiddo, Hazor and Gezer. For many, the governor himself could not attend as he was directing the defence of his city against Kemet's enemies; some of whom were there in the throne room along with their representatives.

I saw them that day for the first time, men in great woolen robes, their faces clothed in hair, black beards textured in ringlets, their eyes full of hate though their words were honeyed. One by one they advanced and bowed before the throne of Kemet, offering greetings and words of friendship even as their armies wrought destruction in our vassal lands. Zimrida of Sidon was there, as was Mutaril the Hittite and Prince Itakama of Syria, all looking greedily about them as if dividing up the riches of Kemet already.

Akhenaten greeted them all civilly though you could tell from his droop-eyed expression that he was bored, having no real interest in politics or the proper govern-ance of a great kingdom. His mind wandered, no doubt to his beloved sun god, and it was at such times that

Nefertiti stepped in. Another commoner like my mother Tiye, Nefertiti was loved by a king and raised to become full queen. She sat on a great throne just slightly lower than that of her husband and despite her lack of formal training, carried out her duties with sense and energy. She found the proper phrases to greet each person, affording them dignity and respect without relinquishing an iota of the respect due to her. My brother Akhenaten was king because he was raised to it; my sister-in-law and cousin Nefertiti was queen as if she was born to it.

Nefertiti at this time was just past the height of her beauty. Twenty-seven years of age and having had six children, though she suckled none of them, having wet-nurses to carry out that tiresome duty; the years had taken their toll. Makeup was now called upon to cover rather than accentuate and her gowns, while still filmy and sheer were gathered in folds to downplay the swell of a belly or to hide the sag of once glorious breasts. Her husband, in his male disregard for such things, still insisted she show herself and had statues and paintings commissioned that laid her ageing body bare for all to see.

Such artwork was peculiar to my brother's reign and to the city of Akhet-Aten. Most Kemetu art is tomb work and shows men and gods in stylized formal poses, shoulders wide and facing the viewer even if the person is doing something to one side. I have often thought the pictures unrealistic and stiff. Evidently my brother did too, for he gathered artists around him who would inject realism into their work. In fact, he insisted upon it, even to the extent of portraying himself as a misshapen man-woman.

Much has been said about my brother and his body, mostly by his enemies. It is true that his skull and face were long, and his hips wide like a woman's, his thighs swollen, but in most ways he was as other men. If he is represented in paintings and statuary with breasts and a great belly it is no doubt due more to good food and lack of exercise than to a womanly disposition. He was recognized as being virile, having fathered six daughters at that time. It is with the gods whether a man fathers male or female children and perhaps it is the revenge of the gods that Akhenaten only had daughters. Certainly the events that precipitated his downfall can be laid at that door.

This realism in art blew through Kemet like a cooling breeze off the river after a day of sweltering heat, yet it lasted for only a dozen years. The old gods needed to return, yet with them has come the old conservatism. I have tried to foster the new art and have had examples painted on the walls of my tomb by an old man, Djetmose, a pupil of Bak the son of Men who was foremost artist and sculptor in my brother's city. I came across him many years later in a distant land, exiled for his heretical beliefs. By one of those tricks the gods like to play on us, he had once been a sculptor in Akhet-Aten and had achieved a brief measure of fame when he created a bust of Queen Nefertiti that was so realistic, so beautiful it was the talk of the city. I do not know what became of this bust. No doubt it was destroyed with so many other wonderful works of art that suffered by association with my brother's reign.

The audience in the throne room came to an end and we all moved on foot out into the street to greet the people again. No longer in formal procession, the royal family mingled with court officials and governors, though the police still kept the crowds at a distance. This was more what I was used to, wandering the streets rather than being carried aloft. I found myself next to Smenkhkare just before we got to the Great Temple.

"So, little Handmaiden of the Aten, you have found yourself a new name and a new family." He grinned and, putting his arm about me, gave me a quick hug.

I smiled back and reached up to give him a kiss on his cheek. At fifteen, my brother Smenkhkare was a handsome youth, muscled and bronzed, with a fine mind and a ready wit. I loved him totally and longed for the day when he would be king and I would be his queen. "I still prefer the name Scarab."

He leaned closer, using the noise from the cheering crowds to cover his words. "Put away Scarab the girl for now. Take up your life as Beketaten the princess of Ak-het-Aten. A king ... and a queen ... must learn about the palace as well as about the common people."

"Will you stay here and teach me?"

He shook his head, leading me through into the great open spaces of the Temple. "I cannot. I must return to Waset when Tiye goes back. You are to stay here at court and become as one of Akhenaten's daughters."

"I don't want to stay. I want to go back with you."

Smenkhkare drew away from me and looked at me seriously. "We cannot always have what we want, sister. Stay here and learn. Grow up. I shall have need of you one day."

Before I could ask him what he meant when he said he would need me, my brother was gone, slipping through the crowds. I stared after him with tears in my eyes until I became aware of a man in the crowd, a farmer from his sun-blackened skin and leathery hands, who stared back at me, a leer on his face. I turned away hurriedly, feeling my face and breasts flush with embarrassment, and gave my attention to the ceremonies.

The king was in full flight, singing his songs of praise to his god, oblivious to the onlookers and the restlessness

349

of the crowd. Expecting the rituals of the god Min, there was voiced puzzlement from the crowd concerning the hymns of praise. Eventually the songs died away and the king withdrew from the altar. Immediately, servants of the temple ran out with armloads of sleeping mats and spread them all over the floor in front of the altar. A buzz of interest arose, the crowd pushing forward against the police cordon as they strove to see what was happening.

Ay called for quiet and as the noisy crowd started to subside, started to speak. "Good citizens of Akhet-Aten, worthy people of the Two Lands and noble visitors. Traditionally, the Heb-Sed festival is a time not only when the strength and fitness of our king is shown for all to see, but also a time of renewal, for Kemet, for our king and for our people, when every man and woman present at the festivities may celebrate their own festival of renewal by offering up a sacrifice of their body. In the past it was offered up to Min, but now, in the knowledge that comes from the light of the Aten, any who choose to do so may, with the king's blessing, partake of the Min fruits here in the Temple of Aten."

The mutterings and comments from the crowd had been rising in volume as he spoke but the roar which greeted his last words sent a shiver through my body. I did not recognize it at the time but the sound of the mob was one of raw lust.

"The king will not stay to observe these rites but will retire to the palace with his family."

Ay's words were almost drowned by the cheering as the crowd surged forward toward the altar. With difficulty, the police cleared a path for the royal family and the nobles, their sticks rising and falling. The foreign observers came with us, their faces a mixture of disgust, disdain and prurient interest, the mix, I suppose, a result of their different cultures and experience. I looked back as I half-ran through the portals of the temple, the police and soldiers trotting alongside. All I could see was a heaving mass of humanity, many already naked, women as well as men, caught up in a maddened lust that would shame the beasts of the field. And all this beneath the open sky rather than in a private chamber.

I have seen the love expressed between a man and a woman many times in Waset when I traveled the city with my brother but never the act of copulation. What I glimpsed as I left the temple was that act, but I did not see love and it saddened and frightened me, for I saw truly, for the first time, the violence and darkness that lies in the centre of men.

Chapter Twenty-Three

"It is all lies, your majesty." Zimrida of Sidon shifted in his chair and stared across the room at his accuser, Maltiri, ambassador for Abimilki of Tyre. "By all the gods, I wish only to bring some peace and stability to the area. There are bandits everywhere ..." He turned to Akhenaten who sat in his raised throne regarding the proceedings with obvious boredom. "Your majesty, surely you have heard of the bandit raids?"

Akhenaten nodded, trying unsuccessfully to look interested. "Yes, I am plagued with letters about the situation. I have already given orders that the problem be dealt with."

"How?" Maltiri shot to his feet and stared at the king, the colour rising to his face. "My master Abimilki has written to you many times asking that you send troops, or if you will not do that, to send gold that he might raise his own troops."

"Surely we can settle this matter amicably?" Akhenaten grumbled. "Maybe you just need to build more temples to the Aten in your territories. When people see the benefits ..."

"What dung-eating benefits?" Maltiri screamed, his face turning red, flecks of spittle flying from his lips. "We had a temple in mainland Tyre and that fornicating son of a whore Zimrida burned it to the ground." Zimrida smiled and Maltiri's face reddened. "There is your problem," he pointed a shaking finger at his enemy. "Kill him and my city is safe."

"I would remind you of whom you address, Maltiri. Let us observe the proprieties and keep our arguments

352

civil." Maya the chancellor spoke softly but with an edge of steel in his voice.

Maltiri fought for control, taking a deep breath. "My apologies, great king. The magnitude of the problem overwhelms me, particularly when the solution is so simple. Troops, gold or just remove Zimrida of Sidon from the equation."

Akhenaten smiled. "I do not take offence at hasty words, Maltiri. The peace of the Aten calms me and enables me to see the inner good that lies in all men. I cannot send troops, as I have said before. My aim is peace, not war. Surely that is desired by all men. As for gold, well, you shall have some. I have a beautiful statue of my great father Nebmaetre you may take back to Tyre. It is similar to the last one I sent."

"My lord, that was but beaten gold over carved wood. My master needs much more gold if he is to defend his city."

"And lastly," Akhenaten raised his voice, overriding Maltiri's objection. "Whatever dispute you have with Zimrida of Sidon, I suggest you end it soon. Zimrida," the king inclined his head graciously toward the Sidonian leader, "Has assured me many times by letter that he has no designs on Tyre but merely seeks to quell the trouble in the countryside."

"And you believe him? My lord Akhenaten, he is the cause of the trouble. He and his master Aziru, son of Abdiashirta."

"No man is my master," Zimrida rumbled. "Though I am ever mindful of your masterful policies." He smiled warmly at Akhenaten.

"Well, we can solve this once and for all," Akhenaten said. "My lord Zimrida, will you take an oath on the Aten

353

who sees all; that you have no designs on Tyre and seek only peace?"

Zimrida got to his feet and bowed toward the king, then toward the glittering image of the sun disk on the wall behind the throne. "I do so swear, my lord. I desire only peace." He sat down again, smoothing his dark robes, a pleasant smile on his face.

Akhenaten beamed. "You see, if men are honest and god-fearing, all troubles can be overcome."

"If you believe that you are an even bigger fool than you look," Maltiri muttered, sitting down again.

Ay caught the sense of the words and frowned. Secretly, he agreed with the Tyrian ambassador, but nothing was going to convince his king. He, and others in the council, had tried to open Akhenaten's eyes to the political situation but he refused to see.

Tutu, the minister of foreign affairs, arose and addressed the king and the gathered envoys. "Great king, and nobles, I must at this time, protest the words of Maltiri of Tyre. No doubt he spoke without due consideration when he slandered the name of Aziru, son of Abdiashirta. I have in my possession many letters from the Amorite king protesting his love for Kemet and his innocence of all charges made by self-seeking men. He has not asked for gold like so many others represented here," he said, looked pointedly at Maltiri. "But he has actually sent gifts of copper and many fine horses to his brother Akhenaten. Is this not so, Sutau?"

The overseer of the treasury nodded. "That is so."

"He has no copper mines in his territories," growled Wahankh of Gezer. "Did he rob the mines of Sin to get it? I remind the king that he owns the copper mines of the land of Sin."

354

"Aziru is a loyal ally of Kemet," Tutu said firmly. "As is his father.'

"Why is it then that my patrols find evidence of Amorite incursions, right down to attacking the trading caravans a day's ride north of Gezer? That is not the act of an ally."

"You have proof these are Amorites?"

"There are sometimes survivors. They identify their assailants as Amorites." Wahankh grimaced and cracked his knuckles. "I suppose you have an answer for this too?"

Tutu nodded sagely. "Bandits. Maybe even deserters from the Amorite army."

"Why do you defend him, Tutu?" Maya asked. "Surely Aziru has shown his colours already by not coming to the aid of Gezer, Megiddo and Hazor?"

"I have been in constant communication with him on this matter. He is very concerned with the bandit problem. Aziru lacks gold. Without it he cannot pay his troops. If he cannot pay his troops, they will desert. If he has gold he can then act as he greatly desires to act – protecting Kemet's northern borders."

"Very well." Akhenaten nodded his head as he made his decision. "I shall send gold to Aziru so that he may guard the north. Many deben of fine gold."

Wahankh snorted. "Send many deben of fine gold to me also then, Waenre. Also to Yabatiri of Akko, Iduma of Hazor, and all your other loyal vassals that we too might defend Kemet against her enemies."

"My lord king," Sutau interposed. "The treasury is not bottomless. Unless we cut back on the building program here in Akhet-Aten, there will be no gold to send north."

355

"Good," Ay muttered. "Then maybe we can forget this nonsense."

Akhenaten frowned. "You have something to say, Divine Father?"

"We should talk about this in private."

"I disagree. If I put this off you will try and talk me out of it," he went on. "I will not curtail the building program. The glory of the Aten is reflected in the magnificence of his city. I can think of no more vital work than the glorification of god."

"But the gold must come from somewhere," Sutau protested.

"Then it shall come from the army. Why should we pay troops to sit idle when the gold can more profitably be spent on Aziru's army. He will defend Kemet so our army becomes superfluous." He turned to the scribes sitting cross-legged on the floor next to the throne. One of them, a mere lad, was scribbling furiously, his goose-feather quill scratching across a roll of papyrus as he endeavored to keep up with the argument. The older scribe sat still and attentive, his blank papyrus open on his lap.

"Apy," the king said. "Take down my decree." He waited until the royal scribe had completed the obligatory honourifics that must precede any formal pronouncement. "The army budget is henceforth cut by one part in ten and a sum of gold of five hundred deben in weight shall be sent north to King Aziru the Amorite with a letter of friendship. You know the phrases, Apy. Prepare it and have it ready for me to see by dawn tomorrow." He turned back to the waiting ambassadors. "Do not think that I am ignoring your pleas, noble lords, but as you have seen, the wealth of Kemet is limited. We must spend our gold first where it will do the most good. We have had a bad harvest this year ..."

Ay quickly rose to his feet. "My lord king, you should ..."

"Where I come from that is a sign of the gods' displeasure," Mutaril the Hittite commented.

"That of course could not be the case here," Akhenaten said firmly. "Aten is our only god and he is not displeasured."

Ay subsided again, sitting down heavily on his chair.

"Of course, lord king." Mutaril inclined his head in agreement and sat back, smiling.

"As I was saying, noble lords, Kemet has had a bad harvest but as soon as the taxes come in we shall have plenty of gold for all who wish Kemet well."

Chancellor Maya curled his lips in a sour expression. "There will not be many taxes this year. If the harvest is bad, the people have nothing extra to give. They must eat, and find seed for next season."

"I have confidence my tax inspectors will find what is needed. Everyone must realize that Aten comes first."

"They already give half in taxes," Sutau said. "One quarter of their production to the treasury and one quarter to the temple. Back before the reformation they only gave one part in ten to Amun."

"Are you saying you would rather be giving to false Amun?"

"No, my lord king. I can see the truth of Aten. What I am saying is that if you tax the people too hard, there will be trouble. Already some resent Aten and long for the worship of the old gods."

"I will not listen to this heresy, Sutau. You will keep silent and do your duty. Find the gold I need to send to Aziru. More if you can so I can complete the city."

"My lord." Ay stood and confronted Akhenaten. "These are matters of internal policy. It would be best to

357

conduct such conversations in private. I am sure my lords Mutaril, Zimrida and Itakama would rather not listen to such mundane details as the harvest and taxation."

"We are among friends, Divine Father. Do you imagine our friends would use this information in an improper way? Well, do you? Maya, Sutau? What about you, Tutu?"

The chancellor and treasury overseer said nothing but Maya refused to look at either Ay or the king and Sutau bit his lip in vexation as he realized he had been talking candidly in front of the Hittite minister.

Tutu shrugged. "They are not our enemies and why should we hide things from our friends?"

"Then I think perhaps we owe these nobles an apology."

A low cough from the doorway to the throne room turned heads in the silence that followed the king's remark. A servant stood just inside the room, his eyes wide in his pale face. "My ... my lord Akhenaten," he quavered. "I br ... bring a message from the queen."

"Not now," Akhenaten snapped. "I am busy, come back later."

The servant half turned to go before swinging back to face the king again. "I must tell you, my lord."

"Oh, very well then. What is it? Hurry up, I am busy."

"My ... my lord ... I ..." The servant looked anxiously around the room at the now-attentive ambassadors and ministers of the king's council. "I must tell you alone."

Akhenaten sighed. "Find out what he wants, Divine Father. The fool will carry on like this all day unless you do." As Ay crossed the chamber, the king turned back to the ambassadors and his ministers. "As I was saying, I think there are apologies due and ..." His voice tailed off as the realisation hit him that Ay was one of the ones he thought needed to apologize. He glanced toward the doorway.

Ay bent over the servant, encouraging him to tell him the message from the queen. The servant hesitated and Ay pointed out testily that he was not only the king's Tjaty but also the queen's father and that if anyone was worthy to hear the message, he was. The servant nodded and whispered quickly, flinching back as if expecting a blow.

Akhenaten saw his Tjaty stagger and clutch the servant for support before turning and staring back at him. In seconds, the sprightly old man had aged and his eyes glittered with unshed tears.

"Divine Father," The king half rose from his throne. "What is the matter?"

A sob ripped from the old man's chest. "Meketaten. Oh, my lovely girl ..." Ay stumbled across to the king and unmindful of protocol, threw himself into his arms, gripping Akhenaten tightly. "Meketaten has died," he howled.

The king stood holding Ay for long seconds before his face quivered and collapsed into tears, the two men gripping one another as grief shook their frames.

Mutaril at once stood and bowed toward the king. "With your permission, king Waenre Akhenaten, I and my colleagues will withdraw. It is not seemly that we should intrude on your grief."

The other ambassadors and governors scrambled to their feet and on a signal from Chancellor Maya, exited the throne room. Maya looked at the two grieving men for a few moments, then approached them softly, laying his hands on them with compassion.

"Go to the queen. She will have need of you."

"Yes." Akhenaten pushed Ay back and turned resolutely to the door. His face, streaked with kohl and malachite where his makeup had run, gave him a wild and distraught look. "Yes," he repeated. "The queen will need me." He set off in a shambling run.

Maya grabbed the Tjaty and pushed him toward the door. "Go with him, Ay. He needs you."

Ay turned his tear-streaked visage to the chancellor. "She is my grand-daughter too." His voice shook. "Who will comfort me?"

Maya nodded. "You are right. I will accompany you. But let us hurry."

The two men set off at a run toward the women's apartments. Already the news had spread through the palaces and they passed servants and officials wearing a variety of expressions from stunned disbelief to calculating, and some very real outpourings of grief for the loss of the young princess. From the queen's palace came the sound of wailing, the screams of horror and desperation making the men's necks prickle with dread.

The doorway to the princess' suite was blocked by women, keening and tearing at their clothing, scratching faces and arms with sharp nails. Ay pushed through roughly into the first room then past servants into the bedchamber that had been Meketaten's. The bed was rumpled and soiled and the stink of sickness permeated the air. Already flies were gathering, their drone adding to the horror of the scene.

The body of Meketaten lay on the bed, arms thrown back and head at an angle, her eyes wide and staring. Flecks of blood-stained spittle covered her lips and chin and spotted the bed linen. Akhenaten was on his knees beside the bed, clutching the body of his daughter to him, a formless keening issuing from his lips. The queen sat at the foot of the bed, haggard and aged, her eyes staring sightlessly at the floor. Ay wiped his eyes then crossed to the bed and put his arm around Nefertiti's shoulders.

"Daughter." He shook Nefertiti gently. "Daughter, it is I, your father. What has happened? I did not think our beloved Meketaten to be so ill. Where are the physicians?"

Nefertiti looked up at her father. "She was so bright and beautiful," she whispered. "Her name meant 'protected by Aten' – why did he not protect her?"

Akhenaten's cries increased in volume and he clutched the body of his daughter more tightly. Ay spared him a shuddering glance before turning back to Nefertiti.

"Why did she die, daughter? What do the physicians say? I thought she only had a bad cough, maybe some light fever. A strong young girl should be able to throw that off easily."

Nefertiti turned her head away from the bed, refusing to look at either her husband or the body of her daughter. "Look at her, father. It is plague."

Ay drew back involuntarily. "Plague? It cannot be – can it?" He took a grip on himself and examined the naked body sprawled on the sheets partly under her grieving father. The body was pale and waxy, save around the face which was smeared and streaked with blood. The sheets by the head were stained with blood too, as if blood had been vomited up recently. He nodded reluctantly. "It may be. I have seen plague before. Sometimes there are swellings and dark splotches on the skin, other times blood is thrown out." He looked around the room and at the crowd of servants and women crowding the door of the antechamber, their cries starting to grate on his nerves. "Where are the physicians?"

Nefertiti looked up again, her face quivering anew. "With Tasherit and Setepenra. They are sick too." She put a hand up to her mouth and coughed; the sound and her words sending a chill through her father.

Ay squeezed his daughter's shoulder and strode through into the antechamber once more, then turned and walked along to the other girls' bedchambers. He stood in the doorway of one and saw the little princess named for her beautiful mother, Neferneferouaten-tasherit – the little Beauty of the Beauties of Aten – shivering naked on her bed despite the heat of the room. The little girl cried out in pain, coughing and wheezing, fighting for breath so her eyeballs stood out with the effort. Beside her stood an old man in a long white robe, his straggly gray hair falling down around his shoulders. He was hunched over, gabbling some long complicated phrases. On the other side of the bed, Beketaten and Meryetaten sat, holding the sick girl's hand and stroking her sweating body.

"You should not be here," Ay snapped. "Meryetaten, Beketaten. Leave now. Go to your own rooms." The princesses got up meekly enough and ran out of the room.

The old man turned, breaking off his gabbling. "Eh? Who are you? What are you doing here? You interrupt my treatment."

"I am Tjaty Ay and this girl's grandfather. Who you are might be more to the point."

The old man drew himself up and stared down his long nose at Ay. "I am Shepseskare, court physician to king Akhenaten."

Ay nodded. "How is she?"

"That is with the gods."

"But she has the plague? How do you treat the plague?"

"Plague? Why would you say that? Are you a physician? No, she has a fever and a cough. I have no doubt she will respond to my treatment."

"Her sister has just died of the plague."

"Yes, yes, I know, but that does not mean to say this girl has the same affliction."

"Two days ago, princess Meketaten came down with a fever and a cough, today she lies dead in the next room, of plague." Ay pointed a quivering finger behind him. "This little girl was with her, looking after her. Now she also has fever and a cough. Do you mean to tell me you do not see a connection?"

"Come, come, Tjaty. I do not tell you how to govern Kemet; that is not my area of expertise. Well, medicine is not yours, so do not tell me how to diagnose sickness or cure people. How could there possibly be a connection between them?" He uttered a short laugh. "Or do you think the disease just jumped off one girl and onto the other?" Shepseskare shook his head, his gray locks swinging. "Illness comes from the gods ... er, well, in this case I suppose we should say god. Anyway, I have prescribed prayers. If we say them often enough, and correctly, I am confident she will live."

As if in answer, little Tasherit cried out weakly and sneezed, a spray of bright blood covering her pillow. Ay stepped forward and wiped his grand-daughter's face gently with the edge of the sheet. She moaned, her fever-bright eyes wandering, unfocused.

"What else have you prescribed, Shepseskare?" Ay asked, controlling his temper.

"There is nothing else that will work. The prayers are to Sekhmet though I of course address them through the

363

Aten. I can prescribe tinctures and oils for the pain, but only prayer will cure her."

"What of frankincense mixed with honey and milk? I have heard that can be used."

"I think I would know if that would be useful, Tjaty. Now I really must ask you to leave. This girl is sick and needs my prayers." Shepseskare resumed his mumbled prayers, turning his back on Ay.

Ay bent over and kissed little Tasherit on her fevered forehead before walking quietly from the room. He leaned in the doorway and looked back, tears pouring again from his eyes.

"Uncle?"

Ay turned to see Beketaten standing a few paces away. She wore a coarser weave linen shift that hung from her slim shoulders on thin straps. It was altogether less revealing than the gossamer-thin garments worn by the whole royal family. Ay thought it more suitable under the circumstances and felt his heart warm toward the girl. He smiled, wiping away his tears.

"Will she be all right, uncle? The physician would not tell us."

"I don't think he knows, Beketaten. It is with the gods now." He saw a puzzled expression on the girl's face and considered his words carefully. "Should I say it is up to the god, Aten, instead?"

Beketaten now thought carefully and Ay hid a small smile. *A girl who does not rush into words*, he thought. *I wonder who taught her that.*

"It is the king's decree that the Aten is the only god," Beketaten said slowly. "Yet for countless years Kemet has had many gods. Does saying they don't exist remove them? Dare I say that the king is mistaken?"

364

"Dare think it, but do not say it. Not yet. There may come a time ..." Ay's voice trailed off and he looked beyond Beketaten to the next bedchamber. "What of Setepenra?"

Beketaten shook herself. "She is very sick, uncle."

"What of the rest of you?"

"Well enough, I think, though the queen has a cough, as do I. It may not be anything. There were many coughs and fevers in Waset when I left there. Even the old queen ..." Beketaten stopped, blushing. "My mother, uncle – your sister. Even she complained of fever and a headache. She was feeling very poorly when she left for Waset yesterday."

"We will hope it is nothing, Beketaten, for all of you. Now, there is a physician with Setepenra?"

"Yes, but not like any physician I have seen. He does not pray at all."

"Really?" Ay smiled again, enjoying the talk with his young niece. "I would like to meet him."

The physician proved to be a young man dressed in an ordinary kilt of medium quality linen. He wore sandals and armbands of woven jute fibers around the biceps of his arms. When Ay and Beketaten entered the bedchamber, the young man was bent over the little girl in the bed, with what looked like a short cow's horn connecting her chest with his left ear.

"What are you doing?" Ay asked.

"Shh!" The physician waved an arm at them, motioning them to keep silent. After a few moments he straightened up and gently turned the little girl onto her stomach. Setepenra, though conscious, made no sound, her body limp and yielding.

"What are you doing?" Ay asked again.

365

The young man grinned. "Hello again, Scarab." He contemplated the older man. "And you are?"

"I am Tjaty Ay and this child you are attending is my granddaughter. I would like to know who you are and what you are doing. You are supposed to be treating Setepenra for the plague."

"Nebhotep. I was listening to her heart but now I am going to listen to her lungs. And yes, I am treating Setepenra for the plague."

"Listening to her heart? What do you mean? It talks to you?"

Nebhotep laughed, his young face breaking out into a cheerful grin that made him look like a mischievous teenager. "It talks, Tjaty, but not in words." He eased Setepenra onto her back again. "Have a listen, like this." He demonstrated how he used the hollow cow's horn.

Ay looked warily at the horn then bent his head over the little girl, fitting the tip of the horn, its sharp end cut off and filed, into his ear and putting the broad end onto the spot indicated by Nebhotep. He listened.

"What is that? It sounds like a temple drum, played very fast."

"It is her heart."

Ay stood up and handed the horn back to the physician. "What is it doing and why?"

Nebhotep shook his head. "That I do not know. The heart is supposed to be the seat of emotion and intelligence. Why it should make a noise is a mystery to me. It is not the sickness, as healthy people also have beating hearts, though the beat is slower, more like the temple drums."

Ay frowned, his mind racing as it tried to assimilate this new information. "And the lungs? You said you were going to listen to them too. Do they beat also?"

"Listen for yourself." Nebhotep turned Setepenra over and motioned for Ay to repeat his performance with the cow's horn. "What do you hear?"

"I don't know. It is faint but it is not a beat, it is a bit like the wind in the palm fronds when they clatter together or ... or ..." He cast his mind about for a likeness.

"Like a sheet of papyrus crumpled in the hand?" Nebhotep took a small piece of papyrus sitting with other pieces covered in scribbled notes from a table and crushed it in his fist, the dry fibers crackling audibly.

"Yes. That's it," Ay exclaimed. "A sort of crackling sound. And we all make this sound?"

"No. Only if you are very sick and you have a sickness of the lungs. I do not yet understand why the lungs of a sick person should sound different from those of a healthy person but I am working on it."

"And is this work of any help in curing my little Setepenra?"

"No." Nebhotep shook his head. "She will die before sunset." He turned the princess over and made her comfortable, stroking her forehead gently.

Ay sat down on the edge of the bed and held the little girl's hand. Beketaten stood behind the head of the bed and directed a gentle breeze down on the fevered child with a small reed fan. Setepenra looked blearily up at the older man. "Unc'e Ay?"

"Yes my little blossom, I am here, and so is Beket."

Setepenra swallowed and dissolved into a minor paroxysm of coughing. She settled back down against the pillows, panting. "It hurts, Unc'e," she whispered, closing her eyes.

Ay leaned forward and wiped away a fleck of blood from the corner of her mouth with a scrap of cloth. His eyes misted over and he looked back up at Nebhotep.

367

"There is nothing you can do? There is no cure for plague?"

"I have been treating her, Tjaty, but there are no recognized remedies for plague." He hesitated. "There is something that sometimes works if you catch it before the blood starts. I have tried it on a few people in the city."

"How many lived?"

Nebhotep moved over to the table near the bed and started going through a large wicker basket. "One."

"Out of how many?"

Nebhotep shrugged. "Fifty or more. I told you, the problem is catching it early enough. Most people don't call for a physician until they start spitting up blood." He pulled out several linen packages from the basket and unrolled them.

"Fifty? I had no idea there was so much plague in Akhet-Aten."

"More every day. For some reason it started when the first of the foreign visitors arrived. The first person I treated was a member of the Syrian party."

"What is this treatment? A lot of prayer, I suppose."

"Actually none at all, though you can pray if you like."

Ay looked at the young physician shrewdly. "You sound as if you do not believe in the gods."

"Shall we say I am unconvinced?" Nebhotep turned from the table and his examination of the contents of the packages. "I have always relied on my skill, my knowledge, cleanliness in all things, and trial. I listen to my elders," he smiled faintly. "And sometimes I find something worth hearing, especially from country midwives. Does my disbelief matter, Tjaty?"

368

"Not at all." Ay looked back at Setepenra, who had fallen into a troubled sleep. "What is this treatment?"

"Milk, boiled with honey, frankincense, a few other herbs that are regularly used for minor ailments, a little bit of hippopotamus dung. Personally, I think the dung is optional."

Ay grimaced. "It sounds foul."

Nebhotep grinned. "Oh, it gets worse. That sort of concoction is fairly often used. My innovations are the boiling and mould. An old woman of Men Nefer told me about that. She says that consuming large quantities of the blue-green mould that grows on rotting bread and fruit will cure internal diseases if you catch them early enough. She even puts the mould on wounds and claims it speeds healing. I have not tried that yet."

"But your mixture works?"

"Yes, sometimes."

"Sometimes is better than never." Ay leapt to his feet and strode purposefully into the antechamber. He grabbed two servants in the doorway who were staring with interest into the bedchambers and half-dragged them back into Setepenra's room. "Tell them what you need, Nebhotep. Enough for the royal family first, then the palace."

"They will not take it, Tjaty. I have found people to be very conservative unless they feel as if they are dying and it is too late by then."

"Let me worry about that, Nebhotep. As Tjaty I can command anyone except the king and queen – and maybe even them. Tell the servants what you need."

"Very well. I need a large pot full of milk, enough for two hundred people to have a cup full each. Start a small pot also with enough for twenty. Place the pots of milk on a fire and bring them to a boil – it must be boiling,

369

that is very important. While the milk is heating gather together honey, frankincense, elderberry, heavet fruit, asif plant, cucumber flowers, green dates, garlic and a little hippopotamus dung. I will come down to the kitchens and prepare the mixture myself when the milk is boiling."

The servant gulped. "Whe ... where do I find hippopotamus dung, sir?"

"From a hippopotamus, I would have thought. Go to an apothecary at the House of Life. He will certainly have some." Nebhotep chased the first servant off then took the other one to the table, where he showed him the contents of one of his linen packages. "This is green mould. It occurs on bread and some rotten fruit. I want you to go into the city and collect as much as you can. Make sure it is green mould, not white or black. Bring the loaves and the fruit intact. Don't try and remove the mould. You'll need some helpers, as I need a lot of it. Five bushel baskets at least."

The servant departed with a papyrus note from Ay charging everyone to obey the man's demands without question.

"I'm glad you thought of that, Tjaty. Left to my own actions, he would have returned in an hour or two without anything."

"There's no point in having power if you can't use it," Ay observed.

"Uncle, I need to sit down. I'm not feeling very well." Beketaten put the reed fan down and came around to the side of the bed and sat heavily on it. "I'm sure it is nothing, uncle. I just feel very tired."

Nebhotep crossed to the bed quickly and put a hand on the princess' forehead. "You are warmer than you should be. Do you have a cough? Any difficulty breathing?"

Beketaten yawned and shook her head. "No, just very tired, suddenly." She leaned back against one of the bed-posts and closed her eyes. "I'll be alright in a minute."

Nebhotep met Ay's concerned gaze. "If you want to pray, Tjaty, pray that your palace servants are quick."

The first batch of milk boiled quickly and Nebhotep left Setepenra in Ay's hands to go down to the kitchens. He returned an hour later with a large jar of the concoction and a copper cup. "You first, Tjaty." He poured the mixture into the cup; green flecks swam in a fetid milky brown fluid.

Ay sniffed it and wrinkled his nose. "It looks foul and smells fouler."

"And it will taste worse. Drink it."

Ay drank and gagged, finally draining the cup. He handed the cup back to the physician. "Thank the gods that's over. It is terrible."

Nebhotep smiled as he refilled the cup and gave it to Beketaten. "You will need to take a cup twice a day for three days, Tjaty. If you are still alive after three days, the medicine has worked. Now, can you get the rest of the royal family to take it?"

"They will if I have to hold their noses and pour it down their throats." Ay watched incredulously as Beketaten drained the cup without obvious distaste. "That was the same stuff?"

"It is not that bad, uncle. Last year when I had lesions in my mouth, the physician in Waset treated me with a milk and scribe's excrement mix. Now that was really foul."

"You do know you weren't supposed to swallow that?" Nebhotep asked gently. "The proper treatment is to apply it to skin lesions after the scab has fallen off.

The physician should have used a mouthwash of milk and baby's urine."

"So I was told," Beketaten said with a grimace. "But you try not swallowing with a mouthful of that."

"Well, it doesn't seem to have done you any harm."

"You are going to give Setepenra some?" Ay asked.

Nebhotep shook his head. "She would not be able to keep it down and it is too late anyway. She is dying." He put the cup beside the jar of milk and dipped a cloth in cold water, wringing it out and holding it to the little girl's hot skin. "All we can do now is make her as comfortable as possible."

Ay left Nebhotep and Beketaten to attend to Setepenra's final comforts and, taking the jar and cup, went to dose the rest of the royal family. By sunset, princesses Neferneferouaten-tasherit and Setepenra had joined their elder sister Meketaten in death. The palace was filled with the sounds of grief and not inconsiderable amounts of retching as the palace staff followed the royal family's example and started their first dose of medicine under the supervision of Nebhotep and Ay.

Chapter Twenty-Four

The plague in its two forms swept through Akhet-Aten with the same ferocity as the country as a whole. Only about one in ten people actually caught the disease, misfortune striking some families but not others, but everyone was affected as an already tottering economy foundered. Nobody could explain the hit and miss incidence though it was noticed that the areas around the docks and the city granaries had a higher incidence of the swelling plague whereas areas near the temples had more cases of the bleeding plague. Nobody thought it relevant that mice and rats teemed around the docks and granaries and the temples were places where large numbers of people congregated. One in ten caught the disease but of those that fell ill, half of the swelling plague victims died and nearly all the bleeding plague sufferers. Perhaps the one thing that prevented the plague from being totally destructive was that people shut themselves away when they sickened, limiting deaths to their nearest and dearest.

The bleeding plague struck the palace especially hard but the death rate was only moderate. In fact, it was heaviest among the royal family, but only in the first days of the sickness. Three of the young princesses died but while others got sick, Nefertiti and Beketaten most of all, none died after administering Nebhotep's medicine. The palace staff suffered a one in three loss to the bleeding plague and one in four to the swelling but this was considered an act of mercy by the god or gods. Some, even among those families that lost members, offered up quiet but heartfelt thanks that they were themselves spared. The population of Akhet-Aten as a whole felt the Aten had spared them and deepened their faith, but in Kemet, and especially in Waset, the plague was seen as a judgment by the gods against the Heretic King.

Amun's city of Waset escaped lightly but one death in particular brought an agony of grief to a city that had suffered so much in the past year. Queen Tiye had complained of a cough while in Akhet-Aten for the Heb-Sed festival. This was followed rapidly by headaches, chills and muscular pain, but she embarked for the voyage back to Waset the following day. The cool river breezes would calm her, she thought. She woke up the next morning in her stateroom on the royal barge 'Aten Gleams' as it forged slowly upriver, her body racked with pain and firm but tender swellings in her groin, armpits and neck. The skin over the swellings was smooth and red but despite their hot look, was quite cool to the touch.

Alarmed, the ladies of the Queen's bedchamber sent urgent word to the barge master who put in at the nearest village to seek help from a local physician. He came, he saw, but could do nothing except apply a poultice of scribe's excrement mixed with milk and honey. The physician went away scratching a flea bite and reciting the proper prayers but either he made a mistake in his recitation or else the village scribe whose night soil container had been raided for its valuable contents was lacking in virtue, because the queen died at noon.

The body was packed in natron and the barge master put off immediately, determined to carry the queen's corpse to Waset as quickly as possible. Three days later, while 'Aten Gleams' was still many thousands of paces from its destination, the village physician fell ill with a fever. Another three days and he was dead, most of the villagers following him into the West before the month was out. One of the few survivors was the scribe with the inefficacious excrement.

Waset was stunned when the barge pulled into the royal wharf with its sad cargo. Many of the rowers were also sick and two who died had been tipped overboard to float away and do mischief downriver. Tiye, no longer queen, was dispatched to the royal House of the Dead to be properly prepared and Smenkhkare, as eldest scion of the *Per-Aa*, or House of Amenhotep, stepped in to arrange the burial. Despite his youth, and only with the help of Huya, royal scribe and steward of the great royal wife, he organized the opening of Nebmaetre's tomb and the preparation of a niche within it for her. He also brought in the goldsmiths and ordered some splendid gold ornamentation for the nested coffins. Word was sent by fleet chariot overland to Akhet-Aten but a message came back that Akhenaten would not attend his mother's funeral. He had made a vow never to leave the City of the Aten.

Tiye was buried with her husband Amenhotep in his golden tomb. Despite the presence of guards at the entrance to the holy burial valley, thieves had broken into the tomb and stolen many items, though thankfully had not penetrated as far as the sarcophagus. The queen was laid to rest in an anteroom and the entrances filled and sealed once more.

Even before he buried his grandmother, Smenkhkare acted more like a king than a young prince, taking charge of the city and setting up procedures to deal with the plague now making itself felt near the docks. Using the old Amun Legion, now called the Waset Legion, he isolated the waterfront, preventing anyone from entering or leaving. Corpses were packed in natron in the warehouses on the docks and sulphur was burned. Smenkhkare had heard that sulphur fumes cleansed the air and he was prepared to try anything to help his people. The

fumes smelt terrible and sent people coughing and choking and large numbers of rats succumbed.

Whether the isolation or the sulphur worked, or
whether the disease just naturally disappeared, within
three months of the 'Aten Gleams' docking in Waset,
plague had gone from the city. The population spontaneously celebrated, cheering the young Smenkhkare whenever he showed himself.

It was at about this time that his great-uncle Aanen
came to see him. The priests of Amun, of whom Aanen
was Second Prophet, had long been in hiding. The god
himself was outlawed and, under orders from Akhenaten,
even the name of the god had been chiseled from many
monuments and inscriptions. His priests, while technically under sentence of death if they set foot in Waset, had
not been pursued too diligently by the army or the Medjay. Too many citizens were secret worshippers of the
old gods, Amun especially, whose city this was. So the
priests remained, calmly moving about the city, and the
authorities quietly looked the other way. Until the plague
faded from Kemet and Aanen arrived one morning at the
palace requesting an interview with prince Smenkhkare.

Smenkhkare received the priest in his private chambers, not wanting to make the visit an official one. He
was learning that a lot of the skill of ruling a city involved
knowing when to be circumspect. There were many spies
of Akhenaten, dedicated followers of Aten, even in the
palace, and Smenkhkare had no desire to stir up enmity
by openly supporting Amun. By receiving Aanen in his
private chambers, he could pass off the visit as an informal one by a relative, his great-uncle. A servant showed
Aanen into Smenkhkare's private reception room.

"Uncle, it is good to see you. You are well?" Smenkhkare noted the plain robe and the unkempt wig, effec-

376

tively disguising the man. Unless you knew him you would never guess he was a priest of Amun.

Aanen had thought long and hard about this meeting, consulting with the other Prophets of Amun. Smenkhkare, as brother to Akhenaten, was an as yet unrecognized heir to the throne given the Heretic only spawned daughters. Surely that lack of sons was a judgment of the gods? On the other hand, there was no predicting the actions of the present king; perhaps he would decide on somebody else to succeed him. Ay was a possibility. The man was certainly thirsty for power and was already Grand Tjaty of the Two Lands now that Ramose was dead.

Not the least of Aanen's problems this fine morning was how to address Smenkhkare and whether or not to bow to him. Strictly, as Smenkhkare held no official position in Waset, Aanen outranked him and should not address him in any way beyond calling him by name or as 'nephew'. On the other hand, the young prince could be the answer to their ongoing problems and should be handled with courtesy and honour. At the last minute, Aanen decided on the latter.

"Prince Smenkhkare, you do me much honour." Aanen bowed deeply, even extending his hands at knee level as one would to a superior.

Smenkhkare flushed and stepped forward to raise his uncle to his feet. He dismissed the servant and led the old man to a chair near the window. "Uncle, there is no need for that. You are Second prophet of Amun and a family member besides."

Aanen smiled to himself at the prince's words. "Then let us talk as family members."

"Excellent. You will have some wine? I have a fine jar of Syrian vintage here." Smenkhkare poured two cups and passed one across to Aanen. "What shall we drink to?"

"To Ma'at? Our dear Kemet could use some stability and order."

Smenkhkare nodded and drank, then looked carefully at the old priest. "Do you talk of Ma'at, meaning the goddess; or of Ma'at, meaning order?"

"They cannot be distinguished."

"Then such words should be used with caution, uncle. You know as well as I that the palace and city are full of spies."

Aanen grinned. "Who better than I to know of caution?"

"Yet caution is not something the priests of Amun practice. I hear many things that happen in the city."

"Yes, I was forgetting how well you know the city and the mood of the people, Smenkhkare. So you must know that the people have accepted the king's god in name only."

Smenkhkare raised an eyebrow and sipped from his cup. "The temples of Aten are well attended."

"Of course. They act the part for the Heretic, yet if he died tomorrow, the Aten temples would be deserted the day after."

"Now that is dangerous talk," Smenkhkare said in a flat voice. "I would remind you that Akhenaten is the rightful king and my brother. As a loyal subject – and as brother, I give him my full support."

"I know. I did not mean it as it sounded. But the plague has swept through Kemet leaving thousands dead, including three daughters of the king. Our lives are in the hands of the gods and who knows what tomorrow will bring."

Smenkhkare got up and walked past his uncle to the window where he looked down on the garden where he had first met his sister Beketaten years before. "Yes, who knows what tomorrow will bring," he murmured. He watched a pair of swallows swooping and flitting above the ornamental pond, catching insects. Somewhere among the eaves of the palace would be their mud nest, probably with chicks inside. The prince sighed, thinking of more carefree days. Once, he would have gone looking for the nest, just to see the parents feeding their young.

"Why did you come here, Aanen?"

"To see my young nephew, of course. Why else would I come?"

"You have never come to see me ... Uncle. I have had visits from your brother Ay and your sister, my grandmother; but never you. Why is that?"

Aanen put down his empty cup and looked at Smenkhkare's back. The young man half leaned out the window, apparently looking at something below him. "The duties of a Prophet of Amun are onerous ..."

"No more than those of a queen or a Tjaty. Why have you never been to see me – yet now you decide to. What has changed?"

Aanen controlled his breathing and fought his desire to get up and pace, not wanting to show his anxiety. "Kemet has changed."

Smenkhkare waited but his uncle said nothing more. After a while he said, "Go on."

"You are correct when you say we have never been close. To me, you have always just been another one of my sister's children and not even an important one. The prince Tuthmosis was the heir, then later the younger

Amenhotep. Why should a baby begotten by the king on his daughter occupy my mind?"

Smenkhkare turned from the window and leaned back against the edge. He folded his arms across his broad hairless chest. "Family feeling?" he hazarded with a faint smile.

"Then came Akhenaten," Aanen said, ignoring the prince's comment. "Yet still while the old king lived, Kemet remained much as it was. There have always been favourite gods and the story of their rises and falls in popularity could occupy us for hours. There was no reason to suppose the Aten would be any different except for the king changing his name."

"And by doing so, signifying he no longer held Amun in high regard."

"Just so. This *Per-Aa*, this Great House is a House of Amun. Its destiny is tied to the god yet how can it survive if the god is passed over? We have seen the Heretic try to destroy the gods, even attempting to chisel out Amun's name. The Aten will not protect Kemet, he shines on all lands equally. Only Amun can truly protect us."

Smenkhkare walked to the table and poured himself another cup of wine. He held the flask out questioningly to Aanen and when the old man nodded, crossed over and filled his cup too. Putting the flask down, he sipped, appreciating the full body of the wine. "So why do you come to me?"

"Who else is there to go to? The Heretic has no sons, nor any to succeed him. You are his brother, and you have proven yourself worthy of being king. What is more important, you are untainted by the heresy of Aten."

"What of your brother, Ay? Or of my brother, Tu-tankhaten?"

"Ay is ambitious and hungry for power. I am sure he would like to become king but he is also a realist. He is a commoner, without any royal connections."

"Commoners have become king before."

"Not often, and only in times of great turmoil. And never while a royal male exists."

"Are you saying Ay would seek to remove me?"

Aanen shook his head. "Not even Ay would do that. He knows that the best he can hope for is to control a king. He achieves a lot with the Heretic; he would hope to do the same with his successor."

"Me."

"Or your brother Tutankhaten, though his name speaks against him."

"Names have been changed before, also by a brother."

"That is true, but he is still a child and unproven. You have shown yourself a friend of Amun."

"And you would seek to make me king in place of my brother Akhenaten?" Smenkhkare threw his cup to the floor, the wine splashing Aanen's robes. The young man glared at the priest, his colour rising. "What would you have me do, priest? Plunge in the sword myself? Or do you favour poison?" He whirled and strode to the doorway, yelling for the palace guards. "This is rank treason, Aanen, and I cannot, will not, ignore it. Guards!"

Aanen got up so quickly he knocked the chair to the floor with a clatter. "No, no, you misunderstand me, Smenkhkare. We do not want you to replace the king, just dilute his influence."

Behind him, Smenkhkare could hear the guard running up the corridor towards the royal apartments. He looked at his uncle through slitted eyes, still angry but in control again. "What do you mean?"

"The removal of the king by assassination would throw the country into chaos and hand our beloved Two Lands to the Hittite. Nobody wants that." Aanen started to talk faster as the shouts of the guards drew nearer. "We had in mind a co-regency, the Her ... Akhenaten and you. Within months."

"Why would the king agree to that?" He held up a hand as the first guard charged up, his sword drawn. "Wait. Stand fast." Smenkhkare walked forward a few paces and lowered his voice so only Aanen could hear his words. "Why would he do that?"

"He wouldn't, of his own initiative, but he could be persuaded. Akhenaten is blind to the chaos he causes but even he can at last see there are troubles. Ay can convince him to make you co-regent and put you in charge of Waset."

"Would I want that?"

"Think of it, Smenkhkare. Akhenaten refuses to venture outside of his city, preferring to while away his days with pleasure and his god. You, on the other hand know the common man and recognize the need he has for the old gods. You would be king to the rest of Kemet. Bring back the old worship, slowly of course, but stabilise Kemet, increase funding to the army, and counteract the blindness of the king. You would not be acting against your brother but rather, saving him, allowing him to follow his god unhindered while the rest of Kemet gets back to normal." Aanen's eyes flicked to the doorway and the soldiers blocking it with drawn swords.

"Why would Ay do that? What does he gain?"

"He thinks he gains influence over a young and untried prince." Aanen ventured a slight smile. "You and I know different. Under your leadership Kemet can become strong again. The gods will renew their blessings and everyone will achieve peace and prosperity – not just a few Atenist sycophants and nobles, but even the peasants and labourers."

Smenkhkare stared at Aanen for several minutes before walking past him to the window, once more staring down into the garden. His fingers drummed on the balustrade. He turned, nodding. "I will think on this. Where can I contact you?"

Aanen felt his knees weaken with relief. "At the temple of Amun, in the caretaker's cottage. He will know where to find me."

"Guards," Smenkhkare said, forcing a smile to his lips. "My uncle wishes to leave the palace. Please escort him to the palace gates safely." He bowed slightly to Aanen and watched as the old man left, guards hemming him close as he left.

At the palace gates, Aanen gathered his plain robe about him and hurried off toward the city, not even glancing toward the open gates of the defaced Amun temple. He penetrated deep into the city, nobody paying him any attention, until he came to an inn close to the Street of Whores. Inside, he looked around the small dimly-lit room with its bevy of drinkers and dice-players, spotting the man he sought in a corner; his back turned, hunched over a pot of beer. He walked over.

"Mahuhy."

The young entrepreneur looked up in surprise, then a calculating look came over him. "Aanen." He nodded, smiling. "A beer?"

"No thank you. He is here?"

"Nearby. Are you sure you will not have a pot? It really is rather good."

"No. Take me to him."

Mahuhy shrugged and drained his own pot before leading the way out into the bright sunshine. "This way." He led the older man around the corner into the Street of Whores.

"He is down here?"

"Why not? Who would look for a high priest in a whorehouse? Then again, maybe they would." Mahuhy laughed at his joke, and then again at Aanen's expression.

They entered the whorehouse through a side door, Mahuhy nodding pleasantly at the old woman in the entrance before leading him up long flights of stairs to an upper floor. Around them could be heard the sounds of women engaged in the pursuits of their profession. He stopped and indicated a rough and splintered door. "In there." Turning, the young man sauntered away, his fingers jingling a few pieces of copper in his purse.

Aanen pushed through the door and saw a man in a plain robe and a wig sitting on the low bed flicking at something on the lumpy straw-filled mattress. He closed the door and bowed low. "Hem-Netjer, may Amun shower you with blessings."

"You took your time," Amenemhet growled. He sniffed. "Is that wine I smell on you? He received you then?"

"He did, though he played down the family connection."

"What did he say? Will he do it?"

"He is thinking on it, but I believe he will."

Amenemhet slapped at his leg and picked something off the mattress, squeezing it between the nails of his forefinger and thumb. Aanen heard a tiny crunching sound and blood squirted. "Cursed bedbugs." The High Priest looked up impatiently. "When will you know?"

Aanen shook his head. "A day, maybe two. I do not think an ambitious young man will delay long. From his look he will do it."

"Then I will send a messenger to Ay. The sooner we get this under way, the better for all of us."

"You think having Smenkhkare as co-regent will really help the return of Amun and the temples?"

"We discussed this, Aanen. If it does not, then we will seek another solution. There is always another prince, one who may be more amenable to our suggestions."

Chapter Twenty-Five

Life in Akhet-Aten gradually returned to normal when the plague left. Many of the rock tombs to north and south in the surrounding cliffs found occupancy earlier than intended but for the poor, only shallow graves in the desert sands gave their relatives any semblance of hope that their loved ones might enjoy the pleasures of the afterlife. Life went on. Widows and widowers found new partners, children found themselves with different parents or with grandparents suddenly gone, yet food had still to be found, clothing supplied and debts paid, pleasures eked out of meager incomes. After a few months, the people of Akhet-Aten realized that they still lived in the best place in Kemet, near their king, and if he could go on, so could they.

Akhenaten had suffered his first setback in his privileged life. The last thirteen years had been nothing but a time of joy for him. Although set about by the cares and worries of managing an empire, he had managed to leave most of that to a succession of other people; his father first, then Tiye, his mother. After her, Ay and his council had taken the troubles of the land upon themselves, leaving him free to worship his god, seek beauty and enjoy the delicious body of his lovely young wife and the wonderful daughters they had produced.

His three young darling daughters; Meketaten, Neferneferouaten-tasherit and little Setepenra lay in the city's House of the Dead for the required seventy days, then had been laid to rest in their tiny rock tombs. Meketaten had her own as she had lived long enough for construction of the rock chambers to be almost complete. The two younger girls shared the tomb prepared for their older sister Meryetaten. The funerals were perfunctory, not because of any lack of love or desire to deny the deceased everything they would need for their journey through death's dark doors; but solely because the complex and mysterious rites pertaining to the old gods were absent. Aten was the only god painted on the walls, prayers to Aten were the only ones written on scraps of papyrus hidden among the folds of the mummy cloths, and hymns to Aten were the only sounds heard in the tombs.

Queen Nefertiti withdrew, with her three surviving daughters, after the funerals and kept to herself, shunning the public life and her strange husband. Akhenaten also withdrew, mostly into silence. He spent long hours alone in the wasteland close to the valley of the royal tombs, talking to his god. Striving to understand how the Aten could deal such a dreadful blow to his only son, the king stared into the bright sky, squinting into the glare, endeavoring to see the face of the Aten. He would stumble back to the palace, his head pounding with pain and brightly coloured images of the Aten dancing in front of him. Cold compresses eased the pain, along with an anointing with oil in which the skull of a catfish had been fried. His eyes were soothed with brain of tortoise mixed in honey, the sticky mess being applied externally.

One afternoon, as the king lay groaning with pain in his darkened bedchamber, attended by Shepseskare the physician, Grand Tjaty Ay came to see him.

"Leave us, Shepseskare. I must speak with the king."

The physician looked enquiringly at Akhenaten. "My lord?" When the king waved a hand in dismissal he bowed and left the bedchamber.

Ay drew up a chair and sat down on it, close to the bed. He examined the king's blotched and sunburnt face below the wet linen compress and the revolting-looking sticky mass on his eyes. "Akhenaten, we must talk."

The king groaned and put a hand up to his temple, touching it gingerly. "How have I offended the Aten, Divine Father? Why has he taken my daughters from me?"

Ay still felt grief for his dead granddaughters but the pain had eased. Other things concerned him now. "The Aten did not send the plague, Waenre. Who knows why these things happen? Perhaps you should focus on your three surviving daughters and your wife. You do not see much of them."

"Nefertiti keeps to herself. She even refuses me the solace of her body. My daughters too. They lock themselves away in the queen's palace."

"They grieve too, Waenre, and they need their husband and father by them now. You should be comforting them, not spending your days staring at the sun."

"I want to see the face of the Aten. I want to look into his face while he tells me why he took my daughters."

"The Khabiru say no man can see the face of their god."

"But I am his only son. Surely a loving father will allow his face to be seen?"

"And have you seen the face of the Aten, my king? In all the weeks of your penance, have you seen his face?" Ay shook his head before realizing the king could not see him. "No. All it has got you is pain and despair. Leave this fruitless search for a reason and come back to a family that needs you and a land that needs you too."

Akhenaten said nothing for a long time. He rubbed his temples with his fingers and when he got the sticky honey-tortoise brain mix on them, wiped them on the sheets. At length he sighed deeply. "Perhaps you are right, Divine Father. I should not hide myself away."

Ay smiled. The first of his two tasks had been accomplished. "Go to your wife and daughters, beloved king. Love them and comfort them. All will be well again."

"I fear my Nefertiti has cooled toward me somewhat. She avoids me, she no longer attends upon the Aten at the temple and she finds excuses not to lie with me."

"She grieves for her children, Waenre. Perhaps she even seeks to blame the god for the tragedy. You must make an effort. Talk to her, be loving."

"Yes. Perhaps then we will have other children. Sons even. It is possible."

"That brings me to the point of my visit, Waenre."

The king smiled gently, his first in many months. "What? You did not come out of concern for your king?"

"That too, of course." Ay hesitated, collecting his thoughts. "My lord king, you are thirty-five years old and have been married for fourteen years. You have been blessed with beautiful daughters but alas, no sons. My lord, sons are necessary if you are to keep your family on the throne of Kemet."

"Then the queen and I will have to have more children. Perhaps my physician can recommend a potion that will result in sons."

"I pray that that will be the case. However, even if you had a son by this time next year, my lord, it would be another fifteen years before he was old enough to mount the throne. Sixteen years is a long time to leave Kemet hostage to the vagaries of fate, and you would be an old man. And what if you do not have a son?"

"I cannot see what else I can do, Ay. Either I have a son to succeed me or ... maybe Meryetaten could become king after me. There have been female kings before.

389

Why, my ancestress Hatshepsut became king despite her sex."

"It would not be advisable, my lord. Queens have a way of inciting power struggles and Kemet needs stability."

"How then? Do I find some nobleman to marry Meryetaten? Who is there that is worthy to join my family? Besides, the throne would pass from my family to another."

"I was thinking more in terms of finding a successor within the family."

"Who? Do you mean yourself, Ay? You are not royal, much as I love and respect you."

"I do not mean myself, Waenre. I have no ambitions to rule."

"Then who?"

"There are suitable princes." Ay breathed deeply, clearing his mind for the essential arguments. "Your brothers Smenkhkare and Tutankhaten."

Akhenaten said nothing but he sat upright, taking the damp cloth from his head and used it to wipe the honey and brain mixture from his eyes. He stared blearily at Ay, pressing the backs of his hands against his eyeballs and blinking several times. "I still see the sun disk," he complained. "But in strange colours. It obscures your face Ay." The king folded the sticky cloth and laid it on the small table beside the bed. "Tutankhaten is but a baby."

"But Smenkhkare is not. He is a fine young man trained in all the arts of government. Fifteen years old and managing the city of Waset with a deft touch."

"Smenkhkare? Fifteen already? It scarcely seems possible." Akhenaten shook his head, wincing and lowering his head into his hands in pain. "You say he is competent?"

"Indeed he is. He is learned in the laws and he has the skills of a scribe. I have also made sure he is a priest of Aten. He knows the city well and the people love him as your brother." Ay's voice took on a cajoling tone. "The people of Waset know that you have made Akhet-Aten your home and will never leave. They accept this though they are grief-stricken that you will never live among them as the kings of your family have always done. If you raised your brother to the co-regency it would bring stability to Waset and maybe even the whole country. It would also leave you free to rule Akhet-Aten without having to worry about what went on elsewhere."

"That is tempting. Would he accept the co-regency?"

"I cannot imagine him turning down such an honour, despite his avowed intention of living a life of learning and worship of the Aten. I am sure he would recognize his duty to Kemet and to you."

"Really, Ay? I had not thought him so devoted to Aten. Well, this bears thinking about." Akhenaten got up and staggered across to the curtained window, waving away Ay's attempt to help. He pulled the curtains apart, uttering a low cry of pain as the late afternoon light speared his tender eyes. He turned back into the room, shielding his face from the light.

"What if I have a son later? I would want him to be king after me."

"Who knows what will happen by the time he reaches an age to be king? Make him a co-regent also. Either way, your line is assured."

"I would like to have my descendants on the throne though, and Smenkhkare, while my brother, is not a product of my loins. And what if he has a son? Will he not want him to succeed? I am starting to think this is

391

not such a good idea, Ay. Perhaps I should just concentrate on having a son with my queen."

"Marry Smenkhkare to Meryetaten."

"Eh? What did you say? Smenkhkare and Meryetaten?"

"Why not? He is a prince of the blood and she is your eldest daughter. If he is made co-regent, the marriage confirms him as heir and if they have a son, he will be of your loins and king."

"Yes, by the Aten, that is a wonderful idea." Akhenaten paused and frowned. "But they hardly know each other and they certainly are not in love."

"Does that really matter, my lord? Oh, I know you and my daughter are in love and you were when you got married, but that is a rare and beautiful thing. It is not given to everyone to experience such love."

"My mother and father did. He had many wives but he always loved my mother Tiye most of all." Akhenaten sat down on the bed again, his expression boyish and wistful. "I would like my daughter to be in love when she marries."

"That is noble, my lord, and quite possible. Smenkhkare is a handsome young man and Meryetaten a beautiful young woman. How could they not fall in love? Bring him here, make him co-regent and betroth him to your daughter. Let them marry next year. I am positive they will have fallen in love by then."

"You think this is the answer to my problems?"

"Yes I do. Yours and Kemet's."

Akhenaten nodded, making up his mind. "Then let it be so. Send a courier to Waset immediately. Bring Smenkhkare to Akhet-Aten and I will make him co-regent. Then I will betroth him to Meryetaten. They can marry next year."

"A wise decision, my king," Ay said with a smile. "Once more you have shown the wisdom that makes our Two Kingdoms great."

"I thought this was your idea, Ay? Did you not say ...?" Akhenaten paused and peered myopically at his father-in-law. "Surely you suggested Smenkhkare?"

"My lord, I only voiced what was already in your mind. Many times you have commented on the problem and come up with possible solutions. If I have played some small part in bringing your ideas together, then I shall deem it a great honour."

"You are too modest, Divine Father." Akhenaten lay back on the bed and closed his eyes. "I have a headache from all this thinking. I will rest. Go and send the courier to Waset and if you see Shepseskare, send him in. I need some more catfish skull oil."

Ay bowed his way out of the king's bedchamber and hurried away in search of the physician, well pleased with himself. Instead of Shepseskare however, he found the young physician Nebhotep.

"Have you seen Shepseskare? The king has a headache and desires more catfish skull." Ay hurried past then stopped and turned back. "Perhaps you could see him. You know how to make catfish skull oil, don't you?"

Nebhotep grimaced but nodded. "I was instructed well. However, catfish skull is nearly useless for headaches. The older physicians swear by it, but that is only because they refuse to look for better methods. I favour willow bark myself."

"Well, I will leave the king in your hands. I have other matters to attend to."

Nebhotep watched the Tjaty trot off down the corridor, heading toward the servants' quarters and the stables. He turned and sauntered toward the king's bedchamber, nodding pleasantly at the guard who greeted him and thanked him. The guard had sampled loose women indiscriminately and developed a case of the pox. After trying various home remedies, none of which worked, he had consulted Nebhotep with his last piece of copper. The physician had prepared a paste of cinnabar and bade him apply it to the sores morning and evening. A month later his genitals were scarred but otherwise in fine working order, as numerous city women could since attest.

"Frequent a better class of brothel, Khay," Nebhotep told him. "Or you will need my cinnabar again."

Khay grinned and let him through into the king's bedchamber.

Nebhotep found Akhenaten lying eyes shut on the bed with the late afternoon sunlight streaming across him. He coughed to announce himself and crossed to the bed, sitting down on the edge.

"Ah, Nebhotep. I was expecting Shepseskare. My headache has come back and I need more catfish skull oil."

"I can give you something better than that." Nebhotep unrolled his small physician's bundle on the table beside the bed and took out a small packet of dark brown powder.

"What's that? Dried dung or bat's guts or something equally horrible?"

Nebhotep laughed. "Nothing that exotic – or useless. This is just powdered willow bark. I warn you, it tastes bitter. I usually mix it into honeyed milk for children. I could send for some, if you want."

Akhenaten grimaced. "Now I will have to take it unhoneyed. Get on with it."

Nebhotep poured a measure of the powder into a cup and added water. "It needs to soak in. Leave it a few minutes." He dipped a cloth into the pitcher of water and wiped away a crusted deposit from the corners of the king's eyes, then sniffed the rag. "Tortoise brain? It won't do you any good, you know."

"Why are you different from the other physicians, Nebhotep?"

"Because I choose my remedies rather than just following old ones blindly. Now, let's have a look at your eyes." Nebhotep turned the king's head gently to face the light and drew back the reddened lids. "How is your vision?"

"I keep seeing the sun's disk, even when I close my eyes. Different colours. It makes it hard to see things around me."

"You know people have been blinded looking at the sun? Man's eyes were not made to see the glory of the god." Nebhotep completed his examination. "I can give you a wash that will sooth the inflammation, but I can do nothing about the images. They may fade with time or ..." he hesitated. "Or you may start to lose your sight."

Akhenaten lay silent for several minutes before sighing gently. "I am in the hands of the Aten."

Nebhotep picked up the cup of water and swirled it, noting the colour of the liquid. "This is ready now." He held the cup out and Akhenaten shifted into a sitting position and took it. He sniffed doubtfully, and then sipped the brown liquid.

"*Aagh*. That is foul." The king swallowed the tiny sip and almost gagged. He looked at the physician reproachfully and drank again, forcing the liquid down. When he reached the dregs he handed the cup back and belched.

"Could you not have put honey in it anyway, without telling me children needed it?"

Nebhotep stifled a smile. "I am sorry, my lord. However, I think you will find your headache easing within minutes, especially if we darken the room." He got up and crossed to the window, tugging the curtains across.

"I wish all my problems were as easily fixed," Akhenaten murmured, settling back against the headrest and closing his eyes.

"The problems of the body I can attempt, but the problems of the state I must leave to my king and his ministers."

"It is a problem of both body and state, Nebhotep. I have no sons."

"Ah."

"Can you remedy that, good physician? Have you a potion in that roll of yours that will make me sire a son?"

"If I had I could make my fortune, my lord."

"Yes, it is as I thought, Nebhotep. It is in the hands of the Aten. If he wants me only to have daughters, then I must bow to his will."

Nebhotep sat down on the bed again, chewing his bottom lip. "I would not presume to argue religious philosophy with you, my lord, but purely from a medical point of view, there may be things you could try."

Akhenaten opened one eye and stared at the physician. "What things?"

"Nothing that would guarantee a favourable outcome but there are many remedies for reproductive problems used by country doctors. For instance, it is said that binding the testicles against the body and applying heated pads can prevent conception when next the man lies with a woman."

"That could be useful, I admit, Nebhotep, but I do not see how that applies to me."

"I merely cite it as an example of a country remedy. More to the point is an examination of many families. Why is it that some men throw male children only, others girls, but most have mixed boys and girls? What is it about their home circumstances that produce this result?"

"You have studied this?"

"I have, though the results are confusing. For instance, many families with boys eat a lot of onions, whereas those with girls eat more lettuce. Of course, this may just be that families with boys send them out to do more physical labour and onions are a staple of the working man, whereas lettuce is eaten more in the home, where the girls are." Nebhotep shrugged. "Then there is the anecdotal evidence. One woman with boys swears it is because she uses a douche of beer just before intercourse, another swears it is by thinking of manly pursuits during the pregnancy, yet another thinks it is the relationship between the birth date and the flooding of the river."

"You think I should have Nefertiti use a beer douche and think of ... of war?"

"It could not hurt, my lord. I suppose what might be more useful is to look at your own family. Sometimes families have only boys or girls for generations."

"There are boys in my line," Akhenaten said hopefully.

"Indeed. Yet the Divine Father Ay has only daughters and your illustrious father had only two sons, but five daughters."

"Four sons, Nebhotep. You are forgetting Smenkhkare and Tutankhaten."

"Yes, my lord, yet if you will forgive me pointing out, your beloved mother, who was sister to Ay who only produces daughters, only had two sons. The young princes had other mothers."

"That is true, but is it relevant? I mean, does the mother really matter? Is it not the man who sires a child in the fertile field of a woman?"

Nebhotep shrugged again. "Who knows? Yet it sometimes happens that if a man is childless he takes another wife and has children. In such a case the woman is barren; her field is anything but fertile. Could it not also be true that a woman's womb is sometimes hostile to male children, only allowing girls to be born? In such a case the identity of the mother would be of supreme importance."

"Hmm." Akhenaten closed his eyes and thought about this idea for several minutes before opening them again and fixing his physician with a look of dawning comprehension. "My father Nebmaetre had two sons and five daughters with his wife Tiye, then he married his daughter Sitamen and had a son, then married his daughter Iset and had another son. He changed the mother, who preferred daughters to sons, and had sons himself."

"That would appear to be so," Nebhotep said cautiously.

"My own wife Nefertiti only has girls. It is obvious her womb is hostile to male children. If I want sons I must marry some other woman." Akhenaten's jaw dropped and his eyes opened wide. "I must follow the example of my father and marry my daughters. My lovely eldest daughter Meryetaten shall bear my son. Maybe even Ankhesenpaaten later, or even my sister Beketaten." The king sat up abruptly and swung his legs over the side

398

of the bed. "This could be the answer to my problems," he said excitedly. "Thank you, Nebhotep."

Akhenaten got up and started dancing, a big grin on his face. Suddenly he stopped and put a hand up to his head. "My headache has gone too. Nebhotep, you solve all my problems. I am going to make you my official court physician."

Chapter Twenty-Six

Nefertiti looked up from the game she was playing with her youngest surviving daughter Neferneferoura when her husband walked into the wide verandah in the queen's palace overlooking the gardens. Crickets chirped in the bushes and leaf litter beneath the verandah and bats flitted and wheeled in the early evening sky. The older daughters Meryetaten and Ankhesenpaaten lay on their stomachs near the edge of the gardens, engrossed in a game that involved a lacquered wooden board and carved stone pieces.

"Greetings, husband," she said with a smile. "Come and sit with us."

Akhenaten looked around the room then stared intently at the older girls, his vision swimming with images of the Aten, before lowering himself to the floor beside his wife. He put an arm around her and kissed her cheek.

"Look, daddy," Neferneferoura said, holding up a battered doll made of rags and wood. "I have a baby brother. His name is Akh'naten too, just like you."

Akhenaten smiled and flipped the little girl's side lock. "You'd like a baby brother would you?"

Nefertiti's smile faded. "Husband, this is not the time to discuss this again," she said in a low voice. "I do not want more children. I thought we were agreed."

"We do need to talk, beautiful one. Send the girls away."

Nefertiti frowned and searched her husband's face before saying, "Merye, take your sisters for a walk in the garden."

"Meryetaten can stay," Akhenaten said. "Ankhese, take your sister Nefer outside please."

400

Ankhesenpaaten took her little sister by the hand and led her down the steps into the garden. They sat by the pool and watched the bats flying over the water, catching insects. Meryetaten moved closer to her parents, intrigued at being included in the talk, wondering what was to come.

Nefertiti got up off the floor and sat down on a wide padded chair, the arms of which were carved to resemble open-jawed hippopotamuses. She regarded her husband coolly. "What do you need to say, husband? We have talked over all this before. When I birthed Setepenra the physicians said it would be unwise to have more children."

"I remember, Nefertiti, my beautiful one. But surely you can see my problem? I need a son to leave the kingdom to. Your father was here today ..."

"I am the eldest, father," Meryetaten interrupted. "Why can I not inherit? There have been ruling queens of Kemet before."

"Don't interrupt, Merye," Nefertiti said quietly. "What did my father say?"

"He wanted to talk about the succession. We had a long and frank discussion about the governance of Kemet."

"With respect, husband, what would you know about governing Kemet? How long is it since you took an interest in anything outside of this city?"

"I acknowledge the great help you have been to me, Nefertiti. You and your father have made my life as Aten's high priest much easier by attending to such dreary matters, but that is not the point. That is not what I want to talk about."

"I am not going to have any more children. I am over thirty and I have had six children. No more."

401

"I do not want you to."

Nefertiti frowned. "Then what did you and my father talk about?"

"He wants me ... well, actually it was my idea ... to bring Smenkhkare to Akhet-Aten and make him co-regent. He can then rule Kemet from Waset. He would eliminate those troublesome priests, look after affairs of state and such and leave me to rule here in Akhet-Aten."

"That is a good idea." Nefertiti's eyebrows rose in surprise, relief tingeing her voice. "And what did my father say?"

"Oh, he agreed. He has sent a courier off to Waset to fetch Smenkhkare. With Aten's blessing we can have the co-regency ceremonies next month."

Nefertiti smiled, getting up and embracing her husband. "Who says you are not a statesman, my husband. That is a wonderful solution. Smenkhkare is your brother so he will be loyal, he is young and handsome and is well loved in Waset, I hear." She hugged Akhenaten again then walked over to stand behind her daughter. "If I might suggest something that would make it perfect – marry him to Meryetaten."

"Your father suggested that too."

"Me? Marry Smenkhkare?" Meryetaten broke in excitedly. "He is very handsome." She blushed and hid her face.

"It would be a very advantageous match for all concerned, darling," Nefertiti soothed. "Your father needs a male heir and Smenkhkare as co-regent would of course become king in time. And you would become queen, child, ruling with him and giving him sons to rule after him. It is the perfect solution."

"Not perfect," Akhenaten said. "But a good short-term solution for the governing of Kemet. I would still like a son of my own body to follow me. Smenkhkare is my brother, not myself."

"I have said I will not have more children."

"I do not expect you to."

Nefertiti stared at her husband, trying to make sense of his words. "What are you saying, husband? You want to have children with another woman? Have you forgotten your holy vow to me, made when we were betrothed? You swore to have relations with me alone, no others."

"I know I did but that was before ... before I knew you could not bear sons."

"Is that my fault? Perhaps the fault is yours. Maybe you cannot sire a son."

Akhenaten flushed. "I am the king. Do not think to lay this blame on me. Besides it is easily tested."

"No doubt." A harsh edge crept into Nefertiti's voice. "And what woman have you chosen to favour with your royal member? I hope at least she is of noble birth."

"She is of the highest. I have decided to marry Meryetaten."

Nefertiti stared, every thought driven from her head. The only sign that the king's words had registered on her mind were her fingernails as they dug into Meryetaten's shoulders.

"*Aah*. Mother, you are hurting me." Meryetaten twisted, pulling away from her mother. Rubbing her shoulders, she backed away to stand in between her parents, looking from one to the other, unsure of what her response should be. "Wh... what do you mean, father? Marry you?"

"Yes, marry me, lie with me and have a son that will rule as king over the Two Lands after me, carrying the word of Aten to all the lands of the earth."

"You are mad," Nefertiti whispered. "Your Aten has finally addled your mind. You have been out in the sun too long."

"What? Mad to want a son to succeed me and carry on my work? It is obvious you cannot or will not bear a son for me, so for Kemet's sake and for the sake of my father the Aten I must look elsewhere for a mother for my son."

"Your daughter? You would impregnate your own daughter?"

"Why not? My father Nebmaetre lay with his daughter Sitamen and had a fine, strong son – Smenkhkare. He then bedded his other daughter Iset and had Tutankhaten. If he had lived, no doubt he would have lain with his daughter Beketaten and had yet another son." Akhenaten started pacing the room, flinging his arms about, his voice getting shriller and louder. The girls in the garden looked up in concern, wondering what was happening. "I tell you, I have had a revelation. It is the union of father and daughter that produces sons. I will marry Meryetaten and have a son to succeed me. Maybe even my other daughters when they are old enough. And Beketaten my sister. There are many fine young women who will give me sons."

Nefertiti trembled and tears made her eyes sparkle in the lamp light. "And what of us, husband?" Her voice shook. "Do our years together mean nothing? Have I not stood by you, even when you ripped Kemet apart with your religion? Have I not given you six daughters, beautiful, loving daughters ..." Tears started to trickle from the corners of her eyes. "Daughters that your god has snatched from us – Meketaten, her name means 'Protected by Aten' – where was his protection, husband? And my little Tasherit and baby Setepenra. Did I give my life and my love to you to have you and your god rip my heart out and trample it?" Nefertiti burst into tears and stood there, head lowered as her tears dripped and stained her gown, her body shaking with sobs.

Akhenaten frowned and glanced around the room, then at Meryetaten who was also starting to cry. "Stop that Merye, there is no need." He paused, and then took a step closer to his wife. "Nefer, my love, there is no need for this. Of course I love you and appreciate the way you have been by my side all these years. It hasn't been all bad though, has it? You are Queen of Kemet, you have power and prestige and riches. You are acknowledged as the most beautiful woman on earth; your likeness is painted by artists and fashioned by sculptors ..."

"And despite this you will cast me aside?"

"I am not casting you aside, Nefer my darling. You will remain as queen by my side. All that will happen is I'll have a son by Meryetaten, your daughter – our daughter – why, it is almost as if you are giving birth to my son."

"What has happened to you, husband? You were once so loving. My joy was your joy and my hurt was your hurt. You promised to love only me." Nefertiti shook her head, wiping the tears from her cheeks and sniffing loudly. Turning, she walked to the edge of the wide verandah and watched as her two youngest daughters played in the darkness by the pool. A nearly full moon was rising over the Eastern cliffs, casting a pale golden glow over the garden. A fish jumped in the pool, the ripples spreading outward and distorting the image of the moon in the still water.

"The Aten has distorted you, husband. You have become so focused, so obsessed with your god that you are as blind to reality as you are becoming by staring at the midday sun." Nefertiti turned back to face Akhenaten, her face set and hard. "I reject your desires, King Waenre Akhenaten. I and my daughters will move to the North Palace tonight. You will not visit us there. You may play your little games with your god in your little city and ignore what is happening around you. I will have no part of it." She turned and called to her daughters. "Come Ankhese, Nefer. Come to your mother." Gathering her children to her skirts, she hugged them fiercely. "We are going to the North Palace, darlings. You like it there, don't you?"

Nefertiti walked past her husband to the door of the anteroom, her arms around her two youngest daughters. "Come Merye." Turning to look at him as she passed, she added. "I think Beketaten had better come with us too. If I left her behind, no doubt she would fall victim to your lechery." She beckoned to her eldest daughter impatiently. "Come Merye."

Akhenaten trembled with the stress of the confrontation but his voice remained calm. "Stay Merye. Stay with me."

Meryetaten took a step toward her mother then stopped, looking anxiously from one parent to the other.

"Stay with me and be queen," Akhenaten said, his voice low and cajoling. "Your mother abdicates her role by leaving me. She is no longer queen. Stay with me and be my queen. I need you by my side."

The girl licked her lips nervously. "Mother?"

"Don't listen to him, you little fool. He only wants to take advantage of you. Do you really want to spread your legs for your own father? You deserve better. Now obey me."

Meryetaten looked at her father. "I would be queen? Really queen? Not just a title?"

"In truth, Meryetaten, Beloved of Aten. I will chisel your mother's name from the monuments and substitute yours. You will be known as 'The Beautiful' and adored by all who see you. You will sit beside me on the throne of Kemet and our son will be king after me."

"I ... I ... mother, I cannot ..."

"You are a fool, Meryetaten, if you cannot see his lies. What do you think will happen if you produce another girl child? He will cast you aside for another."

"I ... I would be Queen Meryetaten." She hesitantly walked over to her father and stood by him, facing her mother. She raised her chin defiantly. "I will be queen."

Nefertiti bowed her head and her body shook once more. Then without another look at her husband and eldest daughter, she swept from the room with as much dignity as she could muster, her younger daughters trailing after her, distraught and puzzled.

***

Three hours later, Nefertiti, her daughters, Beketaten and a whole bevy of ladies in waiting, cosmeticians, mistresses of the wardrobe, cooks, attendants and the many servants that keep a palace running efficiently, had moved over to the North Palace. As this residence already had its own staff, accommodation in the servants' quarters quickly became critical and matters disintegrated into chaos. Nurses hustled Ankhesenpaaten and Neferneferoura off to bed in the aired out bedrooms of the palace and set about preparing ones for Princess Beketaten and the queen.

Rumors sped through the palace, spreading like a dust storm in the howling west wind from the desert. The queen has deserted the king, some said. Others that it was the other way round. A few believed the Aten had commanded the split and one maidservant, who had overheard something from the king's apartments, said he was taking his own daughter Meryetaten as wife. This last idea was shouted down as being too absurd. Yet the princess concerned remained in the old palace and the queen was in a cold fury, snapping at any intrusion into her apartments. Only Beketaten was allowed in.

"Your brother has gone mad," Nefertiti hissed. "He has cast me off despite his vows, and plans to make Meryetaten his queen. He wants a son by her."

Beketaten thought about this for a few minutes. "He ... he will force her?"

"The little bitch has agreed. She wants to be queen and cannot see what this means. She will cast her own mother aside."

"But my lady – sister – you are still queen. How can he do this?"

"He is the king, as he is so fond of pointing out," Nefertiti said bitterly. "He has cast me aside already for that whoring daughter of mine and will no doubt divorce me."

"The people will not support him, lady. You are much loved."

"Oh, Beketaten, you are young and naïve. The people mean nothing. If the king has the army behind him he can do anything he pleases."

"Your father?"

Nefertiti considered. "Yes, my father may be able to help. He is Tjaty, a high priest of Aten and still commander of the local garrison. We shall hope so, for if not, that madman will ruin all of us." She sat down on a couch in her suite and looked across at the young princess standing by the bed. "Do you know what will happen when Meryetaten produces a girl child? Oh, I am sure she will. My husband's member is short and his semen weak. He has not the strength to sire sons and he has the temerity to blame me for our daughters." Her voice rose from bitterness to anger and she got to her feet, clenching her fists in rage. "Do you know what he will do? He plans to force himself upon Ankhesenpaaten and probably little Nefer too – and you, Beketaten. He mentioned you by name."

Beketaten shrank back, shuddering, her hands unconsciously moving protectively in front of her. "No, I cannot. I will not. I am promised ..."

"Promised?" Nefertiti cocked her head in curiosity. "Promised to whom? By whom?" She smiled slowly despite her former fury. "Princess Beketaten – little Scarab – who keeps to herself except when she is with ..." The queen laughed. "Smenkhkare? You have promised yourself to Smenkhkare? Does he know?" She laughed again then shook her head. "It does not matter. Akhenaten means to bring Smenkhkare to Akhet-Aten and make him co-regent. There was talk of marrying him to Meryetaten though that may no longer happen. Either way, little Beketaten, your handsome young man is out of your reach."

"He will not leave me," Beketaten whispered. "He is good and strong and faithful."

"He is a man. He is governed by power and riches and by his testicles." Nefertiti shook her head though she still smiled. "Put him out of your head, Beketaten. We shall send you north I think, to the old king's residence in Ineb Hedj. You will be out of harm's way and later ..." Her voice trailed off and she sat down on the bed again, her attention drifting from her conversation. "Ineb

409

Hedj," she muttered. "Yes, there's a thought. I could raise an army from Ta Mehu ..."

"My lady?"

Nefertiti shook herself. "Go to bed, Beketaten. We will discuss this again in the morning. My father Ay will be here soon and I need to talk to him privately."

Beketaten nodded and crossed the room, kissing the seated queen on the cheek before leaving the room. When the sound of her footsteps had faded, Nefertiti arose and went into the next room where she made use of the water channel toilet now installed in all the palaces. She rinsed her hands in a bowl of water with floating rose petals and dried them on a clean linen towel. Going back into her bedchamber she poured herself a cup of wine and carried it over to the window, where she sat. She stared out over the river, glistening in the bright moonlight, sipping her drink and waiting for her father.

Ay arrived as the moon dipped toward the west, casting its silvery glow into Nefertiti's darkened chamber. Only one torch still burned in its wall sconce, guttering low and throwing flickering shadows over the furniture.

"Daughter?" Ay stood in the doorway, searching the shadowed room for any sign of life.

A shadow moved, flowing up out of a chair beside the window, running toward the door. Nefertiti threw herself into her father's arms with a sob, clinging to him. She overtopped her father by a head but had anyone been looking, there would have been no doubt where the strength in that relationship lay. The wife of the king had been a queen for fourteen years but tonight was just a woman, hurt and bewildered and angry. Her father had been a force in the land since the days of the old king and was now second only to the king in power. As he comforted his daughter, his mind was cool, calculating, seeking the avenue of action that would benefit him the most.

"Father, he has thrown me over for that little slut Meryetaten. How could she do this? How could he?"

"I heard, daughter. Now calm yourself, stop crying. I brought you up better than that." Ay led Nefertiti over to the bed and sat her down. He went back out into the corridor and fetched another two burning torches, fixing them in the place of burned out ones in the bedchamber. The ruddy glow of the resinous torches immediately brought a more cheerful aspect to the room.

Nefertiti in the meantime, wiped away her tears and composed herself. Taking the double lapis and gold earrings from her left ear, and the heavy gold and onyx chain from around her neck, she placed them carefully on the bedside table before crossing back to the main table with its wine and fruit. She poured herself another cup of wine and one for her father too. Handing him his, she drank, looking coolly in his eyes, in control of herself once more.

"What can I do, father?"

"What do you want to do?"

"I want to castrate the lecherous son of a whore," she hissed viciously.

"Be serious, child. Besides, his mother was my sister and your aunt. Do not denigrate her. I repeat. What is it you want?"

"I want to be queen. I want my daughter out of his bed. I want ... I want to humiliate him."

"You can probably achieve some of that. As you know, in Kemet, men and women are equal before the law. He can petition the courts for a divorce but they will not automatically grant it if you contest it. He may be the king but he is not above the law. Without a divorce, you

411

technically remain the queen. I put it to you though, that you may not want the position. He can humiliate you, slighting you in public, flaunting Meryetaten as his chosen wife."

"Stop him bedding my daughter."

"That cannot be done. There is ample precedent that allows a king as many wives as he chooses, from wherever he chooses. Kings regularly marry their sisters and the last one married his daughters. And when it comes to lust, a man's member speaks louder than reason. You will not change the king's mind."

"Then help me humiliate him."

"Can you be more precise, daughter? Humiliate him, how? He is already regarded with scorn by our country's enemies and friends alike for his foreign policies, he is hated by the priests who are slowly building the strength to rebel, and he is hated and feared by almost everyone outside Akhet-Aten. The country is racked by disease and famine, cut-throats roam the land unhindered and the people are not even allowed the solace of the gods. Only the army is still loyal, despite his efforts to disband them, largely because of Paatenemheb. He will not break his oath."

"Then I cannot even humiliate him," Nefertiti said dully.

Ay shrugged. "What would you do if you could? Make him appear a fool? Render his rule impotent?" He licked his lips and glanced across the room to the doorway, lowering his voice to a whisper. "Overthrow him?"

Nefertiti stared at her father. "That is treason."

"There are none to hear us." A buzzing, whirring sound came from the window and the two of them swung round as something large and ponderous flew in, across the room, hitting the wall and dropping onto the

412

bed. Ay laughed nervously, relief making him overloud. "A scarab beetle. It is only Khepri."

"The gods themselves hear us," Nefertiti whispered.

Ay raised an eyebrow in surprise. "You still believe in the gods? I thought you were besotted with the Aten like your husband."

"It was a pleasant enough philosophical exercise, father. It made a lot of sense, but as usual, Akhenaten has taken things too far. It hurts Kemet now."

"Indeed it does, daughter. I am glad to see you have come to your senses. Now, back to my original question – what do you seek to do? Shame him or remove him?"

"Remove? I ... I would not have his life on my hands."

"Who said anything about that? The question is, daughter, what would you do afterward? Say you locked him up for his own safety – would you seek to rule in his stead? Pass the kingship on to another?"

"If I passed it on, I negate my own position as queen. I would rule."

Ay smiled, stroking his chin. "I see. Alone or with a man? A man would gain you more acceptance. Remember the lesson of Hatshepsut."

Nefertiti snorted. "What man is there, capable of rule? I have been queen for fourteen years, ruling alongside my husband. Would you have me bring in an untested boy like Smenkhkare as king?"

"What of myself, daughter? I am already powerful and have effectively been ruling Kemet these last few years."

"You? I suppose you would immediately act like the king and marry your daughter. I think not, father."

413

Ay grimaced. "You may be beautiful, Nefertiti, but I have no desire to bed my daughters. Neither you nor Mutnodjme excite me in the slightest."

"Mutnodjme! I have not heard from her in years. How is she, father?"

"Do not change the subject." He looked at his daughter, past the now-strained beauty to the little girl he remembered, growing up with her sister in Zarw, before he started his rise to power in the days of Amenhotep. He relented his harsh tone, adding softly, "She is well, but she will not stir from the estates outside Zarw. She sends her greetings, as always."

"And I mine, father. Tell her when next you see her."

"So what about it? Will you accept my strength, daughter? You rule Kemet from the throne; I rule it with the help of the army from behind the scenes."

"The army would help you? I thought you said Paatenemheb was loyal."

"He is, but when he is presented with the fact, he will go along with it. I am commander of the local garrison. I could disarm the Medjay and capture the palace. We force Akhenaten to publicly abdicate, naming you as his successor until such time as you can find a suitable husband. With my influence, the nobles, the priests and the people will accept you. What do you say?"

"When?"

"As soon as possible. Before Smenkhkare can get up here. Say two weeks, the night of the new moon, at midnight?"

"What about Smenkhkare? Will he be a problem?"

Ay smiled. "I think I can handle an untested youth. And if he proves intractable, well," he shrugged. "There are alternatives. So, you agree to two weeks?"

"That simple?"

"Of course not. There is a lot to plan. We cannot afford for anything to go wrong or for the king or those loyal to him to catch wind of this. But two weeks allows us enough time. Are we agreed?"

Nefertiti stared at her father's power-hungry look. She felt a moment's qualm, but forced it down. Nodding, she said just one word, "Agreed."

Chapter Twenty-Seven

I would like to say I acted calmly, like the adult I had become, but in hindsight I did not act, I reacted, to the news of the queen's dismissal and the possible fate the king had in store for me.

When I arrived in Akhet-Aten with my mother Tiye, I was simply Scarab, a small child on the brink of adolescence, thrust into the company of my royal cousins, a seemingly tight-knit family with no apparent pretensions of their exalted position. Then Meketaten died, the plague swept through Kemet, my mother succumbed on her way back to Waset and I found myself adopted by Akhenaten and Nefertiti as one of their 'garland of daughters'. This adoption was presaged by my presence in the great procession of Akhenaten's Heb-Sed festival where I took the place of the sick Meketaten. I saw the inscriptions later that recorded all six of the king's daughters present at the festival. In the eyes of almost everyone, I was already indistinguishable from the other princesses. I grew up fast, responsibility thrust upon me, and I became a woman. Or rather, I thought I became a woman. How far short I fell was only made apparent to me in those days and nights following the full moon of Nefertiti's withdrawal from the palace.

The night of the withdrawal I accompanied the queen and her two younger daughters to the North Palace, unsure of what was happening, but the emotions of those around me catching me up in the chaos. Then Nefertiti called me into her presence and told me of the danger I was in, and of her own predicament before dismissing me. I went to the bedchamber set aside for me and lay

416

down on the bed in the darkened room, but I could not sleep.

I thought about my beloved Smenkhkare and what it would mean to him, to me – to us, if he became co-regent. I knew he had promised to make me his queen but if Akhenaten gave him his daughter Meryetaten to be his queen, he would have to agree, and where would that leave me? But wasn't Meryetaten now Akhenaten's queen? She could not be the wife of both men. In our Kemet, a king may have more than one wife, but a queen could not have two husbands.

What would the Tjaty Ay do when he found out? He was undoubtedly the most powerful man in Kemet, probably more powerful even than the king, seeing as how Akhenaten kept himself locked away in his city of the Aten, refusing to think about the troubles of the out-side world. And he was Nefertiti's father. The history of our family is filled with intrigue – husband against wife, brother against sister, mother and son, father and daugh-ter – it is that way, I suppose, in any royal house. So it was not a given fact that Ay would side with his daugh-ter. If he did, then what? Could he use his power to force the king to recant? Nefertiti would remain queen but then Smenkhkare would have to marry Meryetaten. And if Ay sided with the king? Then all was chaos but my be-loved was mine. Could I put my happiness ahead of Ke-met's?

I had to know. I could not lie here in the dark, tortur-ing myself. I would go to the queen and wait with her for her father. I got up and stood naked in the silvery light of the nearly-full moon streaming through my window and thought about my course of action. If I went to the queen after being dismissed by her, she would send me back to bed. For all that I thought of myself as an adult –

417

I lovingly stroked the newly formed curves of my naked body – in her eyes I was still a child. At twelve I was old enough to marry but I was younger than her eldest daughter. I could not go to her tonight.

What then? I was determined to know what the most powerful man and woman in Kemet intended. Could I ask a servant? A slave? Would any be allowed near enough to eavesdrop on what would be a highly charged conversation? Very unlikely but ... the thought came crashing back in upon me. Eavesdrop. Could I somehow overhear their conversation? I felt guilty at the thought. I do not know how it is in other lands, but in Kemet we value our privacy, even in the presence of others. The king and queen could talk, perform bodily functions or even make love in the presence of servants yet the servants would ignore what was going on, shutting out sights and sounds. To deliberately spy on others was extremely bad manners. I had been brought up better than that.

I put on a kilt and a shoulder wrap and left my room, moving cautiously through the unfamiliar corridors of the Northern Palace. The paintings on the walls were more complex, the colours brighter and the furnishings more sumptuous than anything I had seen in the main palace. Few servants were around as the hour was close to midnight; those that were hurried about their business, wanting their beds. Few torches burned and I was able to use the deep pools of shadow to tip-toe cautiously toward Nefertiti's apartments. It was as well I was cautious as I failed to see the guard until I was almost on him. I froze, my heart pounding loud enough for him to raise the alarm.

When after a few moments I saw he had neither heard nor seen me, I slipped carefully, very carefully back. Moving in the shadows I put several more paces

418

between us, and then the sound of footsteps sent me scurrying behind an ornate gilded chair.

Ay strode along the corridor toward me. He is a short man, thickset, no more than my own height though I am not yet finished my growth; yet he exuded power. His head, rounded, showed his age quite clearly as his once-shaven skull was now covered with short white stubble, his face creased and lined, his eyes hard and unyielding. I remembered that he was my mother's elder brother and father to Nefertiti, who was now nearly thirty-five years.

He passed me without a sideways glance and continued up the corridor to where the guard, stepping from his shadowed alcove, challenged him.

"See we are not disturbed."

"Yes, Lord Ay." The guard saluted and stepped back into his recess, now fully alert. I knew I could not get past him.

I withdrew myself, back to my room where I sat on my bed and pondered the problem of gaining access to the queen's apartments. Then I remembered the garden. Both her room and mine faced west, toward the river, with a small garden bordering both. Maybe I could use the cover of night and the shrubbery to get close enough to hear.

Climbing over the window sill, I let myself down carefully into the bushes and squatted there for a minute, listening. All I could hear was a murmur of sound from the North Wharf area and the minute sounds of animals. I heard a slow rustle from the dry leaves near me and my mind at once thought of snakes. This was a royal palace; it was quite possible that Wadjet, the coiled cobra of the king waited in the dark, ready to strike at the enemies of Kemet. But I was not an enemy.

"I am Beketaten, daughter of Nebmaetre Amenhotep, and sister of Neferneferure Waenre Akhenaten, and before the gods of Kemet I do no evil," I whispered, holding my hand low to the earth. The rustling ceased and I knew Wadjet would let me live.

Bent double, I ran across the open ground to the bushes under Nefertiti's window and hid, pressing up close to the stonework, my head just below the sill. I could hear a murmur of voices, but indistinct. I would need to get closer. I stood, keeping to the corner of the window and peeped over the edge.

Ay stood near his daughter in the middle of the room, drinking wine from a cup. I thought I could detect the faint aroma of spices from the wine jug and guessed it was the spiced Syrian wine the queen favoured.

"Help me humiliate him," Nefertiti said; her voice low and vicious.

Her father laughed and drank from his cup. "How would you have me do this? His enemies and friends alike scorn him for his foreign policy; the priests hate him, as does almost everyone outside of Akhet-Aten. Our country suffers and the people are not even allowed the solace of free worship. Only the army is loyal, because of Paatenemheb. He will not break his oath."

"Then I cannot do that?"

"What would you do? Make him appear a fool? Render him impotent?" Ay leaned forward and lowered his voice so I missed what he said next, and Nefertiti's response. I strained to hear and my foot slipped, shaking the bushes. A large scarab, motionless on a leaf, took flight, lifting its horny wing covers and launching itself into the lighted room. It hit the far wall and fell onto the bed.

Ay laughed; the sound overly loud after the whispers, his mirth scraped raw with inner tension. "It is only a scarab. Khepri."

Nefertiti must have said something because Ay asked incredulously, "You still believe in the gods?"

I dropped back down into the shrubbery, my heart thumping wildly. I breathed deeply, calming myself and when I dared to put my head up again the conversation had taken on a sinister aspect.

"Will you accept my strength, daughter?" Ay growled, his voice low and dripping with a lust that sent shivers along the hairs of my arms. It spoke of a hunger, not for a woman, but for power. "You rule Kemet from the throne, I rule with the army from behind."

I could feel my heart starting to pound again, this time from real fear. If they had found me outside the window before, I would have been shamed and lost their trust. If they found me now, I would die, for they were surely talking treason. I could feel Ay's powerful hands at my throat, crushing and breaking, and I swallowed convulsively, stifling a sob. I almost ducked away then but I thought that if it was to happen, I should know when the thunderbolt was due. I stood, to listen again.

"I could disarm the Medjay and capture the palace. We force Akhenaten to abdicate, naming you as successor."

"When?"

Ay stroked his chin, his hooded eyes considering. "As soon as possible. Before Smenkhkare can get up here. Say two weeks, the night of the new moon, at midnight."

I heard Nefertiti agree as I slipped away into the night.

I lay in my bed that night, shivering with fear, unable to sleep. I knew enough of history to know that kings

421

often met violent deaths and when kingdoms fell, no-one was safe. What should I do? What could I do? I was a twelve-year old girl – well, a thirteen year old woman almost, but alone. If only Smenkhkare was here; he would know what to do. Could I get word to him? Ay had said the coup was to be in two weeks time, before Smenkhkare could get here. How far away was Waset anyway? I had traveled downriver once, from Waset to Akhet-Aten by royal barge, and the trip had taken ten days. What about by land? How long would it take a messenger to get there and Smenkhkare back again? Who could I trust enough to send? I had far more questions than I had answers.

I dozed fitfully and woke with the pre-dawn chill on my naked body. Pulling the goose feather coverlet over me, I ignored my bladder and lay in the gray light marveling that I had not thought of the answer sooner. I would take the message to Smenkhkare myself. I would travel overland to Waset and bring the tidings of the rebellion. Smenkhkare would hear it from my own lips and furthermore, I would be safe in Waset. Now all that remained was how to do it.

Throwing off the coverlet, I ran over to the toilet and sat down, suddenly in great need. The toilet was one of the new running water designs and when I finished I lifted the sluice gate and watched as my water was carried away.

I dressed in a warm robe and sat by the window. The sun rose behind the palace, throwing a dark shadow clear across the river, but as I watched, the shadows moved, sweeping back toward me, the sun climbing above the eastern cliffs. The cliffs were a problem. Akhet-Aten lies in a crescent shaped plain on the eastern bank some ten thousand paces long. There are ways out of the plain but they call for a difficult passage up the valley that houses the royal tombs or past the quarries. Both routes would be guarded. That left only the river as a means of escape.

The river meant a boat but I knew I could not hope to row upriver against the current. Perhaps across the river to the farms and villages and hire someone to row me south past the cliffs. I could then angle inland and intersect the main road running across the desert to Waset, cutting off the great loop of the river. A horse would be useful, I thought, though I had never ridden one. Nor had most Kemetu, I remembered. We use horses, but mostly to pull war or hunting chariots, seldom riding them. In fact, couriers are the only people I have seen astride a horse. Well, I could learn, couldn't I? How hard could it be? And what would it cost to hire one? I started looking around the room and in my meager belongings for valuable objects.

I looked at the assortment of necklaces, bracelets and brooches dubiously. I had no idea of the worth of my jewelry, never having bought anything of my own. Well, it's either enough or it's not. What else am I going to need? Food and water. There are bound to be watering places, oases or something, but how far apart? A big bottle of water then, but not too big, I may have to carry it a long way. I went back to the window and sat down again, thinking hard about what I would need, until the servants came to bathe and dress me for the new day.

Chapter Twenty-Eight

Ay was up with the dawn and making plans. Used to rising in the pre-dawn darkness when he fulfilled his duties as a high priest of Aten in the lesser temple, he found it hard to break the habit. His duties as Tjaty and adviser to the king, as well as his myriad functions within the court now occupied his time, forcing him away from the temple.

This morning, unable to sleep past his usual time, he had paid another visit to the North Palace, talking to Nefertiti as she sat at her cosmetic table, three of her ladies in attendance. She sent them out of the room and they talked briefly.

"Play the injured wife. Do nothing else. I stress that, daughter, nothing else. Let it be seen that you have been wronged, but outwardly be humble and restrained."

"What will you do?"

"I have plans to make for a royal marriage." Ay coolly regarded his daughter's pale face and smiled. "It will happen anyway. If I can delay his lust it may work to our advantage. There are many things that need to be in place before the new moon. Leave it to me."

Ay entered the king's palace not long after dawn as the morning services to the Aten were finishing in the Great Temple. He hurried through toward the servant's quarters, the bustle of people in the corridors parting before him almost without thought. Ay never even saw the men and women scrambling out of his way, his mind fixed on what he had to do. He found Nebhotep the physician eating his breakfast of barley bread and beer in the small refectory for minor court officials. Waving to him to remain seated, he pulled up a chair and sat down.

424

"Good morning, Nebhotep." Ay glanced around at the smattering of other people in the room. None were close enough to overhear, but he lowered his voice anyway. "You are knowledgeable concerning the royal monthlies?"

Nebhotep raised his eyebrows and put down his barley bread, swallowing his mouthful. "Er ... yes, Tjaty Ay. Er ... may I enquire ..."

"Specifically, when will the princess Meryetaten become unavailable?"

Nebhotep hesitated. "I'm not sure what you mean, Tjaty. Do you mean when will her monthly bleeding occur?"

"Yes." Ay nodded impatiently and, reaching over, broke off a piece of Nebhotep's loaf. "If she was married, her husband would refrain from intercourse then, would he not?" He popped the bread into his mouth and chewed, feeling the tiny fragments of grit crunching under his teeth.

"Normally, yes. A woman becomes ritually unclean at that time." Nebhotep thought for a few moments. "I believe the princess Meryetaten's bleeding is expected within days. Why?"

"You will not have heard the news yet but the king will marry his daughter Meryetaten, having put away his wife Nefertiti. In the interests of this union producing a son, I have consulted with the priests of Min and they have divined a day that is favourable for the marriage. It is the evening of the new moon." Ay broke off another piece of the barley crust and chewed, talking around the food. "Naturally, I cannot go to the king and tell him a false priest advises him to delay his marriage, but his physician could present the date as a medical recommendation."

425

"I have heard rumors." Nebhotep took a drink from his cup. "Why would the king accept the news coming from me?"

"Because you will not tell him the choice of the day comes from a priest. You will tell him that medically, she will be most fertile on that night." Ay looked at the physician searchingly. "Do you have a problem with that?"

"No," Nebhotep said after a pause. "I will not lie, Tjaty, but it would be advisable to wait until the bleeding is past. I am not sure of the meaning of a woman's bleeding save that it is a signal that she is not with child. It would seem logical to give her womb the maximum time to conceive."

"Good. I will make sure the king sends her to you for an examination. You will recommend this date. Be sure of it, the evening of the new moon. You may spin some tale about the waxing moon inducing increased conception if you wish."

"That will not be necessary. I do not subscribe to superstitions."

Ay smiled and got up, pushing his seat back. "Thank you, physician Nebhotep. You will be doing the king and Kemet a great service."

Well, Kemet anyway, he thought as he hurried off.

Akhenaten had returned from the temple when Ay got back to the king's apartments. Changing from his special robes of greeting into a less formal open kilt that fastened beneath his sagging belly, Akhenaten greeted his Tjaty.

"Divine Father, I heard you went to see Nefertiti last night. How is ... how is my wife? Is she angry?" The king's dressers bowed and left the room.

"Chastened, my lord. Knowing that she said things to you in the heat of passion that she now regrets."

426

The king nodded and wandered over to his toilet, positioning himself on it, his kilt around his waist. "If she will apologize, she may return to her palace." His colour rose in his face and a muffled splash carried faintly.

"My lord, I believe this is what she desires, but she asks your indulgence to let her remain in the North Palace until your marriage. She says she needs to come to grips with her new status, her new position at court."

"Granted." Akhenaten got up and examined the contents of the bowl, then flushed it. "I am sorry if this affair offends you, Divine Father. I know it must be difficult when I put your daughter away like this."

Ay bowed, his face calm. "The king's will is my desire." He smiled faintly. "I know what trouble women can be, my lord, even such a beautiful one as my daughter. Besides, how can I be offended when you only put my daughter aside in favour of my granddaughter?"

Akhenaten smiled broadly and walked over to his Tjaty, throwing his arms around him. "I shall have to call you Divine Grandfather now, I suppose." He turned and clapped his hands. At once a servant appeared in the doorway. "Bring food and drink. I will break my fast."

The king waited until the table in the anteroom had been set and food laid out. He dismissed the servants and started eating. "We will celebrate my new marriage tomorrow. In the Great Temple, I think. Naturally we can only invite those nobles actually in Akhet-Aten but ..." He broke off as he caught sight of Ay's shaking head. "You disagree?"

"It is not my place to disagree with the divine will, my lord, but I do have one concern."

Akhenaten stopped eating and wiped his fingers on a napkin. "Oh? What?"

427

"Last month at about this time – I cannot remember exactly when – I remember the queen, I mean Nefertiti, made a remark which I paid no great attention to at the time."

"And that was?"

"Your daughter Meryetaten was undergoing a painful ... er, time of the month. You understand what I mean, Akhenaten? About a woman's time of the month."

Akhenaten grimaced. "Yes. It is a most tedious affair and interferes with my pleasure considerably."

"If I am right, then Meryetaten is about to have her time again. It would be most unfortunate if this happened on your wedding night."

"Indeed it would." The king pondered this problem. "But you are not sure of the day? Would Meryetaten know?"

"Possibly, my lord, but young girls are often silly and forgetful and this is a matter of great importance. I suggest that we have Nebhotep the physician examine Meryetaten. He will be able to advise us as to her condition."

Akhenaten nodded and resumed his breakfast. "See to it, Ay. Now, is there anything else?"

"Another letter has arrived from Shubbiluliuma. He desires another gift of gold as a token of friendship."

The king groaned and waved his free hand dismissively while picking a fistful of dates from a golden dish. "Does he think I am made of gold? Tell him no ... no, don't tell him that. Put him off. Send him a gilded statue like last time but say more will follow. We must appease these kings if Kemet is to have peace."

"As the king wishes. There is also a thief, my lord. He was caught breaking into the tomb of Ramose. Nothing was taken but he caused some damage. Do you want to preside over the court hearing today?"

"You do it, Ay. I don't want to think about such things. I am going to spend the day composing a new hymn to the Aten to be sung at my wedding."

Ay bowed. "I shall look forward to it."

He left the king eating breakfast and found the overseer of nurses.

"You have heard the king will marry Meryetaten?"

The overseer bowed deeply. "I have, Tjaty Ay."

"He wishes the girl to be examined by Nebhotep the physician. Deliver her to the physician's chambers immediately."

He then went in search of Mahu, the chief of the Medjay, mentally ticking off the preparation points in his head. Mahu was harder to track down. The Medjay barracks were deserted despite the early hour and Ay did not find the chief until mid-morning. In the end, he came across the burly chief of the Medjay at the Southern tombs where he was supervising the resealing of Ramose's tomb. Although the sun blazed in the heavens, the cliff face and a small area of ground beneath remained in shadow. The dust from the repairs to the mud brick wall still hung in the still air, the acrid scent reminding Ay of death and tombs.

"Ay! Good to see you," Mahu called out in greeting. "Rumors are thick in the city. Is it true the queen, your daughter, has been put away?"

"It is." He shrugged. "As the king wishes." Ay indicated the tomb where, some twenty cubits above them in the sheer rock face; two builders were applying the last few trowels of wet mortar to the bricks filling the tomb entrance. "How did he get in?"

"Lowered himself from the cliff top. We think he had an accomplice though he hasn't admitted it yet." Mahu wiped the sweat and dust from his forehead with a rag,

429

his head scarf with its stripes of office slipping as he moved. His thick white tufted eyebrows stood out against his tanned skin.

The builders smoothed the last of the mortar over the repairs and clambered down from the scaffolding, helping the old priest of Aten and the overseer of mortuary buildings to ascend, carrying their official seals. The old men selected a smooth area of fine-grained mortar and pressed the seals of office in.

"I have heard this robber is part of a larger gang," Ay remarked casually.

"Where did you hear that? He is a young man, Amoy by name. He has a brother called Emsaf, whom I believe was his accomplice, though he cannot be found. There is no evidence they are part of a gang."

"Nevertheless, my sources have informed me they are."

"Who are your sources? Let me question them."

"That I cannot allow, Mahu. You know how it is, if I did not protect their identities, they would not trust me."

Mahu grunted and watched the priest and mortuary official climbing slowly down from the tomb. "I suppose you are right. They are trustworthy?" He shrugged and nodded a greeting to the priest as he walked past them toward the city. "I can question Amoy, I suppose, but it does not make much difference whether he acted alone or with others. He will still die for his crime."

"True, but there is more." Leaving the builders and their labourers to dismantle the wooden scaffolding, Ay sauntered back down the dusty trails toward the workmen's village and the centre of town, Mahu beside him. "The gang is meeting soon to divide the spoils of their many ventures. It would bring you much praise if you could capture them."

"There are many gangs. Why should this one bring me fame?"

"My informants tell me it is led by Bennu. You have heard of him?"

"I have. That would be a coup indeed," Mahu grinned. "I am never averse to either fame or gold. Where is this meeting? And when?"

"North and east of the city, about six hours march. There is a small valley with a cave and a small spring."

"I know it. Why so far out?"

"Who knows? My informant tells me they meet there on the night of the new moon. He thinks there will be much booty."

Mahu rubbed his hands together absently, his mind busy digesting the information. "How many in this gang?"

"About fifty I am told."

"That many?" Mahu shook his head, regret showing in his eyes. "Then I cannot do this. It would take my whole Medjay to capture them and I cannot leave the city unprotected."

"It would only be for a few days, Mahu my friend, and I would make sure the army garrison kept order in the city."

"Why do you not use the army to catch your thieves then?"

"I could do so, of course, and now that you mention it, perhaps I will. I merely thought you would like the credit for the capture. Well, I shall lead the army out there, capture the brigands and confiscate their booty. No doubt I will become rich from the haul."

"Do not be hasty, Ay. You are an old man and un-suited to such work."

Ay yawned. "Not so old," he said, slapping his firm belly. "But I could just get the garrison commander, Neshi to do the work."

"That pretentious idiot? He'd arrive too late or lead his troops to the wrong place. If he did get there, he'd let half of them escape." Mahu laughed and threw an arm around Ay's shoulders. "No, you let me do it and I'll make sure the job is done correctly."

"I don't like to put you out, old friend. Besides, it would leave the city unguarded, like you said."

"It would only be for two nights, three maybe. And while the troop commander is incompetent, the soldiers are good enough. All they have to do is stand around in two's or three's on the street corners and there won't be any trouble. Akhet-Aten's a very quiet city really."

Ay pretended to think about it and with a show of reluctance, agreed. Turning down the Medjay chief's offer of a pot of beer, he excused himself and set off for the military barracks in the North City near the Customs House.

It was a long walk in the midday heat and dust and by the time he arrived, Ay was sweating profusely and his kilt and headdress were stained and wet. He acknowledged the challenge of the guard on the gates and walked into the officers' rooms on the cliff side of the barrack square. Here he found a junior lieutenant sitting with his feet up, feeding seeds to a gaudy parrot in a copper-wire cage. The officer looked up as Ay entered the room.

"Yes? What do you want?" Recognition dawned as he asked and he shot to his feet, the parrot screeching in alarm. "Sorry, sir, I did not know you." He saluted; his body rigid.

"At ease, soldier. I have just walked over from the city centre and I'm hot and dusty. I need a bath, a fresh kilt and headdress and a large pot of beer. Find those things for me and bring them over to the bath house."

"Yes, sir." The officer ran to the door.

"One other thing, soldier." The man halted and looked around. "After you have done that, find Commandant Neshi and tell him I want to see him."

Ay left the officers' quarters and walked across to the bath house, picking up a towel at the door. He walked into the deserted wooden building and found one of the stalls with a full tub of river water. Disrobing, he sat on the bench by the tub and filling a ladle with cold water, tipped it over his head. He gasped with the shock, but immediately felt better, the liquid sluicing away the dust and the sweat. Ladle after ladle followed until his whole body felt cool and refreshed once more. The waste water drained away into stone-lined channels that run under all the stalls, discharging the water out into a main drain that emptied into the river.

The lieutenant arrived with a change of clothing and a pot of cold beer, taking Ay's clothes away to be quickly laundered. Following the officer's directions, he went looking for, and soon found, the garrison commander.

"Tjaty Ay," the commandant effused. "You honour us by your presence. When Lieutenant Baqet told me of your arrival it was all I could do not to rush down to the bath house to welcome you."

"Then I am glad you restrained yourself," Ay commented. He stuck a finger in his ear and wiggled it about in an effort to get rid of some water. "Your baths are in good order, by the way."

"Thank you Tjaty. A word of praise from you is like a drink of cold water on a hot day. It is something ..."

"Shut up Neshi," Ay interrupted. "I am a busy man and I do not have the time to listen to your drivel." The

433

commandant subsided and Ay sat down on the only chair in the room. He looked keenly at the now apprehensive Neshi.

"Can you remember your oath of loyalty, commandant?"

"Of course, Tjaty Ay." He thought for a moment then drew himself erect. "I, Neshi, commandant of the garrison of Akhet-Aten ..."

"Don't recite the whole thing, Neshi. I told you I don't have the time. Just tell me who you swore to obey."

"Why, King Neferneferure Waenre Akhenaten of course."

"Very good. And ...?"

"And the General of all the armies, Paatenemheb, and my immediate superior."

"Who is?"

"You, Tjaty," Neshi ended triumphantly, a great smile on his face.

"Very good indeed, Commandant Neshi," Ay said with a trace of sarcasm that was entirely lost on the military man. "Now, I want to put a hypothetical case to you ..."

"A what, sir?"

"A 'what if' scenario. For instance, I might ask you 'what if the Hittites invaded the city'? You would then give me an answer. What I want to know ..."

"I'd send for help immediately sir and take all my men down to defend the main palace. Those Hittites are good fighters so I'd need the help of regular army units."

Ay sighed and closed his eyes. "Let's try again, Neshi. What if a group of rebels simultaneously – that means 'at the same time' – tried to take over both the North Palace where the queen lives and the main one where the king lives?"

Neshi frowned. "I would have to split my forces, which is not good. I'd detail one of my officers to guard the queen while I took the main force south."

Ay nodded. "Probably a better plan would be to guard the queen yourself and let me take most of the men to guard the king. Your men would obey me unquestioningly, wouldn't they?"

"Of course, sir." Neshi looked shocked. "They all know you as the General in charge of the city. They would give their lives for you. You are held in great respect."

"That is good to know, Commandant Neshi. And it eases my mind that such an efficient officer controls the garrison." Ay got up and gripped Neshi's forearms tightly for a moment, before moving to the door. Turning in the doorway he lowered his voice confidentially. "That 'what if' about the rebels is not real, Neshi, but something like it could be. I have heard a rumor that a known Syrian assassin has been seen near Ineb Hedj. Probably there is nothing to it, but if I came to you one night with a sudden need for your troops, it is good to know you are prepared."

Neshi saluted. "We are yours to command, Tjaty Ay."

"Good man. Not a word to anyone though, not even your officers. There are spies everywhere and while I trust your officers, who can be sure of the servants?"

Ay left the North barracks with a smile on his face. The day was even hotter and dustier than before. He considered stopping in at the North Palace to talk to Nefertiti, but decided against it. *The fewer people who know my plans, the better*, he thought. If he had stopped, he might have seen a young girl in a servant's kilt hurrying out of the palace in the direction of the waterfront.

435

Chapter Twenty-Nine

It wasn't too difficult to get the things I thought I would need for my journey to Waset. One of the advantages of living in the palace is that everyone knows their own place and their duties and assumes everyone else does too. As a princess I had the added advantage of having nobody question me. However, I knew that if I stepped outside the palace I would attract attention unless I could disguise myself in some way. A grown woman might have had some difficulty but a slip of a girl was beneath anyone's notice. Being new to Akhet-Aten and never having been in the North Palace before the previous night, the only way the majority of the servants could know my rank was to pay attention to my bearing and clothes. Change those and I would slip into anonymity.

Changing my bearing was not hard. I was reared as a little no-name non-entity in Waset and only had to shed the last few months as one of the garland of the king's princesses. Clothes were a little more difficult. My fine white linen dresses would give me away instantly, so I needed a servant's utilitarian short kilt. Most girls around the palace went bare-breasted and thought nothing of it, having been reared to that condition, I suppose. I was still very conscious of my newly swelling breasts and was thankful for the concealing dresses I could wear. However, if I was going to disguise myself as a servant girl I would quickly have to learn to ignore my chest. I would need a warm cloak to shield me against the cold desert nights, so I could use that for concealment sometimes.

I found it was not easy to get a servant's kilt. I wandered down to the servant's quarters but the closer I got, the more attention I received, and people started asking me how they could help me. I couldn't very well just say I wanted a servant's kilt – or rather, I could have got one for the asking but I couldn't risk word getting back to Nefertiti or Ay. In the end I watched as the laundry was carried down to the river in great woven-rush hampers for washing and returned to the grounds behind the palace to be spread out on the grass to dry in the sun. The clothes were unguarded as nobody would seriously want to steal a low quality kilt. I grabbed one and folded it quickly, slipping it under the half-open top of my gown before hurrying back to my room.

The cloak was easier. I complained of the cold at night when I was sitting up, to the controller of bedding and he found me a lovely dark blue wool cloak with tiny embroidered scarabs around the edge. I knew as soon as I saw it that Khepri was guiding me and that I would succeed.

My plans for my escape were vague as I had no real knowledge of what lay outside the city. I could see the river and the farmland on the far side from the palace windows but the docks were hidden from view. Boats plied the waters, small sailed craft beating up against the current, triangular sails taut; or smaller ones with people working oars. I would have to steal – well, borrow really – one of those to get across the river. I wondered whether I should see if I could find one before it got dark. I dithered for a while, in reality not wanting to change into my short kilt without my concealing top. In the end, I changed quickly, tossed my wig on the bed and slipped out of the window before I could stop to think about it. Anyone seeing me would hopefully take me for a servant in my plain kilt though I could not resist fastening the coarse linen weave with a copper pin that had a tiny lapis scarab beetle attached.

I ran across the road and just missed my uncle Ay. He was striding down the road from somewhere to the north and luckily had passed the palace when I darted out. I hurried into the cover of the streets leading down to the waterfront, trying to resist the temptation of folding my arms across my chest. Nobody else seemed concerned with their nudity or mine and I gradually relaxed.

The river's edge had once been vegetated, no doubt, lined with grass and rushes and in the slower parts of the current where back-eddies rippled the clear green water, water lilies had once flourished. No more. Industry had torn the vegetation and scored the mud which was now littered with the refuse of the city. The river flowed from south to north, past the thousands in Akhet-Aten, depositing things I did not want to think about at my feet. I looked up and down the river bank, idly watching the watermen at their work, noting the presence of upturned boats on the land and others floating, tied up to mooring posts sunk into the mud. Wharves extended out into the river and large boats were tied up to them, crowds of men, mostly naked, loading and unloading boxes and bales.

I wandered up and down the bank, trying to look as if I belonged there, very conscious that a household servant had no business being idle on the riverbank. I found a small upturned boat at the southern end of the waterfront area and pushed against it, testing its weight. It moved easily, rocking, and I felt encouraged. Perhaps it wouldn't be too hard to push it into the water.

"And what would you be after, little miss?"

I jumped and spun round. A naked man, one of the labourers unloading the freight by the look of him, stood a dozen paces from me, his bale on the ground beside him, a look of curiosity on his face.

"Nothing," I said.

"Ain't nuthin' for yer round 'ere." He looked me up and down slowly, a smile appearing that turned into a grin, then a leer. "Unless yer lookin' ter makes a copper or two."

I had run naked most of my life though not since I started to become a woman, and I have seen plenty of naked men before, though not quite like this. I have been looked at too but his look made me feel naked in a way that I didn't like. His member, hanging flaccid as these things normally do, twitched, catching my attention. As if it felt my eyes on it, it grew and started to stand out. I watched, horrified, wondering what was going to happen.

"So yer likes it, little miss?" He glanced around, judging the distance to his fellow workers. "Lie dahn with me be'ind the boat, little miss, an' yer can earn a copper." He moved toward me.

I backed away, dodged around the boat, then as he came after me, laughing, ran for the shelter of the buildings. I glanced back as I entered the first street. He had not followed but was shouldering his bale and starting back toward the boats. I hurried back to the palace and made it back to my room without being accosted again.

Night made the river front an alien place. I stood on the mud with a star-emblazoned night above me, the sounds and smells of frying fish drifting from the city behind me and the heavy, oily lap of the river in front of me. As I stood there trying to pluck up the courage to move, the moon rose over the desert cliffs behind, casting a pearly glow over the river and the upturned hummocks of the boats. A rope creaked somewhere on the wharf and I heard a muffled laugh and voices. *Time to go.* I worked my way along the bank to the south, hoping to find the small boat I had seen earlier but things looked unfamiliar and I couldn't find it. I reached the end of the mudflat that delimited the waterfront area and was about to turn back, wondering if I should leave it another day and do some more scouting first, when I saw a small, almost circular boat attached to a mooring post about ten paces from the shore. I could even make out what I thought was an oar, poking over the side.

I lifted my small bundle of possessions – cloak, sandals, headscarf, bread, empty stoppered jug, jewelry – onto my head and stepped out into the cold water. The slimy mud between my toes made me think of eels and I prayed to Hapi not to send any my way. The river bottom fell away rapidly and by the time I was halfway to the boat, the water was wetting the hem of my kilt. I balanced my bundle with one hand and fumbled my skirt off with the other. Water swirled over my waist and almost to my chest by the time I heaved my belongings into the bobbing boat. I then tried to pull myself in and met a problem. I could heave myself out of the water and half into the boat but the sides dipped alarmingly and water slopped over the edges.

Standing quietly in the water again with my hands gripping the edges of the boat, I thought about my situation. I worked my way upriver, hand over hand along the side until I was at the point where the rope attached the boat to its mooring post. Gripping the slippery wood, I clambered awkwardly upward until I was grasping the post, my hands and legs wrapped around it, my bottom just touching the water. I reached out gingerly and pulled on the rope, tugging the little craft closer. When I judged it close enough I hesitated, then pushed backward from the post, grabbing for the boat with both hands.

I fell into the boat, sending a cascade of water in over one edge. I scrambled in and lay on top of my bundle, breathing hard as the boat rocked violently, sending the stars above swaying back and forth. When the motion damped down I sat up and looked around, sure that somebody must have heard or seen me. Nothing stirred on the river bank and after a few anxious moments I rescued my bundle from the water in the bottom of the boat, propping it up out of the way. With luck, the wool would not have let too much through. My kilt was soaked though. I might just as well have kept it on.

Taking the oar in my hands, I put the blade in the water at the rear of the boat and waggled it back and forth experimentally, much as I had seen fishermen on the river do. It didn't seem too hard. Untying the rope, I pushed off from the post and the current tugged at my little craft, pulling it down toward the wharves. The oar seemed to have less effect now that the boat was free to move in the water but with a lot of splashing and sweat, I managed to ease past the wharves and the tied-up boats and out into the river.

The lights of the city fell behind me, the river front area moving steadily past as the current swept me out. I was alone on a vast expanse of still water, the lap and gurgle of the river the only sound. The glow of the rising moon washed out the stars and cast a path of gold on the water leading back to the darkened palace. I almost decided to go back but the current caught me and carried me past the cliffs and out of sight of the city. I waggled my oar, sculling it back and forth as I had seen the river men do, but I must have been doing something wrong as it seemed to have no effect. I was stuck, adrift on an endless expanse of river with no way to reach the other side. I pulled the oar back in and put my head in my hands, feeling very sorry for myself.

It seemed like hours later but it cannot have been because the moon had scarcely moved, when my little boat rocked violently. My first thought was of a crocodile, and I screamed. The rocking motion was repeated, and again, but I saw no wicked jaws, no eyes lit up like lamps or thrashing tail. Instead the surface of the water rippled over a wide area, moving faster and whispering. The boat bumped and tipped, slewing round and I gripped the sides in a panic. After a few minutes I could see the boat did not appear to be moving, though the water flowed by faster than ever. I eased my cramped fingers off the sides and picked up the oar, lowering it over the side. It touched bottom almost immediately and I knew I had grounded on a sand bank. Now, in the moonlight I could make out the dark humps of vegetation along the shore, very close. I decided to risk wading ashore, so I fastened my sodden kilt about my waist and stepped over the side. The boat, relieved of my weight, bobbed up and started to float away. I made a despairing grab for my bundle and just hooked my fingers in the cloak, yanking it overboard. I fell headlong as the boat swept away.

Spluttering and gagging I made it to the riverbank with my bedraggled bundle of possessions and collapsed on the mud, panting. A splash upriver made me think of crocodiles again so I picked up my bundle and made my way inland. I was cold, despite the warmth that came from the proximity of the river. I thought about putting my cloak on but I realized I would then be left with a number of objects to carry instead of one bundle. I hadn't planned this well.

The moon was nearly overhead now but I gauged my position by the river and headed south, hoping to see the lights of the city before too long. The going was hard, there being no tracks or paths to follow, just hillocks and hummocks of grass and a few trees. Abruptly my feet slipped from under me and I fell with a splash into shallow water. Sure I had not approached the river unknowingly; I sat up in surprise and looked around. A narrow strip of silvery water, straight-sided, led away on either side. I stared at it uncomprehendingly for several minutes until I realized it was man-made. I was sitting in an irrigation ditch.

An irrigation ditch meant farmers and farmers lived in a village. I was nearing my first destination and suddenly I was less sure of myself. Back in the palace when I came up with the plan, I imagined myself as a self-assured young princess imperiously demanding to be shown the way to Waset, then graciously handing out jewelry to grateful farmers on completion of their duty. Now that I was here I thought of how I must look – a wet, bedraggled, muddy servant girl clutching a bundle of obviously stolen goods, attempting to flee her master's service. I nearly cried again, until I thought of the plot against Akhenaten and how I must carry word of it to Smenkhkare in Waset. Steeling myself, I scrambled up the banks of the ditch and looked to the south. Faintly, I heard the sound of a dog barking, and I knew the village was near. I shouldered my bundle and set off.

Chapter Thirty

Two thousand men of the Re and Heru Legions crouched in a shallow gully in the pre-dawn coolness of the north Sin plains looking toward the foothills where a sprinkling of camp fires betrayed the presence of the Amorites. Paatenemheb's army, though small, was seasoned and mobile. The cuts forced on him by a slashed army budget and Akhenaten's short-sighted policies had been offset to some extent by judicious pruning of the less efficient parts of the army. Although at less than half strength, the two legions comprised battle-hardened soldiers led by officers dedicated to preserving Kemet's borders. Djedhor, senior commander of the Red company of the Re Legion, had been promoted to Commander of the whole Heru Legion, while Paramessu had risen to command the Re Legion. Although he now had four companies under him – Blue, Red, Black and Green – he still wore the woven blue scarab of the Blue company on his military kilt, though his garment was now of fine white linen rather than military brown, as befitted his rank.

Amorites had been raiding the northern borders of Kemet for years but in the last six months the depredations had become extreme. Skilled in hit and run tactics the northern soldiers would roam in small mobile groups, killing and burning, then disappear into the back trails and mountain passes at the first hint of the Kemetu forces. Paatenemheb had marshaled his Legions at Hut-waret in the Delta before marching out to bring the Amorite army to battle. He was confident his disciplined forces could cut to pieces the Amorite rabble. With luck, Aziru son of Abdiashirta would be leading his forces and he

444

could rid Kemet of one of its worst enemies. He longed for the day he would have Aziru's bloody head on a spear.

The gray clouds in the east turned to pink and the sky lightened, washing out the last of the stars and rendering the campfires inconspicuous, though thin smoke trails flew from some of them. Paramessu stood with Djedhor on a low knoll to the right of the ranks of soldiers, staring out over the plain.

"Nice and simple," Djedhor growled. "Forget these fancy tactics. Just give me a good straightforward set piece and I'll wipe them from the face of the earth."

"You'll have your chance," Paramessu observed. "Minmose and the General will be in those hills ready to sweep down on them. With luck they'll panic them right out onto the flat where we can get at them."

"I don't know why we couldn't just challenge them to a battle in a civilized fashion," Djedhor grumbled. "Instead of chasing them all over Sin and Syria, herding them like so many cattle."

"We had to get them together," Paramessu explained, though he was sure Djedhor already knew the answer. "Otherwise it's just like trying to catch ducks with hand nets. A lot of work for very little result. This way we have herded them together and we can crush them like an egg between the General's hammer and our anvil."

The sun rose, pushing its way up through a low bank of clouds. As colour returned to the land, the breeze turned, shifting from the north to the north-east, bringing with it the faint sounds of battle, metal on metal and men's cries.

"General Paatenemheb has engaged the enemy," Paramessu said softly.

445

"And there they come." Djedhor pointed, a wolfish grin splitting his otherwise dour features. A dark stain spread down from the foothills and onto the level ground, resolving itself into streams of fleeing men as it came closer. "Why don't they turn and fight?" he said. "Are they all cowards?"

"They will fight," Paramessu predicted. "They flee the enemy behind but when they become aware of our presence they will stand."

"It will be a slaughter," Djedhor grinned. "Re and Heru lie in front of them and Ptah harries from behind. Not only are they outnumbered but they are caught between the very jaws of Set."

"Hardly seems fair, does it? There's only a thousand of them and nearly three thousand of us."

"Who wants fair?" Djedhor snarled. "Give me the opportunity to kill Kemet's enemies."

Paramessu judged the distance to the front ranks of the Amorites, mentally pacing off the distance to the Kemetu soldiers crouched unseen in the gully that lay across the enemy's line of retreat. "I think it is time to join our men." Together they descended from the knoll and bending double to stay out of sight, ran to their places at the forefront of their troops.

"Get ready, Re Legion." Paramessu counted off the seconds, estimating the proximity of the approaching Amorites. "Steady, men, steady." He glanced toward Djedhor and nodded. Djedhor, as senior officer, had the honour and right to call the attack, but being a sensible if somewhat violent man, he allowed his fellow legion commander to exercise his own tactical talents.

"Up Heru!" Djedhor screamed, leaping to his feet. His men erupted from the gully with a loud roar of anticipation, Paramessu and the Re Legion a split second behind them.

From the point of view of the fleeing Amorites, it was as if the earth had spewed up armed men at their feet. Before they could even raise their shields or draw sword, lift spear or fasten helmet, the Kemetu legions were upon them, bronze blades flashing, bright spears thrusting as the twin gods of war and death feasted.

The ragged wave of Amorite soldiers burst on the breakwater of Kemetu bronze and was hurled back in confusion. The Re and Heru legions advanced, their disciplined training kicking in as they stepped, stabbed, hacked and stepped again. Overwhelmed, the Amorite soldiers died or retreated.

Then the Ptah Legion hit them from behind. Paatenemheb and Minmose had harried the last of the Amorite raiders, pressing with superior numbers, herding them south toward the main Amorite camp. As the two enemy forces joined, the Ptah Legion fell on them and forced them in a disorganized retreat into the plains of slaughter.

The three Kemetu legions met as the enemy fled in small groups, scattering for their lives. A small troop, marginally more organized, fled north, slipping around the Ptah Legion, racing on foot for the cover of the hills. Paramessu saw them when he stopped to survey the battlefield, watching his men dispatch the wounded enemy, the army surgeons start to attend to the Kemetu wounded. He screwed up his eyes and put a hand up to block the low sun. A glint of gold caught the light and a red banner fluttered in the distance.

"Aziru," he hissed. Paramessu turned and shouted to Meny, a Greatest of Fifty. "Meny, bring your Fifty, at the double." Without waiting to see if he was followed, Paramessu set off to the north, leaping over bodies and

447

dodging around groups of bloodied and tired soldiers. Tucking his short sword into his belt, he slung his small war-shield over his back and concentrated on his running.

Skirting the last of the bodies, Paramessu glanced over his shoulder and saw Meny, together with a dozen or so of his men, strung out behind him. He nodded grimly and scanned the ground in front of him, trying to discern how many fled from him and where they were going. The Amorites had about equal numbers but were more tightly knit, clustered about a central figure, their retreat slowed by the pace of this one man.

"It must be Aziru," he muttered.

A thousand paces ahead, the Amorites turned slightly to the right, heading up a broad dry stream bed. From his long forays into the area, Paramessu knew the stream turned to the left then split into numerous gullies before rising to the ridge ahead. There was ample cover further up and he and his men would find it hard to follow if the Amorites had any archers. He knew if he was to have any hope of reaching Aziru it would have to be before they reached the ridge.

Instead of veering right, Paramessu continued straight ahead, forcing his tired legs up the slope of the hill shoulder, away from the dry stream bed. The slope became steeper, scattered with boulders and loose rock. He skidded and slipped, almost falling, forcing himself upward. His leg muscles ached and his breath came in great rushing blasts, the sweat pouring off him, but he reached the crest of the shoulder. He stood panting at the top, holding his side and grimacing at the tight pain. Looking down he saw the dry stream bed where it turned to the left and the scrambling figures of the Amorites almost directly below him. He could not cut them off but he would be close behind them if he could descend fast.

Meny and the first of his men were about fifty paces down from him, making heavy going of the loose surface. The rest were further back but coming on as fast as they could. It would have to do. Paramessu pointed down over the crest, waving Meny on, before plunging down the slope toward the tail of the fleeing Amorites.

Several heads looked up as rocks plunged down the slope ahead of the Kemetu commander. A shouted order and four men dropped back to intercept Paramessu, the rest hurrying on. Paramessu looked up, a cry of frustration passing his lips as he saw a man who undoubtedly was King Aziru, disappearing up one of the side gullies, climbing for the ridge line. Not watching where he was going, his foot caught on a rock and he pitched forward, landing hard on the loose surface and careening downward in a shower of rocks.

Paramessu landed hard on the rocky floor of the stream bed, and lay half stunned. Rocks clattering ahead of him gave a warning and he rolled over onto his knees, shaking his head to clear it. He looked up as a shadow fell on him and, without thinking, threw himself to one side, a spearhead clanging off a rock beside him. Scrambling to his feet, he snatched his sword out just in time to deflect another stab by the spear. He backed away, the spearman coming after him with a grin on his face, his weapon probing. Another Amorite spearman followed, scrambling over the boulders to outflank the Kemetu.

Paramessu slipped his small war-shield off his back, his eyes never leaving the spearman's face. The bright point of the lance bobbed and weaved in the periphery of his vision. A flicker in the man's eyes and Paramessu leapt forward, his shield raised, blocking and forcing the

449

spear upward, the sharp bronze point still managing to score a bright line of blood across his shoulder. His sword stabbed forward and caught on the plates of the man's leather and bronze armor, deflecting to the side. Closing with the Amorite he hacked to the side and up and felt his blade bite deep into the man's armpit. Screaming, the man dropped his spear and fell, his life blood pulsing out over the rocks.

Whirling, Paramessu was in time to dodge the spear of the second Amorite. He was forced back, blindly stepping over rocks, slipping in loose stones. He blocked a thrust and saw he was being backed toward the other two Amorites who, armed with swords, were advancing to cut him off. A cry came from up the slope and a stone cracked and ricocheted off a boulder near the spearman. Paramessu saw the man's eyes glance toward the slope and he threw his sword hard, catching the man on the chest with the hilt, knocking him back. Throwing himself forward, he grappled and wrestled him to the ground. He gripped a rock and swung it hard, again, the first blow landing on the man's shoulder, the second on the side of his head. Blood spurted and the man cried out, his hands feeling blindly for Paramessu's throat. He swung again and the man's skull bones collapsed with a wet sound like a melon bursting.

His breath coming in great whooping gasps, Paramessu glanced up the slope to see Meny and the first of his Fifty sliding down the slope toward him. Others followed and Paramessu turned back to the two remaining Amorites, suddenly conscious that his sword was lying somewhere on the rocky bed. He swung the shield around to cover him and tensed, waiting for the attack.

The Amorite glared at the Kemetu commander. "You have killed my men, Kemetu. Do not think I will forget."

He spoke in Syrian, but Paramessu understood him. He said nothing but waited, his men coming ever closer.

"Jebu, come away," the other man called. "Hurry."

The Amorite leader stared at Paramessu for a moment then nodded, turning away and running after his fellow. They disappeared into the gully as Meny and the first of his men arrived in a flood of loose scree.

"Fornicating Amorites," Meny panted. "Shall we get after them, sir?"

"No. Aziru is long gone by now. Gather your men and we'll return."

The Kemetu stripped the dead Amorites of their armor and weapons and hacked off the right hands, carrying them away as the troop descended along the stream bed.

Paatenemheb was waiting for his Re Legion commander, along with Djedhor and Minmose. He eyed the two hands thrown on the growing heap nearby. "You got him?"

"No sir. He dropped back a rearguard to cover his escape."

"But it was Aziru?"

"I think so. I didn't get close enough to be certain but he wore gold."

Paatenemheb nodded. "We did well today." He addressed all three commanders. "But these Amorites are but the first bite of the loaf. The Hittites are coming, gentlemen, make no mistake. We will need more troops than we have at our disposal to meet them in battle."

"What can we do if the king will not pay to build up the army?" Djedhor complained. "We need gold. Our own troops' pay is in arrears as it is."

"Petition him again, General, it is the only way," Minmose added.

"I have tried, but I will try again." He looked at his commanders searchingly. "What else can we do to prepare? I want ideas."

Minmose shrugged. "Fortify Gezer. The Hittites will have to travel down the coast road and lay siege to Gezer. They cannot invade Kemet and leave that garrison in their rear."

"Meet them in the field before they reach Gezer," Djedhor growled. "My fornicating Heru Legion is a match for any Hittite army."

Paatenemheb allowed himself a small smile. "I'd back them at odds of three to one, Djedhor, but not even your men could handle odds of thirty to one."

"Strip the other garrisons then," Minmose added. "Take all the men out of Hut-waret, Djanet and the Sin forts ..."

"Five hundred more at most." Paatenemheb shook his head. "What else? Paramessu, any ideas?"

"The Nubian battalions stationed at Qerert."

"Gods, Paramessu," Minmose interjected. "They are all that stand between us and the southern hordes."

"Who have been quiet this past twelve-month. We could take them if we don't make too much of a fuss. Bring them north, meet and crush the Hittites, then have them back in place before the Nubians know they are gone."

Paatenemheb pursed his lips. "A bold plan. How many would you take?"

"The garrison at Qerert was recently cut by more than half. Even so, I could find a thousand men, I'm sure of it."

"Not enough, but better than nothing."

"Then let me recruit among those laid off. I could find a thousand more."

"And pay them with what?" Djedhor asked. "Our troops are virtually fighting without pay now. You won't get soldiers to sign up again without at least silver in the hand – preferably gold."

"There are gold mines near the Nubian border."

"The king's," Djedhor said. "You are not thinking of robbing the king?"

"I was thinking merely that the king will eventually see sense and release enough gold to pay for Kemet's defence." Paramessu smiled disarmingly. "Perhaps we could make a small withdrawal against that time. Say, six month's pay?"

"A year would be more like it," Paatenemheb grunted. He held up a hand to forestall Djedhor's protest. "But I cannot countenance robbery. You must go down to Qerert and see what you can do just on a promise." He stepped between Paramessu and Djedhor, turning his back on his senior commander. "You will go to Qerert for me, and raise me an army?" The general's mouth twitched in a smile and the eyelid of one eye drooped.

"Yes sir. I will leave at once."

"Good man." Paatenemheb turned to include the other commanders. "Speed is essential. Take a small group with you, say a Fifty. Stop for nothing. It is now just past the new moon, with luck you should be down at Waset by the next new moon, Qerert perhaps eight days later. It will take you longer to return, but with the help of the gods we should have an army back here within three months."

"And what will we be doing while he's doing that?" Djedhor asked.

"You will take your legion north past Gezer. It is essential we have warning of the Hittite movements.

Minmose, you will take the Ptah and Paramessu's Re to Gezer and fortify it. You know how to do that."

"And you, General?"

"I will appeal to Akhenaten once more. I will head south with Paramessu." Paatenemheb grinned at his commander's expression. "Don't worry, I won't slow you down. You will go on ahead and I'll bring another Fifty down with me more slowly. I'll meet up with you again on your march north." He saluted his commanders. "You have your orders, gentlemen."

Taking Paramessu aside after the other commanders had left, Paatenemheb handed him a papyrus scroll. "You will need this authority to bring the troops up from Qerert."

Paramessu's eyes widened. He unrolled the papyrus and scanned its neat columns of writing. "You knew? Before I raised the idea you knew we'd have to use the Qerert garrison?"

"Of course. It is the only logical thing we can do." He grinned. "I was confident you'd think of it."

"You could have told me."

Paatenemheb shrugged. "No need. Now, I want at least three thousand men. Akhenaten has bled this army dry too long and I mean to rectify matters. Take men you can trust but hit the gold mines at Kemsah – you know them?"

"I know where they are though I've never been there."

"Don't kill anyone if you can help it but get what gold you need then raise me an army at Qerert. You can do it?"

"I can try."

"Do more than try." Paatenemheb clapped his commander on the shoulder. "Oh, and one other thing. If you make a pig's arse of the robbery and get caught, re-member I cannot be involved. I won't lift a finger to help you. Let's face it Paramessu, my life is worth infinitely more to Kemet than yours."

***

Paramessu made better time on the road than he thought he would. The General and his men slowly fell behind, but Paramessu, together with Meny and his Fifty, ran onward. By the time they crossed out of the Sin plains and into the desert roads of Kemet, they had taken to traveling at night. It was cooler and they could cover greater distances. The moon waxed and on the night of the full moon they found themselves about fifty or sixty thousand strides to the north and east of Akhet-Aten, moving south on the great caravan road toward Waset.

Chapter Thirty-One

Farmer Pa-it and Asenath his wife sat on a wooden bench outside the door of their one-room hut in the tiny village of Akhet-Re. He sipped on a large pot of weak beer while she leaned against him, enjoying the peace and quiet in this hour between finishing the evening chores and bed. A small fire in the dirt outside the hut supplied a little heat to dispel the evening cool and a little light to push back the shadows. Around them, village life wound down for the day. A soft murmuring came from the half-dozen huts in the little community, the gentle flicker of firelight leaking from the edges of the curtained door-ways or through chinks in the wattle and mud daub fabric of the walls. Sounds of normal, everyday human life. Voices raised in laughter briefly, the chatter of children as they were put to bed, and the squall of an infant mingled with the bleating of sheep and goats in the pens close to the huts and a shuffle and low from the village milk cow in its pen further out. A young pup scuffled with an older, almost blind dog in the dust of what could be called a street but was in fact just a wide space between the huts. The pup barked excitedly as, snapping and snarling, they rolled and lunged, their tails telling of pleasure and contentment. An old tom cat sat in the shadows watching them languidly before closing its eyes and dozing.

Pa-it and Asenath's two daughters, Enehy and Imiu, were no longer at home. In the thirteen years since the building of Akhet-Aten across the river, the economics of the region had changed. A huge market had opened up right on Pa-it's doorstep and the city bought all the produce the little farms could grow. The farmers of Ak-het-Re, unlike so many other workers of the land, bene-

456

fited from the new king's regime, though the loss of the old gods worried them. Pa-it for one still greeted Khepri and Re each day, but silently in his own heart.

Materially, the villagers thrived. Pa-it could afford a dowry and his eldest daughter Enehy married and moved downriver with her new husband, starting a family of her own on another farm. Imiu had left the land and found a job as a lady's maid in the city. The sons, Min and Khu were adults now and lived, by choice, in a lean-to attached to the back of their parents' hut. The youngest son, named for his father, was usually referred to as Pa-it-pasherit or little Pa-it, to distinguish him from his father.

The elder Pa-it was now nearly fifty and the oldest man in the village. Though Akhet-Re was not large enough to warrant an official village leader, with the concomitant duties of keeping the peace and tax gathering, the other farmers looked to him for guidance in most things that involved the community.

Pa-it yawned and stretched before draining the last of the beer. He belched, stifling it politely because of the presence of his wife. "Bed, I think, Asenath." Still he made no effort to get up, sitting contentedly watching the dogs play in the dust. The older dog broke off his play and stared fixedly at the darkness toward the river, his ears cocked. The pup took the opportunity to lunge again at the old dog's muzzle, then yelped as the dog snapped hard before turning its attention back to the darkness. After a moment the pup quieted, sniffing the air before erupting into a volley of barks, running forward to the edge of the firelight then back again. The old dog growled gently and Pa-it got up, picking up a stout wooden staff from the ground beside him.

"Min, Khu, Pa-it-pash, get out here. Asenath, go back inside. Barak," he snapped at the young dog. "Be quiet." The pup ignored him and barked again.

"What is it?"

"I don't know, but I'd like you inside. Min, Khu, where are you?"

The curtain across the doorway of the hut was pushed aside, sending a shaft of light over the darkened street. Two young men, short but wiry, pushed out into the open and looked enquiringly at Pa-it. A taller youth followed them, his untidy shock of black hair and large eyes lending him a look of having just awakened.

"What is it, da?" the youth asked, looking around the village. The young dog let loose another barrage of barks and Pa-it-pash snapped his fingers. "Barak. Stop that." The pup immediately dipped its tail and came running to the youth, pushing between his legs then turning to face the darkness, quivering and whining softly. The older dog stayed where it was, silently, listening intently.

"Someone, or something, coming from the river," Pa-it answered.

"We'll take a look." Min grabbed a burning branch from the fire and whipped it back and forth to make it burn brighter. He started toward the darkness where the dogs pointed. Khu picked up a mattock and followed him, as his older brother walked into the darkness, his brand held aloft, casting a dubious light into the shadows.

Pa-it, and Asenath, for she had joined her husband outside again, heard a cry of surprise from Min, followed by a laugh from Khu and almost immediately three figures emerged into the light of the street fire. Between the two young men walked a young girl, not much past puberty, wearing a short servant's kilt and toting a bundle of blue cloth. The girl walked hesitantly up to Pa-it and

458

bobbed her head, a worried look on her face. She glanced at the old woman standing behind him, then at the youth with the dog. The pup growled and edged forward, sniffing at her legs. After a moment its tail started wagging.

"And who might you be, young miss?" Pa-it asked.

The girl hesitated then said, "Scarab, sir."

Pa-it smiled. "That's a funny name for a girl. Where do you come from?"

Scarab waved vaguely in the direction of the river. "Downriver."

Min guffawed. "More like 'in river' you mean. She's soaking wet and covered in mud, da."

"I fell in," Scarab snapped. "I'm cold and I'm hungry and I'd like to warm myself by your fire before I go ..." The girl's voice trailed off and she looked around at the men and woman. "I ... I can pay."

"We don't charge for the use of a fire," Pa-it said gruffly. "We'd be happy to give you a bit of food too. Nothing fancy," his eyes drifted over her body, noting the soft hands, the shaved head and, despite its muddy state, the expensive blue wool cloak of her bundle of possessions. "Nothing like you're used to, I'm sure." He nodded at his wife, who ducked back inside the hut. "If you'd like to partake of our hospitality, young miss?" Pa-it indicated the door.

Scarab ducked through the doorway and found herself in a single large room. Sleeping mats occupied one end, with a cooking fire beneath an opening in the roof for the smoke to exit, providing the only light. A low wooden table sat in the middle and a variety of pots and baskets lined the wall nearest the cooking fire. The woman ushered her to the table, putting a piece of coarse bread and a handful of ripe dates in front of her.

"I'm Asenath," the woman said. "Do you want a drink?"

"Please. A little wine would warm me."

Asenath snorted. "Wine? What sort of house did you work in? We don't have no wine here, never have. Water'll have to be good enough for you."

"She never worked in any sort of house, Asenath," Pa-it said quietly, following the girl in. "She may be wearing a servant's kilt but look beneath the mud, look at her hands. She's never worked in her life."

Scarab blushed and ducked her head, nibbling at the piece of bread. She gasped as Asenath grabbed her hand and drew it into the light.

"Soft," she said. "You're right, husband." Asenath released Scarab's hand and reaching out with calloused fingers, turned the girl's face to the fire. "Who are you? Are you some nobleman's daughter or mistress, running away?" She looked up at her husband. "She'll bring trouble, husband. Mark my words."

Pa-it grunted, motioning his sons to the other side of the table. He squatted by the doorway and regarded the girl for several minutes as she ate her meager meal. "You are too young to be some man's mistress, young Scarab, so I'm guessing you are a daughter running away." He grimaced, his voice getting flintier. "What was the reason? Daddy wouldn't buy you another brooch?"

"My parents are dead," Scarab replied. "I live with my brother in the pal ... I live with my brother."

"In the palace? In Akhet-Aten?" Pa-it frowned. "You are the sister of a court official? What is his name?"

"Da?"

"What is it, Khu?"

"I seen her, Da. Last year when I was in the city for the festival. She was in one of them huge chairs carried

460

by slaves. Of course, she was in fine clothes and all but I'm sure it were her. Someone said her name were Meke-something."

"Carried in the procession with the king? Meke? Meketaten, the princess?"

"Think so, Da. It were her though. Not as pretty as the others but still nice to look at."

Scarab scowled and poked her tongue out at the young man. He laughed and pulled a face in retaliation.

"Is that true?" Pa-it asked. "You were being carried in the Heb-Sed procession?"

"She's not Meketaten," Asenath said. "Meketaten was one of the king's daughters and she died last year, just after the festival."

"I never said I was Meketaten," Scarab said indignantly. "Though I was carried in her chair."

The older son Min leaned forward and tapped the table. "Then what was you doing in her chair? They only carried the king and queen and their daughters in the procession."

Scarab felt like she was being backed into a corner. "I ... I'm not a daughter. I'm a sister."

"What's your real name, child?" Pa-it asked gently.

"Beketaten," Scarab whispered. "Please don't tell anyone I'm here. I ... I'll leave immediately and no-one will know." She started to get up.

"Stay where you are child, nobody's going to hurt you." Pa-it glanced across at Min. "Go and ask Ankhu and Menna to join us. Apologize for the lateness of the hour but don't say anything about young Beketaten here."

Min nodded and left. After he left a silence fell on the hut. Scarab finished up her dates, spitting the stones out into her hand and lining them up neatly on the edge of

461

the table. Asenath gathered them up with a grunt of annoyance and threw them in the fire, then wiped a rag over the table to clear the crumbs. The males sat or squatted and looked at the girl with curiosity.

Two men ducked under the door lintel and straightened up. One was an older man with an arm twisted and gnarled by some ancient accident. His hair, despite the lines and wrinkles was jet black and wavy. The younger one was tall and thin, with a sour expression as if he had a mouthful of vinegar. Min followed the two men in and stood in one corner.

"Ah, Ankhu, Menna," Pa-it said. "Thank you for coming. I am sorry to disturb you so late but we may have a problem – as a community, that is."

"Who's the girl?" The younger man tossed his head in Scarab's direction.

"She says her name is Beketaten."

"So?"

"Don't be slow-witted, Menna," the older man with the twisted arm said. "I know of only one Beketaten." He stared at Scarab. "Youngest daughter of the old king Nebmaetre. Is that you, girl?"

Scarab nodded.

"Thought it might be." Ankhu grinned. "Nobody outside of the nobility in Akhet-Aten is going to take on an Aten name. You know the king's not exactly loved, don't you?"

"Be cautious, Ankhu," Pa-it said quietly. "She is sister to the king."

"Does anyone know she's here?" Menna asked.

"She came in alone, bedraggled and muddy from the direction of the river. I think she ran away, but I don't know why. I called you both here because we have a problem. If they come looking for her ..."

"And they will," Menna growled. "There'll be a huge hue and cry for the king's fornicating sister."

"Watch your tongue, Menna." Asenath hissed. "Small wonder you cannot find a wife."

"As I was saying," Pa-it went on. "If they come looking for her, we could all pay. 'The people suffer when nobles anger', I think the proverb goes. More so with a king. Nobody is going to worry that she came to us. They'll say we kidnapped her."

"Please," Scarab said. "I don't want to make trouble for anyone. I'll just leave and no-one need ever know I was here."

"That might be a bit late, child. No doubt you have left a trail that the army scouts will follow."

"Not necessarily," Ankhu interrupted. "How did you cross the river?"

"I took a small boat. It went aground on a sand bank downriver and I had to wade. That's when I got all wet."

"They'll find the boat. Now if we put, say her cloak in the river, and rip it a bit, they might think a crocodile took her."

Khu grinned. "We could put some chicken blood on the cloak too. That'd convince them."

"Please, please." Pa-it waved his arms placatingly. "That only diverts attention from the village momentarily. What happens later when they find her?"

"Dump her in the river for the crocodiles, then," Menna growled. "I'll do it."

Asenath stepped between Scarab and Menna. "You keep your hands to yourself."

"We are not going to kill her," Pa-it said firmly. "Sorry, child. Menna is thinking only of the village and our safety, but I promise you nobody here will harm you."

"Well, what are we going to do with her?"

463

"We have two choices. We either let her walk out of here and deny all knowledge of her when the king's soldiers arrive ..."

"Dangerous."

"... or we help her escape so the soldiers don't find her."

"More dangerous."

"Please, I only want to get to Waset. If you show me how to get to the caravan road I'll go and never come back. If they catch me on the east bank of the river, they'll never think to ask here."

"You know how far it is to Waset?"

Scarab shook her head, tears starting to show in her eyes. "I've got to get there, I've got to."

"If you walked, little girl, it would take you a month."

Scarab opened her mouth but no sound came out. Her chin wobbled and she burst into tears. Between her sobs she gasped. "That will be too late. I've got to get there before the new moon."

Asenath put her arm around Scarab, holding her close until her sobs became muffled. She sniffed loudly and wiped her tears away with her fingers, spreading the dried mud on her cheeks into streaks.

"If you need to get to Waset quickly, Beketaten, wouldn't it be better to ask your brother for a chariot? And an escort too?" Asenath handed Scarab a grimy rag.

"Thank you. And please call me Scarab, I don't like my other name." She took the rag and blew her nose loudly. "I can't go to the king. It ... it's too dangerous."

"Told you," Menna said, a note of satisfaction in his voice. "This girl is trouble."

"Be quiet, Menna. Go on, Scarab. Why is it dangerous? Would the king hurt you?"

"No. The king wants to marry me but that's not why it's dangerous."

"Marry you?" Pa-it said incredulously. "But you're his sister."

Scarab shrugged. "My family does that sort of thing. He's marrying his daughters too. He wants sons very badly."

"So why is it dangerous?"

Scarab thought hard. She looked around the circle of faces, Asenath and Khu friendly, Menna hostile, the rest just curious. Taking a deep breath she tried to slow her racing heart and calm herself.

"I overheard the queen and the Grand Tjaty Ay plotting to overthrow the king on the night of the new moon. I can't tell the king because I have no proof and I'm only a girl. He'd call my uncle Ay in, who'd deny it and the king would believe him. Then Ay would have me killed." She paused and looked around again. "So you see, there is no-one in Akhet-Aten I can go to without Ay finding out. My only hope is to get to Waset and tell my brother Smenkhkare. He'll know what to do."

Min whistled. "Sounds like one of those exciting stories you hear on the street corners during festivals."

"But this is no story," Scarab said seriously. "If I don't reach Waset before the new moon, the king will be overthrown and maybe killed."

"Can't say I'd mind," Menna commented.

"Menna! She's the king's sister."

Menna raised his hands defensively toward Asenath. "Sorry little girl. It's just that your brother Akhenaten is not too popular in the countryside. He may be happy with his one god but the rest of us would like our old ones back."

Ankhu shifted in his seat and scratched his leg. "There's another proverb it would be good to remember, Menna. 'The fall of stars brings nothing but trouble.' For 'stars' read 'king'."

Pa-it nodded. "There will be bloodshed. There always is when kings fall. You may not like the present one but will you like this Ay any better? He doesn't sound like anyone I'd like to know. "

"So will you help me?" Scarab asked.

"Help you how?"

"Sell me a horse. I ... I have some jewelry, I could pay for one. If you'd rather," she hurried on, "I could give you a note and Smenkhkare would pay you in gold later."

"Scarab, child," Pa-it's voice was gentle. "Nobody in the village has a horse. What would we want with one? They are only good for riding or pulling chariots."

"Then you can't help me." Scarab started crying again. "The king will die and Ay will come looking for me to kill me too."

Pa-it watched his wife comfort the girl again, drying her tears and holding her. He thought about her predicament and also what had to be done for the safety of the village. The others, his friends and sons, looked at him, waiting for his decision. He made it.

"Scarab cannot stay here. She needs to be in Waset and we need her over the other side of the river as soon as possible. At dawn, Min will take the blue cloak, rip it and put chicken blood on it. He will find a place a little downriver and put it where it can be found. Scarab will stay here tomorrow, inside this hut, not leaving it for any reason. Tell nobody else she is here. If we are questioned it will help that nobody else has seen her. Their denials will have the ring of truth. At dusk tomorrow we will take Scarab back to the east bank and across to the caravan trail. If the gods smile on her a caravan will pass in a day or two and carry her to Waset. There is nothing more we can do."

Scarab looked up through her tears and smiled tremulously. "It will be enough. I thank you Pa-it of Ak-het-Re."

Chapter Thirty-Two

And so I found myself once more on the east side of the river, heading south to Waset and my beloved Smenkhkare. Asenath washed my kilt and headdress, gave me water to wash the mud from my body and fed me, replacing my sodden loaf and filling my water jug. I lost my lovely blue wool cloak though. Min took it at dawn and, as the other farmers in the little community left for their day's work in the fields, hurried off toward the river, the torn and bloodstained cloak over one arm. I gave Asenath one of my necklaces, the lapis one with the silver thread. She did not want to take it but I insisted. It was one I had been given in Waset so I knew she could sell it safely in Akhet-Aten.

At dusk, Pa-it and his sons smuggled me out of the village and took me south, past the boundary steles of Akhenaten's city, past the cliffs that came right down to the water's edge, to where a small boat waited to ferry me across.

"I will row you across," Pa-it said. "I'll take you to the caravan route and leave you there. There is no more I can do."

"There is, da, but I will do it," Khu said quietly. "I am going with her."

"What are you saying, son?"

"Scarab is only a child." Khu flashed a grin at me and my retort died unspoken. "She will need a man to see her safely to her brother." He shrugged. "And I've always wanted to see Waset."

Pa-it gripped his son's shoulders and stared into his eyes. "You are your own man, Khu, but what am I going to tell your mother?"

468

"She knows already, da. Do you think I would leave without saying goodbye?"

Pa-it rowed Khu and me over to the eastern shore and left us on the reed-covered edge. He said nothing, just handing me my bundle of possessions and giving Khu a bronze dagger. Khu hefted his own small bundle then, giving his father a quick kiss, turned and started up the bank towards the sand and rock.

I looked back as we left the grassy verge of the river but Pa-it and his little boat were already out of sight. I heard only a faint splash in the darkness and the sound of insects at my feet. Turning, I ran to catch up with Khu.

I am not sure quite what I expected on my journey. I think probably a proper road that I could make good time on. Certainly nothing like the wilderness of sand and rock that rose before me. The cliffs around Akhet-Aten should have warned me. They are dry and desolate and inhabited by all sorts of scorpions and snakes. The slope we climbed toward the desert plateau that night was like those cliffs, only not as steep. I was thankful for my sandals when we started but by the time we neared the top I realized the difference between proper footwear and the beautifully made but flimsy sandals made for pampered palace ladies. One of them fell apart and the other was chafing me badly, so I took them off and threw them aside.

Khu noticed my predicament. "It'll get easier when we get to the top. There's less rock and more sand."

I saw the rocks did not bother his bare feet so I did not complain, biting back the pain when my soft feet met a hard stone. He was right though. We crested the slope and looked out over the rolling hills of sand gleaming silver and black in the light of the moon, seeming to stretch on forever. I looked back at the inky darkness of

469

the river far below us, invisible with the moon behind me.

"How far to the caravan road?" I scanned the gleaming sands hopefully for a broad, plainly marked road, not seeing it.

"With luck we'll be there by midnight. You won't see it until we are almost on it. Over there somewhere." Khu pointed slightly south of east.

We headed off into the desert, keeping to the tops of what I learned were dunes, as much as possible. The ridges were fairly firm and we could make good progress, but every so often we had to descend the dune when the crest curved away from our intended route and then we sank into the soft sand up to our knees. We stopped after an hour or so to rest. Already it was impossible to see where we had come from and our footprints were not visible further away than twenty paces. A gentle wind stirred the sand grains, filling in our tracks, losing us in the wilderness. At least it was not hot. I sweated when we moved, particularly on the hard trek up and down the faces of the dunes, but when we stopped, exposed on a crest, the wind rapidly chilled me. I shivered but I no longer had my thick blue wool cloak, only a thin threadbare gray one given to me by Asenath.

"Go easy on the water," Khu admonished as I raised my water jug to my lips again. "There's a well of sorts at the rock fort but we may not get there until dawn."

"A fort? Will there be soldiers there?"

"No. It's just called a fort because there is a ring of large boulders. There is supposed to be a well there too. I've never been there but I met a man at the festival last year who had, and he told me about it."

"But there will be a caravan there?"

"Maybe, now come on." Khu got to his feet and brushed the sand off the back of his kilt. "We have to keep moving. We don't want to be out here in the sun."

We reached the caravan road as the moon started its downward slide toward the west. For a moment I was unaware of the difference but I found I was walking on packed gravel and sand, no longer the shifting sands of the desert. I stopped and looked to left and right at a barely discernible ribbon of road that stretched out into the night.

"This is it?" I asked, disappointment in my voice.

Khu nodded and pointed. "South. Come on."

I was tired and my feet were sore, my calf muscles aching, but I followed, unwilling to show myself as a weak pampered girl. Khu offered to carry my bundle as well as his but I refused, determined to show him I was strong. Later, I wished I had let him relieve me of my burden, particularly as my hobbling pace became slower and slower, and more and more often he had to stop and wait for me to catch up. Dawn came, pink light leaking over the horizon, the moon paling in the west.

"We can't be far," Khu said, shading his eyes, staring along the road. "We have been slower than I hoped but we should still be close." I silently blessed him for saying 'we' instead of blaming me for our slow pace. We trudged on, weary but now slightly afraid as the sun rose swiftly, dispelling the desert night chill. Back in Akhet-Aten I would just be breakfasting, eating cool fruit and bread on a shady verandah, but here I had a swallow of tepid water, the sun already rippling the air around us. The sand beneath my feet started heating and I knew I would soon be missing my sandals.

At last, just as I was starting to panic, my feet feeling as if they were blistering, we saw the rounded boulders of

471

the fort ahead of us. I was all for rushing forward, wanting to get into the meager shade and replenish my water, but Khu held me back.

"We don't know who might be there. Other people use this road beside traders. There might be soldiers, or even worse, bandits." He advanced slowly; scanning the road ahead and the boulders for movement, for any sign of life, but saw nothing. He beckoned me and I joined him, limping and sore.

The rock fort was set back from the road about fifty paces and an old well, stone lined and fitted with a wooden cover, sat in a slight depression near the boulders, its low surrounding wall almost topped by the drifting sand. Khu lifted the lid and dropped a pebble in, listening for the delayed but satisfactory plunk as it fell into deep water, the sound echoing up the hollow column of the well. The air in the shaft was cool and moist and very inviting.

"How do we get it?"

"There must be a rope and bucket somewhere," Khu replied. He wandered off to the rock shelters and presently came back with a small bucket and a rope coiled over his arm.

The water was sweet and cold and tasted like a fine wine after the tepid liquid in our water jars. We emptied them out and, after we drank our fill and washed the dust off our bodies, refilled them. I soaked my headdress and put it on. It cooled my head delightfully.

Khu looked around at the desert and along the empty road in both directions. "We must wait here for a caravan."

"But what if one doesn't turn up?" I asked, dismayed at the prospect of just sitting around doing nothing. Having started for Waset I wanted to continue. "Can't we walk?" I asked, forgetting the blistering sand and my lack of footwear.

"I don't know where the next water is," Khu explained, shaking his head. "It's easy to die out here. No, we wait for a caravan." He led the way back to the shifting shade of the rock fort and stretched out where he could watch the road. "Get some sleep. I'll wake you at noon."

I knew I was too excited to sleep despite walking all night but to please him I lay down in the shade and closed my eyes ... and woke with the sun in my eyes. "Is it noon already?" I asked, squinting against the glare.

"Mid-afternoon. I didn't have the heart to wake you. You were snoring like a pig."

"I was not." I worked my mouth, trying to get the saliva to flow. I swallowed a few mouthfuls of water and looked at my companion as he sat there in the shade, yawning. "Have you slept?"

"No. If you are up to keeping watch, I'll get some sleep."

"Of course I am, but why do we have to watch?" I said, matching his yawns. "Won't a caravan make enough noise to wake us?"

"Caravans aren't the only people in the desert." Khu yawned again and rolled over, presenting his back to me. "What if your uncle Ay found out you were going to Waset an' sen' sol'ers affer 'ou?" His voice drifted and slurred. "Or bandiss?"

"What was that?"

He didn't answer, his breathing deepening and slowing. After a while Khu started snoring and I turned my attention to the desert and the deserted track. The sandy desert is one of the most boring places I have been, though at the risk of getting ahead of myself I must say I found plenty of interesting things there later in life. At the time, I found the lack of anything happening sent me to sleep. After drifting off and jerking awake a few times I got up and wandered around, exploring the rock fort. Aside from a scorpion under a rock and a slight shifting of the sand near another, there was no sign of life. The rudimentary shelters under the boulders were primitive and dirty and showed signs of repeated occupation. I supposed the caravan traders slept the night here sometimes. A pile of firewood occupied one shelter. I wondered at someone leaving precious fuel behind, but thought that caravans might leave supplies behind for other travelers on the road.

There was one shelter that was more interesting. Formed from a jumble of boulders with another making a curved roof, a thin angled crevice receded into shadows. I peered inside and taking a stick I found near the stone-circled ashes in the open area between the boulders, I poked into the darkness in case there was a snake. Nothing moved or made a sound so I went in. It was a tight squeeze but I am a slim girl so I managed it. I doubted that Khu could enter though. All I could see was a dimly lit sand floor and the bright slash of light in the entry passage. I came out and wandered off, paying it no further attention.

Nothing else in the rock fort interested me so I went back to where Khu lay in the shade, snoring. I grinned and thought up a couple of choice descriptions of his noise to tell him when he woke. The afternoon passed very slowly and I looked at Khu impatiently, wanting him to wake up. I tossed a small pebble at him, hitting him on his hip, but he just grunted and turned over. I felt guilty so I did not throw another. Instead I sat facing the road north with my handful of pebbles and made a competition of throwing the stones at a stick lying in the sand. I got rather good at it. I found my natural inclination was to throw from the shoulder, using my whole arm and swinging my body, usually missing my target by several paces. Then I remembered how I'd seen Smenkhkare throwing years before, using a flick of the wrist. I tried it, and with practice, got better. After a while I was hitting my target two times out of five.

So engrossed was I with my game that I did not notice the riders until they were quite close. Already I could make out details of the clothing of some dozen horsemen as they moved at a slow walk from the north, the late sun throwing long shadows over the sand. The men appeared dirty and unkempt, and I remember thinking that they must have had a long journey. Then I wondered where their trade goods were. There were no pack animals, just the horses they rode. I felt unease grip me and I stood to get a better look. I suppose the movement caught the eye for one of them yelled and pointed.

I dropped and ran over to Khu, shaking him awake. "Riders," I yelled. "Coming this way."

He leapt to his feet and ran out into the open, took one look at the horsemen spurring toward us and pushed me back. "Run!" He whirled to face the men as they came through the gaps between the boulders, only paces away.

I hesitated, then as he yelled again for me to run, fear seized me and I raced back to our little rock shelter. I grabbed my meager belongings, saw Khu's old bronze dagger and snatched it up too and ran for the cover of the rocks. Looking back, I saw Khu fall beneath a rider as they urged their horses past, toward me. I dropped my bundle but still gripping the dagger ran between the boulders, the rock crevice I had found earlier beckoning me.

A rider rode past me, the hooves of his horse throwing sand up in my face. With a yell, he jumped from his mount and lunged for me. I dodged and he slipped and fell. The dark crevice loomed ahead and I threw myself at it, feeling the man's hand flick my kilt as I scrambled in, squeezing past the smooth stone surfaces. The man yelled and tried to follow, his hand scrabbling and clawing after me. I slashed with the dagger and he withdrew cursing.

All I could see now was the bright splash of light from the crevice entrance. The sounds from outside were muffled but I could hear voices. Nobody came near me for many minutes, then I heard the sound of the well cover scraping back and the splash of the bucket. I suddenly realized I was thirsty and looked for my water jar before remembering I'd dropped it along with everything else I owned. All I had now was the kilt I wore and Khu's dagger.

Remembering Khu's dagger made me aware that he had his problems too. Or was he past his? I'd seen him fall beneath the horse. Did this mean he was dead? I cried at the thought but was confused about whether I cried for him being dead or for me being alone.

Alone? There were a dozen men out there. Bandits probably, certainly not people I could trust. I was young and fairly trusting but I'd overheard stories of what lawless men did – my mind shied away from the thought. Instead, I forced myself to think about my present situation. They couldn't reach me in here and even if one of them was small enough to wriggle in after me, I could stab him with my dagger. On the other hand, there was only one way out. Maybe I could sneak out after dark?

Maybe they'd all be asleep and I could escape? To where? My mind latched onto all sorts of romantic and daring possibilities – stealing a horse and riding to Waset; finding soldiers and leading them back here.

Then reality came crashing back. I was a twelve year old girl, well, almost thirteen, but still young and almost totally without experience of life outside the palace. I had no water, no food, I didn't know how to ride a horse and I'd be willing to bet there would always be a guard awake and alert. After all, they knew I was here and sooner or later...

A shadow fell over the remnants of daylight entering my little refuge. "Come out, girl." A pause, then the voice called again, a touch of amusement in the tone. "You'll have to come out sooner or later. You must be getting thirsty."

I didn't reply, just crawled deeper into the shadows. I could hear low voices but not what was being said. The shadow came again and a grimy, bearded face peered in, trying to see me.

"Don't make me come in there and get you, girl. If you come out you won't be harmed." Someone laughed behind him and he turned; anger in his voice. "Keep quiet you motherless turds." Then back to me again. "Come on girl. We have a fire against the cold, we have food and drink and warm blankets. It gets cold at night. I won't let them touch you."

His eyes must have grown accustomed to the darkness because he suddenly reached out and grabbed my foot. I screamed and slashed with my dagger. He released me with a curse and fell back. The voices came again, my attacker louder and more vocal though I found I could not make out the words. I heard a command, then silence.

477

The shadow again, though the light behind him had lessened. "Last chance, girl, or we kill your man."

My heart felt as if it cramped in my chest. "How ... how do I know he's alive? I s... saw him fall."

"Scarab." It was Khu, without a doubt. "Scarab, stay there, don't ..." A blow and silence.

"He's still alive, Scarab," said the voice. "For now. But if you don't come out I'm going to start cutting him. He'll be a long time dying and you'll have to listen to him screaming."

My mind blanked out and my vision blurred. I felt warm liquid on my leg and knew I was in the grip of panic. I leaned back against the rock and struggled for breath.

"Have it your own way," the voice said. "Strip him boys. Time for a little fun."

"No. W... wait." I fought to calm myself, knowing there was no way out. I could stay holed up in my cave, eventually dying of thirst and heat, but then Khu would die, painfully. Or I could come out – but then what? "You ... you promise you won't hurt him ... us ... if I come out?"

The man laughed. "On my word of honour, girl."

"You'll let us go?"

"Have I not said so?"

I thought about it again but nothing new occurred to me. I had to come out and trust this man. "Stay back, then. I ... I will come out." The shadow backed away. I put the dagger out of sight in the back of the cave and edged out into the dusk where I stood alone in the middle of a circle of leering men.

Chapter Thirty-Three

"She's gone, I tell you."

Ay stood in Nefertiti's chambers and stared at his daughter as she paced like one of the lions in the cages in the Waset palace gardens. "And why should this concern me?"

"Is it not obvious? She knows."

Ay turned and went back out through the antechamber and looked into the corridor. He returned and closed the great cedar wood doors. He did the same with the door to the queen's bedchamber, before crossing to the window and looking out. Satisfied, he confronted his daughter.

"How could she know? Have you told anyone?"

"Of course not, father. Have you? What plans have you been making? Has one of your conspirators talked?"

Ay shook his head. "Only I know the reason behind anything I have set up. It will go as smoothly as I have planned if you don't lose your nerve. Besides, there is no reason to suppose her disappearance is connected."

"Then why has she gone?"

"At the moment we do not even know she has. Tell me what you know, from the beginning."

Nefertiti took several deep breaths, calming herself. She crossed to the window and looked toward the river, staring into the distance. "The maids went to rouse her this morning, to bathe and dress her. She wasn't there." She held up a hand as if to forestall comment though Ay had not stirred or even drawn breath to speak. "She is a young woman, a girl still, and nobody took much notice. She was off somewhere, playing, or with the other princesses. But she did not turn up for the noon meal, nor had Ankhese or Nefer seen her. The overseer of the keepers of the jewelry came to see me when it was discovered Beketaten's jewelry was missing."

"So she's wearing her jewelry."

"A man's comment," Nefertiti muttered under her breath. "Would she wear three necklaces? And a dozen bracelets? The colours clash too."

"Very well, I will accept what you say about the necklaces. Go on."

"She left all her clothes behind, except a blue wool cloak she had requested the previous day."

"Curious. Still, what makes you think she knows something?"

"The night before last the king goes insane, I walk out and we make plans to remove him. The next night Beketaten disappears, apparently wearing nothing but her jewelry and a blue wool cloak. You do not think this is even a tiny bit suspicious?" Nefertiti glared at her father.

"I think your concerns are premature. Still, if it will ease your mind, I will make a search for her."

Ay left the North Palace troubled. He did not like coincidences and this business with Beketaten was too much of a coincidence for comfort. Still, even if she had heard something, what could she do? Who could she tell? He crossed the road and sat down on a stone bench inside one of the city's parks determined to think the problem through before acting.

There are two possibilities. Either she heard nothing or she heard something. If she heard nothing then there is a simple explanation for her absence. She has gone shopping or is on some other frivolous female errand. One of those fool maids miscounted her clothes and she is not wandering the streets naked after all.

But what if she did overhear us — never mind how? Who would I tell if I was her? The king? She is his sister, after all. He may listen. Who else? Ay racked his brains, thinking of all the senior court officials and who might be powerful enough to move against the Grand Tjaty. He couldn't think of anyone. *Who outside the court then? If they were in Akhet-Aten?*

Paatenemheb and Smenkhkare. But the general is off somewhere in the north, who knows where? Smenkhkare is in Waset – maybe ... but how does she get there? Only two ways, overland or by boat. Overland she needs a horse or a caravan – check if there have been any horse thefts, or caravans leaving since yesterday. Boats? What has left for Waset in the last day?

Ay sat back on the bench and nodded. *The other thing I have to decide is – do I bother? She cannot possibly get to Waset and tell her brother, then have anyone here to stop me in less than a month. She cannot stop me, so why should I care?* He scowled. *Because the little bitch thinks she can stop me. Well, I'll find her and she can try telling her brother from the underworld.*

He got up and hurried back down to the main palace, where he rounded up men dedicated to his service, giving them instructions. "You have until sunset. No later. I want something definite from each one of you, now move."

All except one returned by the appointed hour and reported, quietly entering the Tjaty's private chambers and leaving again by a side door.

"There have been no horse thefts in the city, nor any sold to a girl."

"Nobody in the city has seen her."

"A man at the wharves may have seen her yesterday but the girl was wearing a servant's kilt."

"A barge left for Waset yesterday afternoon."

"No caravans have arrived or left the city."

"A rowing boat was stolen last night."

481

Ay sent for Mahu, the chief of the Medjay. "The princess Beketaten has robbed the queen of a costly necklace and fled the city. I know, it is hard to believe, but you must find her, and quickly. And quietly too, use only trusted men. She has either stowed away, or maybe paid for passage, on the barge that left for Waset yesterday; or else she stole a rowing boat and may be headed either up or down the river." Ay got up and came around his desk. Taking Mahu by the shoulder he leaned close, talking quietly and confidentially. "Mahu, treat her with care when you find her and let her talk to no-one. In fact, it would be best if you had her gagged immediately you lay hands on her." He sighed and sat down on the edge of his desk. "It pains me to say so, but she made a threat against the queen's honour and threatened to go to the king unless she was paid off. I don't know what she might say, how she might blacken the queen's name if she was given the opportunity to talk."

Mahu shook his head, his great tufted eyebrows coming together in concern. "I don't know what comes over young people these days. She is so young too."

"I know, Mahu, but I know I can trust you to act with finesse. I must talk to her before she talks to anyone else, even your policemen. Can you do this for me?"

"I can, Tjaty Ay. If she is to be found, I shall find her for you and return her safely, unheard by any."

The chief of the Medjay organized the search immediately, sending a fast boat south in pursuit of the barge, his instructions odd but clear. His men would obey to the letter rather than risk his wrath. Other boats were sent up and down river with instructions to search the riverbanks and to ask of any river man they came across, the whereabouts of the princess Beketaten.

The search was cut short by the fall of night but resumed the next morning at first light. By noon the fast boat returned empty-handed from its interception of the barge and the men joined the riverbank searches. At noon, an empty boat was found lodged in the reeds five thousand paces downriver and near it, a blue wool cloak, ripped and bloodstained. Mahu returned to the palace to make his report.

"The owner identified the boat and the North Palace Controller of Bedding says the cloak was the one given to her the day before."

Ay nodded. "Could she be alive still?"

Mahu shrugged. "Possible, but unlikely. Even a skilled boatman would not be on the river in a small craft alone at night. The currents, the shoals, can be treacherous."

"And the crocodiles."

"Well, it is not usual for them to attack a boat, but if she stepped ashore near one ..." Mahu grimaced. "The cloak is ripped and covered in blood. I do not think she lives."

Ay thanked the chief of the Medjay and escorted him from the palace. "Thank you, Mahu, for your dedication and your discretion. I will have an ox brought round to the Medjay barracks tonight. Perhaps you and your men will enjoy my gesture of thanks." He went back inside and shut the door to his room before breaking into a smile of satisfaction. *Whether Beketaten heard something or not, it is immaterial. She will not be telling anyone.*

Chapter Thirty-Four

I saw Khu lying still on the sands in the desert twilight and it was all I could do not to run to him. Instead I
looked round at the circle of men, resisting the urge to
hide myself from them, until I found the face of the man
who had spoken to me. He was short, not much above
my height, but broad and muscular. He was probably the
hairiest man I had ever seen, certainly hairier than any
normal Kemetu. Long black hair hung in greasy locks
that merged with his unkempt beard. Chest, belly, arms
and legs likewise were covered in a mass of black hair, a
brown, military style kilt his only apparel, though he also
had a belt with short sword and dagger.

I was reminded of one of the powerful half-men of
the lands beyond Nubia that one of the expeditions
brought back from the South in the days of my father.
The man lived for many years in Waset but had to be
caged as he spoke no language and walked on all fours.
He was immensely strong though gentle, for he ate no
meat, only fruit and leaves. This man before me looked
like the half-man but infinitely more dangerous. I had no
doubt he was a meat-eater and not at all gentle.

"My ... my friend," I said. "Is he alive?" I struggled to
keep my voice calm and even.

"For the moment." The man grinned, yellowed and
decaying teeth showing through his beard.

"And you will honour your word and let us go?"

He roared with laughter, his men joining in after a
beat. "Have I not said so, little girl? But first, join us at
the campfire that we may show our hospitality." He
grabbed me by the arm and propelled me toward the
clearing where I could see the orange glow of a camp

484

fire. Two of his men dragged the unconscious body of Khu, the rest of them ambling along joking and laughing. I heard some phrases that would have made me blush had I not been so scared.

Standing me in the light of the fire, the hairy man and the rest of the gang stared at me, examined me from head to foot. I did blush then but fought not to cry. I thought of my brother Smenkhkare and that cheered me. I was a royal princess; I would not let these common men see my tears or my terror.

"So, your name is Scarab, little girl? A strange name for a girl."

"My ... my brother calls me that."

"I am called Bennu," the hairy man rasped. "Perhaps you have heard of me?" I shook my head and he scowled. "I have a certain reputation in these parts." He walked around me, then lifted my hand and felt it with his hard, horny one. "Soft hands, Scarab, yet you are a woman – well almost," he laughed. He dropped my hand and grabbed my breast, giving it a painful squeeze. I squeaked with alarm and jumped back a pace and he laughed again.

"What do you work at that your hands are so soft, Scarab?"

"I ... I live in the palace."

"A lady's maid or something then?" I nodded and a different look came into his eyes, avarice replacing lust. "Perhaps the lady concerned would pay to get you back. Would you agree, Scarab?"

I thought about a ransom demand being sent to the court in Akhet-Aten. Ay would pay it immediately but I would be no better off in his hands than I was in Bennu's. I shook my head.

485

"There's only one person who would pay a ransom for me. My brother at the court in Waset. I was on my way there to see him. I ... I am sure he would pay to get me back ... and him." I pointed at Khu.

"And who is this boy? Someone else we can ransom?"

"Yes."

"Who is he? Your lover?" The men standing around laughed.

I blushed. "He is a friend who was good enough to accompany me on my journey. I would ask that you honour your word and release us."

"A young girl with small but ripening breasts alone in the desert with a young man she calls her 'friend' but insists is not her lover." Bennu leered at me, lust back in his eyes. "Do you bring all your 'friends' out to the desert, Scarab?"

"I have told you he is not my lover. I do not have any lovers. I never have had. I am betrothed to ..." I hesitated, thinking desperately. "... To a friend of my brother. Both he and my brother would pay to get me back ... unharmed." I felt rather than heard a ripple of interest among the men and wondered whether I had made a mistake. Then I knew I had.

"A virgin?" Bennu said softly. "It has been a long time since I had a virgin."

I trembled, though the flickering light and shadows of the campfire masked my fear. "My ... my brother is very wealthy. He will pay to get me back but I must be unharmed."

"Oh, you will not be harmed, little Scarab," Bennu purred. "Who knows, perhaps your future husband will be delighted he is marrying an experienced woman rather than an untried girl."

"No. You promised to ..."

"I lied. Now take that kilt off and let me see what I will be enjoying."

I stepped back hurriedly. "No. Please."

Bennu moved. Before I could do anything his hand reached out and tugged at the hem of my servant's kilt. The clasp popped free and even in that moment of stress I registered the gleam of reflected fire on the little copper pin as it flew off to land in the sand. My kilt was ripped off me and I stood naked in front of them all. Bennu licked his lips and stared. With an effort, I forced my hands to my sides, refusing to cover myself, knowing it to be a useless act.

"Do not do this." Trembling harder, I knew only the truth stood between me and ... and I didn't want to think of that. I also knew that the truth would be dangerous for me and Ay would kill me, but I knew I had to try.

"My real name is Beketaten, princess of Akhet-Aten and sister to the king. He would pay a fortune to get us back but his army would hunt you down and kill you if you harm us."

Bennu gaped, then threw his head back and roared with laughter, slapping his thighs. His men joined in too with guffaws and many ribald comments.

"I like your wit, Scarab, but choose a tale a trifle more likely. Can you imagine a princess alone in the desert, accompanied only by a peasant lad?" He shook his head, wiping tears from his eyes. "Now join me on my blanket and we shall have some sport."

"What about the rest of us, Bennu?" A few of the other men joined in.

"You'll all get your turns, but tonight she's mine. Amuse yourselves with the boy if you like." Bennu reached out and grabbed me, hauling me toward him. I gasped and swung my free hand at his head but he moved and my hand only slapped him lightly. He laughed and crushed me to his hairy chest. His mouth found mine and his stinking breath filled my lungs.

Gagging, I pulled back, my fingers searching for his eyes. He released me, slapping my hands away, then pinned my arms and slobbered over me again. My stomach heaved and I threw up over him before collapsing to the sand, gasping for air.

Bennu stood over me staring down at the thin vomit matting his chest hairs, then with a roar of rage he picked me up and hit me in the side of the head, sending me reeling away. He strode after me and hit me again, this time in the stomach. I doubled over and collapsed, my vision turning red as I struggled to draw breath. He leaned down and hissed in my face. "You will beg for mercy before dawn, Scarab, but there will be none."

Grabbing my thin arms, he dragged me back to his blanket by the rocks and threw me face down onto it. I whimpered and tried to crawl away but he hauled me back, holding my hips and lifting my bottom into the air until I was kneeling in front of him, my face ground into the blanket. I felt my legs parted and I cried out, despairingly.

"Someone's coming, Bennu." A hoarse shout came from the edge of the rock fort. "I can hear feet – many, and metal jingling."

"Eh?" I heard muffled movements behind me and my hips were released. I slumped sideways and looked round through tear-blurred eyes.

The camp was in an uproar, though a silent one. Bennu was snapping out commands, stark naked, though with his covering of fur it was hard to tell. His erect member rapidly wilted. Most of the horses and men

488

melted back into the darkness, dragging the still unconscious form of Khu with them, though four remained
out near the fire.

"They will have seen the fire so someone must remain. I cannot stay; my face is too well known." Bennu
spared a quick grin. "If they are few we can take them."
He strode back and, picking me up, hauled me back into
the shadows. "Keep very quiet, little Scarab, and I'll let
you live," he hissed. His dagger eased close, its point
pricking my throat.

I looked out on the hollow between the rocks where
four men now sat around the fire, their horses hobbled
nearby. I heard the fast, steady beat of running men on
the beaten earth of the caravan track and the jingle of
metal came louder, a counterpoint that sounded like music. Ay had discovered I was missing and sent men to
find me. At that moment I welcomed the thought, even
knowing it meant my death. Some things were worse.

A few minutes later I found out I was wrong. These
were not the garrison soldiers of Akhet-Aten but lean,
hard men from the north. Regular army I judged. They
poured into the rock fort, weapons drawn, a tall man at
their head. Taking up positions facing outward the soldiers remained alert, watching the darkness. The tall man
strode forward into the flickering light and stood in front
of the four gang members, looking down at them.

"Just four of you? Anyone else nearby?"

"No." The man who had been left as leader got to his
feet, though he kept his hand far from his sword. "And
who are you?"

The tall man ignored the question, flicking his eyes
around the clearing. "There are signs of more than four
horses."

489

The bandit shrugged. "A group of horsemen came through just on sunset. They watered their horses and rode on. South." He grinned. "You can catch them if you hurry."

The tall man stared but said nothing. He turned to the man standing next to him. "Meny, have the water jars filled. We move out in five minutes." The man hurried off, snapping off orders. The well cover came off and the bucket was lowered and raised several times, the gurgle and splash of water a welcome sound. I stirred, feeling the need to wash the sour taste of vomit from my mouth.

At once, Bennu's hand covered my mouth and he half-moved over me, crushing me into the sand with his weight. "Do not even think it," he hissed.

The soldiers finished their watering and the tall man nodded as Meny reported. "Fall the men in." He turned back to the bandits by the fire, his eyes casting over the empty space once more. Something caught his eye and he bent and picked up my bent copper kilt pin. He held it up to the light and examined it before straightening the metal between his fingers, seemingly without effort. He attached it to his own kilt and walked back over to the bandit. "Describe the men who were here at sunset."

The man shrugged again. "They were just men. Traders I think."

"Any women?"

The man frowned and his hand twitched nervously. "Er, no."

"Meny," the tall officer called, his eyes on the face of the man in front of him. "Fall the men out. Take a detail and search the rocks. Weapons out."

I knew my life depended on the next few moments. I bit down hard on Bennu's fingers, tasting the hot blood in my mouth. He let out a grunt of pain and his grip

490

slackened slightly. I screamed, muffled against his hand, then wrenched my head to one side and screamed again, piercingly.

I caught a glimpse of the hollow below as I rolled away, Bennu grabbing for me, his dagger snaking out. I scrambled further, into the shadows. The bandit by the fire had flinched at my scream and his hand moved toward his sword, but the officer did not even see it. His own eyes were fixed on the man's eyes and at that flicker his own sword was out and plunged deep into the bandit's belly. Without waiting for orders, Meny waved the soldiers in to the rocks and shouts erupted, followed by the clash of metal.

Bennu forgot me and scrambled to his feet, dagger in one hand and sword snatched up in the other. He stepped out silently between the rocks, rage on his face.

The officer below had turned and fought the other three men by the fire. One lay dead already and another fell, clutching his leg as I watched. He swung away from me, turning his back on Bennu unaware. The bandit leader hefted his sword and gathered himself. I threw myself at him, trying to grip the hair of his legs in my fingers. He shook me off with the ease of a dog shaking water from his coat and I fell against the rock with a gasp.

It was enough though and the officer turned from the last of his three opponents as Bennu charged down the slope, meeting that first blow with upraised sword. He reeled back, the shock of Bennu's weight and his forward motion almost overwhelming him. Metal clashed and gleamed in the fire's light but after that first attack, the tall officer no longer retreated. Armed with only his short sword he held the bandit at bay, blocking sword thrusts and slashes, his height giving him an advantage of reach over the shorter, stockier man. The officer pressed forward now, driving Bennu back.

I saw movement and looked around at the shadowed rocks. Soldiers crowded the perimeter of the rock fort, many of them lounging against the boulders and watching the contest below. For a moment I felt anger that they would stand back and allow their officer to fight alone, but then I realized he needed no help.

Bennu was in trouble and realized it. Robbed of his surprise attack he knew he had met superior skill if not strength. Glancing around he saw he was alone among the enemy and anger filled him. He threw his sword at the officer and as he moved to avoid it, charged in, dagger held low. They collided and the bandit's weight threw them back, toppling to the sand beside the fire. Grappling, Bennu's dagger sought out the officer's life, whose hand strained to hold it back. The other hand, still grasping the sword, beat ineffectually at the bandit's hirsute back while Bennu's left hand slipped between them to his enemy's throat.

The watching soldiers pressed forward, a low hum of concern issuing from half a hundred throats, and one or two stepped forward, swords half raised. Meny signaled them back and advanced to within a pace of the struggling pair before squatting down.

"Do you need any help, sir?" he enquired matter-of-factly.

Bennu looked up, startled and the officer dropped his sword and jabbed up at the bandit's eyes with his fingers. Bennu howled with pain and reared back, loosening his hold. The officer slammed the hand holding the dagger sideways, into the embers of the fire, eliciting another bellow of pain and anger. He scissored his legs and with a heave, rolled over, tipping his opponent full into the fire.

A shower of sparks went up and a billowing cloud of smoke, rank with the stink of burning hair. Snatching up the fallen dagger, the officer slipped it in between Bennu's ribs and thrust hard. His agonized scream cut off abruptly.

The officer stood up and dusted himself down. "Don't ever interfere in my fights again, Meny," he said. Then he grinned and clapped the man on the shoulder. "But thanks." He scanned the hollow and the cheering soldiers. "Casualties?"

"None sir. A dozen dead, bandits by the look of them, and one young lad alive. The doctor's seeing to him." Meny signaled to the soldiers to remove the stinking body of the bandit from the flames. All of the bodies were carried out of sight behind the rocks.

Khu is still alive, I thought. I stepped down from the shelter of the rock, forgetting I was naked and felt many eyes seek me out.

The officer stared at me then smiled. "I believe I have you to thank for that warning." He turned to the officer Meny. "Find a spare kilt and cloak."

Within minutes I was seated on a blanket on the far side of the fire, an oversized kilt fastened about my waist and a warm cloak around my shoulders. The officer came over from where he was talking with Meny and another man and squatted beside me, curiosity in his eyes. He was tall and slim, though broad across the shoulders. To my young eyes he appeared old though I later found he was only in early middle age. His hair was dark and his skin a lovely coppery colour. Despite my ordeal I felt a quickening of interest for this man.

"May I know the name of my benefactor?" I said in a voice that still trembled.

493

"Paramessu, son of Seti. I am commander of the Re Legion, Northern Army. And you, miss?"

"I ... I am called Scarab. Thank you for your ... your rescue."

"Ah, the little lapis scarab on the copper kilt pin. I wondered what a woman's pin was doing out here. You are unharmed?"

"Thanks to your arrival, Paramessu. How is Khu – my companion?"

"He will live. The army doctor says he has a nasty lump on his head but he is already conscious and complaining of the pain." He laughed. "That is always a good sign."

I nodded and smiled, feeling very tired and a bit light headed.

"What were you doing out here?" Paramessu went on. "This is not the place for a young girl."

I yawned and excused myself. "I don't know why I'm so tired," I explained.

"Probably a reaction to your ordeal. As to my question ..." He waited for my answer.

"I am on my way to Waset to see my brother."

"And you decided to walk? Does your brother know you are coming?"

I shook my head. "I hoped we could get passage with a caravan."

Now Paramessu shook his head. "Well, Scarab, your little adventure is ended. I am heading for Waset myself, and beyond, but I cannot slow myself down taking you. I will have Meny take you and – Khu, you said his name is – to Akhet-Aten."

"No!" I jumped up and backed away. "I cannot go there."

"Sit down Scarab," Paramessu said gently. "And tell me why not."

"I ... I cannot." He waited quietly and I relaxed and sat down again.

"I am not your enemy, little Scarab. I do not want to harm you but I must leave soon and I cannot take you with me. Nor can I just leave you here. If there is something you are afraid of in Akhet-Aten you must tell me." He moved then, sitting down and leaning back on one elbow, stretching his long legs out.

His white though travel-stained kilt moved and I saw a small blue-threaded embroidered scarab on the edge. In that instant he ceased to be a stranger and I knew the gods had brought him to me, not just to save me from Bennu, but for another reason.

"Send your men out of earshot and I will tell you."

Interest made his eyes flash. He looked at me curiously for a minute then instructed Meny to move the men back from the fire. Meny raised his eyebrows but obeyed without question.

"All right, little Scarab. What is so important only I may hear it?"

"My name is Beketaten, youngest daughter of Nebmaetre and sister to the king. I overheard a plot by ... by the queen and Tjaty Ay to overthrow the king."

Paramessu did not laugh, nor did he frown. He looked intensely at me and asked in a quiet, controlled voice, "Why did you not take this to the king?"

"Because I am counted as nothing in the court of Akhet-Aten but Ay has the ear of the king. All I would get for my trouble is death – and my brother would still be overthrown."

"Then why Waset? Were you seeking to save your life?"

495

"My brother Smenkhkare rules in Waset. He will know what to do. I sought only to tell him so he may act for the best."

Paramessu leaned back and stared up at the night sky and the star-studded body of the goddess Nut. After a few moments he spoke again, without looking at me. "You swear by the scarab, sacred to Khepri and Re, that what you say is true?"

"I do. May all the gods of Kemet curse me if I lie."

"When is this coup to take place?"

"On the night of the new moon."

"Ten days. My fifty men will not be enough to stop this, and my errand is just as urgent. What use would it be to save Kemet's king if Kemet were lost?" He thought for several more minutes. "I will take you to Paaten-emheb, my General and Meny will carry out my mission in Waset." He got to his feet and grinned down at me, his face suddenly youthful. "Can you ride a horse?"

Chapter Thirty-Five

Meny marched his Fifty out within the hour, armed with the letter of authority from Paatenemheb and also his verbal orders concerning the gold from the mines at Kemsah. He was not happy with his instructions but he would obey.

"I will meet you in Waset a month from the new moon, Meny. Bring plenty of men. Kemet will need them." The Fifty also took Khu with them, on a litter made from spears and a couple of the bandits' blankets.

"At least I'll get to see Waset," he told Scarab.

"I'll get down there when I can," she promised. "Then I'll show you the city sights."

Paramessu and Scarab stayed at the rock fort until the moon rose.

"We travel by night, Scarab. It is cooler, and also the waning moon will be a continuing reminder of our deadline." Paramessu was persuaded with difficulty to continue calling her Scarab, instead of her proper name. It was safer, she insisted.

It was also safer to walk, she said, after her first experience on the back of a horse. Being so far off the ground and having no control of her motion was unnerving. She clung to the animal's neck with a death grip, her legs clenched and her muscles taut. Paramessu shook his head and suggested a different tack.

"We ride together, on the same horse. The other one can trot behind us so we have a fresh mount."

Paramessu started off at a walk, with Scarab clinging to him behind. After a while he kicked the horse into a trot but she found it difficult to stay upright and he was forced to slow again. She gripped him so hard that first

497

night that his arms were bruised the next day, the imprints of her fingers clear.

They stopped just before dawn in a rocky gully Paramessu estimated was near the cliffs above Akhet-Aten. He fed the horses a handful of grain from the saddlebags and whatever scraggly bits of grass he could find in the dry streambed. Water was a problem, and would be until the road north angled closer to the river valley. However, the horses had to have water so he doled out every drop they could spare. In the meantime, Scarab took the blankets and found a spot in the meager shade cast by the precipitous sides of the gully. While she slept, Paramessu thought about her riding problem and came up with what he thought would be a solution. Later that afternoon, after she woke, he fashioned a belly girth from a piece of rope, sat the girl on the horse's back and pushed her feet under the rope. She hung on with her hands, and with her feet also anchored, rapidly gained confidence. He led the horse around in a walk, then a trot, increasing its speed at her command. When they left that night, Scarab was able to hang on despite the bounce of the gait and they made a good distance that second night, though still riding two to a horse.

This time they pushed on until the sun was well above the horizon, the heat of the day steadily increasing. Paramessu drew rein on a ridge crest and pointed to the north and west where a faint darker stain smeared the rolling red of the desert.

"The river," he said. "I was hoping to be here a bit earlier but we have a decision to make. The main road north keeps to the high plateau of the desert. It is less traveled but the going is faster. Also, there is not much water. The other road goes to the river and is used by many people. The main advantages are pasturage and water."

"What do you think we should do?" Scarab looked longingly at the distant river and licked her dry lips. She shifted the cloak about her shoulders, feeling the sweat starting from her skin beneath the heavy material. *I wish I'd brought one of my thin tops*, she thought. She wasn't quite comfortable wearing nothing above the waist in front of this man, though she felt a rather worrying desire to. "We're going to need water soon, aren't we?"

"Yes, and feed for the horses." He considered a moment longer. "When I left Paatenemheb he was heading down to Ineb Hedj. He was to follow along within a day or two as he had business with the king. The only question is did he come back out to the desert road or is he going upriver, either by road or by water." He shook his head. "I don't know but I'd guess the river."

"How long to the river then?"

"Too long in this heat. We'll rest here then strike down tonight. With luck we'll be there before dawn." He turned the horses and rode back down into the hollow between the ridge and the surrounding dunes. An intermittent trickle of water had stained the rocky slopes at some time in the past and encouraged the growth of stunted grasses. Though dry now, the vegetation provided sparse forage. Paramessu hobbled the horses and turned them loose to graze.

Working up the slope he scanned the surface rocks, looking for loose stone and signs of life. He lifted a few slabs, letting them fall again before moving on. At last he grinned and pointed.

"Here. Help me move this rock."

Scarab scrambled up the slope, trying to adjust her cloak to cover her while keeping her arms free. With a grimace she gave up and put the cloak to one side, not looking at Paramessu as she gripped the rock where he indicated. They heaved and the slab tilted and rose until it was vertical, balancing on one edge. Scarab held it in place while Paramessu moved smaller rocks into position. They then lowered it, the edges grinding down, the rocks shifting and settling.

"I think that is stable. Stand clear a moment." Paramessu scrambled up on top of the slab and tentatively jumped on the spot. Nothing moved and he did it again. He nodded and jumped down. "It'll do." He ducked under the slab and started clearing away loose stones and earth.

"We're going to sleep here?" Scarab looked doubtful. "What if it comes down? I think I'd rather sleep out in the open."

"Up to you of course, but look here before you decide." He pointed to the dark earth floor of the tiny shelter. "There's been a water seep under here recently, hence the forage grass. The water attracted insects – I saw some small beetles. The earth is still faintly damp and a lot cooler. I really think you'd be better off here."

Scarab allowed herself to be persuaded and Paramessu rigged up the blankets in such a way as to increase the shade without cutting out too much of the faint breeze that stirred the hot air. They ate, drinking sparingly from the last water jar, then crawled into the shelter. It was a tight squeeze and Scarab tried rather self-consciously not to touch the muscled body of the soldier. She lay awkwardly, pushed up against one side of the shelter, staring up at the disconcertingly close underside of the rock slab, waiting for sleep but very aware of the man's presence.

Presently, Paramessu fell asleep. His breathing deepened and his muscles relaxed. Scarab rolled over on her side, propping herself on one elbow and studied the sleeping soldier. *He's really not bad looking*, she thought. *Really old, but he looks young and defenceless asleep.* She smiled and reaching out, traced the muscles of his arm with a fingertip. *I feel safe with him.* She also felt a strange warm feeling in the pit of her stomach but did not know what that signified. Sighing, she rolled over onto her back and closed her eyes.

When she awoke, she was alone in the shelter, the angle of the shadows telling her it was late afternoon. She lay and looked at the flattened earth next to her for a few moments, smiling to herself, then scrambled out awkwardly, straightening and pulling at her kilt quickly. Paramessu was down with the horses, adjusting ropes and packing their bags. He looked up as she approached.

"You slept well."

Scarab yawned and stretched her arms high and back, then blushed as she realized the effect her action was having on Paramessu. "Are we leaving soon?" She looked down and traced a pattern in the earth with a toe, not wanting to meet his eyes.

"Yes." Paramessu controlled his expression though he felt like grinning. "I left out the last of the bread and water by the shelter."

Scarab nodded and hurried away. She broke her fast then went behind some rocks and squatted briefly before removing the blankets from the shelter and walking slowly back to the horses. Paramessu took the blankets and the empty water jar and packed them. He held out her cloak but Scarab shook her head.

"Later maybe, it's too hot now."

Paramessu mounted the horse and reaching down, swung Scarab up behind him. She tucked her feet under the girth rope and slipped her arms around his waist, taking a firm but gentle grip. Paramessu said nothing, kicking the horse into motion, up over the crest and onto the trail that led toward the distant river.

The smudge of vegetation and water was further away than it looked and the river was still only a thin strip of burning red reflecting the setting sun as it plunged into the mouth of Nut on the western horizon. The heat leaked from the air quickly when night fell, though the sand and rock still retained heat. Scarab felt chilly but refrained from pulling out her cloak, snuggling closer to the broad muscular back of Paramessu. His heat warmed her, the feel of her breasts rubbing against him strangely disturbing and motion of the horse lulling her. She dozed, dreaming she was back in the rock fort but it was not Bennu beside her on the blanket. It was Paramessu and she no longer felt afraid.

The horses stopped and she woke; the stars bright above her and a feeling of damp in the air. "Where are we?" she asked sleepily.

"On the edge of the cultivated land. We made better time than I thought." Paramessu swung his leg forward over the horse's neck and slid to the ground, lifting Scarab down. "We'll stay here until dawn."

"I thought we were traveling by night."

"Only in the desert. We can't afford to miss Paaten-emheb, so we need to talk to people, find out whether he has passed yet. Don't worry, it'll be cooler by the river – warmer at night too," he added.

They spread their blankets under the stars and the half moon that rose in the east, its phase indicating it was close to midnight.

"Time's running out," Paramessu commented. "We can't allow less than five days to get to Akhet-Aten, so we must find Paatenemheb within the next two or three days." He yawned and soon they fell asleep to the sound of the horses ripping the fresh green grass hungrily.

The next day, Paramessu set the girth rope on the other horse and rode alone, with Scarab following behind on her own mount, learning to control the beast with reins and feet. She was disappointed not to be holding the soldier – her soldier – once more, but was also exhilarated at her independence. They reached the river and rode along the well-worn paths and minor roads, through farm land and past small villages and the occasional town. Paramessu nodded to those he met, occasionally asking for news of troop movements. Nobody had seen anything and Paramessu slowly became more worried. To distract him, Scarab edged her horse alongside his and asked questions, drawing out the details of his youth, his life in the army and his aspirations. She added in comments, tales of her childhood and stories from the palace at Waset and more from Akhet-Aten. Paramessu had never seen the new capital city and quizzed her on every aspect, disappointed she did not know more.

"Sorry, Paramessu," she said once again. "I lived in the palace and didn't get out into the city much."

They stopped in a tiny farming village and bought food, eating it beneath the shade of a palm tree at noon as the horses dozed, standing head to tail, and their swishing tails keeping the flies at bay.

"I'm unsure what to do," Paramessu confided. "Paatenemheb obviously hasn't got this far but now I'm worried he is either still in Ineb Hedj or else has taken the desert road."

"Is it far to Ineb Hedj?"

503

"Another four days if we ride hard but every hour we ride puts us another hour further from Akhet-Aten. The figures are starting to work against us."

Scarab leaned back against the trunk of the palm tree and chewed a grass stalk. A cool breeze blew off the water, ruffling the folds of her headdress. She watched an ibis as it flew past, flapping its way steadily downriver.

"I wish we could fly," she murmured. "Then we'd have plenty of time."

Paramessu watched the bird until it was out of sight, then grinned and pointed at the rippled water. A small fishing boat slowly beat upriver, tacking against the current, its small white triangular sail catching the breeze. "Maybe we can fly another way. It is downriver to Ineb Hedj, with the current, maybe as little as two days if we sail through the night."

Scarab looked up in surprise. "Can you sail a boat?"

He shook his head. "No, but there are people all along this river who can." He thought for a moment longer. "There are two problems with taking a boat north. We'd have to leave the horses and if we sailed at night, we could go right past Paatenemheb in the dark. Never mind, I think we have to try."

They found a boat that afternoon and traded the horses for passage downriver to Ineb Hedj and a handful of copper. The boatman was pleased with the trade, the horses being worth as much as his whole boat, and agreed to ferry them down as fast as current and wind would take them. The gods must have been smiling as the breeze, which had been from the north all day, backed to the west and freshened, and by late afternoon the fishing boat was forging down the river, a white bow wave foaming in front and a wide wake spreading out behind. The boat heeled over in the wind, sometimes sending the water cascading over the sides, upon which the master of the boat would ease away from the wind a trifle and his boy would frantically start bailing.

Scarab sat up in the front of the boat, her cloak flapping about her, her face lifted, breathing the fresh air laden with the scents of reed and rush, farmland and thicket; watching the banks glide by so effortlessly. Paramessu sat in the stern with the boat's master, questioning him about aspects of the boat's construction and handling.

At dusk, they put into a small village and tied up at the tiny, rickety wharf. Paramessu and Scarab went ashore to find food and to ask about the movements of any soldiers. Again, there had been none.

"Could he have slipped by unseen?" Scarab asked.

"He could, if he was traveling alone, but he had a Fifty with him and that many men are noticeable. Unless we go by them in the darkness. I think we cannot risk sailing through the night."

They stayed overnight in the village, Paramessu paying for beds and a meal with a piece of copper. Scarab drew a few curious looks as few servant girls had shaved heads, though after several days away from amenities, a reddish-brown fuzz of hair was beginning to cover her scalp. Begging a piece of copper from Paramessu, she sought out and hired a sharp bronze knife to shave her head again. Paramessu stifled a laugh when she came back into the rooms and completed the job, smearing ointment into small nicks in the scalp. She wore her headdress for the remainder of her stay in the village, only taking it off when they were back on the river.

The next two days passed slowly. Paramessu no longer talked to the boat master but sat staring at the eastern bank, fidgeting and muttering to himself. They camped on the river bank, no town being in sight at dusk. Then,

505

at just after noon on the second day, he spotted a column of men trotting south along the river road ahead of them.

"There!" Paramessu yelled, pointing. "There they are. Put in boat master, quick as you can."

The boat master turned to shore, hauling in the sail and the craft grounded in the reeds a hundred paces in front of the column. Paramessu leapt out and trotted up the bank to intercept the column as it slowed then halted.

Paatenemheb stood at the front of his men, breathing hard, his face set, the muscles of his jaws jumping. "What in the name of all the poxed gods of the underworld are you doing here?" he roared. "Have you taken leave of your senses? You're supposed to be in Waset by now." He stared beyond his subordinate commander to the boat and the young girl walking up the bank carrying two bundles. "Gods, man, you've even brought your whore with you? Friend or no, Paramessu, I'll break you to the ranks."

Paramessu walked up to his commanding officer and saluted. "General, I believe my news will excuse my behavior," he said calmly. "If not, I will resign my position."

Paatenemheb glared at the commander, then nodded tersely. "Very well, I will listen to your explanation." He looked beyond him to the girl in a servant's kilt and headdress. His brow furrowed. "Who is she? She looks familiar."

"Scarab, sir ... er, princess Beketaten."

"Beketaten? I don't know a Beketaten. Do you mean Meketaten?"

"No sir, Beketaten. The youngest daughter of Nebmaetre and Tiye, sister to Akhenaten. You might remember her from Nebmaetre's burial though she was only a young girl then."

506

"Ah, yes, I remember now." Paatenemheb ran his eyes over the princess. "She's not so young now, is she? I hope you have been behaving with propriety, Paramessu. She may well figure prominently in future dynastic arrangements."

Paramessu flushed slightly. "Yes sir."

"Well, what's this all about then?"

"Sir, Beketaten overheard a plot to overthrow the king."

"Please tell me you didn't jeopardize the defence of Kemet to come running to me with news of the latest rumor being peddled in the streets? Gods, man, if I reacted to every rumor I'd do nothing else."

"Sir, I believe this is more serious. Listen to Scarab ... er, Beketaten. She heard the plot from the instigators."

"And they are?"

"Queen Nefertiti and Tjaty Ay."

Paatenemheb stared at Paramessu then at the girl. "Ay?" he asked softly. "Yes, I could almost believe that." He nodded and walked over to a stand of tamarind trees, beckoning the others to join him.

"So, princess Beketaten, you overheard Tjaty Ay saying something?"

Scarab put down her bundles and straightened, trying to remain calm in the face of one of the most powerful men in Kemet, one who also had the reputation of having the worst temper.

"Yes, sir. I heard Ay talking to his daughter Nefertiti. They were plotting to overthrow ..."

"You are saying Queen Nefertiti is plotting? The queen? Whatever faults the woman has, disloyalty is not one of them. She loves the king."

"She is no longer queen. The king is determined to have a son and means to marry his daughter Meryetaten.

They may already be married. The queen has been put aside."

"What exactly did they say? Think carefully because I don't want misunderstandings here."

Scarab thought back over the last few days. Much had happened but the words were still fresh. "Ay said that Nefertiti would rule Kemet from the throne and he would rule from behind it with the army."

"He said that? Well, we shall see. I am General of all the armies. What else did he say?"

"He said he would disarm the Medjay and capture the palace, forcing my brother to abdicate, naming Nefertiti as successor."

"And when does this take place?

"Midnight on the evening of the next new moon."

"Five days from now," Paramessu said quietly.

Paatenemheb thought hard, searching the girl's face for even a trace of doubt or guile. He did not see it. "What I find hard to understand is why they should discuss their plans in front of you."

Scarab blushed. "I ... I ... they did not know I was there, sir. I was in the shrubbery underneath the queen's window. I know I should not have been listening but I was anxious to know what was going to happen."

"Did your mother ever tell you what happens to eavesdroppers, Beketaten?"

"Yes sir," she whispered.

Paatenemheb grinned. "Well, not this time. I pray we can intervene in this matter." He shook his head, his white shaggy hair flying. "Five days. We shall be lucky to get there." Abruptly he turned and ran back to the road calling for his Leader of Fifty, Ankhtify.

"Lighten the loads, Ankhtify. Weapons only. Leave the bed rolls, food, water jars, spare clothing. We travel

508

light and fast. We have to be in Akhet-Aten within five days."

The general walked among the men as they started throwing everything aside, holding on to just their weapons. He talked as he walked, exhorting them and encouraging them. "We have an opportunity to serve Kemet, men. I'm calling on your greatest speed and if we succeed, men will talk about this march for years. But I don't want you to do this out of duty alone. A good soldier deserves his pay, and outstanding ones like you men of Ankhtify's Fifty deserve a reward. I'm offering a deben in fine gold to any man who is with me when we reach Akhet-Aten." A wave of cheering broke out. Paatenemheb nodded and walked back to the front of the column, the road and verges littered with baggage.

"Sir," Paramessu gestured at Scarab still standing under the tamarind trees. "You'll have to detail a squad to look after the princess."

"I wouldn't trust any of them," the general said with a grin. "No, you brought her this far. You can take her back." He turned and waved to Ankhtify. "Move out men, double time."

Paramessu watched the column break into a run and disappear within minutes into the dust cloud they generated. Gloomily he walked back to Scarab. "Come on, we'd better see whether our boat is still there. I think we're going to need it."

Chapter Thirty-Six

The moon rose over Akhet-Aten an hour before dawn, a thin crescent of silver hanging in a night sky already readying itself for the rebirth of the sun. One more day and the moon would rise at dawn, almost invisible and new. The night before that dawn was dedicated to the marriage of Akhenaten and his young daughter Meryetaten.

To some it seemed incongruous that the marriage of the king ruling under the sun god should be tied to the phases of the moon, but as it was well known that women were ruled by the moon, it was accepted after some initial discussion. What was not discussed, or at least not in public, was the idea that this new queen-to-be, Meryetaten, would, through the influence of the moon, have some hold over Akhenaten and his sun god Aten.

The celebrations started at dawn on the day that would culminate with the night of the new moon. Though couriers had gone out to all the cities of Kemet, with others reaching as many towns and villages as possible with the news, few outside of the capital cared. The actions of king Akhenaten, locked away in his city of the sun, had less and less effect on people as the empire of Kemet crumbled and law and order fell into ruin. In Akhet-Aten though, the people celebrated. Their king, whom any man or woman could see on a daily basis in the temples or streets, meant something to them. He may be strange in his habits and beliefs, but his presence brought wealth to the city and free food and drink on the holy days – of which there were many. This marriage of the king to his eldest daughter was just another occasion on which to enjoy the king's largesse.

The king, as usual, greeted the dawn with a service in the Great Temple. When the hymns had died away, Akhenaten, as high priest, swung straight into the dedication of his marriage to the Aten. His previous marriages – even though only one had been consummated, such was his love for Nefertiti – had been complex affairs, involving many of the gods, notably Amun and Min. The king, working with Ay over the previous ten days, had come up with a streamlined service that eliminated the need for the complex rites in various temples dedicated to the old false gods, offering himself and his bride to Aten alone. Most of the day's activities involved the populace and the court, rather than the king and his daughter-bride. They also involved large amounts of strong beer and wine. Akhenaten had queried the need for this, especially as he would have to provide for the city, but Ay insisted.

"My lord, this is a day of great joy for your people. Let them eat and drink and dance and be riotous. How many times in a man's life does he see his king marry the woman who will be mother to Kemet's heir?"

"That is true, Divine Father." Akhenaten smiled smugly, stroking his long chin as if in considered thought. "But I would not have all about me drunk."

"Then I shall remain sober for you, great king. The knowledge that I have served you faithfully is my meat and drink."

Following the dawn services and the first rites of dedication, the citizens streamed south to the cattle yards where huge slaughter pens had been set up. Hundreds of oxen were killed and dressed, slabs of bloody meat handed out to all comers. Trestles on the street corners handed out huge conical barley bread loaves, radishes, onions, lettuces and huge jars of strong beer were broached. By noon, the festivities were in full swing, people feasting around fires that had been lit in the middle of the wider streets, and dancing to the sound of flute, lyre, drum and raucous voice. Within the palace, the celebrations were less boisterous, though amphorae of Syrian wine mingled with jars of beer and a wonderful array of baked goods and delicate meats and vegetables were available for the hundreds of court officials, servants and any relatives they could smuggle in. Even the slaves were allowed a portion, as long as their enjoyment did not interfere with their work. Sutau, overseer of the treasury, wandered the corridors of the palace with clenched fists and an agonized expression, computing the cost of the feasts and estimating the drain on the already diminished treasure rooms.

The king celebrated again at noon, leading a party of high officials, priests and city councilors in another long song of praise to Aten, before repairing to the city for rest and relaxation in the hottest part of the day.

The festivities continued in the city unabated. More and more people became drunk, fights broke out, and in the absence of the medjay – Mahu having led his men out of the city to capture the bandit Bennu – the local garrison had the pleasure of breaking a few heads and restoring a semblance of order. Ay smiled as he watched the soldiers at work. Neshi was under instructions not to let his men drink today. They would get their reward in the days to come.

Ay went over to the North Palace during the king's rest time and found Nefertiti in an almost empty palace. Only the most loyal of her ladies remained with her, the rest having vanished as the festivities started. Nefertiti received her father in her private suite.

"Are you sure you would not rather be drinking with the king, father?"

"Come, daughter, this bitterness does not become you. The king will do as he wants and it is up to the rest of us to obey his commands." Ay looked pointedly at the two ladies standing by the window with properly downcast eyes. "Bid your ladies depart. I need to talk to you."

When the ladies had left, closing the doors behind them, Ay cracked his knuckles and sighed heavily. "Gods, I'll be glad when this day is over. That new marriage service the king has devised must be the most boring one ever. There is not much you can say to the Aten once you have praised his shining face and his bounty. Nothing about marriage, that's for certain."

"Imagine how little I care." Nefertiti plucked at her gown, smoothing down the pleats and flicking imaginary dust from its pristine white surface. "I suppose that little bitch is lording it over everyone?"

"Meryetaten? No, she is being quite circumspect. She seems to be making an effort to be pleasant."

"I am surprised. Well, no matter. I wish her joy for her one night of wedded bliss." Nefertiti laughed, cruelty rather than mirth tingeing her voice. "I shall enjoy sentencing her tomorrow. What do you think it should be, exile or prison?"

"I'd leave it a few days, daughter. There are other more pressing matters to occupy us after tonight."

"Oh? What?"

"The army for one. Nobody can rule Kemet without the army."

"I thought you had the army in your wallet? Have you not got the loyalty of the garrison?"

"The local garrison is not the army. I'm referring to Paatenemheb, General of all the armies. I would not put it past him to refuse us and try and reinstate Akhenaten. He could do it too if he had his legions behind him."

513

"Can we bribe him?" Nefertiti sat down and looked out of the window to hide her sudden concern.

"Not exactly, he boasts high moral standards. However, he is primarily concerned with Kemet and the security of our borders. We can make him some offers that he might take, if not for himself, then for Kemet."

Nefertiti turned to her father, shaking her head. "I don't understand."

"Gold to build up the armies again, allowing the worship of the old gods to return – and a marriage that would tie him to the royal house with adamantine bonds."

"Who?" Nefertiti shifted uncomfortably on her chair. "You are not thinking of ... I would refuse. I will marry royalty or nobody. You mean one of my daughters?"

"One of your daughters might be acceptable but they are too young for an old man. The answer is simple – Mutnodjme."

"My sister Mutnodjme? She would not agree. She values her solitude and chastity."

"She will agree. I will see to that. Anyway, I must look for suitable arguments to convince Paatenemheb not to act against our coup. We can be thankful he is on the northern borders and will not hear of tonight until weeks have passed. By then our position will be more certain."

Nefertiti got up and crossed to the table, pouring herself a cup of wine. She offered her father a cup but he refused.

"Water only, I stay sober until after tonight."

She handed him a gold cup of cool water, and sipped her own spiced wine. "Akhenaten will always be a danger, won't he father? As long as he remains alive he will act as a focus for disaffection."

"You've changed your mind? You want him killed now?"

"No. He is still my husband and ... and may the gods preserve me, I still love him. I cannot kill him – or cause him to be killed," she added, seeing Ay's face. "Yet neither can I let him live."

"Well, leave it for now," Ay said smoothly. "Who knows what tomorrow will bring? We will imprison him until we decide."

Nefertiti nodded, putting the subject of her husband's fate to one side. "When is the actual marriage ceremony?"

"Two hours before midnight. He will take his bride to bed, consummate the act and be asleep by the time I strike at midnight."

Nefertiti laughed. "Five minutes would be enough time for that man. But what about his attendants?"

"They will not be in any state to interfere. I have made sure the wine and beer is flowing freely that all may toast the king's nuptials. I'm surprised you haven't heard the noise from the city."

"And your forces are sufficient?"

Ay smiled. "Tonight, ten men could take Akhet-Aten and capture the king. I shall have a hundred, less ten under the command of that dolt Neshi who thinks he will be coming to guard you against possible assassins. Be suitably grateful." He drained his water and put the cup back on the table. "I will leave now, daughter. Stay here quietly, gather your strength." Ay bowed, a mocking smile on his face. "Tomorrow I will greet the new ruler of all Kemet, Queen Nefertiti."

Nefertiti opened the door for her father and walked out through the deserted corridors to the front columned portico of the palace.

"One other thing, father. What of Smenkhkare? The king sent for him to come and be crowned co-regent."

"Leave him to me. For one thing he cannot possibly be here for a day or two, for another he is young and inexperienced. I will bind him to my will."

"He is Akhenaten's brother."

"He will see reason." Ay shrugged. "Or I will remove him."

Ay left the North Palace and walked rapidly back to the main palace, threading his way through crowds of drunk revelers. As the alcohol intake increased, morals decreased, and on a day when everybody's minds were focused on the union of man and woman, a certain amount of licentious behavior was already becoming apparent. Ay saw at least three copulating couples out in the main street alone. Bonfires blazed and the smell of roasting beef filled the air.

The king was awake and waiting impatiently for his Tjaty.

"Where have you been, Divine Father? I have been thinking about tonight's ceremony. Originally the exchange of vows was to take place immediately after the sunset song of praise, then the feasting and entertainment delayed the bedding of my new bride until nearly midnight. I thought instead, I could bed her, then we could come out for the feast." The king grinned and winked at his Tjaty. "I am the king after all. Surely I can bed my wife when I please?"

"Of course, my lord, the king can do anything he pleases." Ay bowed. "Equally of course, I cannot guarantee a son will result from an earlier emission of the royal member."

Akhenaten frowned. "What difference can an hour or two make?"

516

"It does not seem reasonable, I agree, but I have spoken to Nebhotep the court physician and consulted three Syrian soothsayers. Nebhotep says Meryetaten will be most fertile just before midnight, and the soothsayers all agree a son is prognosticated should you impregnate her at this time. The feminine influence is stronger earlier in the night." He paused and tried to look bored. "Still, what is the certainty of a son compared to the king's instant gratification?"

"Hmm. I don't like you consulting soothsayers, Ay. They follow false gods."

"These ones are priests of their sun god. I have no doubt that in their own muddled way they are actually worshipping the Aten."

"You think so? Well, perhaps I can wait another few hours. After all, a son is worth a little delay."

Ay bowed again. "A wise decision my lord."

The sun set and Akhenaten led his inner court in the farewell praises of the Aten, their hymns almost drowned out by the cheering and drunken revelry from the streets outside. Torches were lit and the king, of necessity, turned the proceedings over to another high priest of Aten to conduct the official marriage ceremony. Some of the rituals of marriage remained, though most had been adapted to meet the pure truth of the Aten's light.

Meryetaten entered the temple precincts, dressed in the finest, whitest gossamer-thin linen gown, so sheer it billowed like mist around her. She was decked in gold; a heavy golden ankh of life around her neck; the queen's high crown upon her head; necklaces, bracelets and brooches of fine gold and costly jewels adorning her slim young body; expensive perfumes filling the air with exotic scents; the elaborate makeup turning her face from the eagerness of youth to an impassive mask as she advanced

517

slowly to meet her father-husband. Twenty young girls similarly arrayed, though with simple gold jewelry and with wildflowers adorning their elegantly styled wigs, danced in front of the bride in a stately pavane of homage.

Akhenaten and Meryetaten clasped hands and stared into each other's eyes for a moment before advancing toward the altar of Aten. Together they offered up bowls of smoking incense, the sweet heavy aroma mixing with the flowery scents of perfume, ascending in blue-white clouds into the glowing night. A gong sounded, echoing and reverberating through the temple and the high priest Tjetaten called out for all those who had an interest in the holy marriage to come forth to witness the union of man and woman and god.

The royal couple sat on great padded chairs next to one another and the high priest of Aten nervously sat opposite them. He cleared his throat and read from a prepared parchment.

"Let it be known that on this day, King Nefernefer-ure Waenre Akhenaten bestows the title of Queen of the Two Lands on Meryetaten, that bestowal superseding all others and rendering any previous assignment void. Let it be known further that Meryetaten, as Daughter of the King's Body and God's Wife shall share in the governance of the kingdom, her word being law over all save the king."

Tjetaten then passed the parchment to an assistant and, leaning forward, started to go through, in great detail, Meryetaten's duties, both as queen and wife. "You must be hardworking, honest and truthful; earning praise for your amiable nature. You must give affection and love to your husband, and accept them back. Your duty is to give your husband children, to love and care for the-

518

se children, to provide a stable and calm household and to make yourself loved by all who see you. Furthermore, as queen your womanly duties are intensified. You must be divinely feminine, charming, strong of will yet pleasant of character; adorning yourself with plumes of contentment; showing affection and a pleasant disposition to all your subjects; the sound of your voice a delight to all who hear you."

The priest next turned to Akhenaten, his nervousness returning. He swallowed, making an effort to remember that in the marriage service a king was just a man like any other. "You will hold this woman to be a companion, a helper, and a wife. You will love her with your full devotion, withholding nothing, neither your body nor your love. She is your equal in all things save for the governance of Kemet. You will honour her always, love her always, and never seek her hurt or displeasure. Seek always to please your wife that you may enjoy all the days of your life."

Tjetaten took a small barley loaf still warm from the ovens from a golden tray held by a junior priest and ripped it in two, handing the pieces to the king and his new queen. They ate, passing the fragments to each other. After the ritual bites had been swallowed, the pieces were passed to the guests. Wine followed, rich wine from the vineyards of the Delta, in two ornate goblets, passed around in the same way as the loaf. Akhenaten and Meryetaten stood and drew close, opening their mouths. They breathed in turn, inhaling each other's breath. Finally, a glowing coal was brought from Ay's hearth in a beautifully painted pot. Normally, the parents of the bride would provide the ritual fire but as Akhenaten was the father and Nefertiti, the deposed queen was the mother; Ay had agreed to stand in. Meryetaten took a dry sliver of camphor wood and held it to the burning ember until it sprang into living flame. She then held it aloft before passing it to Akhenaten who in turn held it up briefly before placing it back in the painted pot.

"In the eyes of Aten, in the eyes of these gathered nobles, let it be seen that King Akhenaten and Queen Meryetaten are truly married." Tjetaten stood and spread his arms wide, facing the guests, who immediately broke out into a chorus of cheers.

A procession started. It had been intended that the procession should wind through the streets of the city, allowing everyone to see the new queen in all her glory, but the scene outside had turned ugly, the drunken citizens on the verge of riot. The procession instead made a hurried turn and headed back to the palace for the marriage feast.

The Great Hall of Justice had been prepared for the feast. Long tables stood in the centre of the hall and ornately carved chairs were laid out around them. Servants abounded, all dressed in their cleanest, neatest attire. The king and queen entered first and advanced to the raised dais, taking their seats on the golden thrones. Nobles entered and took their places, their rank and position at the court dictating where they sat.

Servants brought around great ewers of scented water, pouring them over the guests' hands into other great copper vessels carried by other servants. Wine was served, watered and straight; rich sweet wine from Syria, spiced wine from the Delta, honeyed wine from Zarw and two separate wines from the river valley with bouquets redolent of fruit and herbs. Beer was offered, poured from great jars into beautifully ornamented faience cups. Milk too, and water, though few partook of these common drinks.

Meat was abundant, the tables literally groaning under the weight as long lines of servants brought in the smoking meats from the kitchens, cuts of beef, mutton, and goat. Geese and pigeons were everywhere, swimming in their rich fat, river fish and sea fish too. The guests ate with their hands, ripping the food into manageable portions, the grease running down chins, staining garments. Bread, crusted and golden-brown, soaked up the rich juices and gravies, the sharp fresh tastes of onion, garlic, lettuce, radish and cucumber accenting the meats. Coriander, dill and mint added to the tastes. Scented water flowed in abundance again, preparing the guests for further culinary delights.

At last the feasting slowed and the remnants of the meats were removed for the enjoyment of the court servants. Fruits appeared; grape, fig, melon, date and pomegranate to cleanse the palate and through it all the drinking continued.

Akhenaten stood, Meryetaten getting to her feet a moment later. The king seemed to have difficulty standing and leaned on his daughter-wife, a vacuous grin on his face. Meryetaten looked confused and unsure of herself for the first time, the heat of the feasting hall having smeared her makeup.

Ay smiled to himself. *A child in her mother's makeup*, he thought. *Well, I wish them well for tonight at least.* Advancing, he caught the king's attention and bowed low. "My lord Akhenaten, and Queen Meryetaten. May I have the honour of conducting you to the marriage chamber?"

"Ah, Divine Father," the king said loudly. "You may indeed. It is time to impregnate my wife at last."

"Indeed it is, my lord." Ay moved to the side of Meryetaten and whispered in her ear. "Do you wish me to

521

give the king a sleeping draught? You need not go through this ordeal tonight."

Meryetaten said nothing for a moment, before gathering her thoughts, her face twisting into a sneer. "You presume too much, Tjaty Ay. I may have been your grand-daughter once but now I am queen and I outrank you. How dare you suggest that I act in any way but that of a dutiful wife? I shall be bedded by my husband and bear him a son who will reign after us."

Ay kept a straight face and bowed to his grand-daughter. "As you wish it, your majesty. Forgive my presumption." He led the way out of the feasting hall and along the wide, crowded corridors to the king's suite. Ribald remarks followed them, the drunken guests giggling and laughing.

Ay watched the chambermaids turn down the great bed and undress the king and queen. It was his duty to see the act consummated, so he could bear witness that a child born to the queen had issued from the king's loins. He looked on, his face impassive as Akhenaten mounted his daughter. He stood silent when she cried out in pain, sobbing as the king took his pleasure. Then, after the king rolled off, the act complete, Ay walked backward through the doorway, drawing the great cedar doors closed after him.

"It is accomplished," Ay told the guests waiting out in the corridors. A great cheer erupted and the men and women drifted off to find more wine.

Two hours, Ay thought. *Two hours and Kemet is mine.* He hurried off to set his plans in motion.

Chapter Thirty-Seven

By midnight on the night of the new moon, the sober people of Akhet-Aten were in bed. The rest were in an advanced state of inebriation, still valiantly striving to make the most of the free food and drink. The street bonfires had burned down to ashes and glowing embers and the streets were littered with refuse and vomit. Packs of dogs fought for the scraps, ignoring men and women lying around the streets as if strewn by storm winds.

Paatenemheb's first thought as he entered the city behind the Great Temple was that he was too late. The coup had taken place and a great battle been fought and he was seeing the aftermath, dead bodies littering the capital of Kemet. Then he saw a body move and a quick examination proved that the 'bodies' were in fact people sleeping off the effects of overindulgence.

He straightened, feeling the bone weariness deep within. His legs ached and the previous five days passed like a blur in his head, running through the heat of the days and the cool of night, sinking exhausted into sleep by the side of the road during the hottest part of the afternoon. He started with fifty men but that number fell steadily as soldiers, though professional and fit, dropped by the road, succumbing to heat exhaustion, agonizing cramps and festering foot sores. One man died of snakebite after throwing himself down on the grass during a rest period, not seeing the cobra. He died screaming but quickly. Paatenemheb led twenty-seven men out of his original fifty down the steep, craggy valley that was the resting place of the Aten's family, and into the city of Akhet-Aten.

Twenty-seven exhausted men, he thought. *And a garrison of a hundred. Well, we shall test their loyalty soon enough.* Paatenemheb got Ankhtify to organize his men back into ranks and they marched through the slumbering streets to the palace. The buildings were in darkness save for a low-burning torch in the doorways and in some of the main passages. Few people moved within the palace, a handful of servants and slaves who gaped at the sight of the famous general and his armed men.

Leaving his command in the vestibule, Paatenemheb took Ankhtify with him and marched through to the king's chambers, where he found the guard deep in wine-soaked slumber. Hauling the man to his feet, he slapped him hard, rousing him.

"I could have your life for this," Paatenemheb roared. "Sleeping on duty – and drunk too. Where is the king? If he is not safe I will kill you myself."

"S... sir, he ... he is safe. H... how could he not be? It is his we... wedding night. Who would disturb him?"

"Fool." Paatenemheb let go and the guard fell to the floor. He strode over to the great double cedar doors and threw them open. A solitary torch burned low and in the dim light he could see the rumpled bed and two still forms on it. Walking over to the bed, he looked down at the body of his king and hesitated. Then, with a deep breath he grasped the king's foot and tugged.

"Waenre Akhenaten. Rouse yourself, for your life. Akhenaten."

"Eh ... what?" The king rolled over, his features sagging and his eyes unfocused. "What is it? Who ... who is that?"

"Paatenemheb. Rouse yourself, Akhenaten. Your life is in danger."

The king sat up, Meryetaten waking too and pulling the sheets around her. "What danger?" He rubbed his eyes and stared up at his general. "And why are you here? You are supposed to be in Gezer."

"I got wind of a plot to kill you, Akhenaten, and hurried down here. It appears I was in time."

The king swung his legs over the side of the bed and stood. Picking up a kilt from the neatly folded garments on a small side table he wrapped it around his waist. "I think you must be mistaken, general. There is no plot. Who would want to kill me? I am universally loved. Why, even the king of the Hittites loves me." Akhenaten smiled tentatively.

Paatenemheb closed his eyes briefly, resisting the urge to shake his king. "We can talk about the love of the Hittite king later, my lord. For now, we need to get you to a place of safety. Be assured, the plot is real. I heard of it from a witness of its planning."

"And who is supposed to want my death?"

"Ay and Nefertiti."

The king sat down again. "Ay? Impossible. He is my chief counselor and my right hand. And Nefertiti? She is my queen. Why should she seek my death?"

"But I am your queen," Meryetaten whined, putting her arms about Akhenaten. "You made me your queen, father. Remember? She is just jealous."

"Yes. Yes, that is true. It could be, Paatenemheb. I could perhaps believe it of Nefertiti, though never that she desires my death. She loves me. As for Ay – no. I will not believe that of him."

Paatenemheb shrugged. "Well, no matter who is or who is not guilty, we must first ensure your safety – and that of your ... your queen," he added, his lip curling in distaste. "I can then investigate the matter."

525

Akhenaten nodded. "Yes, without me there is no Kemet – and my queen too, of course. Already she carries my son within her body, I know it. I was a lion tonight, Paatenemheb, a rampant wild bull. You should have seen me."

"I regret I missed it," the general muttered dryly. "Now please dress and accompany me. We must get you somewhere safe."

Akhenaten fastened a cloak about his shoulders and put on a pair of sandals while Meryetaten dressed. "You have your army with you?"

"Twenty-seven men." Paatenemheb shrugged. "It will have to do. It will do if none can find you." He ushered the king and his new consort out into the vestibule, where Ankhtify and the rapidly sobering guard waited.

"Where do we go, sir?" Ankhtify asked. "The rebels will search the whole palace."

"The Tjaty's suite," Paatenemheb replied with a grim smile. "With the gods' help it will be the last place he will think of looking."

"Aten's help, general," Akhenaten said peevishly. "How many times do I have to say it? There is only one god."

"I think that dangerous policy has about run its course. Now if you will follow me, time is running out. It must be close to midnight." Paatenemheb cut off the king's remarks and set off along the corridors at a fast walk, his sword in hand. They reached Ay's suite without incident and found the chambers deserted. "Too much to hope he might still be here. I could have nipped this rebellion in the bud. I wonder where he is."

"The North Palace?" Akhenaten guessed. "Nefertiti withdrew there."

526

Paatenemheb left Ankhtify to guard the king. "Secure the rooms. Use an inner one without easy access to windows. Barricade the doors. I'm leaving you twenty men." He clasped his subordinate firmly, kissing him on the cheek. "You are a good man, Ankhtify. I won't forget this night."

"Sir, if you leave me twenty that's only six to take with you to confront the enemy. It's not enough. Leave me fewer, I'll manage somehow."

"All twenty-seven would not be enough if the local garrison has forgotten where their loyalty lies. No, your duty is to defend the king's person and sell your lives dearly." Paatenemheb snapped his fingers and grinned. "Of course, there are Mahu's Medjay. They are at least half-trained. I'll get round there first." He hurried off, leaving Ankhtify to organize the defences.

Mahu was not in the barracks, nor were any of his men. Paatenemheb scratched his head. "Gods," he muttered to himself. "Are they in the plot too?" He thought for a minute then called over the men. "Who is the ranking soldier here?"

One of the men shrugged. "No-one, sir. We are all just troopers in Ankhtify's Fifty."

"Your name?"

"Mintu, sir." The man saluted.

"Very well, Mintu. You are Acting Leader of Ten." He smiled. "Though you only have five for now." He took Mintu by the elbow and led him aside, lowering his voice. "We have a serious situation on our hands as I'm sure you already know. Ankhtify guards the king but I must make an attempt to stop this rebellion before it gets going. I had hoped to enlist the help of the local Medjay but they may be on the side of the rebels. They are not here, anyway."

527

"What about the city garrison, sir?"

"That is the key. The rebels may have subverted the army, in which case our only option is to take as many with us as we can. I believe this will be the case as it seems incredible that Ay would attempt this without support. On the other hand, it may be that he has taken command and somehow persuaded the officers to forget their oaths."

"So what do we do, sir?"

Paatenemheb smiled mirthlessly. "We march on the army barracks, disarm them and take Ay and the rebels into custody – the seven of us."

Mintu gulped, the darkness hiding his trembling body. "That ... that will not be easy."

The general laughed. "It will be nigh on impossible, soldier. Never mind, we die for Kemet and our king. Can you think of a better way to go?" He clapped Mintu on one shoulder, feeling the man's fear. "Obey my commands immediately and in every detail, Mintu, and we shall get through this. We have one chance and I mean to take it. Don't let me down."

"N... no sir, you can count on me and my men."

"Good man. Now, come on, we march north."

Paatenemheb led his men back to the Avenue of the Aten then through the darkened streets toward the North Palace and the army barracks. They carried torches and marched in step, deliberately and purposefully.

"Always give the impression you are in command, Mintu. Men who are unsure of themselves are more likely to fail."

Any men they met on the way they cautioned to get inside immediately. There were not many as the silence in the city and the presence of armed soldiers warned those sober enough to pay attention that something was amiss.

They neared the North Palace when the tramp of feet ahead of them and the wavering light of torches warned of the approach of a body of men. Paatenemheb stopped his men and formed them into a line across the road, bidding them throw their brands on the ground ahead of them. He strode out ten paces and glancing back at his own men could just see his six soldiers standing, armed and ready, in the flickering light. He could see nothing behind those six and hoped that the approaching men would likewise see nothing.

The approaching men marched out of the darkness and hesitated when they saw the figure of Paatenemheb standing stolidly in the road ahead of them. Ay, who had been behind the front ranks, pushed forward as the city soldiers slowed.

"What is the matter? Why have ..." Ay caught sight of the general and stopped abruptly, his men following suit, eyeing their commander and the general uneasily. "Paatenemheb," Ay croaked. "Wh... what are you doing here? I thought you were on the northern borders."

"So I was, Ay, until I heard word of treachery."

"Treachery? What do you mean?"

"What would you call rising in arms against the king?"

Ay said nothing. He stared at the lone man confronting him, then at the six men just visible beyond him. He licked his lips and shifted his weight, his eyes flicking back to the general and away again.

"You have brought the army down with you?" he asked.

Paatenemheb nodded calmly. "Enough to quell a rebellion." He raised his voice, pitching it so the men behind Ay could hear. "The king is guarded as we speak, by men trained for and hardened by battle. It is my hope

529

that the men I see before me, the city garrison of Akhet-Aten, know where their loyalties lie and have turned out to defend their king."

A murmur of voices broke out and Ay shouted to override the babble. "Every man here knows his duty, Paatenemheb. There are no traitors to Kemet here."

"And to the king?"

Ay made no answer but hurried forward, catching Paatenemheb by the arm and leaning close, his voice low. "What is your part in this, Paatenemheb? You stand to lose the most by the continued reign of Akhenaten. I seek only a strong Kemet, one that can regain its rightful place among the nations."

"And to do this you would do what? Kill the king? Or just imprison him?"

Ay hesitated. "Who said anything about that? I want what is good for Kemet, nothing more."

Paatenemheb shook his head. "I will have no part of this." He stepped away from Ay and called out "Mintu, Leader of Ten. You will detail five men and take Tjaty Ay into custody pending my investigation." Stepping past toward the city garrison, he continued. "Soldiers, you have been brought out tonight needlessly and with dubious intent. I ask you to recall your vows of loyalty to the king and to myself as Commander General of the Armies. You will return to barracks. The situation is in hand."

"No," came a strangulated cry from behind him and Paatenemheb heard the whisper of bronze on leather as Ay dragged his sword out. Without turning, he gave a crisp command. "Archers. If that man takes one step forward you will kill him." A heartbeat, then, "Mintu, take the Tjaty into custody. Take him to the Medjay barracks and place him under close guard. Report to me at the palace afterward."

"You are making a mistake," Ay screamed. "Men, help me ..."

Paatenemheb whirled and saw that Mintu and his men had almost reached the Tjaty who stood, sword in hand a few paces behind him. "Mintu, if he says one word more, you will bind and gag him. Take him away now." Ay was bundled away into the darkness and a few seconds later Paatenemheb heard a cry of surprise cut off abruptly. He found he had been holding his breath and turned to face the city garrison alone.

"Who is the ranking officer here?"

"I am sir, Lieutenant Baqet."

"Where is Commander Neshi?"

"He took ten men to guard the queen, sir. In the North Palace." Worry tinged his voice. "Er, general sir, is it true about Tjaty Ay? He told us that we were marching on the palace to put down a rebellion. Now you are saying he was behind it?"

"Are you loyal to the king, Baqet?"

"Of course, sir." Baqet stiffened to attention. "And to you as my commanding general."

"Then you and ten men will accompany me to see the queen. She and the Tjaty have conspired against the king. This conspiracy will be investigated and if indeed the Tjaty believed he was acting for the best, you can be certain the king will be merciful. In the meantime I will have order in the city. Have the rest of the men return to barracks. They are not to leave without my express command. Do you understand?"

Baqet saluted and in a flurry of shouted orders, sent the main body of garrison troops marching back to their barracks. He waited with his selected ten men to accompany Paatenemheb. When the general started walking toward the palace, he turned and looked toward the guttering torches in the street.

"What about your men, general? Will they be accompanying us?

Paatenemheb smiled. "No." He turned back to face his supposed army and called out loudly, "Blue Company of the Re Legion, you will await my return in perfect silence. Let none pass." He whirled and strode past Baqet. "Well, come on then, I do not have all night."

Neshi's men challenged them as they entered the palace and without breaking stride, Paatenemheb rode over their challenges with a bellow. His anger and the presence of Lieutenant Baqet reduced them to confusion and they trailed along behind Baqet's little force as Paatenemheb strode toward the queen's apartments. More guards stood outside the apartments and again they were thrown into confusion by the attitude of the general and the presence behind him of their fellow soldiers. Paatenemheb threw open the doors and marched in to find Nefertiti and Neshi drinking wine together in the vestibule to her bedchamber.

Nefertiti rose to her feet, her wine goblet falling with a clash to the tiled floor, the wine spilling out in a pool at her feet. Her hand went to her throat and her eyes widened. "What is the meaning of this intrusion? How dare you ... Paatenemheb? Where ... what are you doing here?" Her eyes flicked behind her to the knot of soldiers outside the bedchamber, all wearing the insignia of the city garrison. "Are those Neshi's men with you? Where are your own? Neshi," she wheeled to face the garrison commander who was just rising to his feet, a puzzled look on his face.

"They are my men, Nefertiti," Paatenemheb growled. "I am General of all Kemet's armies. They obey me – as your father has just now found out."

Neshi cleared his throat. "Er, general, there seems to be something amiss, by your demeanor. Is it anything I can assist with?"

"What do you mean?" Nefertiti said. "Where is my father?"

Paatenemheb ignored Neshi, focusing on Nefertiti. "Your father is in custody already and will face the king tomorrow on charges of sedition and treason. You also will face charges."

Neshi paled. "I say, general, this must all be some ghastly mistake."

Nefertiti gathered her composure and stared contemptuously at General Paatenemheb. "You dare to accuse me? The queen? You must be mad. No-one will believe you."

"I have a witness to your words. To the plans you made with your father, in this very room, on the night of the full moon."

"Impossible," Nefertiti sneered. "My father and I were alone. And I state now, in the presence of Commander Neshi that I am innocent of these heinous charges ..."

"I did not say the witness was in the room with you. Only that you were overheard."

Nefertiti laughed. "So you will trot out the testimony of some slave or palace servant who has no doubt been tortured or bribed to bear false witness. Do you think the king will weigh their word against mine? I am the queen."

"My witness is more royal than you, Nefertiti. She will be believed."

"Royal? She?" Nefertiti's laugh faded, to be replaced by a frown. "Beketaten? That little bitch Beketaten lives? She is your witness? I will kill that little bitch. She ..."

"Silence!" Paatenemheb roared. "You are under arrest for treason, madam. You will sit down and utter no further word or I will have you gagged."

Nefertiti's lips trembled and abruptly she sat down, covering her face with her hands.

Paatenemheb at last turned to Neshi who gaped at him. "Commander Neshi, are you a loyal servant of the king?"

Neshi opened and shut his mouth several times, looking at Nefertiti then back to the general. "Yes," he squeaked.

"Do you also recognize my authority over you, as General over all the Armies of Kemet?"

"Yes." Neshi nodded.

"Then here are my orders to you, which you will obey without question. You will return alone, now, to the army barracks where you will find your men awaiting you. You will lock the gates and barricade yourselves inside and stay there until I or Commander Baqet says you can leave. Do you understand?"

Neshi nodded then looked questioningly at Baqet. "You mean Lieutenant Baqet?"

"He is promoted temporarily to Commander. He will assume command of the city garrison until such time as I can determine your part in tonight's events. Neshi, you will now obey my orders."

Neshi saluted, his face very pale, and marched out of the room, his back straight, refusing to look at his men.

Paatenemheb called Baqet into the room. "You are promoted to the rank of Commander of the city garrison. However, your command tonight is the twenty men you have here. You will secure this woman, the former queen Nefertiti, in her suite. Guards are to be posted outside the windows and doors. She is allowed one lady in waiting but once she has entered she is not to be allowed out again. No-one is to have access to these rooms and there will be no form of communication between anyone in these rooms and the outside. Neither you nor your men will answer if you are spoken to, nor will you speak. Is that understood?"

Baqet nodded, smiling. "Yes, general, I understand."

Paatenemheb nodded. "Very well, post your men. I will wait here until the guards are in place." He waited until the man had left the room before addressing the woman on the chair, his voice cold and impersonal. "Your rebellion has failed, Nefertiti. If the king is just, you will die. If he is merciful, you will be banished. Either way, I will see to it that you are punished for your treachery." He nodded at Baqet when he returned and then walked outside, checking the disposition of the guards as he went. Paatenemheb left the palace and walked down the dark streets toward the main palace, relief washing over him. When he came to the empty place where one of six torches still smouldered in the dust, he picked it up and blew on it, encouraging the flame.

"Blue Company, Re Legion," he called out into the empty street. "I thank you for your service, and dismiss you." Paatenemheb solemnly saluted before roaring with laughter. Still chuckling to himself he set off with brand held high toward the palace and his king.

Chapter Thirty-Eight

For the first time since Akhenaten moved to the City of the Sun, he did not offer the morning hymn to his god in the temple. Another priest offered it in his place as Paatenemheb refused to let the king out of Ay's chambers.

"Until I know how far the poison has spread, I cannot guarantee your safety, my lord. I ask you to remain within these rooms until I can convene a court and put the conspirators to the question."

"Who are these conspirators?" the king asked.

"Tjaty Ay and his daughter, your wife Nefertiti. I told you this last night."

"Did you? I don't remember. Well, never mind, I'm sure they did not do it."

"They have admitted it, or at least Nefertiti has. Ay fell short of confessing but I have no doubt he will when my men start on him."

"No." Akhenaten shook his head vehemently. "I will not have them put to the question. They are my family; mother and grandfather of my dear girls. I will not have confessions wrung from them by torture."

"It is customary in cases of treason. We cannot put a man to death unless he confesses, and he is not going to confess unless we persuade him."

"I'm not going to put Nefertiti to death," Akhenaten said, a shocked expression on his face. "Nor Ay. I shall probably forgive them. I'm sure it was a temporary aberration. Yes, I'm sure that was it. They merely lost sight of the love of Aten. I will recall it to them."

"I would strongly advise against that," Paatenemheb grated. "If you forgive them they will try again."

"Nonsense, Paatenemheb. I listened to you last night because I was still befuddled with sleep, but I have had a chance to think today. Both Ay and my wife love me dearly and would never hurt me. You are mistaken and I will prove it to you in a court of law. Bring them both here this morning and I will judge them myself."

"Gods above and below, I cannot do that, my lord. A trial takes time. I have to bring the witnesses together for one thing and the chief one is still en route to Akhet-Aten. She won't be here for another day or two. Then there are the statements from the palace officials, servants and slaves. Some of them may have seen or heard something and it will take time to make enquiries."

"I don't need witnesses or statements from anyone," Akhenaten said with a smile. "I will have them swear to tell the truth on the Aten himself. No-one can lie under those circumstances. Now go and fetch Ay and Nefertiti. Oh, and by the way, tell the servants I shall want my breakfast immediately."

Paatenemheb groaned but could see Akhenaten's will on this matter was unshakeable. "As you command, my lord." He bowed low and left the chambers, walking quickly to the Medjay barracks where Ay was held. He found the barracks still bereft of Medjay but Ankhtify had Ay locked in a windowless stone cell.

"Good morning general," Ankhtify said. "That was some bluff you made last night. I thought for sure somebody was going to discover you only had six men."

"It did work rather well, didn't it? But you're wrong about the number of men, Ankhtify. I had thousands." Paatenemheb smiled at the complete look of mystification on his Leader of Fifty's face. "Everyone knows I command all of Kemet's armies. Nobody expects to see

537

me except at the head of an army. All I did was foster that impression."

"Well, it worked, sir. When Ay saw there was nobody behind us, he almost had a fit. I had to knock him out to keep him quiet. I hope that was all right, sir?"

"Perfectly. Now, how is he feeling this morning?"

"Angry, sir." Ankhtify hesitated then hurried on. "Permission to speak, sir?" He waited for the general's nod before continuing. "I know we caught the Tjaty at the head of the city garrison, marching toward the palace and he looked guilty, but ... he is not acting guilty this morning."

"How so?"

"As I said, sir, he's angry. I have seen men accused of far less serious crimes go to pieces when captured. They plead and whine and make excuses, but Ay does none of these things. He orders us to release him so he can protect the king. He is enraged that we will not obey him."

"Ay is a general of the army and a brave and resourceful man," Paatenemheb commented. "Do not expect him to act as lesser men would. Still, that is interesting. I think I will see for myself."

Ay's cell was dark and stuffy, a revolting smell emanating from a pottery jar in one corner. Old rotting straw covered the floor, from which came muffled squeaks and scuffles. Ay sat in one corner, his head resting on folded arms on his knees. He looked up as the door creaked open, spilling a shaft of daylight into the dank cell.

"Come to gloat, have you, Paatenemheb? You are making a big mistake, one of the biggest of your entire career." He pushed himself to his feet with a grimace of pain and leaned against the far wall, scratching at one leg.

"Really? Suppose you tell me what my mistake is."

"No, I don't think I will. Bring me before the king and I will tell him. Then you will find yourself in the wrong."

"Well, you will get your wish, Ay. The king is going to judge you himself. I managed to persuade him not to put you to the question ... yet." Paatenemheb smiled as if mildly amused at Ay's expression of horror.

"He would not do that. I am the Divine Father."

"A pity you did not think of that earlier. You will not be tortured if you tell the truth. Akhenaten will make you swear on the Aten that you tell the truth and he may believe you, he is easily persuaded. However, I am not that easy. If I suspect you lie, I will have you questioned most thoroughly on my own authority. Do not think the king can protect you."

"You think highly of yourself," Ay sneered. "Almost as highly as if you were king in place of that short-sighted fool. Is that your intention? To use this as an excuse to take power – keeping the king in custody for his own protection?"

Paatenemheb barked out a derisive laugh. "I am an army officer dedicated to Kemet's protection. I do not want to become king and I have no claim to the throne, whether by family or marriage. Rather I could believe it of you." The general scratched at his leg below his kilt, then again below his knee. Looking down he saw a tide of tiny black specks seething in the mouldy straw and ascending his legs. He stepped back rapidly, toward the door, slapping at his legs. "Come now, Tjaty Ay. You are called before the king to answer charges of treason."

The Hall of Justice stood almost deserted. Soldiers guarded the doors, refusing either to let anyone pass or even speak of what took place within the chamber. King Akhenaten and Queen Meryetaten sat on the official thrones of the judges at one end of the Hall, on a raised dais. The usual array of courtiers – scribes, fan-bearers, and servants were missing, the only other people in the room were guards made up from Paatenemheb's men. Others had straggled in during the night and he now commanded forty-two of his own, in addition to the city garrison. In the continued and inexplicable absence of Mahu and the city Medjay, Commander Baqet had his men all over the city organizing a cleanup and maintaining order.

Paatenemhet led Ay into the Hall of Justice alone. Ankhtify and a small squad of soldiers had formed a close guard around the Tjaty as they escorted him from the cell to the Hall. Ay acted as if it were an honour guard, giving all sorts of unnecessary commands to Ankhtify, which the Leader of Fifty ignored.

Paatenemheb closed the doors behind him and the Tjaty, whereupon Ay rushed forward into the chamber with a glad cry. He ran toward the dais then, as the guards around the thrones stepped forward, spears lowered, he threw himself to his knees, his arms high and extended toward his king.

"Divine Akhenaten, I thank the Aten that he has kept you safe. I have spent the night in an agony of worry that I would not be there beside you to ward off your enemies."

Akhenaten waved back the guards and smiled down at his Tjaty. "Ay, Divine Father, it saddens me to see you in this state. Arise and seat yourself." He snapped his fingers and a guard brought a stool, helping the old man to his feet and sitting him down facing the king.

Ay smoothed down his crumpled and stained kilt. "It grieves me to appear before you like this, my lord, but I hurried over as soon as I could, not even stopping to bathe or change my clothing. I beg your indulgence, Divine Akhenaten ... and of course, my queen." He inclined his head toward his granddaughter Meryetaten who sat fidgeting on the other throne.

"He had no choice in the matter," Paatenemheb growled, coming across from the doors to stand behind Ay. "He spent the night in a cell where, if it is your judgment, I will return him."

"Thank you, General," Akhenaten said. "I am aware of your accusations, but I am here to dispense justice, not you. Now, Divine Father, you have been accused of sedition in that you did plot with my wife Nefertiti to overthrow me, and of treason in that you attempted to carry this out last night. What do you have to say to these charges?"

"Divine Akhenaten, I could no more dream of overthrowing you than I could dream of overthrowing the living Aten. You are my life and I would willingly give my life for you. If you think that I could ever rebel against your loving and beneficent rule, then execute me now and I shall go to my death singing your praises."

"No, no, no. Divine Father, cease this, I beg you. I have never doubted you for an instant. But you have been charged and I must be seen to be just to all my subjects." Akhenaten turned to where Meryetaten sat staring into space. "Is that not so, beloved wife?" Meryetaten just shrugged and started playing with a massive gold ring on her hand.

"If I might question him, Akhenaten?" Paatenemheb said, and without waiting for permission, addressed the Tjaty. "Ay, did you or did you not hold a conversation with Nefertiti, your daughter, to discuss how you might remove the king by armed force, setting Nefertiti on the

541

throne as sole ruler and yourself as the power behind the throne?"

Ay swiveled on his stool and looked up at the powerfully built general. "I did not. I deny any such activity. Why would I do such a thing?" He turned back to the king. "My lord, you have showered gold and praise upon me in abundance. Why would I be so ungrateful?"

"There is a witness to this conversation."

Ay glanced around the Hall. "A witness?" he asked cautiously. "Then where is she?"

"She? You know the witness to be a woman before she is produced?" Akhenaten asked. "This implies you knew the witness to be there."

Ay shrugged. "A guess, my lord. I believe this witness might be your own sister Beketaten, whom we all fondly know as Scarab. A delightful child but a willful one who has fallen into bad ways recently."

"What do you mean?"

"She stole a valuable necklace from your wife Nefertiti and vanished from the city. I instituted a search for her but could find no trace. I feared she had died as her cloak was found in the river." Ay looked at Paatenemheb with a smile. "The news that she is alive gladdens my heart."

"And mine," Akhenaten added. "Though I wish somebody had told me of this before. I did not even know she was missing."

Paatenemheb snarled and came very close to Ay, leaning over him. "Beketaten told me that she overheard you and Nefertiti in the former queen's bedchamber discussing your plans."

"I deny these charges. Bring her before me and let us get to the bottom of this," Ay replied, stifling a yawn.

542

"Where is this child?" Meryetaten also yawned but did not bother to hide it.

"Yes, Paatenemheb," Akhenaten queried. "Where is Beketaten? I would like to hear this from her own lips."

"She is not here. I left her five days ago near Ineb Hedj and came as quickly as I could, praying I would be in time. I left her in the charge of my deputy, Paramessu, to follow at their own pace. I expect them in a few days." Paatenemheb paused, then, anger creeping into his voice, went on. "That is why I wanted these proceedings delayed, my lord – so that I could assemble my witnesses."

"I'm bored," Meryetaten whined. "I want to go and see my jewels again."

Akhenaten smiled at his daughter-wife. "Soon, lotus petal. This is part of being a king and queen – listening to the cases brought before us. And this case is important. Your grandfather has been accused of a terrible crime."

"So let him off. You are king, are you not? You can do anything you want."

"That is true, but I must also do what is just. If I just let him off, people might wonder whether he truly was innocent or whether it was because he was of my family."

"I put my faith in your divine justice," Ay said piously. "But is it just that I am accused on the word of a young child and am denied the opportunity to question her myself? There is a very simple explanation for what she thinks she heard."

"And that is?" Paatenemheb growled. "You said Nefertiti would be on the throne and you the power behind her. What could you possibly mean by that, other than discussing how to divide the spoils?"

"My lord king, when you dismissed Nefertiti and banished her to the North Palace, she summoned me. Naturally I went as she is my daughter and at the time I believed her still to be the queen. Was I wrong to perform this loyal act?"

"Of course not, Divine Father. Go on."

"Alas, my daughter was very angry and shouted and screamed and said a lot of things that did not make much sense, but after a while she quieted down. It was then that she said things that disturbed me." Ay broke off his narrative and put his head in his hands and made a sobbing sound. "Divine Akhenaten, do not judge her harshly I beg you. Rather would I suffer unjustly than have my lovely daughter suffer for an injudicious word uttered in anger."

Paatenemheb started clapping slowly. "Very moving, Ay," he said sourly. "You will move us all to tears. Get on with your tale."

"*Shh*, Paatenemheb, let him speak. Go on, Divine Father."

Ay took a deep shuddering breath and looked up, his eyes red from rubbing, though still dry. "My lord king, she ... she said ... Great Father, do not force me to bear witness against my daughter. Let me bear the blame. Kill me and let her go free."

Akhenaten fluttered his hands in agitation. "No, no, Divine Father, you are becoming upset." He turned to one of the guards. "Bring wine for my Tjaty. Hurry!" He waited impatiently while the guard ran to obey the king, dropping his spear to the floor with a clatter. The guard handed Ay a cup of wine.

"Thank you, my lord," Ay said. His hand trembled as he raised the cup, spilling a few drops of wine. He drained the rest and set the cup on the floor.

"Now, Divine Father, you must go on. I charge you to tell the truth, no matter how painful it might be. I ask this of you as my beloved Father."

544

"For you then, great king," Ay said, his voice low. "Though it breaks my heart, I will relate to you my daughter Nefertiti's words." He paused as if gathering his strength. "My daughter asked me to help her kill you."

"No!" Akhenaten recoiled in horror. "She would not do such a thing."

Meryetaten stopped playing with her gold ring and looked up, suddenly displaying an interest in the proceedings.

Ay nodded slowly. "I regret to say it is the truth, my lord Akhenaten. She wanted to hire an assassin immediately, claiming that the people would follow her as ... as she was the true founder of the worship of Aten anyway."

"Lies," Akhenaten muttered. "Lies. She always followed, never led."

"Of course, my lord. I knew that to be the truth and I immediately tried to counsel her. I managed to talk her out of hiring an assassin ..."

"And where would she find an assassin, I wonder?" Paatenemheb mused. "Now you I could understand. You know plenty of dubious characters."

"Alas again, my reputation suffers through the associations I make to safeguard my king." Ay shook his head sorrowfully though he glared at the general from under his bushy eyebrows. "As I was saying, my lord, I talked my daughter out of killing you but she immediately started to tell me of her plans to seize the kingdom and imprison you. I went along with it solely to learn who her other conspirators might be."

"And were there others?"

"Yes my lord. She named Sutau, the overseer of the treasury. I know, Divine Akhenaten, I could not believe it either and except for her statement, I have no proof of his involvement."

"So when you said you would be the power behind the throne?"

"I thought if she would accept me, she would not look to others less loyal than myself. If I was trusted ..."

"Who would trust you?" Paatenemheb muttered.

"... then I would learn of her plans in good time so I could stop her. My lord, last night I was leading the city garrison to the palace to guard you against the rebels, when Paatenemheb here waylaid me and threw me in a vermin-infested cell. It is only by the grace of the living Aten that the rebellion came to nothing."

"Or perhaps I ended it by arresting the ringleaders?" Paatenemheb commented.

"A moving story," Akhenaten said. "I believe you Divine Father and I am thankful that I have such loyal ministers. Sutau disturbs me though. I never suspected him of such things."

"Nor should you now, Akhenaten. Ay is not loyal; he is a conniving backstabber who thinks nothing of betraying his own daughter to save his skin. Let me put him to the question. I will soon ascertain the truth."

"There is no need, general." Akhenaten shook his head and gestured to his father-in-law to stand. "Ay, do you solemnly swear on the living Aten and the hope you have of everlasting life in his sight that the words you have uttered tonight are true and without blemish?"

"I do, my lord king. May I be struck blind and live without the glorious sight of Aten if I have lied."

"Then that is good enough for me. No man can lie with the name of Aten on his lips." Akhenaten stood up and came down from the dais. He embraced Ay, kissing him on both cheeks. "Divine Father, I find you innocent

546

of all charges against my person. You are reinstated without prejudice to all your positions within my government. It is my heartfelt desire that you join me at dawn tomorrow to offer up the hymn of praise in the Great Temple."

"You are not serious?" Paatenemheb broke in. "He has said nothing that can be substantiated. At least let me confront him with his daughter, or with Sutau." His fists clenched and he became red in the face. "Why did he try to kill me last night? He drew a sword on me and only the actions of my men prevented it."

"Did you, Divine Father? Is there truth in this?"

"My lord, I confess this freely for I have told the truth in all things. Yes, I drew a sword on Paatenemheb but this was only because I believed there might have been others recruited by Nefertiti that I knew nothing about. Here was a man who sought to prevent me from guarding you. For one awful minute I believed he was a traitor and I drew my sword." Ay sighed deeply. "I was one old man against a squad of professional soldiers. What could I do?"

"You acted correctly, beloved Father." Akhenaten embraced him again. "However, Paatenemheb, you are correct also. I must confront Nefertiti and find out the depths of her iniquity. Please go and bring her to me that I may judge her."

Paatenemheb controlled his anger, working his rage off by pacing the floor of the Hall of Justice. He started to say something further, to argue his case again, but he refrained. After a few moments he bowed curtly and left.

When he was gone, Ay sat down again and bowed his head. He sighed deeply. "My lord Akhenaten, please do not put me through this agony. No man should have to see his daughter condemned. Let me leave the room so that I am not unmanned with grief."

"Faithful Ay," Akhenaten raised him up and kissed him again. "Of course you have my leave to go. I would not willingly cause you pain and I promise that if I can I will be merciful to your daughter."

Paatenemheb returned within the hour with Nefertiti and a squad of soldiers. The former queen was pale but composed and though the last few weeks had aged her, adding fine wrinkles to her face and bowing her shoulders, her great beauty was still obvious. When she entered the Hall of Justice, the king sighed as he caught sight of her, his daughter-wife Meryetaten screwing up her face petulantly.

Nefertiti bowed to Akhenaten gracefully but aside from a slight inclination of her head, did not acknowledge her daughter on the other throne. "My lord king," she said softly. "I am happy to see you in good health."

"Are you, madam? I was under the impression you desired my death."

"Never, my lord. I have never desired you dead. Humiliated perhaps," Nefertiti smiled faintly. "As you humiliated me. But never hurt."

"That is not what I have heard from witnesses. Do you deny plotting rebellion?"

"No. But I was led astray. My father is a strong-willed man and as a dutiful daughter I was bound to ..."

"You seek to blame him? By Aten, woman, this is too much. I have heard the truth from his own lips, how you and Sutau sought to dethrone me and take control of the kingdom for yourselves. You must be mad to think the people would accept you."

"Sutau?" Nefertiti laughed, a high clear tinkling melody of pure amusement. "He told you that? And you believed him?" She shook her head, her smile fading. "You are a fool, Akhenaten. You believe only in your Aten and are content to let this precious land of ours fall about our ears. I sought only to correct this."

The king glared at his former queen. "You do not deny wanting to dethrone me? You admit it?"

"Oh, Akhenaten, can you not see what you are doing? Has the Aten in truth blinded you? You trust those who would harm you and put no faith in those who would defend our Two Lands. You dismiss your wife of fifteen years to bed your own daughter – and for what? Sons? What need have you of sons? Marry your daughters to your brothers that our families might continue to rule Kemet. Meryetaten would be perfect for Smenkhkare and ..."

"I do not want to marry Smenkhkare," Meryetaten screamed. "I am married to father and I am queen now, not you, so keep your stupid advice to yourself."

Nefertiti shook her head, a wry smile on her face. She ignored her daughter's outburst and addressed her husband again. "Yes, I am guilty of seeking to overthrow you, husband. I was a good queen and would be again. My father knows how to rule and would be the strength behind the throne, my strength. Together we could have brought peace and prosperity back to Kemet, defending our beloved country against her enemies." She turned to Paatenemheb. "Is that not what you would want, General? To have our armies strong again and Kemet respected rather than being an object of ridicule?"

"I would have Kemet strong and respected, madam, but not at the expense of civil disobedience, of rebellion against Ma'at and the king. I swore to defend Kemet *and*

549

to obey my king in all things. This I will do even if it means stamping you into the dust."

"Then I have failed," Nefertiti said calmly. "And Kemet will continue to decline."

"So you admit it openly, without coercion?" Akhenaten's lip trembled. "You do not deny your treason?"

"If you see it as treason, husband, then I can do no more. Deal with me as you will." Nefertiti bowed her head, awaiting her husband's decision.

For several minutes Akhenaten said nothing. He sat on his throne with head bowed, tears trickling down his face. At last he sat up and wiped his face. "I cannot find it in myself to ... to execute you as I know I should, as the law requires. Instead I ... I sentence you to exile beyond the boundaries of Kemet, never to see our beautiful land again."

Nefertiti sobbed. "Kill me, husband. Do not send me from the land I love."

"I cannot kill you, Nefertiti the beautiful, for the love we once had. But I must be strong and put you from me. It shall be as if you are dead for no man will speak of you, no woman envy your beauty, no child think of you, for you will be no more in Kemet." Tears broke out afresh in Akhenaten's eyes. "Take her away, Paatenemheb. Take her from my sight that I may expunge her from my memory."

"Where ... where will you send me?"

"For now, to the North Palace. Tomorrow I shall decide on your place of exile. Take her, Paatenemheb. Take her quickly."

The king watched in agony as his wife; once the most beautiful woman in Kemet, now a traitor, and soon to be a fading memory; was escorted weeping from the Hall of Justice. As the doors closed behind her, Akhenaten broke down and cried, kneeling on the floor and howling with grief. Meryetaten sat stony-faced on the queen's throne, confused and upset, wanting her jewels.

Chapter Thirty-Nine

I arrived back in Akhet-Aten with some trepidation. Paramessu and I rehired the fishing boat to bring us up-river, but traveling against the current with no rowers, with just the fickle winds in our sail, took a long time. I did not begrudge the delay because I enjoyed the company of this strong, mature soldier. He talked for hours about his father Seti, a judge and troop commander in Hut-waret; about his childhood and early life; about his life as a soldier and commander, and the future of Kemet. In my turn I told him of my life in the court and my adventures in the city of Waset with Smenkhkare. Naturally, my life did not take long to relate but I listened to Paramessu talk all day and night, encouraging him whenever he stopped, asking questions, hanging on his every word. He had this ability to talk as an equal and with him I did not feel like a young girl, but like a woman whose company he enjoyed.

The age difference between us was great, some twenty years, but age means little to us in Kemet if attraction is there. I know I wanted to get to know my Paramessu better, and I think he felt the same. I found myself wishing I was not a princess or him not a commoner. Age difference is nothing to a Kemetu, but the difference in our rank was everything. If I had been a little older I could have taken him as a lover, but never anything more. The man who married me would have a claim on the throne of Kemet, and the king would not allow me to marry outside of the family. My Paramessu said nothing, acted like a perfect gentleman throughout our trip, but I knew in my heart what we both desired. It was not to be though, and I locked my secret thoughts away in my heart. So it was with sadness that our journey came to an end. The moon was already halfway to full when we tied up at the north wharf amid the freight barges, and I found I had missed the one event that would have given me much joy to attend – my brother Smenkhkare's coronation.

He had arrived in Akhet-Aten the day after the attempted coup by Ay and Nefertiti to find the capital city buzzing with rumors. Brought before the king – by Ay of all people who had managed to wriggle out of danger – he was apprised of the reason for his summons. Akhenaten embraced him, acknowledging him, in the absence of a son of the King's Body, as his heir. Arrangements were already in train for the coronation, when Smenkhkare would be raised to the throne as co-regent. This had been Ay's original plan, to install a boy as king and manage him from behind the throne. Then Nefertiti's disgrace had offered him a more pliant puppet and I believe if the coup had succeeded, Ay would not have let my brother live. As things turned out, he was forced to change his plans and my brother became useful again. Smenkhkare was to rule over the whole of Kemet from Waset, with Ay's help, while Akhenaten, though maintaining his position as senior co-regent, would rule over Akhet-Aten and continue to be the sole channel for the grace of the Aten.

The coronation itself was not elaborate. Akhenaten refused once more to allow any of the old gods of Kemet any part in the proceedings, calling on the Aten to bless his brother and to guide him. Smenkhkare persuaded Akhenaten to remove the appellation of Aten in his coronation names though, taking on further Re names instead. He ever had an eye on the reunification of Kemet under the old gods and knew an Aten name would work against him. So my beloved brother became king and co-regent of the Two Lands, Ankhkheperure Djeserk-heperure Smenkhkare. Akhenaten, still suffering from the defection of his wife, and reluctant to share any real power with his daughter Meryetaten whom he now saw as a willful little girl, often addressed Smenkhkare as Neferneferuaten, Nefertiti's former appellation, even to the extent of calling him this in official inscriptions. It was regarded as another sign of Akhenaten's failing mind.

The city celebrated the coronation but the festivities were strained. Even a populace as carefree and hedonistic as Akhet-Aten's, became tired of continuous rejoicing. Nobody in the capital knew Smenkhkare or recognized the abilities this handsome man possessed. There was a feeling of unease too. Rumors of the attempted coup were rife, with much speculation as to the fate of Neferti-ti. Ay, despite his involvement, appeared unscathed and if anything, in a more powerful position than he had been before. The king moved out of the great palace into the smaller North Palace, even moving into the rooms used by Nefertiti so briefly. He withdrew into himself, only venturing out to conduct the morning, noon and sunset services to the Aten in the Great Temple. Refusing any involvement in the running of the country, Akhenaten leaned heavily on Ay's strong arm, allowing this traitor as much power as he had sought through his daughter's coup. Only Smenkhkare stood between him and total domination of Kemet.

I met Ay the day I arrived back in Akhet-Aten. Brought before the king, I saw to my horror that my uncle was firmly in place at Akhenaten's side. The king greeted me with a warm embrace, before inviting me to greet my uncle Ay. Without thinking I blurted out my accusations, not understanding why he had his liberty.

The king looked at me with a sad smile. "Dear Beketaten, I do not doubt that you overheard the Divine Father and ... and that woman speaking. It is because you are a child that you failed to recognize the difference between the treason of that woman and the loyalty of my beloved Ay. He acted bravely on my behalf and has been cleared of all charges." Akhenaten laid a hand on Ay's arm, smiling up at him. "The Divine Father Ay is my strong right arm. Now, embrace your uncle, child, and offer him your apology and no more will be said."

I remained frozen in place but Ay came down from the throne dais and embraced me, letting me feel the strength in his arms and broad shoulders. He kissed my cheek and whispered in my ear. "I shall not forget what you have done, Beketaten." Stepping back with a smile, he released me and, finding I had control of my limbs once more, I bowed to the king and left the audience chamber.

My position in Akhet-Aten had changed, as had my position in the lives of all those I knew. I never really had a father – I have related how Nebmaetre failed in this duty, though through no fault of his own. My mother Tiye paid me scant attention and I had never felt close to her. The nearest I ever came to having a mother was during my few months as one of Akhenaten and Nefertiti's 'garland of princesses' in Akhet-Aten, but now Nefertiti had gone.

It was many years before I found out exactly what happened to her. All I knew at the time was that she had been exiled. One of the conditions by which her husband allowed her to live was that she leave the Two Lands forever. Neither the king nor Ay ever spoke of her again. The memory of her, apart from the paintings and sculptures adorning tombs and public buildings, faded with

555

the passing of time. The only other person to know of her place of exile was Paatenemheb. Two days after my return he left Akhet-Aten with a small squad of picked soldiers and with them went a closed sedan chair, the curtains closely drawn despite the heat. I believe Nefertiti was in it as they headed up the valley of the royal tombs, heading north and east into the desert. There is not much in that direction except the Wilderness of Sin, for Nefertiti would never be allowed into Syria. The danger of her being captured and held hostage was too great. If Sin was her destination I can pity her for it is a barren and demon-infested land, bare rock and sand, almost waterless, inhabited by nomadic shepherds and bandits. Kemet maintains outposts there, lonely copper and turquoise mines where dedicated miners sift the rock for metal and gem, where slaves toil and die, and where soldiers curse their fate and dream of the cool green river valley of home. It is a place where beauty shrivels and the mind turns inward upon itself.

So there was little in Akhet-Aten to hold me there and one good reason – Ay – for me to leave. I decided I would follow my brother to Waset. It was a place I loved, and the two men my heart sang to would be there, Smenkhkare and Paramessu.

I must admit Smenkhkare had changed too. When I first saw him, I screamed his name out loud and ran to him, throwing my arms about him. He was friendly but restrained, disentangling my limbs and, sitting me down, listened as I told him everything. After a while he excused himself and left me feeling let down and puzzled. I took my woes to Paramessu.

"He has changed, Paramessu. He no longer loves me. But why? What have I done?" I wailed.

556

"Of course he has changed, Scarab," Paramessu said gently. "When you played together in Waset he was a boy and you a girl, without cares or worries. Now he is a king and a man, with all the joys and sorrows that go with it. He feels overcome by it all and feels he must face the future alone."

"But I love him. I would willingly face the future with him."

"Yes, and I'm sure he loves you still. Remember you have changed too. When last you saw him, you were an innocent and naive girl but now when he looks at you he sees a woman, strong and resourceful. A woman who has saved Kemet." Paramessu sat down next to me and took my hands in his. "Your brother carries the weight of Kemet on his shoulders and at the moment it crushes him. Be patient and he will grow accustomed to his burden. Then he will realize that his sister Scarab is the most precious item in his treasury."

It was not exactly what I wanted to hear but after thinking about it for a few minutes I realized the future did not look as bleak as I thought.

"Perhaps I should go back to Waset," I said. "Akhet-Aten does not seem safe now that Ay almost rules here."

"I think that would be a good idea, Scarab. Why don't you come with me? I have been put in charge of the escort taking Smenkhkare back to Waset and I'm sure he ... and I," he added, smiling, "Would be happy to have you on the Royal Barge. We leave in five days."

"You are going to be in Waset too?" I threw my arms around his broad shoulders and kissed him. After a moment I felt him return the kiss, then he gently untangled himself and drew back.

"I am not staying in Waset. My duties call me south to Qerert, then north to the Syrian border again."

557

"I could come with you."

Paramessu smiled gently, his voice tender but firm. "I am a soldier, Scarab. I go where my general bids, often living hard and off the land. You are a princess, sister to two kings. Our worlds have touched briefly but now we must go our own ways."

I felt the abyss opening again. "You do not want me?" I said in a small voice.

"More than anything, but your place is at your brother's side and mine is fighting Kemet's enemies."

"You will come back to me, Paramessu?"

"One day, little Scarab, but not soon. Maybe the world will change and a soldier can ... can be with a princess. Or maybe you will change your mind."

"Never," I said, with all the certainty of the very young.

We left Akhet-Aten five days later, aboard the Royal Barge that had brought Smenkhkare from Waset. Akhenaten and Ay came down to the docks to see us off, the occasion formal and filled with pomp and spectacle. The two kings of Kemet bade farewell to each other, the old king weary and bowed, his mind not on the speeches but wandering as he lifted his gaze to the blazing disk of Aten above us; the young king full of energy and enthusiasm, eager to be away from this capital city that was now a backwater of the kingdom.

Ay watched and waited, his cold, calculating eyes sifting and weighing, standing next to Akhenaten. Though older by far, and shorter, Ay looked to be the king, supporting an old bent man as he waved farewell to the future.

We sailed south, the rowers straining to push the heavy gilded barge against the current. Smenkhkare sat on a light wooden chair under an awning set up in the middle of the boat, his face turned to the warm breeze from the south, sniffing the air as if he could read what was to come. He saw me and beckoned.

"Come, little Scarab, sit beside me. We have ..."

Epilogue

"Come, little Scarab, sit beside me. We have ..."

"That's it. The writing runs out at this point." Dani pointed at the wall where the tightly packed hieroglyphs petered out in a patch of flaking mortar close to the bottom of the final wall. "End of story, folks."

"Jeez, you're kidding! That's no place to end a story."

"What happened?" Doris wailed. "I want to know. Did Scarab marry her soldier? Did she become a queen? What do the history books say, Doctor Hanser?"

"I believe you'll find them quiet on that point," Daffyd said in his sing-song Welsh accent. "Very little is known about Beketaten. In fact, I'd go so far as to say this tomb," he gestured around at the walls. "This tomb, if that's what it is, presents a wealth of new knowledge."

"Really?" Bob said, looking up from where he sat cross-legged on the floor. "What was new? I thought archeologists knew just about everything about Egypt. They've been studying it long enough."

Daffyd laughed and pulled out his tin of tobacco from the pocket of his jacket. "Where do you want me to start?" He carefully rolled himself a cigarette and lit it, the smoke curling up into the darkness. "The origins of Aten worship, for instance; or the parents of king Tut; or what happened to Nefertiti. History just says she disappears around Year 14 of Akhenaten's reign. Now we know."

"If it's true," Marc commented. "Can we really guarantee any of this is accurate? It may just be some propaganda exercise written long after the events by an odd bod for some purpose of his own."

"Oh, that would be really bad," Angela said. "Fancy making up a detailed story like this."

"And an exciting one," Doris added. "I want to know what happens next."

"If you can't stand not knowing, you're in the wrong game, Doris," Al drawled. "Archeology often raises more questions than it answers."

"The guy may not even have been an Egyptian," Marc went on. "Maybe he just wanted to hurt their reputations."

"So why hide it away so effectively?" Daffyd blew a cloud of smoke up toward the ceiling of the chamber. "I'll bet we are the first to see this room in over three thousand years. It's a bit hard to hurt reputations this late in the game."

"He was Egyptian," Dani said quietly. "Or rather 'she'."

Marc stroked his luxuriant beard contemplatively. "You think the author really was this Beketaten lassie?"

"Yes, I do. The language and phrasing is New Kingdom despite its informality. There is a wealth of detail about the royal family that just would not be available to an outsider, and the impression I get is partly that of an old woman looking back on the events of her life, and partly that of a young girl actually experiencing these things as she talks."

"If Beketaten became an old woman," Angela said slowly. "Then why does the story break off so abruptly at such an early age?"

"The sudden breaking off is easy. See here?" Dani pointed to the bottom of the wall. "Water has got in at some stage and peeled the mortar from the underlying rock. You can be certain there was more written on this section but it's illegible now." She scanned the previous lines of script, then looked back at the missing section. "I'd say you have her trip to Thebes in this part, probably finishing with her arrival there."

"What a bloody unsatisfying place to end though," Bob grumbled.

"Think about it, boyo." Daffyd stubbed out his cigarette on his tin of tobacco, put the tin back in his jacket pocket and the stub into his jeans. "Here we have a tomb or at least a chamber with a detailed life history of a woman – well, still a girl actually – that ends in Thebes, not Syria." He grinned. "What does that suggest?"

"What do you mean?" Doris asked. "Are you saying she dies in Thebes?"

"Don't be a goose, Doris," Angela laughed. "How can she die in Thebes if she writes this story up here in Syria?"

"So what does it suggest, Daffyd? Are you going to tell us?"

"Doctor Hanser?" Daffyd smiled and made an elegant bow in her direction.

"It suggests this is not the whole story," Dani said slowly, staring at the Welshman. "There is more."

"Where?" Marc asked. "We've examined the whole chamber."

"Perhaps there's another one then boyo."

"Then let me repeat myself – where?"

"Where was this first chamber? Hidden behind a layer of mortar." Daffyd spun on his heel, his outstretched arm describing a full circle. "Everywhere I look I see a layer of mortar."

"Jeez Louise."

Everyone scrambled to their feet and stared around the dimly lit chamber, the light of flashlights and lanterns reflecting off the white walls and vibrant colours in a dazzling coruscation.

"Another chamber," Al chortled. "Of course. Let's get looking, guys and dolls."

"Before you do, there is something I'd like you to think about," Dani said. "We are in Syria, officially on an archeological dig looking for the Neanderthal migration route. We have stumbled on what may be the find of the century after king Tut's tomb, but we are not equipped to deal even with this chamber, let alone anything else that might be here." She looked at her watch. "In case you haven't noticed, the permit for our dig runs out this morning, in about nine hours. If we don't pack up today, the authorities are going to want to know why."

Marc whistled. "We've been here all night? Man, where does the time go?"

"So what's wrong with telling them?" Doris asked. "They'll be pleased, won't they?"

"Probably very pleased," cut in Daffyd. "But not with us."

"Daffyd's right," Dani continued. "We are not Egyptologists. We should never have opened this chamber in the first place. We might be able to argue ignorance of what we had found when we first broke in, but not after this lot. They'll bring in their own team of Egyptologists and if we are lucky we'll read about it in the scientific journals ten years from now."

"And we'll probably be persona non bloody grata," Bob grumbled.

"Language, Bob," Angela corrected with a smile.

"Yup. Last time we get invited to Syria. Damascus gets rather upset with foreigners plundering their artifacts."

"We're not plundering," Angela protested. "We haven't taken a thing."

"Doesn't matter," Dani said. "We entered a chamber of probable historical importance without the proper permits ..."

"We didn't know when we opened it."

"... and having entered it and found out the significance, we didn't immediately stop and notify Damascus."

Dani looked around the gloomy faces of her archeological team. Nobody said anything, the only sound in the chamber being the hiss of the gas lanterns. "We got into this together," she said at last. "So we decide together. What do we do?"

"What *can* we do?" Doris asked.

"It's a good point to start," Marc agreed. "What are our options?"

"Tell Damascus and takes our licks," Al grinned.

"Okay boyo, it's an option," Daffyd said. "But for God's sake be serious about this. It's no joking matter."

"Report it immediately then," Al continued. "We say we just found it accidentally. After all, we do have the mud and earth that fell away from the rock face outside."

"Don't tell 'em. We found it; we should get to excavate it," Bob said vehemently.

"Anything else?" Dani asked. "Any other ideas?"

"Fill in the hole," Daffyd said slowly. "Fill it in, plaster over the entrance and forget we ever saw it."

"You're not serious? You mean you could just walk away from this discovery?"

Daffyd shook his head. "No. It's just an option. We need to think of them all. Another might be to cover it up and come back to try again next year."

"All right," Dani said. "Let me see if I've got this straight. One – we can come clean and hope we don't get

564

chucked out of the country. Minimum result – we never get to see this dig again. Two – we report it as an accidental discovery and never see the dig again. Three – we don't report it, try to disguise our digging and come back next year. That way we might get to see what's in the next chamber ..."

"If there is a next chamber."

"Agreed. Four – we don't report it, just cover it up and forget we ever saw it. Can you think of any other options?" The students shook their heads or muttered denials. "Then we need to vote on this. How many ..."

"One moment, Doctor Hanser," Daffyd interrupted. "What do we do if there is a split vote?"

Dani considered for a few moments. "Majority wins. We all agree to abide by the vote."

"And if it's tied? Sorry, doctor, but it's better to sort this out beforehand rather than arguing about it later."

"If two options are tied, we drop the other options and vote again." Dani looked round the group. "Are we all agreed on the rules? All right, then. The options are – one, own up to deliberately opening the chamber; two, own up but claiming it was accidental; three, a cover up until next year; and four, covering it up and forgetting it." She took a deep breath. "Option one?"

Nobody put their hands up. Dani nodded. "Option two?" Daffyd and Al raised their hands immediately, followed a moment later by Dani. "Three votes. Option three?" Five hands rose. "And option four?" Nothing.

"All right, we have a majority vote for option three," Dani said. "We attempt to cover up our find and come back next year to continue."

"This is stupid. We'll never get away with it."

"Al," Dani snapped. "We voted on this and the majority rules. We cover it up until next year. I want your

565

word that you will keep this secret. Not just you, Al, everybody."

One by one they promised. Dani nodded. "All right, we have a lot to do and not much time. It is nearly three in the morning." She stifled a yawn. "We have to be out of here by noon. They're sending a truck for us. But we need to finish the cover up by daybreak in case any of the camp crew comes snooping." Looking around at her little group, she started assigning duties. "Bob, we need a couple of bags of cement from the camp. Try not to let anyone see you. When you get back, you and Marc will fill in the hole and plaster over it. Al, you and Will see to disguising our activity around the hole. Daffyd, I want you and the girls to go back down to the dig and put it in order. Theoretically we've just spent all night packing up, so you'll have to get going." She clapped her hands sharply. "Okay, chop, chop."

They took a last look around the chamber then clambered through the hole in the mud brick wall, the colourful scenes and glorious writing fading into the blackness as the lanterns and flashlights were passed back into the cave. Al started picking up fragments of brick from the floor and handing them through to Will, who stacked them neatly.

"We have another problem, Dani," Marc said quietly as they stood on the muddy path leading back to the diggings. "Can we be sure they'll let us come back next year?"

"Not for certain, but if our work is not finished here, there's no reason why not."

"Trouble is; we didn't find sufficient evidence of Neanderthal occupancy to warrant another year. They might just tell us to try somewhere else."

"Then I'll have to try convincing them our findings were more meaningful than they really are."

"I hope you are not suggesting we falsify the data, Dani?"

"God no! But I've worked over here the last five years. If there's any reluctance to let us back I'll pull in a few favours, sleep with a few ministers ... joking, Marc!" She punched him playfully on the arm. "Don't worry. It'll turn out okay. I have it on good authority." Her hand found the golden scarab in her pocket and she squeezed it tightly. "The very best."

Bob returned with the cement and the men started the reconstruction of the mud brick wall, using the fragments of the original and adding to it whatever rocks they could find in the cave.

"Save some of the small bits," Marc advised. "And bits of the original mortar coating to grind up. We have to match the wall of the cave exactly."

The brick wall closed slowly and just before daybreak, the men stepped back, eyeing their work critically.

"Don't give up your day job," advised Al.

"It'll look okay when we apply the mortar coating." Bob scooped a trowel of fresh mortar onto the wall and started coating the surface. It went on smoothly and fast and as the gray light of the new day filtered past the great rocky overhang of the cave, they cleared away their tools and stared at the wall.

"It's bloody obvious there's something there."

"Jeez, Al, it's still wet. Look at that bit where we started. It's almost dry and blends with the rest much better."

"Perhaps we could put a bit of mud around as if it was still clinging to the wall where this lot came down?"

Marc pointed at the great wash of mud that flowed out from the wall and over the path.

"Couldn't hurt."

Mud-slinging occurred and by the time Dani came back from helping Daffyd, Angela and Doris clear up the official dig, the section of wall that hid the chamber was covered in mud that matched the spill of debris on the cave floor. She eyed their work judiciously.

"What do you think, Dani?" Marc asked. "Does it pass muster?"

"It'll do." Dani grinned and shrugged. "It'll have to do; we're running out of time." She led her exhausted team out of the cave and down to the little camp where they washed up and ate a huge breakfast before joining the Syrian workmen dismantling the camp.

The trucks to transport the expedition back to Damascus arrived just before noon together with a ministerial car carrying the under-minister of National History, Ahmed Bashir. His purpose was to inspect the site before the expedition was allowed to leave, to check for any damage to what could be an important historical landmark.

Dani and Daffyd led the under-minister down to the dig, passing the covered up wall as they went. They pointedly did not look at the wall and attempted to distract the man but they need not have bothered. The under-minister was concerned only with the mud on his expensive Italian shoes and paid only cursory attention to his surroundings. He signed the requisite forms and Dani and the others boarded the truck for Damascus. Members of the Syrian support crew accompanied them so the conversation on the trip back was inconsequential. Most of them slept, having spent an exhausting night.

Dani was not alone with her team until the airport. She gathered her students into a quiet part of the terminal for goodbyes. "It's been great, guys, quite apart from ... you know. I'll see you all again next year?"

"Hell, yes. I wouldn't miss it." Al said.

"We'll be here, Dani." Marc smiled, his freshly shaven face making him look like a high school kid rather than a post-graduate student.

Nods and brief affirmative remarks came from the rest.

"I think I'm going to be doing some Egyptian research before next year," Daffyd said quietly. "It seems to me we need to get familiar with the eighteenth dynasty."

Dani saw them all off on their flights and sat down alone in the departure lounge to wait for her own. She pulled out the gleaming gold scarab with its spiky Aten and stared at it, turning it over in her hands.

"So it's true, grandmother," she whispered. "All the old tales you used to tell me of Scarab. But now I know who she was – Beketaten, princess of Egypt."

The story of Beketaten, princess of Egypt, will continue in "Scarab – Smenkhkare: Book 2 of the Amarnan Kings"

The Main Characters

The pronunciations given below are hardly definitive. As vowels are unknown in ancient Egyptian, we can only guess at the proper pronunciation. I have tried to select spellings and pronunciations that are common among English speakers. If you prefer another form, please feel free to use it.

Aanen (Air-nen) - second prophet of Amun, brother of Ay

Ahhotep (Ar-hoe-tepp) - a glass maker of Waset

Akhenaten (Ar-ken-ar-ten) - the heretic king

Amenemhet (Ar-men-em-het) - first prophet of Amun, high priest

Amenhotep III (Ar-men-hoe-tepp) - king, father of Amenhotep IV and Beketaten

Amenhotep IV - king, son of Amenhotep III, later changed his name to Akhenaten

Ankhesenpaaten (Ank-kess-en-pah-ar-ten) - third daughter of Akhenaten and Nefertiti

Ankhkheperure (Ank-kep-er-oo-ray) throne name of Smenkhkare

Ay (Eye) father of Nefertiti and brother to queen Tiye, holds title of Divine Father, Tjaty to Akhenaten, priest of Amun and later of Aten

Aziru (Azz-ee-roo) - king of the Amorites

Bakt (Back-th) - third prophet of Amun

Beketaten (Beck-ett-ar-ten) - youngest daughter of Amenhotep III and Tiye

Djeserkheperu (Jess-er-kep-er-oo) - throne name of Smenkhkare

Heqareshu (Heck-ah-resh-oo) - overseer of nurses in the royal palace

Horemheb (Hore-emm-heb) - general of the eastern borders, later of all armies during reign of Akhenaten

Ineb Hedj (Eye-nebb Hedge) - Memphis, the old capital city of Egypt

Iset (Eye-set) - daughter of Amenhotep III, mother of Tutankhaten

Iteru (Eye-teh-roo) - The Great River, the Nile

Iunu (Eye-oo-noo) - Heliopolis, centre of worship of the Great Ennead

Jebu (Jeb-oo) - an Amorite captain

Kemet (Kem-et) - The Black Land, Egypt

Kensthoth (Kens-thoth) - high-ranking scribe of Waset

Khabiru (car-bee-roo) - a tribe from the north; the Hebrews

Mahuhy (Ma-hoo-hee) - businessman of Waset, a pimp

Meketaten (Meck-ett-ar-ten) - second daughter of Akhenaten and Nefertiti

Meryetaten (Merry-ett-ar-ten) - eldest daughter of Akhenaten and Nefertiti

Mutaril (Moo-tar-rill) - councillor and ambassador for the Hittites

Nakht (Nark-th) - apprentice to Ahhotep, glassmaker of Waset

Nebhotep (Neb-hoe-tepp) - court physician in Akhet-Aten

Nebmaetre (Neb-my-tree) - throne name of Amenhotep III

Neferkheperure (Neff-er-kep-er-oo-ray) - throne name of Amenhotep IV (Akhenaten)

Neferkhepruhersekheper (Neff-er-kep-roo-her-say-kepp-er) - mayor of Akhet-Aten

Neferneferouaten-tasherit (Neff-er-neff-er-oo-ar-ten-tash-er-rit) - fourth daughter of Akhenaten and Nefertiti

Neferneferoura (Neff-er-neff-er-oo-rah) - fifth daughter of Akhenaten and Nefertiti

Nefertiti (Neff-er-tee-tee) - daughter of Ay, wife and queen of Akhenaten

Paatenemheb (Pah-ar-ten-emm-heb) - name that Horemheb took to please Akhenaten

Pa-it (Pah-eet) - farmer of village of Akhet-Re (also his youngest son)

Paramessu (Par-ram-ess-oo) - son of Seti, a friend of Horemheb, becomes an army commander

Scarab - nickname of Beketaten

Sebtitis (Seb-tie-tiss) - a minor noblewoman of Waset

Sepat (See-path) - Nome, province

Setepenra (Setter-pen-rah) - sixth daughter of Akhenaten and Nefertiti

Shubbiluliuma (Shoe-bill-ool-ee-oo-ma) - king of the Hittites

Sitamen (Sit-ah-men) - daughter of Amenhotep III, mother of Smenkhkare

Smenkhkare (Ss-men-kar-ray) - son of Amenhotep III by his daughter Sitamen

573

Ta Mehu (Tah-Meh-oo) - Lower Egypt (the northern Kingdom)

Ta Shemau (Tah-Shem-oh) - Upper Egypt (the southern Kingdom)

Tiye (Tee) - wife and queen of Amenhotep III, sister of Ay

Tjaty (Jar-tee) - Vizier

Tutankhaten (Too-tank-ar-ten) - son of Amenhotep III by his daughter Iset

Tuthmosis (Tuth-mo-siss) - eldest son of Amenhotep III, dies young

Waenre (Wah-en-ray) - throne name of Amenhotep IV (Akhetaten)

Waset (Wah-set) - Thebes, the City of Amun

Yuya (Yoo-yah) - Khabiru Tjaty of Tuthmosis IV, father of Ay, Tiye and Aanen

Gods of the Scarab Books

Amun (Ah-moon) - the hidden one; a sun god, lord of the sky and king of gods; became increasingly powerful during the eighteenth dynasty; worship was centered on Waset.

Asar (Ah-sar) - (Osiris); god of the dead; one of the Nine of Iunu

Aten (Ah-ten) - the sun as a disc, distinct from Re; elevated from a minor god in the eighteenth dynasty; became the supreme god during Akhenaten's reign.

Atum (Ah-toom) - Creator god; the unified light; one of the Nine of Iunu

Auset (Ow-seth) - (Isis); goddess of family love and loyalty; one of the Nine of Iunu

Djehuti (Jeh-hoot-ee) - (Thoth); god of the moon and of wisdom; patron deity of scribes and knowledge

Geb (Gebb) - god of the earth and growing things; one of the Nine of Iunu

Hapi (Hah-pee) - god of Iteru (the Nile River)

Heru (Heh-rue) - (Horus); a sky god; the Ascending Light

Het-Her (Heth-her) - (Hathor); goddess of love, beauty and fertility

Inpu (In-poo) - (Anubis); god of death

Khepri (Kepp-ree) - an aspect of the sun god epitomized by the actions of the sacred scarab beetle which rolls balls of dung (representing the ball of the sun) containing its eggs; the Dawn Light.

Khnum (Kh-noom) - god of the source of the Nile; the Divine Potter; creator of human children

Min (Minn) - fertility god.

Nebt-Het (Nebb-tt-heth) - (Nephthys); goddess of secrets and mysteries; one of the Nine of Iunu

Nekhbet (Neck-beth) - vulture goddess of Ta Shemau

Nut (Noot) - goddess of the sky and direction; one of the Nine of Iunu

Ptah (Tar) - god of craftsmen.

Re (Ray) - one of the sun gods; the Mid-day Light; also Ra.

Satet (Sah-teth) - goddess of the inundation of the Nile

Set (Seth) - god of the desert and destruction; associated with the colour red; one of the Nine of Iunu

Sobek (Sob-eck) - the Crocodile god

Shu (Shoo) - god of air and dryness; one of the Nine of Iunu

Tefnut (Teff-noot) - goddess of moisture; one of the Nine of Iunu

Wadjet (Wah-jeth) - cobra goddess of Ta Mehu

Wepwawet (Wepp-wah-weth) - Opener of Ways; the god of war and funerals

About the Author

Max Overton is a writer of historical novels with the award-winning Lion of Scythia trilogy as his first foray into writing.

Born in Malaysia, he traveled extensively through Asia, Europe and North America before settling down in New Zealand. Later in life, he moved to Australia where he taught a variety of courses at James Cook University. From there, he moved to the United States for five years and then back to tropical Australia, where he continues to write.

Max is now in the final stages of a five-part historical series set in ancient Egypt (the Scarab books). He has also written paranormal adventure, paranormal historical and horror novels and he is starting to explore other genres.

You can keep track of all his novels with Writers Exchange E-Publishing on his author page:
http://www.writers-exchange.com/Max-Overton.html